The Thirteen Tribes of Cain Series

 *Book Three*

The Decree

R.J. Craddock

Transcendent Books
Springville, UT

First Edition, December 2022

Also available in eBook form.

Follow R.J. Craddock on Facebook, Twitter, Instagram, and Goodreads for all news and events, or sign up for The Tribe Proclamation at www.rjcraddock.com

Summary: Gwen's back, living the high life while hiding in plain view as a magician in Las Vegas. With her two best friends by her side, her life seems perfect at last... Until Gwen finds herself wanted for breaking both wiccan and human law. Now Gwen can either face a wiccan tribunal for potentially exposing her kind to the human world or fight false charges in human court for murdering all her former lovers. Either way, the one thing that cannot stay in Vegas is her.

Cover design and illustrations by R.J. Craddock of Green Cloak Design.

Cover illustration copyright © 2017 by R.J. Craddock

ISBN-13: 978-0-578-27697-7 (Transcendent Books)

The Thirteen Tribes of Cain Series

The Forsaken

The Offspring

The Decree

(More books to come)

DEDICATION

To my good friend and junior high cohort, Racheal Davidson, aka Rae Gordon. Thanks for being the Morna to my Gwen and vise-versa, whether near or far apart. You believed in me long before I genuinely believed in myself. Thanks, Rae, for being your sarcastic, silly, musical-theater-loving self. You'll always be my own personal Fairy.

The

Decree

R.J. Craddock

Contents

Prologue

olored lights danced in the night sky above the kingdom, casting their glow on the festivities. The light show turned the pale, white palace into shades of red, blue, and gold as the citizens celebrated the crowning of a new king. They honored the occasion by dancing, singing, and performing magic feats in the square before the palace gates.

Wiccan light shows have always been soundless, done with simple magic. No gun powder necessary, the king noted to himself as another silent spray of light erupted. Deverick Hawthorne watched his people from his gilded perch atop a raised platform. His mother and advisors sat on either side of him. The palace loomed over the city to his right, almost as imposing as the weight of the future hanging over him.

Music and laughter filled the air, along with the smell of spiced liquor, which tickled his nose and tempted his thirst. Deverick knew he should be more jovial, but he had not quite recovered from the trauma of the last few days. One moment he was the most gifted young Warlock in his nation, enjoying his wealth and a simple country life, the next, he was the King of all Wicca, and his best friend was now his enemy.

Neither Onan nor his father, Lord DuCall, had attended the coronation, nor were they present that night. He had inquired of his mother, Master of all the Wiccan rumor mill, of the DuCalls' whereabouts.

"My sources tell me they have both left the Kingdom. No one seems to know where they have gone or if they plan on ever coming back," she had informed him with all solemnity.

Internally Deverick shook off the thoughts of Onan, not wanting the heartache that threatened at the very thought of him.

"Son, please try to enjoy yourself!" his mother leaned in to whisper in his right ear, her long black hair hanging over one shoulder in a long braid. "You've earned this." He gave her an answering smile.

"Your Highness."

Deverick looked up to find his royal advisor, Hardenbrook, standing before his throne. "The first families are ready to perform The Dance of Willow. If you'll follow me into the pavilion, Sire."

Deverick arose. Stepping down from the platform, he followed Hardenbrook alone. Not even his mother could go with him into the pavilion. Only the King was allowed to see The Dance of Willow performed.

His subjects called out greetings and gave their congratulations as he walked through the square. A magical shield barring any who might think to get too close to the King.

There is no rush, my darling. His mother spoke in his head, and he looked over his shoulder at her before she was lost to his view by the throng. *You have all the time in the world to choose a Queen.*

I know, Mother, do not worry. I will not fall in love tonight.
Mentally he shared a laugh with his mother before he closed the telepathic connection between them.

He had heard much talk about The Dance of Willow, which was supposed to be a very erotic experience. The last thing he wanted was for his mother to be privy to his dirty thoughts as his potential betroths demonstrated their magical and physical talents for his consideration.

Hardenbrook led him through the crowd to a small booth at the far end of the square. Draped in red velvet curtains, the simple wooden structure gave off a dark, sensual air even from without. Hardenbrook stepped aside the booth, gesturing for his liege to enter. He would wait without for Deverick to return.

The King took a deep breath to steady himself, inhaling the smell of lavender and feminine musk that wafted out of the dark booth. He took only a few steps into the dark enclosure before his surroundings magically changed. No longer was he in a small tent, but instead, he found himself inside a vast chamber, the roof, and walls, made of red velvet. The pavilion gave him the feeling of being in a circus big top. The light was low and moody from enchanted blue flames hovering along the walls. A large circle of glowing white stones rested in the middle of the tent. With his heart pounding in his throat, he stepped over the stones and walked into the middle of the circle.

Suddenly, an ornate black lacquer chair appeared just in front of him. He felt compelled by unseen forces to take a seat and did. A moment later, a siren's call of voices reached his ears from a small archway on the opposite wall of him. He watched as, one by one, thirteen young women entered the pavilion, each singing the same strange hypnotic song.

They all wore loose red robes that covered them from neck to ankle, the lower half of their faces veiled in red satin. Their eyes peeked over the satin mask, blazing in various colors. He saw every shade from green, blue, orange, aqua, pink, and even violet, all with a ring of gold around the pupil. Every one of them wore her hair up in fancy ringlets or braids. He noted a good number of brunettes, a few blondes, and one redhead in the bunch.

They glided around the outside of the ring of white stones until they encircled him. Deverick knew not which way to look. Of all heights and figures, yet so similarly dressed, he could not identify a single woman. He knew those veils hid the faces of girls he had known as a child, some even friends. Others he knew only by name. At this very moment, they might as well be women of an alien race. He shuffled nervously in his chair.

He knew at least one woman who was not present. The one whose face he most longed to see, whose name haunted him even in his dreams. If he could visit her every night and enter her dream world, he would've. But she was forbidden to him; thus, he had stayed away from her all these years.

These thirteen women were the few he was allowed to consider for his bride and future Queen. As the King of his nation, he could not marry for love. He had to marry for power, for prestige.

Amongst the general populace of Wicca, children were betrothed around age fifteen. However, the first families of Wicca, the pure blood, waited to align themselves with the next ruler of their nation.

Finally, the thirteen red-clad women stopped singing their wordless tune. The tent fell silent. He sat there momentarily at a complete loss of words, clueless as to what should proceed. Then, they all started dancing the ancient dance of seduction and enchantment, named after the wife of Wicca from whom they all descend.

He watched them sway their hips and move from one delicate step into another, creating orbs of light and fire between their dancing fingers. He faced the perplexing issue of choosing whom he would consider for his bride.

He would rather duel a hundred warlocks and Witches than face this task.

His final decision did not have to be made tonight. He did, however, have to eliminate all but three of them. When he had chosen the finalists, they three alone would unveil their faces. From that point on, the ladies had up to a year to court him, to convince him that she would be the most suitable choice for his Queen. He was expected to produce an heir for the throne and continue his family's' royal bloodlines. He would need a wife by the end of the year, and a child must be conceived soon after.

No pressure, he thought to himself. The ladies removed their robes of scarlet, and his thoughts scattered like leaves in the wind. Underneath, they wore white straps of material woven over their hips, stomach, and breasts in such a way to show an alarming amount of skin without showing anything at all. Their legs and feet were bare. They kept their veils on as the dance became even more suggestive in its motions. Music came from all around, as if played by invisible musicians.

He found himself driven to the edge of arousal and madness. He could not stand to sit there much longer. He examined them each more closely. He found his eyes kept wandering to the same woman, her violet eyes startling against her pale skin and platinum blonde hair. He felt compelled to choose her and before he knew it, he had spoken to her.

"Comala betaphil dauter un darcnaes." Reaching his hand out to her, he summoned her. The words allowed her access into the enchanted circle of stones, and she entered silently. She danced closer to him, spinning around his chair, making him feel slightly dizzy in more than one way. She unveiled her face, letting the red silk fall to the ground at her feet.

Amethyst Rosenblaze smiled seductively at him as she sat upon his lap, gently caressing his face as she continued to sway to the enchanted music.

Deverick had known her since they were kids; their mothers were old friends. Yet, somehow, it was like he was seeing her for the first time.

Has she always been this beautiful? he asked himself and could not seem to conjure up a single memory of her before that night. As strange as that was, he did not have time to dwell on his sudden lapse of recollection. Her lips were on his as she kissed him. Her breath was hot and scented with herbs, the smell and taste maddening to his senses. He found he could not help himself and wrapped his arms around her to kiss her back. She parted her lips for him, and his tongue entered without hesitation to caress hers.

All at once he was very much aware that they had a rather large audience. He had two more women to choose, yet he was making out with the first. Traditionally, he was only supposed to kiss them briefly as one of the three "chosen" and then the lady was to leave. Then he could choose the others. He was not meant to have much physical contact with his female prospects until he chose one and wed her. Passionate kissing, let alone anything else of a sexual nature, was completely out of the question. These were Wiccan daughters of the first families, the pure blood. They were to stay untainted until their wedding nights, as was their ancient custom. Should he have carnal knowledge of any of them, he would have to marry the lady right away. A lesser blood Witch might be taken for a mistress, but high bloods were Witches of a higher caliber. They were not to be treated like common slatterns.

Reluctantly, Deverick gently disentangled himself from the enchanting Amethyst and her over-powering kisses. Standing, he helped her to her feet.

"Uon onnor mie, ister Wicca." Placing a hand over his heart, he saluted her. Bowing his head down to hers, he lightly brushed her lips with his. When he stepped back from her, he thought he saw anger in her violet eyes, but the look was quickly replaced with a gentile smile.

"Uon onnor mie, fafa Wicca," she replied, bowing, and making the sign of the 'W' over her heart as she backed away from him until she was out of the circle.

Deverick did not wait to watch her leave, instead turning back to the other ladies. Twelve danced outside the circle of stones, barely clothed with faces veiled. They had continued the dance even while he had been distracted. He could sense their feelings. The air seemed thick with jealousy and disapproval. The other ladies did not like that he had chosen Amethyst or of her kissing him in such a manner. Some part of him agreed that his and her behavior had been odd as well, but decided it was of no consequence now.

What's done is done, he reminded himself. *Let us get this over with so I can get to bed and get some sleep.*

Again, he took his seat in the black chair provided and watched the remaining woman as they danced the "Willow."

Next, he chose another of the blondes, one with blue-orange eyes and dirty blonde hair. Again, he repeated the ceremony, speaking the words that granted her access. She, too, revealed her face. This one was called Nabilia Darkhood. They had never met before, but he knew her by reputation. She was known for her beauty and her cunning. She was well-read and clever.

She would make a good Queen; he thought and knew his mother would agree. Giving her the traditional kiss, he spoke the ceremonial words and she spoke them back before she, too, turned and left the circle of stones.

Last, he chose the redhead. The color of her hair and the brightness of her blue eyes set her apart from the brunettes. He felt certain he did not know her, so he picked her as his third and final choice.

Deverick repeated the ceremony for the last time. The woman unveiled her face and introduced herself to be Blythe Linthrobe, a distant cousin of the DuCall family.

Deverick hesitated a moment before he bent down and gave her a kiss. She seemed surprised and pleased that he had chosen her even after knowing she was Onan's kin. Beaming, she gave her farewell and stepped out of the circle.

The other ten ladies bowed to him and left quietly as the enchanted music faded into silence. Blythe left last, and then he found himself all alone in the eerie velvet pavilion.

My work is done here, he commented to himself as he walked back the way he had come. He expected to hear and smell the festival on the other side of the dark entry way as he stepped through. Alas, he neither heard nor smelled anything. To his astonishment, he did not step back out of the booth and onto the square where Hardenbrook should await. Instead, he found himself walking blindly into pitch blackness. He thought he heard a voice behind him and spun around in alarm. Only he did not stop spinning. The darkness continued to turn around him, making him dizzy beyond comprehension until he lost all sense of time, space, and consciousness.

Chapter One

Unusual Champion

The pain is all she knows. It is everywhere and nowhere as if her body is made of it instead of flesh and bone. Gwen has no sense of space or time. The only thing more real than the pain is the weight of the mountain crushing her. She wills her body to move. Nothing. Her eyelids are led, taking effort to force them open. There is nothing but darkness. The smell of blood overpowers the scent of dirt, rock, and water in the air. She opens her lips to take in a breath and tastes blood, the only moisture in her otherwise dry mouth. She coughs, and blood spurts out onto the dark stone surface before her. Instinctively, Gwen moves as if to wipe the blood away from her mouth. She finds she cannot feel her limbs at all.

I wouldn't be surprised if every bone in my body is broken. The realization should cause her to panic, but she is much too befuddled to think or feel just yet.

With effort, Gwen tries to remember where she is or how she got here. Her memory is a fog, her head throbbing fiercely.

It feels as though I've got a concussion, she muses, trying to collect herself.

Flashes of images pass through her muddled mind as everything clicks back into place. Being attacked by Vanita in the park, waking up in Bec LaNuff in her old room, trying to kill Ivan, and then…

Gwen closes her eyes tight, not wanting to recall the events that happened afterward. Nonetheless, Angelo's visage comes to her mind. She will never forget the look on his face before… the sun rose and burned him out of existence.

Choking on the sobs that come unbidden, she cannot keep his screams out of her head. She cannot un-see his charred, blackened body. Her arms still remember the feel of his stiff and lifeless corpse. She groans in pain both physical and emotional, not sure which hurts worse. She lets the tears come now, letting all her agony pour out of her. By the time she is through, she feels like a balloon depleted of helium.

The rage that sent her after Legion to avenge Angelo starts to pump through her veins once more. She recalls the crazed state of mind she had been in when she decided to cut off her own finger. The goal was to sever the ring that bonded her to Legion. Maiming herself had not been of any importance in the heat of the moment. Oddly, Gwen feels the sensation of that missing finger as if it is still there. In some ways it feels more real than the digits she has left.

Everything that happened afterward spins in her mind — Raven being injured, Morna staying behind to heal him as she chased Legion though the fortress — seems a bit fuzzy. However, her struggle with Legion in the pit is clear now.

I'm buried under the mountain, Gwen realizes. *Or, at least what's left of it.*

She recalls releasing the power that tore Bec LaNuff apart. At the time she had not cared about anything other than killing the monster that had enslaved her and murdered her love.

How am I still alive? she asks herself, not completely certain she wants to live at all.

"You're alive because I'm not finished with you yet," a voice answers her unspoken question. It is in her mind just as much as it reverberates off the rocks around her.

Gwen stiffens, knowing instantly the person behind that disembodied voice.

No, not you again!

"Of course, it is me. I have always been with you," the voice replies as the image of the dark stranger takes shape in her mind. The first person the lost orphan had encountered after coming to, wandering in the snow ten years ago. "After all, who else would look after you as I have?" She tries to push his image away. He refuses to let her mind go onto other thoughts. He is everything; there is nothing else.

"Why can't you just leave me alone?" she yells in a pained croak. Her voice echoes and then disappears as if she never spoke.

"What an absurd thing to say." He smiles in her mind, his pitch-black eyes devoid of soul or light. "You are mine, child. You see, I am very heavily invested in the outcome of your little life."

"What are you rambling about?" Gwen's not sure if his words are confusing because the man speaks nonsense or because she has had a few knocks to the skull. "You're nothing more than a figment of my imagination brought on by delirium and depression. The only thing you're *invested* in is seeing me lose my mind!"

"Nonsense," he chuckles. "Everything you have endured, everything you have suffered, I have made possible so that you might become the Witch you were destined to be!"

"Say I believe you, and you're not imaginary. How exactly does making me suffer make me into anything other than a mostly dead freak who no one can love? What kind of destiny are you preparing me for?" Gwen coughs up more blood, her throat aching from the overuse. "Besides, what's the point of going on without Angelo?"

Gwen rages at the dark stranger until she realizes that his image has finally left her mind. She waits for a response from the man, but his presence has left.

She hates to admit it, but she is not relieved to have him go. Without him she is just a trapped thing waiting to die, alone and un-remembered.

* * * * *

Gwen wakes with a start several hours later. The rocks and the little air about her seem even colder than before.

Perhaps it is night now?

"It is." The man's voice interrupts the quiet about her.

"Ah." Gwen groans and grits her teeth. "I thought I had scared you away, boogeyman. Why are you back? Can't you just let me die in peace?" she croaks.

"Of course, I can't let you die, not here anyway," he adds. Thankfully, his face does not invade her mind again, yet still she can hear the smirk in his voice. "You asked before what kind of destiny I was preparing you for?" He pauses. "Do you really want to know? Should I tell you everything and let you choose here and now how your story will end?"

Gwen gulps, trying to clear her throat and force the nerves down into her stomach. Her throat is sandpaper. Her saliva is all but gone.

"Nothing? No smart-ass remark?" The voice laughs lightly. "No, I suppose you are not ready to face the truth. You are not quite twisted up enough inside just yet."

"What?" Gwen reacts, his words sending lava through her numb body to the top of her head. "Not twisted up enough inside? I'm a mess! I'm as good as dead, you idiot! What else can be left for me now?" She yells, not caring that she is depleting her small bubble of air, or the energy left in her shattered frame.

 5

"Vindication, revenge, and power!" His words shake the rocks around her with the might of an avalanche.

Shaking and terrified, Gwen shuts her eyes and braces herself for the mountain to finish what it started. The rumbling moves the rock about her until the weight no longer bears down on her. Gwen hesitantly ventures a peak at her surroundings when the quake finally ceases.

She is no longer pinned beneath boulders. A dim light shines through an opening above her. A long pathway is cleared between her and the hole in the debris, as if this escape route were made just for her. Gwen takes a deep breath of the fresh air pouring into her encasement. It both rejuvenates her and makes her sore. Her lungs, her ribs, her every inch, throb with pain as she struggles to move her arm to reach toward the dim light. *Is that the moon?* The little bit of movement she can muster tears a scream from her throat that does not seem to express her agony. Gwen collapses, giving up on the fruitless task.

"A lot of good providing me with an exit does if I'm still bleeding internally and have bones made of powder," Gwen scoffs.

"Then heal yourself," the dark stranger supplies. She then sees his smile as his face appears in her thoughts like the Cheshire Cat of Wonderland.

"Magic doesn't work in the pit, silly!" Gwen replies, exhausted and defeated.

"Ah, but the pit is no more. The mountain has crumbled and, with it all, its power to confine your abilities has disintegrated. Since you have rid yourself of your wedding band, and your finger, nothing is holding you back."

Gwen is silent a moment as she lets this information sink in. Tentatively, she reaches out for the source of all power. Gwen gasps when she finds the magic readily there and nothing in her way to impede. Without the ring tying her to Legion and without the pit, she has returned to her former self.

Her elation is quickly replaced by an unsettling feeling in her gut. Gwen looks back up at the opening above her with trepidation.

"Why are you doing this? If you enjoy watching me suffer so much, why help me out of this mess?" she asks the man in her head.

"Like I said before, child, I am not done with you. And you have work yet to do."

"You need me for something, right? Whatever it is you want me to do, I won't do it." Gwen calls out to him in as defiant a voice as she can muster in her weakness. "You should know by now that I don't take kindly to being forced into anything."

He chuckles. "Fine, then. Stay down there and rot." Inside her mind she sees him turn and start walking away.

"Wait!" Gwen cannot help calling after him, panic seizing all reason.

"Yes?"

"If I do as you suggest, heal myself and climb out, what will happen next?"

"Hmm. I suppose you will just have to find out, won't you?" She can hear the smug smile in his black, silk voice. "Besides, what choice do you have? We both know you are a fighter; it is not in your nature to roll over and die. You could not give up even if you wanted."

His words ring true, shaking her to the very core. She closes her eyes and quiets her mind, trying to make a rational decision. She contemplates all she has yet to live for and experience, wondering whether it is all worth the possibility of more torture and ruin.

But what if this all is just a delusion? Am I really going to let a specter scare me into dying in a hole in the ground? Is this really how I want my life to end?

"Well?" The dark stranger's arrogant voice interrupts her tranquility, forcing her back to the present.

"What do you want? Just tell me and get it over with."

"No, that would be all too easy. If I tell you, it ruins the fun of letting you figure it out on your own." He shakes his head, his short dark, hair swaying with the movement behind her eyelids. "No, my dear, if you want answers you're going to have to climb out and hunt them down yourself," he finishes with a self-satisfied grin.

"I see. Even with a superior being stalking me, I still must do everything myself. How typical." Gwen says sardonically.

His peal of laughter bounces off the rocks around her. She tries not to shiver at the eeriness of the tone. She sighs, turning her eyes onto her battered and broken body. *This isn't going to be easy, and man it's going to hurt!*

Taking a deep breath, she closes her eyes and gathers as much energy and power as she can from her own store as well as the stone and life around her.

Ah, that is my girl. She ignores his whisper of approval in her head. Instead, she turns her mind toward her memories of her mother and the healing song she taught her.

"*Ba beta lavota*," Gwen sings the words beneath her breath, willing the power to repair all that is damaged. A scorching pain like burning ice sweeps over her. The spell slowly works its way throughout her body. The pain it causes is nearly unbearable. Only Gwen's iron will keeps her holding onto the power through the anguish to see it through to the end. She wails in pain and curls up in a ball when she finishes, waiting for the last tendrils of discomfort to subside.

Once it passes, she uncurls herself and reaches a hand toward the closest handhold. With a grunt, she pulls herself upward, finding foot holes as she scales the tunnel of rubble toward the dim light above.

The stranger is no longer in her mind. For all she can tell, he has gone on to torment someone else.

With renewed vigor, Gwen reaches for the next handhold and the next. Unnatural strength pumps through her muscles as her once-shattered bones miraculously withstand impact of movement as if made of steel. The closer she comes to the top, the cleaner the air becomes. The light grows brighter until she at last pulls herself out of the tunnel and crawls out onto the surface of the ruined mountain.

Heart racing and gasping for breath, she welcomes in the cool night air as she plops down on her back to rest in the dirt. The full moon hangs high above her, a glowing sphere of light in a peaceful and brilliant starry sky.

At last, her breathing returns to normal and her pacing heart slows. After undergoing the strenuous task of healing, and the long climb, her body reminds her that she has other needs in which to attend now.

With a groan, she rolls onto her knees and slowly gets to her feet. Her stomach grumbles at her as if to confirm her earlier suspicions.

"What now, Gwen?" she asks herself, staring down at the valley below her and then glancing up at the ravaged mountain above her. "Where's Raven when you need him?" She starts the arduous trek down to the valley floor. "He's good for a laugh, good for hunting food, and if he were here right now, I could go down the mountain in ease on the back of a warm, furry wolf."

A thought occurs to her that she had not had time to ponder before. *Where is Raven? Where is Morna?* Guilt sweeps over her in a sickening wave. *What if I killed them? What if they're trapped under the mountain just as I was?* The thought brings Gwen to her knees, shaking. She looks back up the way she came, in shock. Gulping down the dread, she sends her mental energy out, searching for any sign of intelligent thought in the region.

She encounters only animal life. One in particular seems to be looking for her.

A bird caws. Puzzled, Gwen looks up to the sky to see a raven soaring in circles above her, its dark shape blacker than the sky behind it, barely perceivable.

"What do you want?" Gwen asks the animal. In response, it swoops down and lands at her feet, shaking its feathers as it settles. He turns his head at an angle to look at her as if posing an unspoken question.

Gwen receives a torrent of images from the bird's mind, sensing he is trying to communicate with her. *Are you she?*

It depends on who you're looking for, birdie. She who?

She who brought down the Mountain of Blood? Gwen perceives from the animal's thoughts. Through his eyes, she sees the mountain fall from without, sees the witches searching the ruins for survivors. The Raven twitches and angles his head as if trying to figure her out.

Then I am she, Gwen replies gravely, not the least bit proud of this tremendous feat. *I am the one who kills hundreds of innocent lives simply to kill one evil creature.*

The raven shows her an image of Morna comforting Raven, who is bound and limping. She sees the bird's eye view of her friends leaving with the other survivors.

You saw this yourself? Raven and Morna are, okay? Gwen tries to ask the raven, using images to convey her meaning.

He understands and caws in affirmation. Gwen senses that he has been waiting for her to emerge from the mountain.

You waited for me? Gwen asks incredulous. *Why? Who are you?*

The raven caws at her twice and then takes flight.

"Of course, you can't tell me who you are. I mean, why am I surprised? No one ever does," Gwen grumbles to herself as she gets to her feet and follows the bird flying above her. She is not sure why she trusts this strange animal, but something tells her he is a friend and that she is supposed to follow him.

Besides, it is not the first time a raven has come to my aid. Could it be the same bird from the times before? Gwen shakes off the notion until she recalls reading about the bird years ago. *Ravens can live forty years in the wild and seventy years in captivity. Maybe it is him?* Gwen tries to recall the details of the other times a raven has been there at the right time and place, without being able to discern if it has always been this same animal. *And you don't know it is a him either, Gwen,* she reminds herself; yet her instincts tell her she is right.

The raven swoops down from the sky into a thicket of trees. Gwen follows, curious. The bird alights on a bunch of fallen trees propped at an angle upon a large boulder. He caws at her as if to say, "this is the place." Gwen notices an opening beneath the tree trunks and smells bread and cheese nearby.

When Gwen hesitates, the raven caws again and nods his head, pointing his beak at the opening below him under the fallen trees.

"Okay, I get it, this is shelter and you brought me food?" Gwen asks incredulously. "Why?"

The bird sends a feeling of safety to her, a warmth that permeates her flesh. At last convinced, Gwen climbs down to the shelter to which the bird has led. Ducking down, she crawls into the dark opening, not sure what awaits her. It is dark within, the scent of bread and cheese growing stronger. Something rough and thin crunches beneath her knees, and Gwen smells rotting leaves amongst the dirt. Finally, Gwen's hand brushes the fabric of a blanket. She crawls out of the dirt onto the soft, dry surface. She fumbles a moment in the dark to grasp the food. She knows it is within reach.

"Duh, Gwen. You are a witch, remember? You can make your own light!" she says to the darkness. "*Illumae*," she whispers. Instantaneously, a ball of soft white light appears just above her head. She shields her eyes with one hand as her eyes adjust. Her little dwelling is a small dirt cave, with dying grass and rotting leaves making up the floor and the fallen trees her roof. The blanket she sits on is knitted cotton in a green and white plaid pattern. Several scraps of old bread and moldy cheese rest before her.

"Where on earth...?" The Raven swooshes in from the caves opening. He pointedly avoids the ball of light and lands on the blanket across from Gwen.

"I see you'll be joining me in this... feast," Gwen quips to the black bird, who looks up at her with his black eyes. "I was just wondering who made this little picnic?"

The raven seems to understand the images in her head and sends back flashes of his own memories.

Gwen gasps. "You did this?" she replies skeptically, seeing in her mind the bird snag the blanket and food from a family campsite on the other side of the mountain. He found the food in the trash bag and piled it upon the blanket. With his beak, he had grasped each corner of the plaid material and dropped it into the middle, enclosing the food within. Once all the corners were in place, the raven had gathered them all in his beak. Flying low and with significant effort, he carried his scavenged spoils to this hideaway. She even saw the bird smooth out the blanket by pulling all the corners with his beak and stomping across the wrinkles with the talons of his feet.

"Why are you helping me?" Gwen asks, completely floored by the resourcefulness this strange animal has exerted on her behalf. "Who am I to you? Why were you waiting for me?"

The raven only caws, nudging a crust of bread toward her with his beak as if to say, "That is not important — just eat up!"

"All right. Beggars can't be choosers. I will eat it." She concedes to the bird, grabbing the crust of bread he offered her and

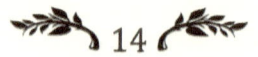

tentatively bringing it to her mouth. "I never thought I'd break bread with a bird," she mumbles before taking a bite of the stale, dry bread.

It is rough and lacking in taste, but it is food. Gwen finds her stomach all too willing to overlook the source of the food and its lack of flavor. Before she knows it, she has eaten half of the bread and cheese. Satisfied, the bird caws at her again, sending the message that now she should sleep.

This is no ordinary raven. He is concerned for me, but why? He must have an owner, someone who taught him how to do all these things. Try as she might, Gwen cannot fathom who could be the owner of this remarkable bird.

Gwen sighs as she makes herself comfortable on the blanket. Laying down to sleep, she uses her arm as a pillow and stares at the bird across from her busily pecking at a roll of bread.

"Weird stuff seems to be the norm in my life."

At this, the raven looks up at her as he chokes down his food. His black eyes meet hers. "I don't have many friends but I'm glad I'm so fortunate as to have such an unusual champion."

Chapter Two

Cat Eyes

T he night seems darker than most, the alley devoid of light. Even so, Raven can see in the darkness like no human ever could. At night, his world has a silver glow about it, illuminated not by the sun but by the energy that flows through all the elements of the earth. Effortlessly, he walks through the dark recesses between the old buildings. This part of Chicago few dare to traverse alone. He is not afraid of death anymore, because he feels nothing.

A familiar smell wafts through the air to his nose: blue bells, sunlight, and dew.

Damn Fairy! Raven grumbles under his breath, knowing she can hear just as well as he can. He thought he had given her the slip this time, but no, yet again she has tracked him down. He does not know how she does it. *Must be some Fairy superpower.*

Ever since Bec LaNuff, the Fairy has been like his shadow. For a while she stayed out of sight, trying to spy on him without detection. She had no choice but to reveal herself when he came across some Vampires in the backwoods of Louisiana.

It was a few months prior. He was wandering the woods after a hunt when he stumbled out of a clearing. He found before him a gang of Vampires tormenting a handful of teenagers on a weekend camping trip. One of the teenage girls had dark hair and green eyes. She looked at him with terror in her eyes as if pleading with him to save her. All he could see was Gwen. With the battle of Bec LaNuff still fresh in his mind, he had charged into the fray with blind rage, not caring one bit that he was seriously outnumbered. He changed into the beast and attacked.

Only after he killed a couple Vampires did he realize that he was likely fighting to his death. That is when the blue Fairy dropped out of the sky into the camp site. The Vampires were stunned by her appearance. She let out a banshee-like scream that shattered the air and drove Raven and the Vampires to their knees in pain. The humans seemed less affected, but terrified.

"Run, you idiots!" she yelled in English to the stunned adolescents. They obeyed her, running off to climb into their SUV barreling down the road. All their camping gear left behind.

Morna then turned and gathered Raven's wolf form into her arms. Without a word, she shot back into the sky. The rest of that evening is still a blur for him, only remembering snatches of images from the wolfs side of his mind.

When he came to the next day, he was human again, naked and lying parallel to a nearby creek. Morna the Fairy was sitting on a rock watching him, her wings glistening in the sunlight.

A sound reaches his ears, pulling Raven out of his thoughts to the present, and his stroll through the alleys of Chicago. His supernatural senses note everything going on around him. Around the bend, he hears a woman's voice followed by male laughter. Raven slows his pace and peers around the corner into the alley beyond.

Two Hispanic men stand before a lone Black woman with her back up against the brick wall. Lit by the dim light of a flashlight, held by one of the two men. Raven observes the woman as if trapped in an unforgiving spotlight. Her coat looks rumpled, her hair half-yanked out of its long brown braid. Her eyes are wide and frantic. She throws her purse at the two men's feet.

"Take it!" In a panic, she wrestles her jewelry off and offers it at her assailants with shaking hands. "Here, take it all! It's just stuff, please, let me go!" she begs.

"What do you think, Big Danny?" One of the men looks to his comrade, awaiting his action. The other man holds a gun limply at his side, eyeing the desperate woman's valuables. For a moment, the captive lady looks hopeful.

"Tempting," Big Danny taps the gun against his leg a few times as he walks toward the woman, his finger on the trigger. He eyes her, openly looking her over as a predator might his meal. "But...

my guys haven't had any fun in a long time." Big Danny steps within inches of her and points the gun at her forehead. She gasps, panting. She closes her eyes and turns her head. He smiles and brushes her face with the barrel of his handgun. The woman whimpers and quakes. "It wouldn't be right to let you go just yet. Once the boys get here, that's when the fun will really begin." He whispers into her face. Her eyes still clench shut out of fear.

To Raven's nose, the woman reeks of fear. It permeates the alley, but not as much as the stench of the men's evil desires. A growl builds from the base of his throat as his anger forms into something dark all its own.

"No… Please, please!" she forces out of trembling lips.

"Hey!" Just as surely as if Raven's voice had been a gunshot, the three people before him react in unison. Big Danny whirls around with gun at the ready. Aiming the flashlight at Raven, the other man stares wild-eyed as he scrambles to find his own weapon. The woman's eyes fly open to stare in awe at Raven. He stands now in the middle of the spotlight in the otherwise dark alley before them. "The lady asked you to leave her alone. That's exactly what you two are going to do. Only you won't be taking any of her stuff with you."

"Oh, is that so?" Big Danny looks at him with mock shock and then turns to his associate. "Hey, Guillermo, I guess we're just supposed to run along because some bum tells us to." His partner laughs nervously. Obviously, he is more intimidated by Raven's impressive bulk and height than his leader. "Hmmm, what happens if we decide not to do what we're told, huh? Big guy?" Big Danny asks, waving his gun around as he speaks.

"Then I'll just have to rip the flesh from your bones till you're dead," Raven replies smoothly, shrugging nonchalantly.

Suddenly a triumphant look spreads across Big Danny's face and Guillermo snorts.

Dispassionately, Raven looks over his shoulder to see four more men standing behind him. Some have knives in their clutched fists. The others carry handguns aimed at his back. They wait for him to speak, to react to their presence. Twenty-year-old Raven says nothing.

"Well, I don't see how that's going to happen since there's now *six* of us and only *one* of you." Big Danny scratches the side of his face with his gun barrel as his mischievous grin spreads wider.

"I've survived worse odds than this, and against real monsters." Raven's voice takes on a deadly edge in the ominous surroundings. "I'll be the last man standing, that I can promise you."

The lot of them laugh arrogantly.

Fools. You have no idea who you're messing with.

Above, Raven senses a shape fly over the moon and tenses. Looking up, he checks to see if his guardian angel is visible. She is not. However, he can hear the faint patter of her delicate wings in the air nearby.

Great! He laments inwardly. *The last thing I need is for her to stick her neck out for me yet again. She'll never let me live this one*

down. I practically walked right into danger after I promised I would be more careful. If he were honest with himself, it was a promise he had never intended to keep. He just did not plan to get caught by Morna when he broke it.

"Look, I know you won't believe me, but I feel I must warn you. I'm not human. The little lady stalking us from the rooftop isn't either." Raven stands square before them, speaking so that none would miss a word. "If you're not scared of me, you should be terrified of her."

A musical little laugh drifts down from above, bouncing off the walls of the alley. Guillermo before him visibly shivers. They all stare wildly around the alley and above to the sky. Big Danny jerks his gun, obviously unnerved.

"No one threatens us!" the leader shouts as he starts shooting his gun at the sky. His men take this as their signal to attack.

Raven lurches to the side as one of the young men behind him dives toward him. His would-be assailant stumbles and lands face first on the asphalt, cussing as his nose snaps on impact.

Another gunshot explodes in the confined alley. Instantaneously, Raven spins around, the bullet missing his left shoulder by mere inches. Crouching on all floors, Raven charges toward the shooter. Yelling out profanities, the boy shoots again, missing as Raven quickly dodges and rolls in a zig-zag pattern. Giving out a guttural growl, Raven knocks the boy over, pinning him to the ground. He rips the gun from his attacker's hand.

Thinking fast, Raven spins to confront the other gang members around him, with his finger on the gun's trigger.

Still glancing upward occasionally as if spooked, Big Danny points his gun at Raven's chest while his second in command, Guillermo, helps the other man off the ground. This man grunts in pain as he holds a hand to his nose, blood gushing between his fingers and down his chin. The other three men turn hate-filled gazes on Raven, matching their leader's grimace. The injured man pulls out a butterfly knife from his back pocket, brandishing the blade with a flourish. Another man aims his gun at him while he hikes up the waistband of his sagging jeans.

"Drop the gun," Big Danny orders. Raven points the barrel towards the leader with a level glare. Big Danny turns to his second in command. "Guillermo, if he doesn't drop the gun on the count of three, kill her." He gestures towards the woman they cornered earlier with a jerk of his head.

Raven glances towards where the woman had been only moments ago. In all the commotion, she slowly inched her way toward the mouth of the alley. Guillermo's sudden appearance puts a stop to this. She screams as the man yanks her by the arm and throws her down on the pavement. She hits the ground with a whimper, mumbling and begging for mercy.

"One, two…" Guillermo pulls out a gun and points it at the woman's head.

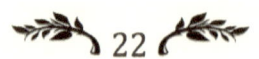

"Okay, Okay Stop!" Raven drops the gun on the ground and raises his hands slowly. "Just leave her alone."

Big Danny smiles. "Cut him up, Joaquin," commands the leader to his knife-wielding companion. "Hugo, you hold him down. If he tries to run, I'll splatter his brains across the alley. Samson, Guido, you keep a look out, make sure no one's coming."

Joaquin and Hugo step forward to do Big Danny's bidding. They smile in unison. Joaquin's bloody broken nose lending him a ghoulish air. Hugo circles around Raven as Joaquin lunges at him with his blade. In a flash, Raven kicks Joaquin's hand, hurtling the knife into the air. The man shouts and buckles to his knees, cradling his injured hand. His friend attacks Raven from behind, pinning his arms behind his back. As Raven struggles free, he hears the cock of a gun. His head snaps up to look at the leader.

A banshee's wale pierces the alley, echoing off the narrow walls. Joaquin screams and covers his ears, curling up in a ball on the ground while Hugo releases his hold on Raven to do the same.

A whoosh of wind and the flapping of wings follows as Morna drops out of the sky right on top of the gang leader. He screams in utter terror, squeezing the trigger on the gun, shooting wildly. The bullets whizz and ricochet off the walls and asphalt. Everyone ducks to avoid being hit by a stray bullet. Morna, looking fiendish in the silvery glow of the moon, clutches Big Danny by the shoulders and shoots back into the night sky.

Raven feels a gust of wind and blinding pain as a bullet burst through his left shoulder. Raven roars as the impact flattens him onto his back.

Recovering from Morna's piercing screams, Hugo and Joaquin stir. The first leaps to his feet, quickly pinning Raven down by pushing a boot heel into his Adam's apple. Raven gasps for breath and struggles. Weakened by his bullet wound, he lacks the strength to force his assailant off. Joaquin quickly joins his companion. Having found his lost butterfly knife, he flashes it at Raven,

"What was that thing?" Hugo demands, pushing all his weight down on Raven, He points his gun in his face cocking it. "Where's Big Danny?" Raven crawls at the man's leg but can't breathe enough to speak. "You tell that thing up there to bring back Big Danny or we'll kill you," Hugo instructs Raven.

Raven just spits at them.

"You hear that? We're going to kill your friend unless you let Big Danny go!" Joaquin calls up into the night sky.

An evil laugh carries down to them.

"No, no!" Big Danny screams. A moment later, he falls helplessly from the rooftops. His screams of terror end abruptly as he collides with the street below with a bone-shattering crack.

Big Danny wails in pain clutching at his broken legs.

Joaquin rushes to his injured friend's side, while Hugo looks at the scene in stunned horror. Raven kicks the legs out from under him, sending the man down hard on his back. He pushes with all his

might against Hugo's leg, forcing the man to lose his balance and stumble backward. With a surprised shout, the gun slips out of his grip and slides across the pavement.

Gasping and wheezing for air, Raven rolls onto his hands and knees, sucking in as much oxygen as he can.

"Kill him!" Big Danny commands with gritted teeth as Joaquin drags him off to the side of the alley next to Guillermo whose, still holding onto the frightened woman.

"Here. Watch out for Big Danny. If that thing comes back, shoot it!"

Guillermo nods, training his eyes on the dark sky whilst holding the barrel of his gun to the Black woman's head.

Before Raven can recover, Hugo gets back up onto their feet. He delivers two swift kicks into Raven's stomach. The impact sends the air out of Raven's lungs again as he collapses onto the ground.

"Got you now!" Joaquin lunges at Raven with his blade ready to plunge into his back. The blade never meets flesh.

Raven hears the others gasps and glimpses a small blue woman appear between Joaquin and himself. She effortlessly twists the man's wrist. He erupts in shouts of pain as Morna's super-human strength crushes the man's bones. The wailing Joaquin drops his weapon. With a swift and powerful kick in the man's chest, the fairy sends the man flying across the alley to smack into the far brick wall. By the time Joaquin lands on the ground, he is unconscious.

Raven hears running footsteps and looks up to see Hugo rushing over to retrieve his fallen gun. The beast inside tears through Raven's mind, taking control.

Just as the gang member curls his fingers around the gun's handle, an animal roars behind him. He spins around to see Raven in his massive gray wolf form. The animal reveals his jagged teeth as he leaps forward. With wide eyes, Hugo fumbles to aim the gun at the beast charging at him and stumbles backward. He crashes to the ground, the gun flying out of his hand as he makes impact with the hard pavement. The wolf lands atop of Hugo, who wails in fear. The wolf ends the man's pitiful noise, clamping his jaw around the man's throat and ripping it free.

With the taste of the man's blood in his mouth, Raven feels the beast rescind into his inner dwelling until the monster decides he is needed once more. When the pain of transformation washes over him, Raven slowly stands on his own two feet in his human form.

"You, okay?" Morna asks, her high-pitched voice soft and smooth, like honey, a strange contrast to her banshee cries.

Warm despite the night air against his naked skin, Raven does not shiver. Keeping his back to her, he glances over his shoulder and nods in reply, his heart pumping in his ears, his shoulder throbbing in pain.

She smiles at him, her blue skin more glorious and stunning to his night vision than anything else around. He watches as her smile fades, and she points behind him.

"Raven!"

"Die, you freak!" Guillermo yells.

Raven turns just in time to watch the young man who had been threatening the woman, standing just a foot before him with his gun in his hand. Just then the other two gang member who had gone off to keep watch come racing down the alley with guns ready. Guillermo aims and pulls back on the trigger. Multiple gunshots rings through the night. Raven closes his eyes and braces himself for the impact of the bullets. He might be able to dodge the other men's attempts but Guillermo is to close for that.

"*Haultia emmitula!*" chants a female voice from somewhere in the darkness.

Raven is stunned by the lack of impact, until recognition surfaces. His breath catches in his throat. He stays still, afraid to open his eyes, lest this all be just a dream. *In that case, I don't ever want to wake up.*

Raven hears more gunshots as the men empty the rest of the bullets in their clips, shooting at someone else in the alley. The new woman laughs, and the young men scream profanities at her as they turn and flee. Their running footsteps fade into the other sounds of the night.

"Wait, you idiots don't leave me here!" Big Danny's words ring out in the still alley. No one answers his command; no one comes back for their fearless leader.

"Sorry, pal, but either they can't hear you, or they just don't care." The familiar voice laughs darkly after addressing the man. Still Raven cannot bring himself to open his eyes.

Raven flinches as a bright light pierces through the skin of his closed eyelids.

Morna gasps behind him. He feels a gust of air as she rushes to the speaker of the enchanted words and the source of the light. He hears the rustle of fabric and wings, imagining that the two women must be embracing. Still, he refuses to even peek.

The click of heels on the pavement echoes off the enclosure as the newcomer walks up to him and stops just inches away.

He takes a deep breath, taking in the aroma of her. She smells of spices, flames, and a hint of wildflowers.

"Sorry to intervene. It looked like you had it all under control for a moment there. Until that last little bit, anyway." She speaks and the sound sends a jolt of bitter-sweet joy through his veins. "What's wrong with him, Morna? Has he developed narcolepsy?" she jokes.

"I have no idea what that is," Morna replies, her bird-like chirp of a voice just to his right.

Something jabs him just under the rips. Yelping, Raven jumps away from Morna and her poking fingers. His eyes fly open to give her a glare. His annoyance dies immediately as his eyes alight on the other woman's face.

"Where the hell have you been?" he shouts at Gwen, half-angry, half-laughing.

With watery eyes, Gwen flings herself into his arms, her shape instantly familiar to his body as he folds himself around her. Her head leaned against his chest. They are both too caught up in the moment to mind his nakedness.

"Sorry. It takes a while to tunnel out from under a mountain, and it's not like you left a forwarding address, you know," Gwen says in her usual sarcastic tone. "And I was busy hanging out with a bird. A raven, actually."

"What?" Raven steps back, holding her at arm's length with a sad smile on his face.

"I'll explain later," Gwen replies.

"What should we do with the woman?" Morna interjects with a nod of her head at the lady whose distress had started the whole skirmish in the first place. The three friends turn to look where she cowers in the corner of the alley, her eyes the size of saucers.

"She has seen us. She knows what we are," Raven points out. Before he can open his mouth to speak again the woman jumps to her feet and bolts toward the opening of the alley and freedom.

Morna moves as if to take flight, but Gwen puts a hand on her blue shoulder to stop her. "I've got this." She dashes forward, heading off the woman to block her escape. The woman comes to an abrupt halt and opens her mouth to scream. However, in that moment Gwen entrances her, taking complete control of the

woman's mind. After a few uttered instructions, she hands the woman back her purse and jewelry.

Raven and Morna watch as the woman slowly rouses. She adjusts her coat, drops her jewelry into her bag, and slips her purse over her arm.

"Excuse me, miss," she speaks in her regular voice. "You really shouldn't be out at this time of night alone," Gwen warns the woman.

"You know, you're right. I'll go home right away." She says before walking off as if nothing happened. She never once looks back and is soon out of sight. The woman picks up her pace, the clacking of her high-heel shoes blend into sounds of the city.

Gwen wears a smug look on her face as strolls over to Big Danny who has collapsed onto his side, panting heavily.

"Well, I don't know about you guys, but I can always go for some grub after a good supernatural ass-kicking." Gwen bends down over the gang leader and he flinches

"Please don't hurt me, please…" he whimpers.

"Oh, relax, I'm not going to kill you. I am going to need your wallet, though," Gwen explains. Shaking, Danny retrieves the wallet out of his back pocket and hands it to Gwen. Straightening, she plucks the cash from its leather folds with a glove-covered hand before tossing it over her shoulder. "Who feels like hitting a diner? Food is on me! Of course, we'll need to get Raven some clothes before we go out to eat." Gwen points this out with raised eyebrows and a smirk on her face.

Raven blushes, laughing awkwardly. Morna giggles.

"This Big Danny fellow looks close enough to your size," Gwen points out. "Sorry, buddy, but looks like I'm going to need your clothes, too," Gwen tells the man in a mock apologetic tone.

Raven shakes his head with a silent chuckle. He quickly moves over to the gang leader's side. With swift hands, he peels the clothing off the man. Danny screams in pain as his injured legs are jostled when his pants are removed. Raven dons the clothes onto his own person. It smells of liquor and blood, but it will have to do for now.

"Let's get out of here," Raven says then pauses to look back at the pathetic man at his feet. "What should we do with him? And the dead guy?" Raven asks the girls. He averts his eyes from the corpse left by the wolf. He pushes down the sense of guilt along with the bile threatening to raise up from his stomach. *He tried to kill you and Morna.* He reasons in his head.

"I doubt anyone will care to see this guy go," Gwen muses gesturing at the dead man. "Big Danny's not going anywhere, but I won't bother removing his memories. No one is likely to believe a word he says anyway. Besides, there was an awful lot of gunshots fired and it will not be long before the cops show up."

As he walks over to join the two girls, Raven cannot help looking over all the changes in his long-lost friend. Gwen is taller than he remembered, dressed from head to toe in black. She still wears her black hair long and straight about her pale face.

As if on cue, they hear sirens in the distance coming nearer. Raven and Gwen turn as if to dash away with their superhuman speed when Morna touches both their shoulders.

"I've got this." She mimics Gwen's tone, gaining her a laugh from both her friends. Before either can protest, she takes them both by an arm and shoots into the sky. Despite her size, her fairy strength is more than adequate to carry them all high into the starless sky and away from the scene.

As they soar through the sky, Raven cannot take his eyes off Gwen, as if she will vanish like a mirage. Looking at her, he feels as though his soul has returned to him, seeing his true self staring back at him in her yellow-green cat eyes.

Chapter Three

New Beginning

The forest of Fort Washington State Park is eerily quiet in the setting Philadelphia sun. Walking amongst old sycamores and dogwood trees, Gwen, Morna, and Raven started their hike from an ordinary looking parking lot onto the Green Ribbons Preserve trail. The paved biking trail ran along the Wissahickon Creek north into the woods. With the beginning of autumn upon them they were frequently passed by cyclists of all ages enjoying the scenery. The sounds of tourists laughing and birds chipping in the trees created a noisy atmosphere. Eventually, the paved path ended, turning back into its natural earthy trail, the cyclists no longer present. The forest grew quieter, and wilder.

Taking the rear, Raven faithfully follows his two companions as Gwen leads Morna and him off the trodden path. They head into the woods without any real direction. Once they leave the trail,

bird's songs vanish. The woods lose all sign of life. After a while, it becomes clear that Gwen is following a long-forgotten path into the mountains.

At her human size, Morna fills the gap between them. The Fairy seems to hear things that are not there. Her head tilted slightly, blue tipped ears twitching. Once they were well out of sight of humans, Morna changed her appearance back to her usual Fairy garb. The blue-skinned girl moves bare-footed in the autumn foliage without making a sound. Her footsteps float just above the forest floor. Her golden hair hangs down her back; between her wings, which hang limply behind her, not quite reaching her calf. Both catch hints of the remaining sunlight. They glisten as if made of gold and diamonds.

Despite the lack of sound or trace of animal life, the forest is alive with smells for Raven, the decaying smells of the turning leaves overpowering him. A sense of death permeates the air. His instincts tell him to turn back, yet he knows Gwen will not join him should he leave. His relentless sense of allegiance keeps him tethered to her. Letting out a deep sigh he continues to follow, whilst his lungs become ever heavier with dread.

Gwen moves with purpose, seeming unaffected by the strange lack of wildlife ambiance or the smells in the woods about them. She does not stop to listen or look at the beautiful setting. She does not seem to care about the gorgeous display of gold light shining through the trees. Gwen has been of one mind and purpose ever since Raven handed her that key. The key Angelo entrusted to him outside of Bec LaNuff before the vampire died attempting to rescue Gwen. *Almost as if Angelo knew he would not live much longer.*

At the time, Raven took the key to soothe the clearly agitated Vampire. Later when the Italian lay charred to death in Gwen's arms, he had been glad to have it to offer her. Before he could, the mountain fortress collapsed with Gwen lost somewhere inside. He contemplated throwing away the key a dozen times in the months that followed. With her sudden reappearance a week ago, he is again glad to give her this one last gift from the one she seemed to love so dearly.

I hope that whatever the key unlocks brings Gwen some semblance of peace.

Abruptly coming to from his musing, Raven realizes that Gwen has stopped. Morna waits expectantly beside her. Raven watches as Gwen wanders toward an exceptionally large boulder with a tree growing right up against it, as though the tree were the rock's conjoined twin.

Gwen tucks a strand of her jet-black hair behind her ear as she studies the bark of the tree. With her fingers, she traces the knots and cracks in the surface as if looking for something familiar. With the slightest nod, Gwen stops her search and pulls the key from her coat pocket. Confidently, she inserts the key into a barely visible crack and twists it. Raven hears a small click and then a whoosh of stale air as part of the tree trunk moves into itself. Gwen stares into the blackness beyond the opening in the tree. Her face is blank, yet her scent is heavy with apprehension.

Morna steps up beside Gwen, placing a small bluish hand on her shoulder. Her touch startles Gwen. She spins around to look at her two friends as if just now realizing that they are even there.

"Should we go in?" Morna asks softly. Gwen looks at her as if struck dumb, a kaleidoscope of emotions dancing behind her eyes.

"After all, we've come all this way," Raven adds, hesitant to step forward but wanting to encourage Gwen.

"Of course," Gwen replies with a weak smile. She turns and steps into the tree. Without hesitation or sound, Morna follows. Raven finds himself standing there staring after them, immoveable.

I haven't been this afraid to enter a place since Bec LaNuff, he thinks to himself. *And that was a nest of Vampires and other monsters. What am I afraid of?* The thought emboldens him, propelling him forward. He finds himself a moment later standing at the opening into the tree.

Instead of looking into darkness, Raven sees Gwen and Morna standing inside a round room filled with enchanted light. Less troubled, Raven steps inside, closing the door behind him.

The tree, it seems, is in fact attached to the boulder and the boulder itself hollowed out into a simple dwelling. With large rock slabs making up the floor, and the walls and ceiling the same dark gray of the boulder, the only color comes from the furnishing. A small wooden cot sits at the opposite end of the room, made up with

ancient quilt and linens. From the smell of it, a feather-filled mattress and pillows lie underneath. Bookshelves made of old, gnarled wood take up one corner. Old, dusty, leather-bound books fill its recesses. Next to the door resides an ancient armchair and end table set around a long-unused stone fireplace. To Raven's astonishment, three long, oval windows in the stone walls look out into the forest.

"The windows only work from within. Don't ask me how; Angelo didn't know the particulars of this place. It was long abandoned when he discovered it a hundred years ago," Gwen answers his unspoken thought, making Raven aware that he has accidently left his mental guard down. Gwen gives him a small smile of understanding before turning away to look at the room.

"When did he bring you here?" Morna asks aloud. Raven knows it is just for his sake.

"Right after you left us at the hermit's cabin near Bec LaNuff. He wanted to show me another safe place." Gwen hesitates a moment, her face falling from calm into complete loss. "His safe place." She whispers the words as if they hurt to speak.

Without explanation, Gwen squats down in the center of the room and works her fingers along the edges of one of the rock slabs in the floor. Raven watches as she digs the dirt out from under one part of the rock. Getting her fingers under it, she uses both gloved hands to pry the rock up enough to slide it out of its place. In its absence Raven sees an opening in the floor, and what looks like a wooden ladder leading downward.

Gwen takes a deep breath before lowering herself down into the opening. She vanishes from view and Raven hears her footsteps on the wooden ladder as she climbs down, into what or where he does not know. Fearless and free as always, Morna steps into the hole, falling without bothering to use the ladder to reach the bottom. Again, Raven finds himself hesitant to follow while the girls seem unafraid. With a nervous chuckle at his own stupidity, he makes his way to the opening and lets himself down onto the ladder.

The ladder is made of incredibly old wood that creaks and protests under his weight. Below him he sees light at the end of a small vertical tunnel. Descending the ladder, he emerges into the lit chamber below. His two companions stand in a room full of closed chests and trunks.

"What is this place, Gwen?" Raven asks.

"Angelo's hoard," Gwen replies, a bit amused. She laughs dryly as she steps up to one trunk. Using the same key that opened the tree's hidden door, she unlocks the trunk, throwing it open.

"What is that some kind of master key?" Raven asks.

"Better than that. It's a Witch's skeleton key. Angelo got it from the Black Magic Market some time ago. It can open anything with a lock, but once it does, it can only be unlocked by this key forever afterwards." Morna nods in understanding.

Stepping up besides Gwen, Raven gasps involuntarily at the gold shimmering coins piled within the trunk. He cannot help but dip one of his hands into the gold coins, letting them slip between his fingers as they clink and clank back into the box. The metal delightfully cold against his warm flesh.

"Are they all filled with this?" Raven asks. He notices that Gwen's face is glowing in the reflective light off the gold.

Gwen nods, giving him a crooked smile. "Now don't go all crazy pirate on me. It's just money, after all."

"Yeah, but a hell of a lot of it!" Raven looks about the room in wonder before turning back to Gwen eyes alight with excitement. "Is this real gold?"

Gwen sighs exaggeratedly, shaking her head in affirmation.

"Wow, Gwen, this is beyond generous of him. Why, you'll never have to worry about money again!"

"Yes, but is this why he sent you here?" Morna asks doubtfully.

"Maybe, but it's not what I came here for." Gwen scans the room a moment, her eyes lighting up for the first time since her return. Gwen is across the room in an instant, pulling from among the trunks an oddly shaped ancient leather case. Gwen sets it atop a trunk and unfastens the clasps to open it. Inside sits an antique red violin. A gold animal head forms the handle, with gold rivets, plates, and knobs.

Gently, as if picking up a sleeping babe, Gwen removes the instrument from its red velvet case along with its bow. After a moment's hesitation, she puts the violin to her chin and assesses the strings. The notes are sour, making both Morna and Raven cringe. With a determined look, Gwen adjusts the knobs to retune the long unused violin. Once done, Gwen plays a short song. The tune is so sweet in its melancholy that Raven's eyes get a little misty. When done, Gwen silently puts the instrument away in its case, staring at it, blind to the world around her. Gwen shudders. Her shoulders slump. Raven watches as a single tear slides down her cheek, falling to the dirt floor.

"Um, we'll give you a moment alone," Raven announces, gesturing to Morna with his head toward the ladder.

"Yes, of course. We will just be waiting for you outside the tree," Morna chimes in with her little voice before following close behind him. In no time, Raven reaches the top of the ladder and climbs out of the hole in the floor. A whoosh of air announces Morna's ascent, and a second later, she appears hovering above the hole. She glides above solid ground and gently lands on the stone without a hint of her footfall.

How on earth does she do that? he wonders for the hundredth time since meeting her. Morna waits for him to stand, dusts himself off, and heads for the door before she follows behind him out of the strange dwelling.

* * * * *

A small eternity later, Gwen emerges from the tree trunk into the full darkness of the woods to find no one waiting. Slowly, she closes the tree door, hearing it lock back in place as the latch clicks. With Angelo's instrument case slung over one shoulder and two small sacks hanging from tie strings on her belt, Gwen makes her way slowly through the moon-lit forest. Sending her mental feelers out into the surrounding area. Gwen locates her friends not far off in the trees just ahead of her. As Gwen approaches, she sees and hears their campfire, the smell wafting to her through the night breeze. *Apparently, Raven has caught a couple rabbits that are now roasting over the fire.*

The rather large, broad-shouldered man and the tiny wisp of a girl sit near each other deep in a quiet conversation, their heads close together as they speak. Raven sits on the ground while Morna perches on a fallen tree trunk. Even with her elevated seat, Morna's and Raven's faces are on the same level. The firelight casts them in its romantic glow.

Gwen's step slows as she watches them. Suddenly she wants to be as silent as her Fairy friend, her attention rapt by the two youths before her.

Well, I'll be a dirty toad! They're in love! Gwen confirms to herself. Unknowing that she is present, neither guards their thoughts, their feelings exposed for her. *Well, maybe love is a little too strong a word for it, but there is a spark.* Morna seems to be burning a

strong blaze for Raven. Gwen senses that although he is very attracted to Morna, for some reason Raven is holding back.

Suddenly she is ashamed of how self-involved she's been since her reunion with her friends. Had she been less depressed and pathetic, she might have noticed the spark between the two before. Watching them now on their own, without Gwen to worry over, they seem perfectly content in each other, as if they are a world unto themselves.

Just now the idea of a Fairy and a Werewolf as a couple seems the most natural thing in the world. A sly smile finds its way onto her lips as she approaches the two. A crunch of leaves must have given her away, for they both look up at her simultaneously. Under normal circumstances they should have heard her ages ago, both gifted with superior hearing and smell.

They were too distracted to notice. Gwen's little smile breaks into a full-blown wicked grin.

"What's so funny?" Raven asks as Gwen finds a seat for herself on the opposite side of the fire from them.

"Nothing, I just had a nice thought."

Are you all right, Gwen? You were in there a long time. The wolf was beginning to worry. Morna communicates telepathically, her voice a pleasant sound in Gwen's head.

I'm fine. I just needed a moment to think, to produce a game plan. The words "game plan" seem to confuse Morna, which makes Gwen laugh inwardly. Settling by the fire, Gwen takes off the violin

case and sets it down beside her, out of reach of the flames. As Gwen moves, one of the sacks on her belt makes a few metallic chimes.

Raven quirks an eyebrow at the sound. "So, what's the plan now that you're filthy rich?"

"I was thinking we should go to Vegas," Gwen responds smugly.

"What? You can't seriously be thinking of blowing real gold on the tables, are you?" Raven exclaims, his horror evident on his tan face.

Gwen cannot help but laugh at him. It takes her a while to stop laughing. When she does, she smiles brightly at her two befuddled friends and replies, "That's not quite what I had in mind."

"Well, then, what do you have in mind?" Raven retorts still confused.

Gwen responds simply by uttering a single phrase: "A little magic and a whole new beginning."

Chapter Four

Blood and Vengeance

*T*he hot wind carries a multitude of scents to her vampire nose. She inhales the intoxicating aroma as the tourists flow around her. She stands on top of a bench set into the sidewalk. Her elevated perch provides her with a clear view of the human buffet while keeping her from being trampled underfoot. A few of the warm-blooded Eden Spawn that pass her look at her curiously. For a moment, she can imagine what she looks like to them.

It must seem odd for an eight-year-old girl to stand on a bench alone, sniffing the air like an animal in the middle of the Las Vegas Strip. Lynette flashes a toothy smile at a black-skinned man who is unfortunate enough to meet her grayish eyes.

"You lost, kid?" the stranger asks, shouting to her over the den of chattering sightseers.

"Yes. I cannot find my parents anywhere." Lynette lets out a little whimper, her big eyes drawing the man nearer as she enforces

her will upon his feeble mind. He stumbles blindly toward her, pushing passers-by out of the way, ignoring their shouts and curses as he makes his path to her bench.

"What hotel you staying in, kid?" the tall, skinny, Black man asks, his eyes glazed over but his mind still working.

"I don't know the name." Lynette lets her voice quiver and her lip tremble for effect. The man reaches out and puts a hand on her shoulder, concern in his bid brown eyes.

"It's okay, kid. Vegas is my home. You describe the place to me, and I'll know which hotel it is."

Quickly Lynette slides off the bench, grabbing the stranger's hand as if a life vest in a squall.

"Thank you!" She looks up at the man with big, watery, doe eyes, pulling him along the sidewalk as she speaks. "It's the one that's shaped like a triangle with a big diamond light on top and the statue that looks like a lion with a person's face on it," she explains in as childish a voice as she can muster.

"That'll be the Luxor hotel and casino. It's just up the street a few blocks." The man's pace picks up as he moves with purpose now. "Don't worry, we'll get you back to the hotel and they'll help you find your parents. You know your room number, don't you?"

Lynette's eyes get even bigger as she shakes her head no, forcing her cheeks to blush.

"That's okay, they can look you up by your parents' name and find the room number easily enough." He winks down at her and gives her hand a little squeeze.

Lynette smiles sadly up at him.

The man leads her through the thronging foot traffic down the Vegas Strip. Weaving through cars, they cross the street. The cabbies honk and yell at them. None of the pedestrians pay them no mind.

The hot desert breeze rushes passed them, tousling the girl's wild brown curls.

"Man, it's hot tonight. But that breeze sure feel good, don't it?" the man next to her asks in a conversational tone.

"Sure does." Lynette agrees although she does not feel the heat or the breeze anymore. She has not felt those kinds of sensations for exactly three years. Today happens to be her undead birthday.

Finally, the Luxor hotel comes into view. Lynette feels the man's warm blood pumping through his veins and through the skin of his hand.

It's now or never.

Lynette stumbles and falls to the sidewalk, the jolt stopping her companion in his tracks.

"Whoa, now. You, okay?" He bends over her, concern wrinkling his dark brow.

"No. I think I sprained my ankle." Lynette tries to stand but collapses to the pavement with a cry.

"How about I carry you the rest of the way?" he asks, and she nods consent. The man bends down and scoops her up into his arms, bringing her with in biting distance of his pulsing neck. The artery bulges against his dark skin, tantalizing her thirst.

He carries her onward until she moans in pain.

"I don't feel so good. Can we sit down a minute?" she asks, spotting an alley just to their left as she mimics a nauseated look.

"We're almost to your hotel. You can wait till then, can't you?"

"No, I can't. I think I'm gonna puke." She makes a funny face and the man's expression becomes a mix of distress and revulsion. He looks about for a place to sit but there are no benches in site.

"Sit me down over there," Lynette suggests, pointing a shaky finger at the dark, empty alleyway, a recess between two stores.

"Oh, all right, but just for a minute, okay? We got to get you back to your parents quick," he insists as he quickly crosses into the alley. He goes as if to set her down on her feet just a few yards from the alley's opening. Lynette yelps as her feet hit the ground.

"My ankle!" she moans. "I need someplace to sit." She demands in a whiny voice.

"Shoot, I forgot about your foot." Her rescuer looks about. His face lights up when he sees an old, worn loveseat set next to a dumpster. "How about right there, kid? It won't smell great but at least you'll be off that ankle."

"Yes, please take me to it."

Without hesitation, the man lifts her and carries her small frame over to the smelly old loveseat. He bends down to lay her upon it, her arms wrapped around his neck as he leans over her. He moves as if to pull away and stand, when … Lynette strikes.

She clasps her arms tightly around his shoulders, forcing him onto her. Before the man can even react, she bites into his jugular, crushing his windpipe while tearing into his flesh with her fangs.

Unable to make a sound, the man struggles to escape her grasp, but the child's strength exceeds his ten times. His blood flows freely into her mouth, pouring into her like a spring freed of a damn. She gulps it down eagerly, her eyes rolling up into her head as she rides the tide of the ecstasy that comes with fulfilling her blood lust.

The man is still, his warm body lying half on top of her as he kneels on the dirty pavement. His breathing slows.

With the last spark of life draining from him, his mind opens to her. His memories flow through her as smoothly as his blood.

His life flashes before her mind's eye. The images pass by at hyper speed, yet Lynette can understand them all with perfect clarity.

His name is Jamal. He owns a dingy strip club off Freemont Street. He has a mother he calls frequently and a feminist sister who despises him and what he does for a living. Jamal lives in a fancy high-rise condominium on the rich part of town and….

Lynette sucks in breath, breaking the flow of blood as she pulls back in shock. Blood splatters across her face and spills down her shirt. She pushes the man off her with a hiss. She sits up in a panic.

The corpse falls to the pavement with a dull thud. Jamal's eyes stare up to the sky vacant.

"That bitch is still alive?" Lynette whispers to herself as her mind reels. Just before she broke contact, she saw an all too familiar and hated face in the man's memories. *The witch from the mountain, the teen slut who her master's maker was so blinded by was this man's next-door neighbor!* "Gwenevere."

The realization rocks her to the core. Quickly she scoots off the loveseat and bends over the dead man. Placing her mouth over his gaping neck wound, she sucks what is left of his life-force.

He is starting to go cold, but a faint glimmer is still left of his consciousness. Lynette sucks it in with his coppery delicious blood, searching for more remembrances of the witch.

A few moments later she releases the man and rests against the dingy sofa behind her. She pants not from lack of air for she needs none, but from the shear excitement of this new discovery. Slowly a sneer spreads across her child's face and a wicked gleam shines in her gray eyes.

"It looks like I'll be staying in sin city just a little longer," she comments to herself. "I'm not the only survivor of Bec LaNuff after all."

* * * * *

The bright neon lights reflect against the sidewalk. Few pedestrians walk the strip in the early morning hours. The sun is just half an hour away from rising. The child cares not. Her attention focused singerly on the advertisement above her flashing on a small casino's electric marquee.

Entranced. The hottest magic show in Las Vegas! "A must see," says Sin City Weekly. Tickets available now at the box office inside.

With a laugh, Lynette stuffs her hands into her pink denim jacket pockets and turns away from the sign. With a skip in her step, the child vampire heads back to her little hole in the wall motel room to plot her glorious revenge. A new purpose in her lonely life has presented itself to her. A reason to go on after losing everything she ever cared about. Now that the initial shock has worn off, it makes perfect sense that the witch survived the destruction of the forsaken fortress once known as Bec LaNuff.

She always was a relentless little bitch.

The wiccan girl was as good as responsible for her abduction from her simple human life and her rebirth unto the grave. Sure, she had not turned her. Luca had, but at the command of his maker Lord Legion, master of Bec LaNuff and head of the vampire nest that ruled under the mountain. However, none of it would have happened if the witch had stayed out of the vampire's way. She should have done what she was told and kept her pointy little wiccan nose out of other people's business. Then Lord Legion would not have needed to abduct Emily Rose. He would not have had any reason to make a child spawn, something forbidden in the vampire world. Emily Rose's rebirth as Lynette had been done as a punishment for the witch's misdeeds. This eternal existence as a child was inflicted on her by Gwenevere whether she saw it that way or not. And if that had not been enough, the same witch later killed her entire vampire family— Lucca her maker, and her siblings Jezebel, Lethawyn, and Ryan.

Hatred boils within her and the child resolves. *I will destroy her whatever the cost!*

Thus occupied, Lynette does not notice the two men trailing behind her. Two blocks later, it becomes apparent to her that she is being followed. She sniffs the air and smells nothing. Her ears pick up no sound from the men's steps. No breath escapes their lungs; no hearts beat within their chests. If she were not a vampire, she would not have known they were there at all. Forcing herself not to glance over her shoulder, little Lynette quickens her step. Finding herself at a busy intersection, she casually waits with the few pedestrians at the cross walk.

With the precision only the undead possess, the child darts into the oncoming traffic. She weaves between the rushing headlights, ignoring the blares of horns as she dodges her way effortlessly to the other side. Not waiting to see if her stalkers followed her example and not caring what the humans might think, Lynette breaks into a run. At top speed, she moves like a flash of light down the sidewalk, a gust of wind shaking shop windows and knocking over tourists in her wake. Slowing down to human speed, the child vampire stumbles into a gift shop. The clerk behind the display case eyeballs her as she makes her way toward the back of the store and into the lady's bathroom.

Immediately she locates the nearest air vent. Leaping toward the metal grate in the ceiling, Lynette hooks her fingers into the metal and pulls the flap open. With her free hand she swings herself nimbly up into the opening, pulling the door closed behind her. Lynette squeezes into the ventilation shaft and becomes still as a stone. If she had a heart, it would be racing right now, thumping against her young chest. Her mind reels with uncertainty and terror.

After a year on the run, she believed she was too smart, too careful to be caught. Apparently, she was wrong. Why else would two vampires be following her now?

In her early days as a fledgling, her maker Luca and her blood sisters had impressed upon her the precariousness of her situation. She was considered an abomination to her own kind. She was an insult to the very foundation of their society. Being chosen to be reborn unto the grave was an honor, one that was not given to just any mortal. Vampires were parasites with humans their bodily host. All forsaken souls were adult of maturity and wisdom beyond this earth. Forcing such a soul to be enslaved within a child's shell was unthinkable. She was useless in the eyes of the great spirit.

Because of this, she had never been allowed to leave Bec LaNuff without one of her undead family. She would have likely lived out the rest of her immortal life under that mountain, never seeing a human city again. If that witch had not destroyed the fortress she would be living there now, safely protected by her nest and the great lord Legion himself. Out here in the human world, she is vulnerable and friendless.

However, she has enjoyed the freedom of being outside the mountain since it's fall. Despite the absence of her maker or her favorite companions leaving her empty inside. She feels most keenly the loss of Ryan, her undead blood sister and Danielle, Legion's child lover. Had the witch not run off with the Italian traitor, Ryan would not have been killed by the werewolves. Legion would not have unleashed his fury on poor Danielle. The Lord of Bec LaNuff had not intended to kill his pet, but he was blinded. By the time he realized what he had done, Danielle's preteen body lay in bloody pieces about the grand chamber. Lynette had always intended to turn Danielle vampire once she got too old to suit Legion's lust of young flesh. The two of them had discussed it often. Her dear friend's death she also laid at Gwenevere's feet.

Lynette nearly jumps out of her skin when the bathroom door burst open with a bang. From beyond, she can hear the screams of the store's attendant as something brutally attacks him. She stiffens, unable to move as she peers through the holes of the metal grate below her. The white tiles of the restroom floor shine in the florescent light, and a faint shadow cast a crossed it. A man stands in the doorway.

Slowly the shadow moves forward until Lynette can see the tops of the man's head as he steps just under her hiding place. Long brown hair hangs to the man's shoulders, his clothes modern but out of place on his dignified frame. He glances about the empty lady's room as if considering where to look first. Lynette dares not move a muscle and watches him with wide eyes.

With the sound of tearing drywall and metal, two hands burst from below and grab her by the middle. With a growl, Lynette tries to fight the strong hands that pull down on her. A gaping hole appears as her body slides out of the broken ventilation shaft. Lynette claws at the metal around her for a hand hold but is thrust down on to the tile floor. Her skull smacks into the solid surface with a deafening crack. Lynette moans in pain. The florescent light above her spins as black dots dance before her vision. When the room stops spinning, she notices two men standing over her, a gaping hole in the celling behind them. The second one has a clean-shaven head and is dressed in gray sweatpants and wife beater tank top. Tattoos decorate every inch of his exposed skin. Even his face is lined with ink as he smiles broadly at her with brilliant white teeth. Smugness and bloodlust shine behind his silver-gray eyes. The other man is the one she saw before. His long brown hair dangles about his tanned face as he tilts his head and smiles coldly down at her.

"Well, hello there, precious. Someone important wants a word with you," he declares with a Spanish accent. Before she has time to react, his companion pulls back a tattooed fist and punches her right in the nose.

Blood and pain encase her consciousness until the world fades, along with all thoughts of blood and vengeance.

Chapter Five

The Black Russian

A cacophony of noises breaks the solace of her delirium. Lynette jerks awake only to find herself still caught in darkness. A sack covers her head like a coffin for her skull. Claws dig into her biceps as two separate personages drag her across a tile floor. Her sneaker's toes catch on the edge of each tile between the grouts. All around her is the swell of jazz music playing, a live band evidently nearby. Peals of laughter, rhythmic footsteps, and the clang of glass add to the thick sounds in the air. Lynette takes in panicked breaths. Although she does not need air, some human habits are hard to break. Abruptly her brisk escorts toss her to the ground. Her already throbbing head smacks hard against the tile. With a groan, Lynette forces her arms beneath herself to regain her footing. The music stops. The laughter and gaiety in the room cease. She knows before the sack is removed from her head that hundreds of eyes are trained upon her. Her skin crawls with unease.

With a whoosh, her concealment is flung away, and her vision regained. And the room becomes abruptly silent. The scene revealed to her is bright, opulent, and reminiscent of the Jazz Age. The room she stands in is set up like a high-end nightclub from the early twenties. Several crystal chandeliers hang from the ornate ceilings. The walls are painted a bold blue with white trimming and patterns. Beneath her feet, the brilliant white tiles sparkle, reflecting the lights above. A grand stage stands before her. Upon this she sees the full jazz orchestra set up, all dressed in their finest black tuxedo with tails. From the smell in the air, some of the band members are human, the rest Vampire.

She stands just before the stage in the empty pathway between several rows of game tables. Everything from modern games like roulette and twenty-one to odd ones she has never seen before. *Are those giant cockroaches lined up in boxes by the far wall? Is that a racetrack before them? Are they racing cockroaches?*

The carousers gawk at Lynette, dressed in every kind of style imaginable. From ancient fashions such as tall, white, powdered wigs and giant hoop skirts, to the modern skinny jeans and t-shirt. Some ware extraordinarily little clothing at all, most of them children of the grave. They all intermingled as if the prominent historical vampire's figures of the ages have joined in this one place to cross the barriers of space and time.

The room remains silent. No one returns to their games; the band does not take up their instruments. No one approaches her. Lynette spins around to face the two persons who dumped her into the middle of this den. She finds herself staring up at the two men who abducted her from the bathroom in Vegas.

"What do you want with me?" Lynette demands, trying to sound commanding even though she is no taller than their navels. The two men exchange a look but say nothing.

Lynette suddenly bolts forward. In a flash, she ducks between the men. She dashes straight for the open doors at the other end of the room, a brightly lit hallway beyond. Panting, she flies out of the room and toward freedom. Abruptly something takes hold of her shirt collar, and she lurches backwards. With a yelp she hits the floor, sliding a cross the white marble. When the child comes to a stop, she finds herself lying at the feet of the man with the long brown hair and the Spanish accent.

"Now where were you off to in such a hurry, *Nena*?" An amused smile crosses his face as he clasps his hands behind his back. Slowly he walks around her in a circle, staring down at her as if examining a specimen through a microscope.

"That's not my name. Just let me go! I'm no threat to you," Lynette shouts as she scurries backward, away from her abductor. He and a few other vampires walk toward her, closing in from all sides. Her back collides with the stage. Trapped but determined to go down with a fight, Lynette hisses at her assailants and strikes out at them with her razor-sharp claws.

"Oh, isn't that cute?" a tall elegant looking blonde woman in a knee length black satin dress mocks to her left. Lynette lashes towards her but misses. "The baby vampire thinks she can fight her way out!" The woman continues addressing the room. The onlookers snicker and laugh, their gray, lifeless eyes trained on Lynette.

"Let's get on with it already, Peyton." The Spanish man exhales an exasperated breath. "She's nothing to us."

"Oh, come on, Dante. How often do we get to torture a child spawn?" the tall, blonde woman with hair down to her waist asks playfully. The smooth ink-covered man who had punched Lynette in the face waits expectantly to Lynette's right. Two more women stand directly in front of the child vampire, one a curvy Black woman with bleached blonde hair in ringlets hanging over one shoulder. She wears white skinny jeans and a white lace peasant top that barely conceals her ample bosom. The other woman looks as though she were in her twenties when she was reborn to the grave. She is skinny and long of limbs. She heavily made up in dark colors with her dyed blue hair done in a short asymmetrical haircut.

"I'm as fascinated as you are, Peyton *Mi alma*," the Spanish man called Dante responds. His shoulder-length brown hair sways, his black boots clicking on the marble floor as he approaches the woman named Peyton. "But we must not keep the king waiting. Now, should we?" He wraps an arm around her waist, and she curls herself around him.

"I suppose you're right, Dante." Her white fangs shine in the light as she smiles.

"But I've never seen one before," protests the skinny blue haired young woman. She looks at Lynette, wide eyed as she moves closer. "She looks just like a real kid."

"Stay back, Nyx," the blonde, Black woman warns. The girl ignores, her prattling on.

"I mean, if I didn't know better, and I was a human I'd totally think…" One strap of her Guns N' Roses tank top falls over her pale shoulder. Her pleather pants squeak as she kneels with an outstretched hand toward Lynette.

The child leaps forward like a viper. Her mouth claps down on one of the girl's dainty fingers. The young woman lets out a cry that echoes through the silent chamber. Lynette twists her head, ripping the digit clean off. Blood splatters across the bright white tiles as Lynette spits the lump of flesh out. It rolls a crossed the room to settle before the Black woman's feet.

Before the finger stops rolling, a gust of air flattens Lynette against the wall. The inked man clutches the child by the neck. She tries to struggle free. The man lifts her up with his iron grip till she dangles several feet off the ground.

Nyx the injured blue haired woman screams in horror staring down at her mutilated hand.

"Oh, stop your belly aching. I warned you," the Black woman scoffs as she bends down to pick up Nyx's severed finger.

"Morgana, show some respect for your Queen!" Nyx shouts between angry gasps. She cradles her bleeding hand in the other.

"Do you want to keep it as a souvenir?" Morgana asks with a laugh, waggling the bloody stump of flesh before Nyx's face. The young woman shoots Morgana a look of pure hatred as she shoves the woman's hand away. Several of the crowd giggle at this but quickly fall silent when Nyx turns to glare at them.

"You wouldn't dare speak to me like that before Lazar!" Nyx declares. "Theobald kill it!" the Queen demands of the man holding Lynette by the neck.

"Enough! Put her down, Theo," Dante interjects. He glares at Morgana, who stuffs the severed finger into her pant pocket, not caring that it leaves a blood trail down the leg of her white jeans. "Like it or not, Morgana, Nyx is your Queen." Dante adds.

"Don't worry, your highness, it'll grow back by tomorrow night," Peyton assures with a flippant air, as if losing body parts is just the course of the day.

"What will grow back?" a deep male voice with a slight Russian accent demands from the open door. Everyone turns to look at the newcomer. A tall Black man with skin like dark chocolate enters the room. He is dressed in a perfectly tailored black tuxedo with a red bowtie and shirt beneath his jacket. The crowd seems to swell with chatter at his entrance. Lynette knows who he is by the way he moves and the way the others react to him. Lazar Taudero, the

Vampire King, also known as "The Black Russian," wears his title as surely as if he wore a crown.

"Lazar!" Whimpering Nyx pushes past Dante to race into the arms of her king. Her stiletto heels click loudly on the marble floor. "That little monster tore my finger off!" she explains as the man a foot taller than she takes her hands into his with all the solemnity one would expect from a father to his child. Lazar kisses her between the eyebrows and whispers words of comfort to his Queen.

"It's her fault," Morgana declares with a huff. "She tried to pet it." The tone of the woman's voice says volumes about how she feels about the king's choice of bride.

"Stop talking about me as if I were an animal!" Lynette screeches, still grappling to get the iron grip of Theobald off her slender neck. "I have a name!"

"We know, child," Peyton quips. "Lynette, Legion's little lost spawn. We know all about you."

"Release her, Theobald," the king demands. Lynette falls like a stone to the hard floor. If she were human, she would have broken her tailbone with the impact. She glares up at Theobald as he slowly steps away to stand by Morgana yet never takes his eyes off her.

"Ladies and gentlemen, I present for your amusement Lynette!" the King announces with theatrical gestures and a broad white fanged smile. Lynette nearly jumps when the band begins to play, the piano doing a dramatic trill as the drummer accompanies, thumping the bass drum rhythmically. "First Dante will interrogate our captive, and then we shall take a vote as to the manner of her execution!" The band bursts into life as if to emphasize the Kings words. The room murmurs with excitement, until the king silences them with a gesture.

The band grows silent but for a violin and cello who accompany Dante's words as if the score to the interrogation itself. The King nods to Dante for him to begin.

"How did you escape from Bec LaNuff?" Dante turns on Lynette, still crumpled on the floor before the stage. "When no other vampire made it out of there alive?" Dante asks with a quizzical brow.

"I left just before the fortress fell." Lynette replies coldly.

"And no other came with you?" Dante continues.

"No. They were all too busy fighting with the wolves and by then it was already dawn," Lynette answers bitterly. Tasting the Queens blood still in her mouth, she spits it out onto the floor at her interrogator's feet. This produces a look of amusement from him, nothing more.

"Yet you still survived? How?" Peyton interjects, her lover seeming comfortable with her intrusion.

"I escaped out of the lower tunnels that lead through the mountains to the other side. I waited inside the tunnel until the sun went down."

"And since then, you've been feeding at will without any one to answer to," the king finishes for her, with a peculiar drawl to his voice.

"I can take care of myself; I don't need a master." Lynette retorts.

"You are to die, Lynette of Bec LaNuff," the King announces jovially. Setting his wife aside, he strolls toward the child. He speaks as though her death is as trivial as a performance on his stage. Despite his cherry demeanor and laughing eyes, she is not fooled. There is no doubt in her mind that the King is even more twisted than Legion was. Mercy is not in his vocabulary. The closer the smiling, well-dressed host comes, the smaller Lynette feels. "Do you know why?" he asks with a too bright smile.

"Because making a child into a vampire is forbidden," Lynette answers mechanically. "But that isn't my fault! I didn't choose this."

"No, but you will die all the same." The king turns his back on her as if to leave. Theo smiles at her viciously and the others look on her with death in their eyes. The band begins a dramatic melody as a drum roll echoes through the opulent room.

"Wait!" Lynette leaps forward as if to touch the king's sleeve. Instantly the five vampires surrounding her leap forward, claws out and hissing. The rest of the room seems on edge. "The witch still lives!" Lynette calls out in desperation.

The king halts abruptly, turning slowly back toward the child. "Stand down," the king orders and the rest of the vampires fall back

as if nothing happened. Turning around, the king makes a cutting motion across his neck at the leader of the band. They too fall silent. The room looks to its king expectantly. "What witch still lives?" A darkness that was not there before fills Lazar's eyes.

"The one who killed my family." Lynette whispers at first, her voice growing louder as she speaks. "The one who fooled the great Legion into marrying her. The witch who made Bec LaNuff fall!"

The room goes still as they all turn amazed gazes on the child. Finally, Dante breaks the silence.

"Impossible. The witches have declared her dead," Dante sputters out angrily. "Sire, don't listen to her, she's just trying to save her own skin." Dante pronounces his judgement.

"No! It's true. Gwenevere lives and only I know where to find her!" Lynette stumbles to her feet to face them all, as if defying the others to dispute her again.

"Peyton, find out if she's telling the truth," the king orders. A moment later, Lynette finds herself in the clutches of Peyton. The woman bites down onto her neck.

Lynette cries out, terrified, until the venom takes effect on her, calming her but not incapacitating her. She is Vampire, too, after all. Almost immediately Peyton pulls back, releasing Lynette. She turns her head and spits the child's blood out onto the already blood splattered floor with a grimace. She turns to her king.

"It's all true," she confirms.

Silent rage seems to fill the air as the vampires all look to one another.

"Then you may have a purpose yet, Lynette. I will let you live, but only if you swear yourself to me, naming me as your new master," the King declares somberly this time, stepping up to Lynette again. The playfulness is gone from him "Do you accept, Child?"

"Yes," Lynette replies in a hoarse voice.

Lazar lets out a moan as his fangs extend out of his gums to full length. Without a word, he puts his left wrist to his mouth and bites. With blood dripping from his dark lips and down his arm, he extends the fresh wound toward her. He gestures for her to do the same. She does, piercing her left wrist as well. She holds her arm up to him. He takes her bleeding wrist to his mouth and she, his to hers. Simultaneously they suck each other's blood. When the King releases her, Lynette feels all but drained. She slumps against the stage, weak. Despite receiving blood from Lazar, because of her diminutive size, he took more from her than he gave.

"You are now bound to me through blood, Lynette, and are hence forth in the service of the King."

"Yes, Master," Lynette mumbles, managing to get herself into a bowing position. She presses her forehead to the floor at his feet.

"Theobald." Lazar jumps onto the stage. The king snaps his fingers, and the tattooed vampire steps up before the stage. "Bring someone for your new blood sister to eat." The king's accent thickens, his Russian influence evident.

Theobald bows and smiles wickedly as he turns and disappears from the room in a flash. Lynette's stomach grumbles at the mention of blood and eating. *A lot of good eating Gwenevere's neighbor did me! Oh well it's not like anyone is going to really miss that guy.*

"Arise, Lynette," her King commands. She finds her body obeying despite her own will. The new bond has already taken effect. She watches her new master closely as he observes the silent audience about him. "Why all the long faces?" he asks, flashing a brilliant smile. "I promised you an execution. I promised you a display of carnage for your viewing pleasure, did I not?"

The crowd looks to one another, confused. Lynette tenses, ready to defend herself at a moment notice.

"My king, you have already declared the baby vampire your new servant and our blood sister," Dante points out with an arched brow.

"Well, of course I don't mean her." Lazar answers his second in command although he addresses his remarks to the room. His voice booms loudly.

"Then who shall we execute, my liege?" The room fills with both anticipation and dread. The humans in the room with enough of their own minds still intact have the good sense to slowly melt into the crowd and out of view of the vampire king. The others, the braindead human servants, just stand their staring off into space, sitting ducks for the kill. "Which of the humans shall we feast upon to mark this occasion?"

"None of them," Lazar announces with an icy tone. "No, today someone has shown great disrespect to royalty. Someone who has repetitively done so for far too long. It's time I rectified this oversight." Lazar hops down form the stage in a single fluid motion. Slowly he does a full turn before the stage, looking several of the vampire present straight in the eye. Once his gaze moves past them, those singled out quickly follow the humans' example and get out of sight. Lazar strolls slowly up the marble walkway between the gaming tables towards the room's arched entrance. His eyes scan the crowd for his victim like a snake stalking its prey. All at once, Lazar spins around and points his long muscular arm toward one particular vampire.

Lynette's eyes, like everyone else's present, hurry to the spot where the king's unfortunate chosen one stands. There standing between Peyton and Theobald, Morgana stares with wide eyes back at her king.

"But my king, what have I done to offend you?" the previously confident Morgana manages out of trembling lips.

In a flash of black, Nyx appears by her husband's side, her pale face, and grey eyes alight with a wicked kind of glee. "Think hard, Morgana. Think very, very hard," Nyx suggests, a sneer in her voice. Lazar wraps his young bride into the folds of his coat and holds her close to him. He never once takes his eyes off Morgana.

"My Liege, I was merely making gest with Nyx. I meant no offense. She has frequently made poor choices and behaved childishly. I was merely trying to warn her of her errors. No disrespect was ever…"

"Silence," Lazar commands, and Morgana's mouth clamps shut mid-sentence against her will. Her eyes grow wider still as she shakes her head and waves her arms before her, as if to dispel the King's ire. "Morgana will serve as a lesson to you all. An insult upon my queen is an insult cast upon me!" Lazar turns and makes this announcement to the room. His voice takes on a wild edge at the end. His frame shakes with his rage. "Kill her. Leave nothing of her behind," the King commands.

Lynette shrinks back from the rest as several vampire advance towards the soundless yet hysterical Morgana. Even her own friends Peyton and Dente join the vampires eager to do their kings will. Several of the vampires from amongst the gaming tables follow suit until a circle of vampires has formed around the doomed vampire woman. Without a warning, the group attacks. In a flash of claws, fabric, blood, and tissue, the assassins converge on Morgana. Her bond to her king and obedience to his will is so great that even in death she makes not a noise. The only sound comes from the hisses and growls of her murders, from the tearing of her flesh and the breaking of her bones.

The spectators about the room cheer them on and laugh at this display of mutilation. The sounds deafening to Lynette's ears, she closes her eyes and clamps her hands on the side of her head to drown out the site and sound of it all.

Someone touches her shoulder and Lynette flinches away. When she looks up, she finds the king standing above her. "Look not so dreary, my child, for we have reason to celebrate! Soon the witch who destroyed Bec LaNuff and killed so many of our comrades will pay for her crimes!" He spins around to address the room with a big, bright smile. The band instantly begins to play a rousing jazz tune behind him. The tension in the room melts and the crowd smiles and laughs, returning to their games and merry making. Several of them rush to the dance floor to move with the music ignoring the blood splattered marble floor beneath their feet.

Lynette does not feel like celebrating. With her head bowed, she stands still, watching the others with distaste. She ventures a glance toward where the ill-fated Morgana stood only moments ago. True to their master's command, they left nothing of her behind. Where her bones and clothing might have gone, Lynette can only imagine. She has never heard of vampires devouring their prey before, just draining them of their blood. Perhaps this is only the sort of thing that happens here in Lazar Taudero's court.

"Sire." Dante steps up to address the king. He turns a happy face to his second in command. "Should I arrange a hunting party to leave immediately to kill the witch, with this child as our guide?" Dante asks his liege in a low whisper.

"No. I have much grander plans in mind than the slaughter of just one witch." Lazar smile broadens and he begins to chuckle, joy and evil mingling behind the eyes of The Black Russian.

Chapter Six

Vanished

The crowds file eagerly into the casino theatre. Humans mill all around them as Jonah Crayborn ushers his little sister, Leona, and his best friend, Thayer, to their seats.

"Five rows from the stage. Not bad," Thayer comments as they shuffle passed the other audience members toward their own red cushioned chairs.

Leona takes the farthest seat. When Jonah goes to take the seat beside her, she gives him a look that only a brother would understand.

"Hey, Thay, why don't you take the middle seat?" Jonah turns to his friend, who is a few inches shorter to his six-foot-two. The scrawny eighteen-year-old, Thayer Blackwool, shrugs, scooting past him. He sits completely oblivious to the significance.

"Not that it matters, really. This whole thing is just ridiculous," Leona huffs, tossing her dirty blonde waves over her shoulder in a classic girly move to attract attention from Thayer.

You're wasting your time, sis, Jonah muses to himself as he settles into his own chair.

"Come on, lighten up, sour puss," Thayer teases, the gold in his lime-green eyes mocking her. Jonah suppresses a laugh as his fifteen-year-old sister glares a hole through Thayer's shaggy ginger head. When, Thayer doesn't give in and stares back, egging her on, Leona rolls her aqua-gold eyes, looking away.

"Humans playing at magic. Honestly, why are we wasting our time and money to watch this drivel?" she asks no one in particular. A few of the nearby audience members give her dirty looks for this comment.

"Because we're in Las Vegas, Leona. Seeing a show is part of the Vegas experience," Jonah replies with a brotherly sigh.

"Just wait till we're twenty-one — then we'll really party Vegas style." Thayer nudges Jonah companionably in the side. The two friends share a look and smile slyly.

Leona looks over Thayer to shoot an unforgiving glance at her brother, a taller dark-blonde version of herself. Fortunately, Jonah is saved by the lights dimming, signaling the beginning of the magic show: "Entranced."

The room goes pitch black; the audience falls silent. Gothic organ music begins to play from the speakers hidden throughout the auditorium. Drums join the music. The intensity of the sounds builds upon each other until the percussive beats transform into a long, smooth roll. When the drums stop abruptly, a single spotlight illuminates the middle of the stage. Within the spotlight stands a mid-size man. He is dressed in a black tuxedo with tails, a top hat, and a green, silk-lined cape, his head down turned. The man looks up into the crowd dramatically. His pale face is in stark contrast to his suit and his oversized black mustache.

"What is magic?" he asks the audience, his voice amplified over the speakers, seeming to come from everywhere all at once.

"It has nothing to do with top hats and capes," Leona mutters. Sitting beside her, a Hawaiian-shirt-wearing sixty-year-old woman with Eighties-style white sunglasses shushes her.

"It was a rhetorical question, Leona," Jonah whispers at her, leaning over his friend. Leona folds her arms and ignores him and the lady next to her. She stares at the Magician on the stage with a snobbish air that seems to say, *Hit me with your best shot.*

"Is magic simply the suspension of disbelief? Is it the fear of the unknown that leads us to believe in the unexplained?" The mustached Magician waves his hand in an elaborate gesture. A classic black and white magic wand appears in his outstretched hand. The music bursts forth in dramatic notes as he unfurls his cape, pushing it behind him as he steps forward in deliberate steps, much like a dancer just before leaping.

"Is there such a thing as real magic?" he whispers. With a wave of his wand, he gestures toward stage left. Fire erupts into the air. He gestures to stage right, and another blast of flames ignites with a thunderous roar. Several of the front and second row spectators gasp in delighted shock. A few women even scream in fright.

"Is it all just sleight of hand, or misdirection?" the man continues in his over-dramatic voice. Suddenly, the man spins. His back to the audience, he walks to the middle of the stage. Green smoke spreads from behind the black velvet curtains. It thickens until it encircles his feet, the wooden stage floor completely hidden from sight.

With a pop, the Magician's form collapses. His cape and top hat fall instantly to the ground without a person to clothe.

The audience applauds and cheers. The top hat begins to hover off the ground. The audience goes silent as the cape rises into another shape. Suddenly the cape and hat spin toward the audience to reveal a woman in a green sequin showgirl dress wearing the Magician's cape and hat. Again, the audience shows their appreciation.

"Or is it nothing more than an illusion?" the woman finishes the man's speech, her voice feminine and dark as a secret.

Modern dance music pumps through the auditorium as the black-haired beauty dances along with it, tossing aside the green cape and top hat in a way that suggests a strip tease. To his disappointment, she takes nothing else off. Jonah looks to Thayer, who likewise looks crestfallen that the show isn't going to go in that direction.

"Give me a break. This is supposed to be a magic show, not a strip club," Leona grumbles as if she can read their thoughts. Jonah and Thayer fight the urge to burst into laughter.

The Magician turned babe dances around the stage. The fire seems to come forth from all over the auditorium at her bidding.

"Not bad pyrotechnics," Jonah observes.

"Are you referring to the flames or her smokin' hot ass?" Thayer whispers into Jonah's ear behind his hand. Jonah busts up laughing, unable to help himself. Thayer grins, bouncing with the music.

Leona sees this and scoots away from him, her face red with mortification.

Jonah laughs and settles down farther into his seat to enjoy the show.

* * * * *

"Thank you all for suspending your disbelief and allowing me to enlighten you this evening." The gorgeous enchantress addresses the audience as stagehands remove the props from her last trick. Throughout the show, her costume changed several times. Jonah prefers her current get up, a black lace gothic romper that shows her skin beneath. Only her breasts and nether region are covered by the lace, but just barely. She wears sexy knee-high black leather boots. Her only jewelry is a gold chain hanging from her neck strung with a large oval medallion. "Our show is almost to a close, but before we part, I'd like to explore one more myth." She tosses her black hair as she pauses for dramatic effect "The Myth of Transformation."

Suddenly she sinks into the floor and vanishes. Techno music starts to play, the theater darkens, and a colored laser light show starts bouncing lights all over the auditorium.

With a bang and a green cloud of smoke, the female Magician appears on the balcony amongst the audience. The spotlight races to find her, encircling her in its glow. Those around her gasp in surprise, offering another round of cheers and applause.

"For my last magical demonstration, I will need a few volunteers from the audience." She speaks commandingly, her voice resonating impeccably throughout the vast auditorium. Hands shoot up all around her. Jonah watches as she deliberately takes her time walking down the stairs and through the aisle to examine her volunteers.

"Hmm ... no one's catching my eye over here. Perhaps I should look..." And again, she sinks into the carpet vanishing again only to reappear without sound or smoke in the isle just four seats away from Jonah. The spotlight searches around the theatre and then finds her as she finishes her address. "Over here." The audience cheers again. The people seated around him instantly start raising their hands, eager to be the one chosen for the grand finale.

Suddenly Thayer raises his hand, half standing up to get the Magician's attention.

"What are you doing?" Leona demands in a harsh whisper, tugging on Thayer's t-shirt to get him back into his seat. "You're making a fool of yourself," she warns. Thayer ignores her, waving his hand about wildly.

The green-eyed vixen turns her gaze their way. She sees the enthusiastic Thayer and smiles.

"Ah-ha, there we are!" the woman announces, winking at them. "Excuse me, sir, might I get by you?" she asks the elderly gentlemen at the end of their row. He kindly stands, as do all the audience members on that row to allow her to walk by. The men, no doubt, don't mind one bit having this hot little number squeeze past them, practically rubbing against them in her skimpy little get up. Jonah can't help wondering if every other man in the room is as affected by her. As she comes closer, Jonah forces himself to breath normally and relax. When she is upon him, he rises from his seat so that she can pass him to get to Thayer but bows his head suddenly, embarrassed to meet her eyes.

"Now what might your name be?" she asks, and it takes Jonah several seconds to realize she's not talking to Thayer but to him. She arches one dark brow at him as if to ask, *Is anybody home?*

"Me? Oh, I'm … Jonah." His voice projects around the theatre, startling him. He swallows the lump in his throat. "Jonah Crayborn." He reaches a handout to her. She looks at it a moment and then smirks at him before shaking his hand.

"So how about it, Jonah. You want to do a little magic?" She catches his eyes, and they lock on, her eyes boring into his soul.

"Witch!" Leona gasps. Thayer, shocked, sinks back into his chair. Yet Jonah is so overcome by this woman's magnetic gaze it takes a moment for the details of those eyes to register in his mind. Dark blue green on the outside, dark green fading into light, a pupil the dark center of a golden sunflower. He gasps, releasing her hand as if her flesh burned him.

She looks startled a moment, shocked, and offended, before understanding dawns.

"Too shy, are we?" she asks aloud. "Never fear, there are plenty of others to choose from." She winks at him before returning the way she came.

His knees give out and he finds himself in his chair again. Thayer and Leona turn identical white faces in his direction.

"She's a..."

"A real Witch?" his sister finishes for him. "I'm surprised you even noticed that with her in that get up and all." Leona scoffs.

"What do you know?" Thayer adds, "A real Wiccan with her own Vegas show, pretending to be human? It's crazy! Why didn't I think of that?" Leona tries to shush him. "I'm just saying it's brilliant when you think about it. She must be making bank!"

"Oh, shut up, will you?" Leona hisses at him.

"What is the problem?" Thayer asks, annoyed.

"It's against the law to perform Witchcraft in front of Humans, remember?" Jonah answers mechanically, his attention on the woman as she picks her volunteer, a short teenage girl with long blonde hair, leading her onto the stage.

"Oh, right." Thayer stares off into space, perplexed. "Well, no one must know. Obviously, none of the Elders have heard of this yet, or they'd have shut her down and taken her away to the tribunal by now," he adds, optimistically.

"What? Of course, they need to know. If we don't report her, we're as guilty as she!" Leona protests. The Hawaiian-dressed grandma hushes her again. Leona turns to tell the old bag off.

"Shhh! She's about to do the last trick," Jonah says, stopping the insults in his baby sister's mouth. Reluctantly, she turns her attention to the stage. The three of them watch as the last trick unfolds.

"Since the world was created, there have been tales of creatures who could change their very shape, shift into other forms. Transformation, they call it. Shape shifters and changelings are just some of their nick names. What if I told you that this myth is, in fact, a reality? That before your very eyes you will see this girl altered into something else?" the enchantress asks the audience, her volunteer facing the crowd with nervous excitement on her heart-shaped face. "Would you believe your eyes? Or would you convince yourselves that it is all just an illusion?"

Several of the audience members shout different replies.

The real Wiccan smiles mischievously at the crowd as the music starts up again. "All right, let's get on with it, shall we?" She winks at them, turning toward the girl as green smoke fills the stage once more.

"Do not be afraid, child," she soothes the blonde teenager. "What is your name?"

"Tiffany," she replies, her voice small and timid. "What are you going to do to me?"

"Nothing bad. I won't turn you into a frog or a monkey," the Witch teases. The girl and some of the audience laugh in response. "Have you ever dreamt about flying?" she asks Tiffany.

"Of course, who hasn't," Tiffany replies.

"Would you like to fly now?"

"Well, yeah! That would be really cool!" Tiffany says, smiling nervously to the crowd that applauds her.

"Your wish is my command, Tiffany." The Witch steps back from the girl walking circles around her as she chants. "*Mythica musa, mythica rae, transformae, wingga transformae skinna, mythica farro, transformae, transformae Tiffany, un farro!*"

With a bang, a flash of fire and green light, the last words are uttered. Tiffany screams arching her back, her face contorts in shock

and pain as wings burst from her spine, just above the hem of her tube top, spreading wide behind her as they unfurl. Blue and silver, they resemble massive butterfly wings.

The audience screams, gasps, cries out in awe. But the show's not over yet. Tiffany looks at the Witch, baffled.

"Go ahead. What are you waiting for? You have the wings, now fly," the woman urges.

"Okay, I'll try." Tiffany hesitantly flaps her new wings, creating gust of air as she slowly begins to hover off the ground. Tiffany looks down at the Witch and then the audience. She looks to be floating ten feet above the stage. Laughing, she spins in the air and flies out above the amazed audience. She flips and twirls in the air. At one point she flies over Jonah, Thayer, and Leona.

"Am I imagining things or is that girl a real Fairy?" Thayer whispers.

"Those wings are too real. Plus, I can't make out a wire. I think you're right," Jonah answers as he stares up at Tiffany.

"So that means we're watching a real Witch practicing real magic in a magic show. Who's using a real Fairy planted in the audience to pretend to be human, who gets transformed into a Fairy?" Thayer laughs. "Wow! Man, she is good."

Finally, Tiffany lands on the stage, laughing and beaming with delight.

"That was amazing!" Tiffany tells the Witch.

"I'm glad you enjoyed it. But all good things must come to an end. I must turn you back, I'm afraid," the Witch announces. She encircles the girl again, chanting. *"Revisa transformae, reunitia humo formatia, Revisa transformae, transformae humo revisa!"* With a burst of light, the girl falls to her knees. Stunned, she makes no sound as her massive wings fold in on themselves and magically disappear. Everyone gasps and cheers; a few members of the audience even give a standing ovation.

"Thank you, Tiffany. You've been wonderful." Gently, the Magician helps Tiffany to her feet. "Let's hear it for Tiffany!" The audience goes wild for the dazed teenager as she makes her way back to her seat.

"Now, I need just one more volunteer; a man this time," the woman announces. Again, hands shoot up all over the crowd. For a moment Jonah considers raising his hand, needing to be near her, wanting her to touch him again. Jonah waits to see if she'll look his way, but she does not. Instead, she chooses a large, muscular guy in his twenties from the second row. He comes up on stage to join her. He looks for all the world like the leader of a biker gang, with rugged features, black leather jacket, and long black hair tied in a ponytail.

"What's your name, sir?" she asks the man.

"Adam," he answers, his voice as tough as his exterior.

"You've heard of werewolves, haven't you?" she asks him.

"Of course, I have," the man scoffs. "I don't believe in all this nonsense, to tell you the truth."

"You don't? Then why did you volunteer?" the Witch asks, not the least bit affronted by his attitude.

"I figured why not?" he replies, shrugging his massive shoulders.

"All right, then. Let's see if we can make a believer out of you." She smiles as she encircles him as well, saying a similar chant as she had with the girl the first time. At the end of her spell, Adam abruptly falls. He lands on all fours, yelling and screaming as his body changes. His clothes rip and tatter about him. Women throughout the crowd screech in horror as they watch the man turn before their eyes into a black and silver wolf.

The animal hears the audience around him and bares his teeth, snarling, looking as though he might charge the people in the front row.

"Calm, Adam. Be still," the Witch commands. The wolf turns to the sound of the Witch's voice. She reaches a handout to him, and, like a puppy, he treads over to her and sniffs her hand. The crowd gives out a collective sigh of relief as she pets the wolf's fur. The giant animal lies down at her feet, docile.

Jonah turns to his friend and sister, seeing in their faces that they are thinking the same exact thing.

"She's a real Witch who has a real Fairy and a real Werewolf pretending to be human, pretending to be in her pretend magic show." Thayer says aloud. The audience is too busy cheering the

Witch on stage to hear his comment. Jonah and Leona nod, both at a loss for words.

"That does it. We've got to get backstage and meet this chick. I mean, she is now officially my hero!" Thayer announces.

It takes a while for the audience's adulations to settle down this time. They all watch as the Witch picks up her black and green lined cape and drapes it over the body of the wolf.

"To protect his modesty," she explains with a suggestive waggle of her brows. The audience laughs. In no time at all, the Witch reverses the spell, turning the wolf back into the man. Slowly he stands up, naked from his shoulders down, the rest of his body covered by the cape. One of the Witch's stagehands enters from stage right.

"Please, find Adam some clothes," she instructs the male assistant. The man's clothes lay tattered by the witch's feet. Some of the ladies in the audience squeal and hoot at Adam as the other man helps him off stage. Even though he has the cape wrapped around him, covering him up, it's obvious the guy is built like a man from the cover of a romance novel.

Jonah and Thayer roll their eyes at this.

Finally, the auditorium goes quiet as the lights dim, leaving the Witch standing in the center of the stage lit by the spotlight.

"Tonight, you have seen utterly amazing things. But nothing will prepare you for the truth." She chants beneath her breath as the organ music plays, rising in volume as the Witch glows from within.

The audience seems to lose their mind as she floats off the ground, her body becoming a blinding light.

"For I am not human, and magic is real." Her voice encompasses the theater, sounding almost as if she were in their minds, everywhere and nowhere at all. "Everything you've ever read about in stories and myths is far more real than you know. Never doubt the supernatural, and never become too entranced with reality, for nothing is what it seems!" After the last word echoes off the walls, the woman becomes a sphere of light more blinding than the sun. Jonah, along with everyone else, shields his eyes. And with a loud bang, the light collapses in on itself, leaving nothing behind. The Witch has vanished.

Chapter Seven

Pain of the Past

"Get out of the way!" Raven roars at the stagehand blocking his path. The scrawny twenty-something boy gives him a terrified look before flattening himself against the wall. Raven ignores him as he tears down the hall and turns a corner. At the end of the hall is a door with a star on it. Its gold paint glares at him as if mocking the terror, he hides behind his dark expression. Raven propels himself forward, not allowing his fear to hold him back. He pauses a second to knock briskly on the door before turning the knob and entering.

Gwen stands before the vanity mirror. Clad only in a pair of black panties, she fastens the clasp of her bra behind her back, her black hair falling to her narrow waist. In the mirror's reflection the strange scar over her heart looks like a fresh wound recently healed over, although he knows the injury that caused it happened over twelve years earlier. Before he met her, from a time she can't even remember. She turns to face him.

"Tada! See? I'm not dead!" she proclaims contemptuously as she walks across the room to her open wardrobe. "You coming or going? Not that I really care if the crew sees me in my unmentionables but, really, it's rude to dress with the door open."

"I'm pretty sure they allow that here in Vegas," he comments as he steps into the dressing room, closing the door behind him.

"In that case I ought to charge admission," Gwen jibes, selecting a pair of dark blue distressed boot-cut jeans to wiggle herself into. The material hugs the curve of her hips, buttocks, and thighs.

Raven laughs lamely at her remark. He makes himself comfortable in one of the rotating chairs at the vanity table, fidgeting with her collection of makeup jars and containers. Raven forces himself to keep his mind clean, avoiding eye contact with her firm, perfectly curved body as she dresses.

Another guy would read into this situation, see it as a kind of sexual invitation and make a move. Not Raven. He figures that after the orphanage, foster care, Bec LaNuff, and over a year of performing together, she's just become numb to the idea of modesty and decorum.

Being a girl, and sexually experienced, she's not as easily aroused as you, Raven reminds himself as Gwen takes a shirt off a hanger and slips it on over her head.

He'd never admit it to anyone except Gwen, but Raven is still a virgin. It's not that he hasn't had opportunities. After all, he has the same needs and urges as any other man. The only difference is that his are aroused by just one face — a face that answers to the name Gwenevere.

However, the right moment to tell her how he feels never seems to come. For the past year, she's been living and working under the alias Ramona Greenly, a twenty-two-year-old from New Mexico. In actuality, Gwen is still only seventeen, and thus a minor. However, her age isn't the only thing holding him back.

She's changed.

He sees a darkness behind her eyes that wasn't there back in New York. Anger, disgust, self-loathing, hatred, and indifference boil just beneath her skin, waiting to erupt. She's fragile still, tender on the inside, underneath her arrogant, cold demeanor. So, Raven bides his time, watching as she struggles her way through the scars to find her own kind of healing.

It's something she must do on her own, he admits to himself reluctantly. *I won't add to her confusion. She has to reach for me first; it must be her move.*

In the meantime, she's had a few flirtations, trivial little relationships that never amounted to much, every single one of them a low life degenerate. Weak-minded fools, Gwen controls, consumes, and tosses them aside with little thought or feeling. It's her twisted way of coping.

By the time Gwen returns to the vanity she has added a pair of black ankle boots and a gray-laced vest to her outfit. Instead of taking the other chair she stands as she quickly re-applies her makeup. All traces of her theater makeup from the show, along with all her clothes, disintegrated while doing her grand finale. Because of this Gwen has over a dozen of her finale costumes hanging in the wardrobe. Each one she only ever wears once. The crew never asks questions. Gwen has entranced them to ignore anything unusual that goes on in the show. Especially anything odd about her, Morna, and Raven.

Raven shivers involuntarily. Most of his anxiety has faded, yet still he's on edge. His right-hand drums nervously on the counter, his legs twitch, and his knees bounce.

"Raven." Gwen stops mid smearing her lipstick to fix him with a knowing look in the mirror. "Go ahead and say it already."

"You need a new finale, Gwen. It's just too dangerous, traveling by light, transporting yourself, whatever you want to call it, it's just insane!"

"I've been doing it twice a day, six days a week for a year now. I still haven't burned myself out of existence," Gwen adds, applying the blood-red cosmetic to her already perfect lips. With her make up all done and her dark, form-fitting attire, Gwen looks like a cross between a rock star and a 1950's pin up girl.

"I just don't understand how it's even possible." Raven stands, pacing toward the door and then turning to pace back to the mirror.

"You turn yourself into a ray of light and then somehow reform in another place? It defies physics, Gwen!"

"Exactly! That's why it blows the audience's minds. It's also why we're becoming one of the most talked-about shows off the Strip, might I add." Gwen examines her face one more time in the mirror, quickly brushes through her long black hair, adds a couple sprays of product for volume, and then turns to leave. "Enough of all this. We're just going to keep fighting over it. Neither one of us will ever concede, so we might as well leave it alone."

"You said I could go ahead and say it, and so I did, and I will continue to say it until you stop behaving like Evel Knievel with a death wish."

Gwen rolls her eyes, shaking her head.

"By the way, what do want to be disguised as for tomorrow's shows? I think it's about time you dressed in drag!"

"No, Gwen. For the last time, nobody cares if the volunteer that gets turned into a Werewolf is always a man and the one turned into a Fairy is a girl. As long as I'm hidden under your appearance spell and Morna can change her skin and hair color at will, no one will ever know that it's the same two volunteers every time. There's no need for me to put on a dress, for heaven's sakes!" By the end of his little speech Raven's cheeks burn, only tinting his tan skin a little as he throws his arms up in the air in exasperation.

Gwen smiles at him mischievously. A wicked little laugh bubbles out of her as she passes him on her way to the dressing room door.

Why must you always tease me? Raven asks mentally, turning on his heel to follow her.

Why do you always rise to the occasion? Gwen asks back without looking at him. For this he has no reply.

Raven follows fast on Gwen's heals as they exit the dressing room, nearly knocking someone over in the process.

A girl squeaks in alarm as he catches her in his arms, saving her from tumbling to the floor. Raven almost doesn't recognize the girl he all but trampled on. Dressed in typical teenage clothes, her face disguised the color of beige. Morna, the five-foot-nothing, ninety-pound Fairy stares up at him with her enormous yellow eyes. He stares back, not sure where he is or what he was about when he hears Gwen's cough.

"Should I leave you two alone?" Gwen teases. Morna and Gwen seem to exchange looks.

Communicating via telepathy, no doubt. Embarrassed, Raven sets Morna on her feet again and steps away.

"Let's get out of here." Raven mutters, side-stepping the two girls and heading down the hallway. Soon he hears their footsteps on the tile behind him.

"You two at it again?" the Fairy asks.

Gwen doesn't reply.

"I saw that guy you were chatting up during the show. Will you be meeting up with him later?" Morna asks suggestively.

"You never know," Gwen replies smugly.

Grumbling to himself, Raven pushes open the backstage door, holding it open for the girls to exit into the dry heat of the Vegas night.

The moment Gwen steps into the alley behind the theatre a sense of foreboding sweeps over her. Morna enters the alley way behind her, followed closely by Raven. Gwen's friends/bodyguards follow her down the alleyway, like twin shadows.

The stage door opens again behind them as a few of the other cast members of the show, file out talking loudly. The three friends watch their fellow performers laugh companionably, all young, talented, and one-hundred percent human. They think the show is just another Las Vegas gimmick. None of them have any clue that the three of them are authentic.

Of course, they don't. Gwen tells herself. *They don't even know our real names. They think I'm Ramona Greenly, for goodness sakes.*

"See you tomorrow, Ramona."

Gwen waves goodbye to Lauren, one of the makeup crew, as she hops into a yellow taxi with her roommates, Suzanne and Deborah, an acrobat, and a pyrotechnics expert.

Raven and Morna follow as Gwen turns a corner headed to the parking lot behind the building.

Gwen's face alights when she catches sight of her transportation across the lot. Her ride is a Harley Davidson Heritage Soft tail. The machine is a thing of power and retro beauty with its white-wall tires and hunter green metal- flecked paint job. Raven has a bike of his own, a more manly version of course, parked next to hers. It's in black, no metal flecks for him. Although so much has changed over the years in their friendship, they still share a love for speed. Morna looks at vehicles with trepidation and avoids the things at all costs.

Behind her, Morna and Raven fall into an awkward yet comfortable conversation about the show. It's the words they don't say, that impregnate the air with sensual tension. Just before they reach the motorcycles, Gwen finds her attention drawn elsewhere.

Is that who I think it is? Her eyes lock on a familiar pair of Aqua gold eyes that stare back at her. Two teenage boys and a girl wait beneath the streetlight at the other end of the parking lot. Each glow with a shimmering, multi-colored aura. Images dance from their minds to hers. *They're Wiccan. Why aren't they shielding their minds from me? Or is my ability just getting stronger?* Lately she's been sensing things she shouldn't and hearing other's thoughts even when she's tries to keep her mind to herself.

"We have company," Gwen announces without taking her eyes off the newcomers.

"I thought I smelled something strange," Morna admits as they all stop next to the motorcycles.

"Me too, but I didn't know what it was." Raven holds onto the handles of his Harley, looking unsure if he should stay or go. "Why didn't either of you say anything about other witches being here?" He gives both girls a curious look.

"I just barely told Morna, a moment ago. Sorry," Gwen sighs. "I wasn't expecting to see them again." She indicates with a nod of her head for her friends to come along. Slowly the three friends start walking toward the three Wiccan youths.

"You know them?" Raven asks in a low whisper, his deep voice like rich molasses.

"No. They just saw our show," Gwen whispers back.

"The blond Wiccan boy is the one Gwen was flirting with in the audience right before my transformation bit," Morna supplements. Gwen feels rather than sees her friends share a look of understanding. Gwen has long learned to ignore her friends' disapproval when it comes to her love life and dating practices.

"Oh, I see," is all Raven says just before Gwen and her supernatural escorts approach the streetlight.

"Jonah, wasn't it?" Gwen asks, hands in pockets, her manner arrogant but at ease.

"Yes, Jonah Crayborn. This is my sister Leona and our friend Thayer Blackwool." The ash blond Jonah indicates his companions. Leona only nods briefly at Gwen and her lot in acknowledgement.

"I'm Ramona Greenly, this is Derick Black and Matilda Cerulean," Gwen introduces. Neither of her friends make any effort

to shake hands with the strangers. Even without her telepathic powers, Raven and Morna seem to register that this is not a social meeting. *Werewolves and fairies have their own ways of detecting danger.*

"I loved your show!" Thayer lunges forward, hand extended. Gwen has no choice but to shake his hand. "I particularly like the finale! I mean…" Thayer's physical contact with Gwen gains him a glower from Raven. Thayer's smile disappears, and he quickly steps back to stand with his friends, shoving his hands back into his pockets nervously. "…It was pretty amazing," he finishes.

"Thanks." Gwen smiles arrogantly at Thayer before turning her cool eyes on the wiccan siblings. "So, what do I …"

"Why are you following us?" Raven interrupts stepping forward to stand shoulder to shoulder with Gwen. His face darkens when he realizes Jonah and the others aren't intimidated by his impressive bulk.

"We're here to issue you a warning." Fifteen-year-old, five foot four Leona speaks up. "Stop performing magic for humans. Or we'll be forced to report you."

"To whom?" Gwen laughs mockingly.

"To the King and the council of elders, you idiot!" Leona steps right up into Gwen's face. Simultaneously Raven growls and Morna hisses at her.

"Leona, don't be ridiculous!" Jonah commands. She glares at her brother as if to say *Stay out of this.*

Jonah glances around to see if anyone is nearby. A few people walk down the sidewalk on either side of the street, but the parking lot is empty except them. No one pays them any attention.

Jonah pulls his sister away, putting himself between her and Gwen. It looks for a moment as if Leona will shove her brother aside, till Thayer puts an arm around her to hold her against him. She instantly settles down, though she continues to glare at everyone and no one in particular.

"Look, no one wants to get you into any trouble, honestly. But the next Wiccan who stumbles upon your little show won't even hesitate to throw you at the council's mercy," Jonah explains.

"I don't like your tone," Raven interjects. The Wiccan and the werewolf boys exchange a deadly look.

"And what would this council do to me, exactly?" Gwen intervenes, drawing Jonah's attention back to her. A gust of wind sends tendrils of her black hair flying across her face.

"It depends on the how long you've been performing and the kind of tricks who've been doing," Jonah answers matter-of-factly.

"Traveling by Light is considered a treasonous act," Leona shouts at her. "The King declared it himself after the Twelve Crossing massacre." Thayer and Jonah shush her earnestly. Lowering her voice, the wiccan girl adds, "The High Council of Elders would execute you without a second thought."

"Look, Kiddos. I'd say I appreciate your concern, but frankly I never really cared for the opinions of others." Gwen pulls out her keys from the front pocket of her jeans, nonchalantly twirling them on her index finger. "I don't live by rules or laws, whether human or otherwise. I don't hail to any kingdom. And if this council really wanted to punish me for practicing my natural born talents, then they'd have to catch me first."

Morna giggles at this, a fiendish noise that makes Leona shudder.

"It's getting late." Gwen smiles, yet her eyes stay cold. "I'm late for a date anyway. Nice to run into you again, Jonah." Gwen's voice speaks the Wiccan boy's name like a caress on his soul, and it has the desired effect.

Too Bad he's a Wiccan, she muses, her eyes lingering long on Jonah's, the look held until the very last moment. She turns and leaves the three Wiccan youths behind, knowing Morna and Raven will depart only after she does.

"What's your coven?" Leona demands. "Or don't you have one? If you're a wild witch, we can't just let you leave."

The three friends stop in their tracks. In unison, they turn to look at the others.

"What's that supposed to mean?" Raven glowers.

"It means that if she hasn't been properly trained in a coven, then she's a wild witch and by the law she can't wander free." Thayer adds in a grave tone.

Raven and Morna react in an identical manner. Their emotions boil, anger flares, and their animalistic natures seem to take over.

"Is that a threat?" Raven asks, baring his teeth like the wolf he is inside. Morna steps slowly toward the others with a deadly look in her eyes.

"Stand down," Jonah commands, eyeing Raven and Morna with the protectiveness of a big brother.

"Or you'll do what?" Raven asks.

"We don't want a fight," Jonah replies smoothly, his eyes steady and sure.

"That may not be your choice," Raven declares, moving with superhuman speed he crosses the gap between them, shoving Jonah hard against the streetlamp behind him. The impact knocks the wind out of the wiccan while denting the lamp post. Gasping, Jonah buckles to his knees.

"*Dasae windah*," Thayer shouts. A giant gust of wind sends Raven backwards. Unable to withstand the force of the magic wind, all six foot four-inches, two hundred and thirty-pounds of Raven rolls head over feet across the parking lot like a tumble weed.

Morna lets out a feral cry and lunges at Thayer. She knocks the unsuspecting Wiccan down on his back, forcing him to release his spell. Morna perches on his chest like a vulture about to eat a corpse. She pulls back her claws to strike.

"*Gainga res, restraint*!" Leona chants with an outreached hand.

Morna screeches and looks about wildly as an unforeseen force takes hold of her, lifting her off Thayer to float into the air. The fairy

thrashes, but the same force restraining her limbs in place holds her stiff as an iron rod.

"Stop it! Release her, now!" Gwen shouts, breathing heavily. Leona ignores her completely, hatred burning in her aqua eyes as she stares at Morna's prostrate form.

A howl pierces the night. Gwen spins around to see a huge black and silver wolf charging across the parking lot towards Leona. The wiccan girl snaps her attention away from her prisoner, eyes alighting on the werewolf.

"Leona, stop," Jonah coughs, struggling to get to his feet. "Enough of this."

"NO! They attacked you!" she retorts. Gwen senses the other Wiccan girl gathering more power. She begins to cast another spell toward Raven, who leaps past Gwen, vaulting himself at the witch.

"Enough!" Gwen shouts. Her voice echoes off the buildings and down the street, filling the night. Her whole body becomes a glowing light as her anger flows from within her in waves of power. Magic words pour out of her that Gwen has never used before. "*Inka captae maeqic, enosa un forsaken*!" The light radiates out of her, knocking the others down all at once.

Leona shrieks as she is flattened to the sidewalk. Her head hits hard with the force. All the power drained, she lay unconscious. Free of the curse, Morna falls to the ground with a crack of bones and a pained cry. The wolf collapses from midair to fall hard on the pavement below. Raven gives out a whimper and crawls backwards to curl around Gwen's feet like a whipped dog. Only Jonah and Gwen are still standing.

Seeing the effects of her power on the others, Gwen quickly releases the energy, the light retreating into her. She pants heavily as she and Jonah's eyes meet.

"I'm sorry. I didn't mean for that to happen," Gwen says.

"Neither did I…"

Thayer stirs and rolls onto his hands and knees, coughing and muttering. A panicked look crosses Jonah's face. His eyes dart from Thayer to Gwen.

"You better go," Gwen commands, her calm returning to her as her heart finally stops racing.

"I'm sorry but what they said is true. You must come with us," Jonah retorts, an empathetic look in his eyes.

"No, I don't." Gwen whispers.

* * * * *

Gwen lays into the bike and takes off down the street, blazing through the neon-soaked streets of Las Vegas. After she entranced Jonah, Thayer, and Leona, Gwen erased their memories of her and took off with her injured comrades. Once she had seen Raven and Morna safely back to Raven's apartment, Gwen left them there to recover. A part of her wanted to stay with her friends. A bigger part of her needed to bury her sorrow, needed to hide from what she is. She needed an escape from reality.

Besides, I'm really late for my date, Gwen rationalized as she hopped on her motorcycle, taking off into the night.

By the time Gwen arrives at her destination, she has worked herself into a frenzy of emotions. Anxious, angry, frustrated, lonely, and a little scared by the Wiccan's warning and the events that transpired. Gwen finds she can't contain the energy building up beneath her skin. She pulls up into the parking lot outside the local's favorite dive bar, The Double Down Saloon. She kills the engine, ditches her helmet, and heads into the bar.

Usually, she gives a little smile up at the white painted letters above the awning that read "The Happiest Place on Earth," and the punk rock skeleton on the front door. Tonight, she's in no mood to smirk at the bar's ironic persona. Gwen skips the line to go in and is waved in at the door by Jimmy, the human pin cushion, and his ever-growing collection of facial piercings. He smiles at Gwen in recognition with a mouth full of metal. She winks at him and moves on without stopping to chat. She passes the bar decorated in women's lingerie and funny signs that read "$20 Puke Insurance" on her way to the pool tables in the corner. Leaning up against a dingy brick wall with a huge "Shut Up and Drink" sign behind him, Gwen spots Michael.

A total hipster from head to toe, he sports a worn brown fedora, big black-rim glasses he doesn't need to wear, with a red and gray plaid long sleeve shirt, skinny jeans, low boots, and a black wool scarf draped around his neck as if an afterthought. A hipster hanging out in a punk rock bar would seem a little out of place, but not here at the Double Down Saloon. Michael sips a beer waiting his turn while his other hipster friends play a game of pool. He hasn't seen her yet, so Gwen takes the chance to observe her latest fling unabashedly.

Michael is a skinny guy, with short black hair, pale skin, and big brown eyes that seem bottomless in their wonder of life. He is the first step in Gwen's new plan to change things around. The first decent non-psychotic sex maniac she's dated since ... well, Angelo. Perhaps if she is honest about it, she would admit that Angelo had been a bit of a sex fiend in the beginning, too. It turned out in the end that he really had a heart of gold underneath that Italian accent and immortal arrogance.

Gwen can't help the sigh that escapes her lips at the thought of the one and only man who ever really mattered to her. The only lover she ever really wanted. Her eyes start to mist. Gwen growls at her own stupidity. Squaring her shoulders and shaking off the pathetic feeling of heartbreak, Gwen charges towards Michael. At the last moment, her date looks up to see her, and a second later she wraps herself around him and kisses him with all the ferocity she has boiling within. She hears his friends' whistle and jibe at them, but she ignores them. Completely consumed with her need to drown her sorrow, Gwen kisses Michael ever more passionately as she attempts to devour the pain of the past.

Chapter Eight

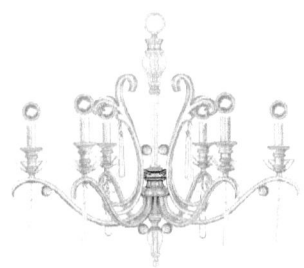

Moving Forward

onah Crayborn wears a black tuxedo, standing in the middle of a gorgeous ballroom, all shimmering gold. Above him several large crystal chandeliers light the room from the tinted glass ceiling. He marvels at the room when suddenly he turns as if hearing her steps. As she walks toward him, recognition lights up his face, melting away Gwen's apprehension at bringing him into her dreams.

"Ramona!" He smiles down at her, gathering her into his arms the moment she is near.

"It's Gwen, actually." She swallows the lump in her throat. She hadn't meant to tell him the truth, even in a dream. Her true identity might be dangerous info to give this Wiccan boy.

"Excuse me?" His aqua-gold eyes shine down on her, and she feels her body relax under their power.

"My real name is Gwenevere, but my friends call me Gwen," she clarifies. "I'm surprised you remember me."

"How could I forget you?" Jonah smiles again, and Gwen can't help but smile back. "I like Gwenevere better than Ramona."

"Me, too." Nervous, Gwen looks about the room, not sure what she had in mind by summoning him. She isn't even sure where here is. This ballroom isn't a creation of her imagination, and she has never seen such a place before. "Where are we?"

"We're in the grand ballroom of the Wiccan palace, in the Wiccan capital."

"Oh. So, this place is real?" Gwen realizes that suddenly their clothing has changed. His suit is now the same aqua as his eyes and her dress, which had at first been black, is now green. *Interesting.*

"It's real, all right. Haven't you ever been to the Wiccan Kingdom?"

"No." Gwen steps away from him to cross the room, precipitously needing to look out the window and see this Kingdom for herself. Jonah takes her hand. When they come to one of the large, arched windows, she releases Jonah's hand. She presses both her palms to the glass, looking out into the night. There, below her, a glowing city grows out of the earth and mountains around them. Gwen gasps and spins around to face Jonah.

"I have been here before, but only in dreams. I didn't realize this was the Wiccan Kingdom," Gwen confesses to him as he steps up to take her in his arms again.

"How can you dream of a place you've never been before?" he asks as he brushes a strand of her black hair behind her ear. His face suddenly changes as if a disturbing thought has just crossed his mind. He releases her and takes two steps backward. Shoving his hands into his pockets, he stares at her in barely concealed horror. "Are you a Dreamwalker? This is your dream, isn't it?" His voice holds a note of accusation in it.

"I have no idea what a Dreamwalker is, and if it were my dream, we wouldn't be in the ballroom, we'd be on the staircase, or in the city, maybe in the attic, but not here. I told you I've never been in this room before," Gwen responds defensively. *Why is he looking at me like that? What did I do wrong?*

"Right. Sorry, I forgot." His shoulders relax, and he takes his hands out of his pocket, looking at the floor for a moment as if trying to decide what to say next. Running a hand through his dark-blond hair, he finally looks back at Gwen. "I get the impression you were not raised in a Coven. Am I right?" Gwen nods. "Look, there's a lot you don't know. You're obviously a Dreamwalker or you'd be doing and saying only the things I would dream up. We're in my head, my dream, but you're controlling it. Dreamwalking is forbidden, Gwen. Only Wiccans who belong to the Dark Circles dare use this kind of magic. It's considered a rare gift and incredibly dangerous."

"Dangerous?" With heat in her cheeks, Gwen scoffs. As she speaks, she stalks passed him toward the ballroom door. "I've been doing this for as long as I can remember, and I've never experienced any real danger. This is all just a dream, Jonah!" She turns at the door to shout. "How can it possibly hurt anyone?"

For the briefest moment, Gwen sees terror on Jonah's face but is too angry to wonder why. Instead, she flings open the door and turns her back on him to cross through it.

"Gwen, no! Don't walk out that door!" She hears his voice shout behind her, but it's too late. Gwen has already stepped past the threshold. Before her, everything is black. Her foot doesn't land on solid ground but seeps into nothingness. Gwen lets out a scream as she falls into endless darkness.

* * * * *

Sweat-drenched and gasping for air, Gwen jolts upright in bed. It takes Gwen a while to settle down, taking deep breaths. Running her fingers through her black, tangled hair, Gwen looks around her in disbelief. She sits in her own bed in her luxury high-rise condominium on the Vegas Strip. Snoring softly beside her, Michael sleeps nestled snuggly beneath the covers. Her side of the bed is a mess. The blankets and sheets are strewn about, and her clothing is twisted and wrinkled, as though she squirmed restlessly as she slept.

I fell asleep in one man's arms only to wander into the dreams of another, Gwen realizes, trying to recall the night before. After Michael drifted off to sleep, she lay staring up at the ceiling, wrestling with self-loathing and feeling unfaithful to Angelo. Gwen felt a sense of comfort when Jonah's face popped into her mind. Willingly, she had slipped into sleep with the intent of dreaming about him. Her conscious must have sought out his consciousness through the world of dreams, and thinking she was conjuring him up in one of her own dreams, she had instead impermissibly entered his.

I've never done anything like that before.

Gingerly, Gwen swings her legs over the side of the bed and gets up. Feeling a bit shaky on her feet, she makes her way to the bathroom to freshen up. She splashes some cold water over her face and looks into the mirror at the pale, thin, frightened girl before her.

I'm a Dreamwalker? What did he mean when he said it was dangerous? Why did Jonah react like that when I stepped through the door? Pondering this, Gwen takes a brush to her manic hair.

A few minutes later, feeling more herself, she enters the bedroom again, this time surer on her feet. *What if the danger wasn't to me, but to Jonah? Did I cause something terrible to happen to him by walking through that door?* The thought makes her skin go cold, but she has no way to know if he is all right. In the waking world, she has no clue where he is, no phone number to call and no idea if he is a Las Vegas resident or just another tourist passing through.

Gwen moves into the front room. Closing the bedroom door behind her, she crosses to her desk and sits. Starting up the computer, she does a search on the name Crayborn in the Las Vegas phone directory. Scanning the names, she finds only three Crayborns in sin city, none of them with the first name Jonah.

Well, duh, Gwen, he's your age, remember? I doubt he has his own house. He probably still lives with his parents. Only problem is he never mentioned their names and you didn't bother digging into his head to investigate his background when he stood right before you because you figured another Witch would feel you in their head. She regrets her decision to respect his privacy.

With a sigh, she slumps back in her swivel-back chair. Maybe Raven can track his scent? Gwen hopes. Restless, she hops out of her chair, snatching up Angelo's red-varnished violin from the alcove where it is displayed. Crossing the room, she enters the glass French doors out onto the balcony. Outside, the hot, dry desert air mingles with the smells of the dingy city as the sun rises in the east. Even living in the nice part of town high above the pollution of the traffic below, Gwen can taste greed, lust, and desperation on the wind. Closing her eyes, she lets out all the tension of the dream into a long sigh. Feeling relaxed and sensing the sun coming up, she tucks the violin under her chin, places the bow to the strings, and plays.

The music floats out over the city, the melody hypnotic and melancholy. When at last the song is finished, Gwen lets the violin rest at her side and opens her eyes. Suddenly, she feels the warmth of arms surround her. She looks down to see a pair of blue hands and arms encircling her waist.

"Good morning, Morning Dew." Gwen smiles as she turns to face her small bluish friend. Morna's head barely reaches Gwen's shoulder, yet her fully extended wings hover well over Gwen's head. She wears her blue Fairy dress made of spider silk, flowers, and leaves. Looking quickly toward the bedroom, Gwen is relieved to see that the door is still closed. "I've got company, you know. You shouldn't just show up like..." Gwen gestures to Morna's wings. "...this."

"I know about your male bedfellow; I can smell the male human rank in the air." Morna wrinkles up her nose in a comical fashion in the direction of the bedroom. "Just give me a moment to change." She steps back from Gwen.

Even though she's witnessed her Fairy friend transform hundreds of times, Gwen is mesmerized as she watches the air around Morna quiver and bend as a shimmering light engulfs the small blue girl. With a sound like breaking twigs and stretching elastic, Morna is transformed. When the process is over Morna stands before her, minus wings with beige skin, looking for all the world as human as anyone you'd meet on the street. Only her long, straight, blonde hair and her golden eyes are the same as they were before.

"Is this better?" Morna smiles smugly.

"Yes, thank you," Gwen laughs. Stepping around her, Gwen closes the balcony doors and crosses the room to replace the violin in its place of honor. "So, what brings you by so early? Shouldn't you be sleeping?"

"You were awake. I could feel you worrying more lines between your eyebrows about something. I thought I ought to see if you were all right," Morna explains with a shrug of her dainty shoulders.

"Just a strange dream." Gwen shakes her head, perplexed.

"That's typical for you, though, Gwen. What made this one any stranger than the others?"

"Well … never mind. It was nothing, I'm sure."

Morna gives her a suspicious look but drops the subject.

"Since you're up anyways, Raven wants to meet for breakfast."

"That sounds great! Let's go. I'm starving," Gwen replies.

"Absolutely. Right after you get dressed." Morna gestures to Gwen's pajamas.

"Right. I'll meet you downstairs."

"Will you be bringing the human with you?" Morna asks with a quirked brow and a little smirk.

"Michael? Well…" Gwen laughs nervously, fidgeting with her long black hair as she glances back to the closed bedroom door. She can feel his mental hum within. He's still sleeping. "Nah, we'll let him rest. But maybe next time."

"Humph, it's not like you to leave a near stranger alone in your sanctuary or leave your place unlocked. What if he needs to leave before you return? Anyone or thing can wander on into your condominium," Morna advises, her serious tone almost comical with her bird-like voice.

"Well, don't worry. He has a key. Michael knows to lock up when he leaves." Gwen shrugs with forced casualness.

"He has a key?" Morna's blonde eyebrows shoot up at this. "This is quite a serious step for you."

"Gall, Morna don't make a big deal out of it, okay?" Gwen exhales with exasperation. "I'm just testing things out with Michael. I'm not getting married!"

"Your love affairs are your own concern," Morna, laughs as she turns to go. "Make sure you introduce him properly to us before too long."

"Fine, all right. You have my word on it." Gwen shakes her head and smiles awkwardly, watching Morna wave goodbye and slip out of her front door.

Gwen grumbles to herself as she hurries barefoot across the hardwood floor. With utmost stealth, Gwen turns the knob of her bedroom door and pushes it open. The room beyond is dark, her blackout curtains drawn tight to hide the dawn. *An old habit I still can't break.* Michael sleeps on his side, his back to the door. Slipping inside, Gwen moves about the room, dressing as quickly as she can. Superhuman speed can come in handy but not when she was trying to be quiet. It disturbs the air too much, causing gust of winds. Still, what is slow for Gwen is three times the speed of the average human and she is fully dressed, ready, and creeping out of the bedroom within five minutes. She stops by the front door to slip on her Converse. Gwen reaches for the doorknob when a door creaks open behind her.

"Where are you off to?" Michaels asks with a yawn.

"Just out for a quick bite to eat." Gwen puts on a bright smile and turns to face him. "Do you want me bring back some coffee?" His hair stands up on one side, his shirt and baggy sleep pants crooked. His bright brown eyes have a sleepy haze to them. *He's adorable.* He scratches the stubble on his cheek and smiles lazily in reply. Gwen turns to go. Before she closes the door, she hears Michael call out "I love you, don't be gone too long!"

Gwen stalks down the hall to the elevator as if the fires of hell are on her heels. She practically bounces as she waits for the elevator to reach her floor. The doors fly open before her with a ding, and Gwen dives inside, ignoring the father and daughter already occupying it. Gwen pushes frantically on the buttons. When the elevator finally lurches downward, Gwen takes deep breaths. Leaning against the back wall of the lift for support, Gwen closes her eyes.

This is a part of being normal, Gwen. She lectures herself in her mind. *If you're going to play this role, you better get used to hearing "I love you" tossed about as a greeting and a parting farewell. Just suck it up and deal with it, Gwen! Other people have panic attacks over natural disasters, starting a new job, or speaking before an audience, but not me. No, I get freaked out by the everyday stuff. I'm uncomfortable with normal.* But that's not the only reasons she's panicking. It hits her that at some point or other Michael will expect her to say "I love you" back. Gwen swallows the rock of doubt lodged in her throat and takes a deep breath.

Once upon a time, all she wanted was to hear those three little words. Now she can barely tolerate them. *It is better to have loved and lost than to have never loved at all,* she quotes sardonically in her mind but doesn't have the energy to even laugh at her own bad jokes. She doesn't have to love her new boyfriend right away, but she is at least willing to try, for her own sanity if for no other reason. With all the sincerity she can muster, Gwen pastes a smile on her pale face. Her friends are waiting. Now more than ever she must be the strong one, the stable one for all three of them. She steps out of the elevator, leaving her doubt behind. With chin up and shoulders square, Gwen fights the sorrow of the past as she forces herself to accept the reality of moving forward.

Chapter Nine

The Show Must Go On

With Morna riding on the back of her Harley, Gwen pulls up to the curb outside their favorite Vegas diner. Killing the motorcycle's engine, Gwen lets the kickstand down. Morna gracefully dismounts the bike. Gwen climbs over the machine, following her friend inside. Even as small and petite as she is, Morna still walks into the diner as if she owns the place. Yet there's nothing is arrogant about the Fairy. Today she wears her golden hair loose down her back, partially covering up her bare back exposed by her usual backless yellow tank top. Her hair ends at her bottom, which makes it almost as long as her blue jean short shorts. Morna fits right in with the other barely clad female patrons. This is Las Vegas, after all.

The funny thing is that Morna would wear the same skimpy get up on the peak of Mount Everest, Gwen muses.

From her time with Morna, Gwen has learned that Fairies' skin naturally adapts to their surrounding climate. Although they can

make their wings look transparent and invisible to mortal eyes, they still need room to move. Unable to make them disappear entirely, her friend constantly sports backless shirts and tube-tops whenever out in public.

Morna's sandals squeak on the tile floor as she abruptly turns and slides into their usual booth. Careful not to bump her undetectable wings against the back of the seat, the Fairy sits erect on the edge of the bench. Morna gestures to the other side of the booth. Gwen smiles at her and obeys, settling into her seat just as the waitress strolls up to their table.

"What will it be to…" The brunette waitress stops mid-word when she looks up from her notepad, recognizing them. "Oh, it's you two again." She smiles, putting one hand on her hip. "Where's the third musketeer?" She looks around the diner for Raven with a flirty smile on her lips.

Morna's good-natured smile melts into an icy glare directed at the clueless waitress.

"He's running late, but he should be here soon," Gwen replies, trying to hide the smirk on her face.

"Do you gals want to get started without him or should we wait for Mr. Tall, Dark, and Brooding?" Out the corner of her eye Gwen notices Morna bare her teeth in what looks like a silent hiss.

"We'll just order for him, Angie." Gwen smiles broadly.

"The usual all around, then?" Angie the waitress asks, beaming back.

"Yes. Thank you." With that, Angie almost skips away, looking up every time the doorbell chimes with an expectant smile.

Gwen turns a knowing look on Morna.

The Fairy doesn't realize Gwen is staring at her; her attention is still on Angie the waitress as she gossips behind the counter with another co-worker.

She's probably eavesdropping on the conversation with her Fairy super hearing, Gwen ruminates to herself. *By the livid look on Morna's face, they must be talking about Raven.* Gwen politely stays out of the two waitress's heads, something she finds harder and harder to do of late. It isn't that she's lost her ability to control her telepathic powers. They seem to be changing, gaining overwhelming strength, as though someone turned up the range of her mental frequency.

Gwen clears her throat. Instantly Morna's head snaps back to Gwen with her full attention.

"Yes?"

"Why don't you just mark your territory and claim the guy already? Seriously, Morna, you can't bite the head off every girl who sniffs around him."

"I know not of what you speak, Ramona." Morna emphasizes Gwen's false name.

"Not a clue, huh?"

Morna shakes her head with a tight-lipped expression as she absentmindedly plays with a strand of her gold hair.

"Okay. Just remember that someday some chick's gonna come along and grab his attention, and then it'll be too late to tell him the truth." Gwen drapes an arm over the back of her seat nonchalantly.

"What truth is that?" Morna shoots back defiantly.

"That you're in love with that big fur ball, you idiot!" Morna's blonde eyebrows shoot up in surprise at this; her mouth opens as if to speak but Gwen doesn't give her a chance. "Both of you are the silliest, shyest people in the world! If you ask me, he feels the..."

"Hey, what's going on with you two?" Raven's rough voice breaks into the tension. Both recoils to find him standing right next to their booth as if appearing out of thin air. The two girls look at each other and back at him at a loss for words. Raven gives them both a stern, yet confused, look. Before he can speak, Angie shows up with a tray full of hot food and cold drinks.

"There you are, handsome!" Angie winks at Raven, whose cheeks instantly change into a deep shade of scarlet. He mumbles a hello and then moves to take a seat by Gwen, who doesn't move over.

"There's more room on the other side, Derrick," Gwen announces, using his alias since Angie is present. Raven looks embarrassed and quickly takes the seat next to Morna, who also looks a pinker shade than normal.

Gwen hates to humiliate her mild-natured friends, but the way the two tiptoe around each other is starting to drive her crazy. For some reason they can't seem to recognize what Gwen saw briefly in the woods outside of Boston two years ago.

I've tried to stay back and let them discover their feelings on their own time, but, honestly, how oblivious can they be?

Angie serves everyone's food and drinks before slipping a napkin Raven's way with handwriting scribbled across it.

"Enjoy your food. Let me know if you need anything else." She pauses a moment, her eyes lingering on Raven before she adds, "Anything at all." With a flirtatious sway of her hips, the waitress walks away.

"Finally. I thought she'd never leave!" Raven says under his breath.

Morna's whole demeanor changes at his remark. A little smile plays at the corner of her lips as she picks up her fork to eat her bowl of assorted fruit.

Raven crumbles up the napkin with Angie's number on it, using it to wipe up some moisture on the outside of his glass before throwing it into the nearest trashcan.

"Nothing but net!" Gwen exclaims as the napkin lands perfectly in its target. This earns her a big smile from Raven. When Gwen looks back at Morna, her smile is gone, and her face down turned, her brow knit together as if she's troubled.

What's wrong, little sprite? Gwen tries to ask mentally, but Morna keeps her firmly shut out of her mind, leaving Gwen to wonder.

Gwen can see why Morna is so smitten with Raven. *He is kind of a babe*, with his long black hair pulled back into a ponytail, his startling gold eyes against his dark tanned skin, and his manly, broad-shouldered build. Apparently, the masculine, hairy, strong silent type is Morna's cup of tea. Gwen has no idea what her "type" is. No one ever bothered to ask her — they just took what they wanted from her. By the time she was mature enough to form such opinions, her innocence had long been taken. Her heart was already broken. Now she just coasts by, picking up a new beau whenever the ache inside threatens to consume her.

"Hey, waitress! Change the channel, will you? There's something wrong with this station," a male patron sitting at the counter shouts. The three friends ignore him, their attention on consuming their meals. "Now there's something wrong with this one, too! Hey, I think your connection is busted or something. You should check the satellite," the same man announces loudly in the diner.

Gwen turns around in her seat and watches as a bus boy walks around the counter to mess with the TV mounted on the wall at the end of the bar. On the screen, Gwen sees channel after channel of broken up sports broadcasts and news bulletins. Each one is littered with static accompanied by a strange voice. Her food forgotten, Gwen scoots out of the booth and wanders toward the television. Her attention is rapt by the words spoken in the strange voice hidden within the static.

"I can't fix it!" the bus boy announces, uttering an expletive in Spanish under his breath. He moves to turn the TV off.

"Don't touch it! Just wait a moment," Gwen tells him. The young Hispanic man looks at her like she's crazy but leaves the TV on as he goes back to his regular duties.

"Derrick! Matilda! You need to come listen to this!" Gwen calls out never taking her eyes off the screen.

A moment later, Gwen senses Raven and Morna step up on either side of her. Together, the three listens to the message in the true tongue hidden within the garbled TV program.

"This is a worldwide announcement brought to you by the HCOE. Attention all the children of The Forsaken. The twelfth tribe has renounced the rule and law of the HCOE and has denounced all association with the Thirteen Tribes of Cain. This statement was released by their King at the sixth hour this day."

"Hey, come on, turn the TV off already it's giving me a headache!" the man at the bar shouts.

"Hey, what are y'all watching? There's nothing there." Angie bobs up in front of them. She looks perplexed between them and the static TV screen. The three friends ignore her, too engrossed by the hidden message to pay any of them mind.

Suddenly the voices change on the announcement. Gwen imagines the one she is hearing now is the voice of the Vampire King himself.

"We, the Vampire, will no longer pledge allegiance to any power other than ourselves. We will not wait for the end of times to reap the rewards of Armageddon. We will not share our throne with lesser tribes or squabble over territories. We will not hide in the darkness any longer. This world is ours for the taking, and the humans' blood, ours for harvesting. We declare war on any who meddle with our designs, human or Forsaken. Let none cross our path or blood will flow in the streets of all the cities of man!"

The original announcer's voice continues the broadcast. "Clearly, they mean to announce their presence to the world of man and openly slaughter at will. In response to the above statement, the HCOE has released a statement of their own.

"Hey, weirdoes, I'd like to drink my coffee in peace if you don't mind! Why don't you find a TV in your hotel room to stare at if you like static so much?" another patron yells from the booth nearby. A few other patrons add their comments to his, a general sense of annoyance building in the diner.

Not wanting to miss a single word of the announcement, Gwen angrily turns on the other costumers in the diner. With her entrancing voice she commands, "Quiet!" Instantly, the whole diner goes still, as the patrons and staff alike all freeze, caught at attention, their eyes glued on Gwen. "Be still and don't move till I say you can!" Satisfied, Gwen spins back around, ignoring Morna and Raven's questioning glances, and focuses on the TV once more.

A third voice, perhaps the voice of the Head of the HCOE, reads the HCOE statement.

"We, the HCOE, will not take this declaration of war and simply stay out of the way. Any Vampire who exposes himself openly to humans or slaughters Eden Spawns unlawfully will be hunted down and executed without trial. However, the HCOE is negotiating a treaty with the twelfth tribe in the hopes that terms can be met, and peace restored to all the Thirteen Tribes of Cain. In the meantime, all members of the other tribes must cease all dealing in the human world and return to their respective clans, nests, packs, and covens immediately! Any of The Forsaken left amongst the mortals may be perceived as a threat to the Vampires and slaughtered without question or reason. The HCOE encourages all The Children of Cain to help negotiations move forward by leaving things to the HCOE. Should any be slaughtered during this delicate time, negotiations may become strained. Further information of this crisis as it develops will be broadcast through the channels available to each tribe."

Again, the original announcers voice resumes. "We, the members of the Intertribal Communication Network, urge all members of the Children of Cain to heed the HCOE's warning and evacuate all human cities and return to your own kind without delay. Thank you, that is all." With that, the static continues but the voices cease. Gwen looks around, glad to see that her spell is still in place. The other occupants of the diner are still frozen.

"What are we…" Raven begins but, deep in thought, Gwen interrupts him.

"Do either of you know what HCOE stands for?" Gwen asks, her eyebrows knit together as she chews absentmindedly on her bottom lip.

"It stands for High Council of Elders, Gwen. They are made up of the kings and queens and advisors of each tribe. They make up the government that rule over all Thirteen Tribes of Cain," Morna answers in a solemn tone, her gold eyes dark with worry.

Gwen as she faces the diners.

"Listen, all of you. Nothing happened just now. The TV is just disconnected from the satellite. There were no strange voices. You did not notice my friends and me doing anything out of the ordinary. Please, go back to your meals as if none of this happened," Gwen commands in a haunting tone. The moment she breaks eye contact, everyone in the diner resumes their normal activity.

Waitress Angie hurries over to the TV and turns it off as the male patron at the bar complains again. None of the other diners give them so much as a glance as the three make their way silently back to their booth, their food now gone cold.

Gwen takes a moment to process her thoughts as she tries to eat the rest of her meal. She finally looks up to finds Morna and Raven both staring at her with identical, yellow-eyed stares.

"What?"

"Well, that's pretty big news, don't you think?" Raven asks, a bit annoyed.

"Yeah, I'll say." Gwen immediately goes back to eating.

"What does that mean for us?" Morna asks no one in particular. "What does that mean for the show?"

The three exchange silent glances. "Nothing," Gwen finally answers.

"What do you mean nothing? We can't just pretend like nothing's going on, Gwen. Those Wiccan kids found us out. What if they tell someone about us or some Vampire moseys into one of our shows one of these nights, huh?" Raven demands.

"Then I'll deal with it," Gwen replies calmly. She shovels some eggs into her mouth as if to signal that the conversation is over.

"Gwen be realistic. Where there is one Vampire, there are many. If we stay and just one finds out about us, you can be sure they will come back with more and finish us off when our guard is down," Morna warns.

"I've dealt with my share of Vampires before, remember? I can handle whatever comes after us. Besides, unlike you two, I don't have a pack or a nest to return to. I never had a Coven! So where exactly do you expect me to go, huh?" Gwen shoots back in a harsh whisper to not be overheard by the other patrons.

Only after the words leave her lips does Gwen think the better of them. Neither of her friends will look at her now, both off in their own thoughts.

"Whatever happens, I will go wherever you go, Gwen," Morna announces after a moment, breaking the awkward silence.

Gwen smiles weakly at this.

"Me, too," Raven adds "I don't know the new pack master very well, and most of the old pack died in..." All three share an understanding look.

"I haven't spoken to a single member of the Fae tribe since I left. I'm not so sure I would be received back into the nest without some repercussions," Morna admits.

"I think that settles it, then," Gwen announces. "We're staying, and the show must go on!"

Chapter Ten

Nocturnal Encounters

Mist fills his lungs, birds chirp, and leaves rustle in the wind. Blades of grass tickle his cheek, dampening his skin with dew drops. Through his eyelids, he feels the warmth of the sun through snatches of shade. Opening his eyes, Jonah finds himself lying amongst the foliage in the woods. Trees sway high above. With a start he sits up, looking about frantically, panting.

"Gwen?" he calls into the stillness of the forest. His voice carries amplified as if in a cavern.

"Yes?" a young woman's voice answers back just behind him. Spinning around on his knees, Jonah finds the dark-haired vixen standing behind him. She wears black leather pants and a revealing corset top. Bosom half exposed, her creamy skin contrasts starkly to her jet-black hair. She smiles at him with a conspiratorial gleam in her eyes. "It's nice to see you again, Jonah." She says his name like a caress on his soul. Inwardly he shivers.

"I wasn't sure I'd see you again."

"Then why did you call my name?" she asks, quirking a dark brow as she looks down at him.

"Optimism, I guess. I was afraid you slipped into oblivion and would never wake up again." Jonah, hops to his bare feet, stepping easily on the uneven terrain. *You never step through a doorway that isn't of your own making in the dream world! You shouldn't be playing with something you don't understand.* "I'm glad to see you're still in one piece." Jonah says aloud.

Jonah notices Gwen's demeanor change, her eyes narrow, her chin set in a stubborn manner. The energy around her sizzles with irritation. Her clothing shifts, mutating into blue skinny jeans and a long-sleeve, red-stripped slouchy sweater. She stuffs her hands into her pockets and lets out a long breath.

"Oh, that. Well, as you can see, I'm perfectly fine," she replies shortly.

Malicious darkness, does she have to be so beautiful? How does anyone think straight with those eyes looking into their soul? He runs his finger though his dark blond hair and smiles. "Yes." He gulps nervously. "I'm glad."

Gwen's supple lips spread into an amused smirk. A pleasant, yet erotic, medley of smells meets his nose as Gwen steps past him — wildflowers, dark honey, cinnamon and burning wood. Their eyes meet for a moment before she steps onto the dirt trail leading farther into the forest. Jonah's heart feels as though it'll stop beating altogether. Sighing, he stuffs his hands into his jean's pockets to stroll after her.

The air has that surreal taste that only exists in the dream world. Sweeter than anything that the real world can ever offer. As if one could taste thoughts, sounds, emotions, and longings.

"So, where are we?" Gwen stops abruptly and turns her green-eyed gaze on him, standing so near him, like she had in the last dream.

"You'll see soon enough." Jonah fights the urge to collect her into his arms again as he did then and take her lips in a kiss. At this very moment, her perfect lips beckon to him. Gwen gives him a knowing smile and licks her lips suggestively, as if she knew what he was thinking. With effort, he tears his eyes away from her mouth and steps around her to continue down the path. "If you can keep up, that is." Jonah smirks back at her.

Before Gwen can mouth to reply, Jonah takes off down the trail at superhuman speed. He laughs as he winds his ways through the trees.

He hears Gwen laugh and the sound of her foot falls as she chases after him. With a whoop, Jonah bounds on. Exhilaration pumps through him as air rushes past him. The uneven terrain beneath his bare feet bothers him not at all. His feet move as if running on air.

"You're going to have to do better than that, Jonah!" Gwen declares, appearing suddenly on his right side, her speed nearly matching his own. Her green eyes are bright, and her hair flaps behind her like black wings. Her jubilation surges around her. Their energies mingle as they tear through the woods side by side, feeding each upon one another's power, magnifying the other's joy. A laugh burst out of him. He presses harder to get the advantage.

His efforts finally pay off. He emerges ahead of Gwen onto the shore of a large sparkling lake. Jonah stops instantly, sand spraying. A stormy sky hangs ominously above. Clear blue sky reflects in the waters still surface. The shoreline is empty of life, just a continual line of trees curving around the lake. His eyes instinctively fall on the small mound of land in the middle of the body of water. A picturesque home resides there. Even from afar it seems vacant, like the void in his heart.

Gwen bursts forth from the trees with a triumphant yell. Caught completely unaware, she is halfway across the surface of the lake before she can stop herself. She pauses to look back at Jonah, perplexed. With a yelp, the girl disappears beneath the surface, sinking into the depths.

Now do I dive in after her or should I just wait here until she realizes she can't drown? Jonah muses. While he contemplates his choices, he toes a rock from amongst the sand at his feet. Picking it up, the stone feels cold and wet in his palm. He flings the rock. Skipping with perfect precession, it bounces across the water. Upon its twelfth skip, Gwen's head pops up just in time to make contact with the stone. A resounding crack followed by an indignant cry from Gwen echoes across the water to Jonah.

"Hey," she shouts at him. "Watch where you're throwing rocks!" Her attempt to sound annoyed is spoiled by a chortle.

"You're fine. It's not like it's a real rock anyhow!" Jonah retorts as he casually steps out onto the water. His feet glide with perfect ease along the liquid surface as he makes his way out to Gwen. With a fascinated tilt to her head, she watches him approach. *I bet she didn't know we could do that in dreams.*

"Real or not that, still hurt," she protests, craning her neck to look up at him.

"May I offer you a hand, madam?" Jonah jests as he reaches down toward her.

"Well, it is the least you can do." With a suspicious look at his hand, she grasps it, almost as if she expects him to trick her. Together they pull her out of the water. "You got me into this mess, after all."

"Hey, you're the one who wasn't looking where she was going." As she emerges, her drenched hair and clothes dry of their own accord. Smiling at this, Gwen stands toe to toe with him on the middle of the lake, their hands still intertwined.

"Whatever you say," Gwen submits. "Now are you going to tell me where we are, or do I have to guess?" Their eyes meet and all at once Jonah can't remember his own last name, let alone anything else of importance.

"Um … we're at…" Jonah shakes his head a bit to dispel the trance of Gwen's yellow-green eyes. "At my home." He points beyond her. Gwen turns to look at the secluded island dwelling with a thoughtful expression. "Well, it was my home … my parents' home. I grew up here. No one lives here anymore," Jonah supplies as Gwen turns to him. A strange mixture of emotions dance behind her eyes. Standing this close, her head comes just above his shoulder. With her face upturned to investigate his face, her lips are now mere inches from his.

"Why doesn't anyone live here anymore?" Gwen asks in a faint voice, even though not a soul is near to hear them speak.

"Because…" *Being here without my parents is too painful to bear,* he admits to himself. Aloud, he continues, "We live with the Blackwools and Aunt Nicola now."

The sky rumbles and gray clouds roll in, over casting the blue sky in mere seconds. The musky scent of rain hangs in the air, yet no drops fall.

Something like sympathy passes behind Gwen's exotic eyes and she smiles weakly. "Well, you brought me this far." She breaks the connection between their interlocked fingers and steps away from him. "You might as well show me around." She smiles over her shoulder. Without waiting for him to reply, Gwen walks across the lake toward Jonah's childhood home.

Why did I bring her here? he asks himself as he reluctantly follows Gwen. Apprehension builds in his gut, filling him like an overstuffed pig. In reality he had only hoped Gwen would appear in his dreams again, but he hadn't exactly planned to expose himself like this to her so soon. *But then I rarely have control of where or when I show up in the dream world,* he tells himself as the two of them step onto the rocky surface of the lake island.

The pale white house looming before them is a cabin. Neither grand nor expensive, it's just a practical, white-washed wood cabin with a porch. A small patch of pine trees circle about it. Wildflowers grow in clumps amongst the sparse grass. White stone steps lead a path up to a faded orange front door.

"After you." Gwen stops at the bottom of the steps, waiting for him to lead the way.

Jonah gulps down his nerves and moves forward. Despite his trembling legs, he finds himself standing before the door with his hand on the brass doorknob. Shadowy shapes are visible through the glass pane before his face. His childish fears and apprehensions wail in his mind, demanding that he turn back. *Leave the past in the past.*

"We don't have to go in, if you don't want to." Gwen speaks up from just behind his shoulder. He can almost feel her body heat even in the dream world. "We could always explore the bottom of the lake," she suggests cheerfully.

"No. We might as well." With renewed assurance, he twists the knob and pushes the door open. Jonah half expects a gust of black smoke to come billowing out as they cross the threshold. At last, they enter the front room without incident. Gwen closes the orange door behind them.

Before him Jonah sees the old familiar rooms of his childhood. White painted, wood-paneled walls, dark wood trim and base boards with rustic wood floors frame large picture windows looking out on the lake line every side, bathing the interior in natural light. A line of hooks juts out from the wall to his right. No coats or hats occupy them. Across from the hat rack, a doorway leads into the kitchen. The living room sits before them with a hallway leading off to the right to the rest of the house. From the entry, Jonah can see that the living room still holds his mother's piano, along with the rest of her favorite bits of furniture. Everything second hand, reclaimed, and repainted to his mother's artistic tastes. All frozen in time the way his mother would've liked it. *I doubt a single piece of furniture remains intact.* Josephine Crayborn's tireless hours of labor and love were destroyed as surely as the woman who had created them. Hesitantly, Jonah steps forward. A floorboard creaks beneath their weight as they pass the kitchen. Jonah smiles to himself.

He can almost hear his mother call his name from down the hall. The loose floorboard always made it impossible to sneak about. Despite being human, Josephine possessed powers of her own: motherly intuition.

Behind him Gwen remains quiet, her breathing warming his neck.

"It's not quite as beautiful as the grand ballroom in the palace,

is it?" Jonah whispers conspiratorially, glancing over his shoulder at her. "But it's home."

"I think it's beautiful." Gwen smiles weakly. Worry and sadness hang around her.

Great, Jonah, your second time dreaming with her, and you take her some place depressing! Stop being a killjoy and liven things up or this will be the last time you ever see this gorgeous creature again.

"What did you do for fun around here?" Gwen asks as she suppresses a laugh. "I mean, when you lived here as a kid?" She hops over the back of the floral sofa in the middle of the room and lands on it in a casual pose. Smiling up at him, she folds her arms behind her head to await his answer.

"The usual things one does when you live on a lake." Jonah replies. "Fishing, camping, canoeing, hiking…" He shrugs his shoulders.

"Conjuring magic, dabbling in the dark arts, and ritual animal sacrifices?" Gwen quips with a quirk of one perfectly arched black eyebrow.

"Only on Wiccan holidays if Father permitted it," Jonah smirks. "The rest of the time my mother home schooled us. My parents never pressured us to learn the craft."

"Really! Why not?" Gwen sits up, looking flabbergasted. "Not that I know anything about the parenting practices of Wiccans, but I just assumed they would train their kids in witchcraft from infancy."

"My mother was human," Jonah admits with a sigh while

running his fingers through his hair. He looks about at the seating available to him before the large rock fireplace. *There is just enough space at the end of the sofa to sit next to Gwen and it's the closest seat,* he considers in his head, *but if I want to avoid the temptation…* He takes three steps and plants himself in the armchair across from the couch. The coffee table safely divides him from the black-haired Goddess. "My father was Wiccan and they believed that it was best to raise us somewhere between the two cultures. That's why we lived here instead of in a coven." He gestures at the house around them. "My father only taught us basic spells unless we showed a particular interest in one form of magic or another. It's not like we were left ignorant of Wicca. We still had every book on the craft available to us in the study. It's just…" His chest constricts as the walls around his long-suppressed agony threaten to collapse. *I will not lose it in front of her,* Jonah tells himself. *Bursting into tears is a deal breaker on a second date … not that this really counts as a date but…*

"Your parents didn't want to force you to choose between being Wiccan or human," Gwen finishes for Jonah with an understanding nod. "It sounds to me like they were really good parents."

Jonah smiles at this, the tightness in his chest lessening at her words. *Now she's wondering what happened to them.* Before his eyes, Jonah sees a red stain spread across the rug from beneath the coffee table. He gulps, averting his eyes from the blood. *Great, Jonah, you cornered yourself right into a sob story. How do I change the subject without seeming like I'm intentionally avoiding the…?*

"So was it just the four of you or do you have grandparents and …"

"Cleo, our little sister, is five years younger than Leona. She's going to be ten soon," Jonah interjects, grateful for the change in subject from the dead to the living. "My mother's family lives nearby just outside of Seattle. We visit my human grandparents occasionally. My father's family are originally from England. Most of his family still lives in the Warwickshire Coven near Alcester."

"Is that where you're living now with your Aunt Nicola?" Gwen gets up and strolls over to the fireplace. She picks up some twisted ginger roots lying on the mantle to inspect them.

"No. I haven't seen my father's family since I was six." Jonah watches as Gwen puts back the root and starts examining framed portraits on the walls. "Nicola isn't really my aunt — we just call her that. She's Thayer's aunt and his family the Blackwools adopted us. They're part of the Monroe Coven in Pennsylvania."

"Hmmm … interesting." Gwen takes a three-piece folding picture frame from off a bookshelf and smiles impishly. "Aha! I knew you must have been a beautiful baby," Gwen jokes in a singsong voice, holding up the old baby photos of him and his siblings triumphantly.

"Ugh, just put that back." Jonah blushes as he hops out of his chair to cross over to her. He swipes the folding frame from her and replaces it on its shelf. Gwen giggles and saunters off toward the dining room. Before Jonah can follow her, she ducks into the adjoining kitchen, disappearing behind the living room wall and out of sight. *Please don't find some embarrassing item in the kitchen. Not that there is that I can remember but still…*

"So, Jonah, do you want to show me your room?" Gwen pops out the other side in the entryway, a mischievous look in her eyes. Frogs leap in his stomach at the thought. Possible scenarios that would result in utter embarrassment to total indecency cross his mind. Jonah stammers, scrabbling for words, when Gwen adds, "Or, should we go searching for sunken treasure at the bottom of the lake?"

"I'm up for it if you are." He sighs with relief, giving her a nervous smile.

"Then come on. What are we waiting for?" Gwen spins on her heels and dashes for the door.

He glances about the living room. The rug beneath the table is as it was, pristine and white. The suffocating weight of the misery that occurred in this room dissipates, allowing him to breathe. Jonah hurries after Gwen.

She left the front door wide open. Gwen takes the white stone stairs down to the edge of the lake. She bounds three steps at a time in carefree leaps. He stops to close the door. Jonah feels his spirit lift, as if leaving the weight of death behind in the confines of the cabin's walls. Quickly he meets Gwen at the shore.

"I'll be Wendy and you can be Peter." Gwen grins as she grabs his hand in a firm grip. Her emerald eyes shine playfully in the reflection of the water. "Let's hope we don't run into any mermaids. I've been known to be the jealous type." She winks at him.

Jonah's heart leaps into his throat at the word mermaid, and he grapples mentally with his own thoughts while trying to conjure intelligent speech. Thankfully, Gwen dives into the lake.

Letting out a startled cry that turns into a laugh, Jonah finds himself dragged along with her. With a splash, they break through the water and plummet below. The rush of icy water closing in on him jolts through his body. Instinctively, they hold their breath before realizing their foolishness. Together, they release their breath. No air bubbles emerge from their lips and yet no water fills their lungs. Gwen gives him an amazed look. With a laugh that seems to defy the thickness of water, she dives deeper. Still joined by hands, Jonah swims with her. They touch down on the dark soil, the texture grainy between his toes. Seaweed and rock covers most of the floor of the lake. All around them, the lake seems endless. Every scent seems thicker and heavier while also diluted, each blending into the next until his nose can barely distinguish between dirt, water, and plant. Looking back to the surface, the clouds seem eons away, as if the cosmos of another galaxy.

With a playful tug, Gwen leads him onward to discover what the underwater world has to offer. Glints and glimmers shine occasionally amongst the underwater plant life. Gwen guides him towards several of these sparks of light — a metal butter knife, shards of glass, coins, and a few tin cans.

There is still so much Jonah doesn't understand about the dream world, and now that he is dreaming with a Dreamwalker, the possibilities seem endless. *This could be for better or worse*, he reminds himself. In his occasional studies with his father as a boy, his father read to him from "The Dreamers Plane."

"While humans experience a subconscious state while they sleep wherein, they dream, they do not cross over into the dreamer's plane unless brought there by a Dreamwalker. Their dreams consist solely of individual experiences and concerns. However, while in this state their minds are open subconsciously to suggestion. Humans' dreams are vessels skimming the surface of the dream plane while Forsaken are the creatures residing in the ocean flowing through the dream plane freely. Dreamwalkers are the ocean itself. They are the dream plane."

No matter how lucid a dreamer he has become over the years, Jonah can never manipulate the dream plane the way someone like Gwen can. Inwardly, the thought gives him pause. Abruptly he releases Gwen's hand. She instantly spins around in the water to face him. She gives him a wink and a playful smirk as if to say, *all is well.*

When she steps away, her foot slips and falls. Soil floats up in a gust around her fallen form, like a cloud of muck. Jonah pushes forward to get to Gwen. Parting the murky water, he finds her sitting atop a large oval reflective surface. Cracks fan out from beneath her, reaching out to an ornate gold filigree frame. The glass shards' pearlescent glow catches the little sunlight from above. Gwen examines the cracks, surrounding her as if half intrigued, half terrified.

What is a mirror doing down here? Jonah answers himself in a heartbeat. *Well, it is a dream, Jonah; stranger things have happened,* he reminds himself wanly.

Gwen tears her gaze from the broken mirror, a troubled look in her eyes. Jonah hefts the slender witch to her feet. Her long black hair swishes about as if doing its own dance. The black tendrils encase his face, obscuring the world. All that he can see is Gwen. Her mesmerizing eyes lock on his. When at last her dark locks settle, the universe seems to click into place. The stars align. Suddenly nothing is impossible. Jonah gathers Gwen into his arms. He brushes a hand through her silky strands and grasps her by the back of the neck. She leans in even as he guides her lips toward his mouth.

A bright light washes over them as a lightning bolt flashes above. The rumble of the accompanying thunder shakes the ground beneath. Jonah and Gwen look up, startled, and watch as the sky quickly returns to its gray color once more. Quietly, they wait for another bolt of lightning to strike.

A flash of light flutters out of the corner of Jonah's vision, startling the Wiccan teens. Gwen clutches his bicep in her sudden anxiety. By instinct to impress along with the sense of uncertainty in the water about them, Jonah's every muscle tenses. Gwen's expression hardens as they peer about for the source of the moving light. The sky above stays calm.

Nothing stirs. The lake bottom seems just as it had a moment ago, peaceful, and serene. Yet an eerie sense of watching eyes surrounds them like a shroud of squid's ink. A flood of guilt watches over Jonah, the weight of a thousand lies threatening to drown him.

Gwen shakes him gently to get his attention. Her hands still firmly encircle his upper arms. Concern flickers behind her eyes. A dark shadow falls across her face. Her eyes widen in shock. Something brushes against his leg. Jonah catches a glimpse of a long, scaly tail with a pearlescent double fin wrap around his ankles. A hand grasps his shoulder and spins him around. Gwen tries to cling to him, yet he slips away from her. From black tendrils to red he is transported.

Red curly hair flays about wildly in the murky water. Unblinking lime green eyes bore holes into his soul. A lady of the sea's body melts from human flesh into an iridescent fish tail. Even as she takes shape in his mind, the Mer maiden opens her mouth. Instead of the voice he has long known, she emits a startling screech. The lake dissipates. A black liquid takes its place, swirling about them. Gwen's voice screams his name in the distance, fading rapidly as the oily liquid consumes Jonah's vision till all he can see is Isla's disappointed eyes.

Gasping, Jonah rolls out bed with a thud. He winces, disentangles himself from his bedding. A glow of light shines through the shroud of sheets covering Jonah's face, bringing light to the darkness. By the time he emerges from his linen cocoon, he finds his best friend and roommate staring down at him from the upper bunk. A glowing orb of light floats just above the ginger teen's hand.

"By all Beelzebub, what are you doing, Jo?" Thayer exclaims. His usually perfectly styled spikey red hair lays haphazardly, adding comic irony to his incredulous yet sleepy grimace.

"Nothing." Jonah rubs his bruised shoulder. "I just fell out of bed," he explains as he flings off his blankets. "I must've had a bad dream."

"Hmph," Thayer yawns and scratches behind his ear. "Must've been a crazy dream, then." He fluffs his pillow before adding, "I've never seen you toss or turn before."

"How would you know? What's that supposed to mean, Thay?" Jonah scoffs as he climbs back into the bottom bunk.

"We've been sharing the same room since we were ten. I think I know how my best friend sleeps," Thayer informs him with an attempt at a sarcastic tone ruined by a yawn.

"And how is that?" Jonah snorts as he smooths his blankets over his body and settles back into his pillow. The room plunges into darkness as Thayer releases the spell creating the orb of light.

"Like the dead," Thayer mumbles. Jonah tenses, his mouth working. "What was the nightmare about?"

"Well … um … it was about your sister," Jonah admits, unable to produce a plausible lie. "Not that Isla is a nightmare or anything. She's a sweetheart, really. It was just … well, I was dreaming about..."

Snoring sounds from the bunk above him. Jonah stares into the darkness as an unsettling realization takes shape in his mind. Not only did he not want to explain to Thayer what he was really doing in his dreams the last two nights, he also had no idea of who he had been with. The raven-haired vixen is clear in his memory, but the details of how he met her or who she really is seem … fuzzy. Despite this, Jonah has no doubt that this woman, Gwenevere, is flesh and blood. They have met in the waking world once before. He falls back to sleep with a nervous excitement. In one world or the other, he must find the truth behind the woman in these nocturnal encounters.

Chapter Eleven

Severe Truth

"The disappearances continue as this abduction epidemic spreads throughout the United States. Terrifying still are the new reports coming in from all over the globe of abductions rising in alarming numbers."

Michael stands in front of the flat screen TV on the living room wall in Gwen's high-rise condo, his attention rapt by the female news anchor reporting on News 3 Live at 3:30. A bowl of Cap'n Crunch clutched in his hands, he shovels spoon after spoonful absent mindedly into his mouth.

"The early theories of a gang or terrorist group being behind all this have been dismissed," the news anchor continues. "As of yet no organization has stepped forwards to take credit. Young and old, male, and female, and of every race and religion, it seems no one is safe from these abductors." Gwen sips her coffee in the kitchen, trying to act natural. Her hands shake involuntarily.

"Authorities are puzzled by these abductions, as there seems to be only one connection between all these disappearances." The lady anchor with a brunette bob hesitates for dramatic effect. "…the time of day. Every single abduction has happened at night and outdoors. Sometime in the hours between dusk and dawn, someone or something is lurking the streets of every major city. There have even been a few reports of similar occurrences in small towns far away from metropolis areas. The FBI is heading up the further investigation and urges everyone to stay inside at night. It has been inferred that a national curfew will be set in place, but the White House has not confirmed this report."

"Can you believe this stuff?" Michael asks as the commercial break brings him back to the present. He goes to take another scoop of his cereal, only to realize his bowl is empty. He turns and walks to the kitchen. His brown hair disheveled, and he's still dressed in his night clothes even though it's afternoon. Michael works nights as a blackjack dealer at the same casino where Gwen performs her show. He passes her on his way to the sink where he dumps his dirty bowl.

"It's pretty crazy," Gwen replies with forced shock. Part of her had hoped that the Vampire decree of rebellion had been all talk. The last couple of weeks have proven this theory wrong. "It's only a matter of time until these people slip up." Gwen finishes the last of her coffee, joining him at the sink to wash her cup and his bowl. "They'll get caught. Those kinds of people always do."

Out of the corner of her eyes, she realizes that Michael is watching her. Gwen ignores this, pretending to focus on drying the dishes and putting everything away. She can't help wondering for the hundredth time if he suspects that she knows more about the whole thing than she's letting on. Perhaps that's just her own conscience talking. After all, how could a Vegas illusionist know anything about such things?

"You really think so?" Michael asks, wrapping his arms around her from behind and drawing her into his chest. She lets him, although the last thing she wants right now is physical contact. She needs purpose, to act. Sitting around watching the world she's grown accustomed to and the people that she's learned to love torn apart is breaking her apart.

"Yes. It'll all work out. You'll see," she tries to reassure as she gently disentangles herself from his embrace and walks into the living room. "Where's the remote? Let's turn this stuff off. It's depressing." Gwen announces as she tears the couch apart in search of the lost remote.

It's more than depressing, it's driving me insane! The weight of guilt in her stomach grows heavier by the day. She can't help but feel responsible for those taken. Only people like her can defend the humans from these monsters. Interfering is forbidden in the name of keeping peace between the tribes. She's been trying to stay out of the world of The Forsaken for the past two years. Challenging the vampires now would put her dead center in the spotlight of both their tribe and her own.

"Here it is!" Michael declares from the kitchen. "You had it with you when you made the coffee, remember?" He brings the remote to her and again she sees concern in his eyes.

He knows something is bothering you. Of course, he does, you're practically living together now. He'd have to be a complete idiot not to notice that. "Thanks. I guess I forgot." Gwen forces a laugh as she takes the remote from him. Just then the news comes back on.

"Police have announced the identity of the remains found recently behind a Las Vegas nightclub last week as Las Vegas local, Roman Moore." Gwen's hand freezes in mid-air, her finger poised above the power button. She stares at the screen. The hair on every inch of her skin standing on ends. "Roman attended the University of Nevada-Reno, for Psychology. He was reported missing last Saturday. Due to the state of his remains, the authorities were unable to positively identify him without a forensic analysis. Roman is just one of many similar murders that have occurred in the last six months, although this is only the second victim murdered in Nevada. Other victims murdered in the same gruesome fashion have been discovered in various cities in the United States. This has the FBI investigating the possibility of a serial killer at work. Although it is unclear how these victims are being killed, the striking resemblance between these cases is startling."

"Gwen?" Michael repeats her name for the third time before she comes to. "Are you alright?" He gently shakes her shoulder as if to wake her.

"What?" Gwen turns to him, still half dazed. "Yes, of course. I'm fine." She shrugs, knowing her act is unconvincing.

"Did you know that guy or something?" Michael asks, indicating the flat screen with a nod. "That Roman Moore, guy?"

"Yes. I did. I haven't seen him in a couple of months, though," Gwen admits, the feeling in her limbs beginning to return.

"Oh. I'm sorry." Michael seems at a loss for words for a moment. "How did you know him? You didn't...."

"We dated briefly," Gwen interrupts him. The walls of her condo seem to be shrinking around her. She drops the remote on the carpet and briskly heads to the door. "It wasn't all that serious, and I didn't know him all that well, really." She doesn't give him a moment to speak. "I just remembered I need to meet with the set designer about some changes to the show." Gwen needs to get out or she'll burst. She grabs her jacket from the hook by the door and her keys from the entry table. She quickly throws open the door. "I'll see you later," Gwen calls back without looking back and is halfway out the door when she feels Michael's hand on her arm. She stops and turns to him, white faced.

"Hey, it's okay. You don't have to hold everything in all the time you know. Talk to me!"

"There's nothing to talk about," Gwen answers numbly, unable to avoid his big brown eyes and the depth of affection she sees there. She swallows hard. "Look, maybe you shouldn't go out tonight. Maybe just stay inside, you know just in case." Before he can protest, she slips out of his grasp. The door closes with finality behind her.

Before she's even on the elevator she finds her mind returning to its new favorite distraction.

Jonah Crayborn.

Ever since the first time she wandered into his dreams, she hasn't been able to stay away. She isn't really cheating, but in the pit of her stomach she knows it isn't too far off. Nothing has happened between her and Jonah in the dream world. Well, not really. Still, being a part of each other's subconscious universe gives them an intimate connection despite the distance between their bodies.

She knows it's wrong, but she can't resist the temptation. He only remembers snatches of what happened that night in the parking lot. In the dream world, he knows her and yet he doesn't. She likes it that way. He can never lead other Wiccans to her. She has made sure of it. With the news of Roman's death hanging about her, Gwen feels the need for an escape from reality more keenly. Tonight, she needs to indulge in the Wiccan boy's vibrant yet peaceful psyche to sooth her own. To pretend she's someone else, somewhere else, anywhere else than her and here.

With the coldness that she's long become accustomed to, Gwen yet again turns away from the severe truth.

Chapter Twelve

Bloody Remains

everal hours later, Gwen is in the middle of her grand finale, the audience in the palm of her hand. She successfully pushed all the nonsense about the Vampire rebellion and running into the Wiccans to the back of her mind. She even managed to pretend that she hadn't heard the news about her last boyfriend being ruthlessly murdered.

Then it hits her. The sudden pain that engulfs her, the darkness that comes with it, is like a punch to the stomach.

Morna, did you feel that? Gwen sends through their mental bond. Currently their minds are joined as they are about to connect their powers so that Gwen may travel by light.

Yes. What should we do? Morna sends back from somewhere backstage, concern evident in her mental hum.

Send me there right now!

No, Gwen. That would be folly. You'll show up weak and naked unable to fight anyone. You don't know what's waiting there for you! Morna speaks reason but Gwen doesn't want to hear it. Strung so tight with the tension of all the madness happening around her, she can barely think twice before throwing herself into the fray.

Fine. Then meet me in my dressing room now. There's no time to lose! Gwen thinks back.

With all the composure she possesses, Gwen finished the show, saying the final lines of the script. "Never doubt the supernatural, and never become too entranced with reality, for nothing is what it seems!" Gwen's voice amplified through the theater defies the terror she feels inside. Then the power surges through her body as their joint spell takes effect.

No matter how many times she's done this trick, the searing pain of transformation has never lessened. She'd never tell Raven just how much traveling by light hurt or how it weakened her. If it weren't for Morna's Fairy herb concoctions, Gwen would be in a collapsed heap on the floor when Raven barged into her dressing room.

Her world becomes light and her body nothingness.

* * * * *

Gwen parks her Harley down the street from her building with Morna stashed away in fairy form in her coat pocket. Raven pulls

up just behind her. Gwen jumps over her bike and heads down the street. Raven follows on her heels.

Police sirens color the street where she lives, reflected off the pavement and buildings. Gwen forces herself to walk instead of running inside, she approaches the entrance. Several police vehicles are parked along the front sidewalk, with an ambulance. *Is that a news van?* Gwen swears under her breath.

Her neighbors all stand out on the sidewalk, talking to a news reporter and her camera man. Men in uniform block off the front doors of the condominium, standing behind yellow tape. Gwen has the power surging inside of her long before the first officer tries to stop her.

"Sleep!" Gwen shouts in her strange tone of voice. Instantly, all in earshot go limp. In unison the reporter, the police, and the bystanders all fall to the ground unconscious. Gwen doesn't give them a second glance as she ducks beneath the yellow tape. Just inside the door Gwen finds more police talking to the night doorman and the super intendant. The moment she walks in the door, they all turn to her.

"Sleep!" Gwen calls out again. The occupants of the lobby drop like flies on the tile floor. Raven enters the revolving door as the last policeman falls. The man snores before he's even hit the floor.

"Don't worry. They'll be fine," Gwen answers Raven's unspoken concern. She didn't need to read his mind to know he was uncomfortable with all of this but more worried about her state of mind. When one knew a person as long as they have, one learns to read the energy in the air around them.

Raven nods but stays silent as he follows her to the elevator. He stands behind her with his hands in his pockets as she pushes her numbers on the control.

Elevator music plays on the speakers, but Gwen's disturbing thoughts drown it out as they ride up to her condo on the top floor. She watches the lights on the control panel hop from button to numeric button as her ride ascends ever upward, her mind a whirlwind of troubling thoughts, emotions, and dark fears.

All too soon, yet not nearly soon enough, the elevator doors open with a ding on the topmost floor, revealing the hallway outside. With a steadying breath, Gwen stuffs her hands in the pockets of her leather coat, careful not to jostle Morna tucked away in her inside pocket. Numbly, she makes her way down the hall with Raven as her shadow.

Gwen turns the corner. Her condo sits at the very end of the next hallway. Several men in suits and police uniforms move about ahead of her. Her unit's door gapes wide open with yellow police tape strung across the door frame. Two men in black business suits, one white and one Hispanic, stand just outside the condo talking. Gwen assumes by their dress and demeanor that the suits are FBI agents.

Just then the two detectives turn to look at her and Raven. Gwen's footsteps slow as she reaches out her mind toward the two men.

Good lord, I've never seen anything so disturbing in my life. His body is just torn to shreds! Honestly, who or what could do such a thing? I don't care what that crazy nun said, there's no such things as Witches and monsters. Someone else did this, not her—

Remember what they told you. She looks harmless but she's lethal and she knows things and does strange things. She's killed before and she'll do it again. If this is the same girl who killed all the other guys, then I must be careful. Keep your mind blank. I'm not sure how close she has to be to hear my thoughts, but…

Gwen forces her control over the men's minds, inserting herself into their consciousness. In a matter of minutes, she has both men's thoughts and memories sorted through and knows all the details of what has occurred. However, she is compelled by her need to see it with her own eyes. Gwen tears her eyes away from her apartment's wide-open door, a gaping tomb, the corpse inside the life she's grown accustomed to. With her eerie tone of voice, she commands the agents, "Follow me."

"By all means," the two men, agents Murphy and Mendez, intone in hollow voices, their faces vacant, their posture stiff.

Ducking under the police tape, Gwen enters the apartment. The scene she sees before her seems so alien, yet so familiar. Her condo is ransacked, every bit of furniture overturned, broken, or even torn in shreds. Glass is sprinkled all over the title floor of her living room and kitchen. A trail of blood smears across the floor leading into the bedroom. A few members of the forensic crew mill about, gathering samples of blood, glass, and other items with metal prongs stuffing them into sterile plastic bags. Two EMTs wait patiently with a body bag on a gurney.

Silently, the two federal agents enter the room behind her and Raven. The others in the room stop to look at the detective, curious and confused why they would let someone into the crime scene. Before anyone can talk, Gwen does.

"You know nothing. You'll forget all this the moment you walk out that door. Go downstairs and wait outside the building. Keep anyone who tries to enter out until I have gone."

The forensic team and the two EMTs go stiff, their eyes wide and hollow. Now all under the spell of her hypnotic voice, they quickly leave without a word to do her bidding.

Gwen knows that the rational thing to do would be to follow the blood trail into her bedroom but finds her feet have melded themselves to the floor. Raven touches her shoulder as if to comfort her, but Gwen doesn't need that just now. Releasing the breath, she hadn't realized she'd been holding, Gwen rips her gaze away from the destruction. She spins around to look at the two agents.

"Well, I bet you have a theory about what happened, right? So, tell me, what happened here?" Gwen asks as the ominous sense of the violence done in the room settles heavily upon her.

Murphy returns half to himself and clears his throat. "Well, there's no sign of forced entry, and all the valuable items seem to be left behind. Besides the vandalism, there's nothing to suggest a burglary."

"And Michael? What about him? I'm assuming his body is in the bedroom?" Gwen gulps down bile.

"Yes, Miss Greenly. Although, as you see by the pattern of the blood in the front room, it looks as though he might have been here when he was attacked and then, after he was injured, he must've been dragged back into the bedroom where it appears he died." Mendez spills everything out as if it is the most natural thing in the world to discuss the case with her.

"And the cause of death? I mean, just from the looks of things in there and by looking at the body, what would you surmise he died of Agent Mendez?" Gwen asks calmly, not really wanting to hear the answer.

"It's kind of, well … it's hard to say really, Miss Greenly." While he struggles to find the words, Gwen sees inside his head the images from his memory.

"He was torn limb from limb. That's what killed him. The remains are scattered about the room in a way that suggests it was done by an animal, yet there are no other signs to support this," Murphy blurts out insensitively. His partner gives him a dirty look but says nothing more.

Gwen stares at them a long moment, blank-faced as she processes everything.

"Besides the fact that the murderer didn't break in forcibly and they left everything behind, is there anything else unusual about this crime scene?" Gwen asks.

The agents look at each other a moment, exchanging silently with their eyes. Murphy turns to her.

"Well, no, not if you consider that it looks identical to the other six killings we've investigated recently."

Gwen gives herself a moment before responding, seeing again in the FBI agents heads other crime scenes of men torn apart in a similar fashion, Roman Moore the most recent. "Are you saying you think this is the work of a serial killer?"

"It looks that way, yes," Mendez replies.

"And you came here thinking that this killer was me?"

"The only thing these seven men have in common is you, Miss Greenly. Every single one attended your show and were rumored to have been romantically involved with you just before their murder."

Gwen and Murphy's eyes lock on one another's while Gwen mentally extracts the names of all the previous victims from his memory.

Cameron Scott

Leo Miller

Palani Kai

Garrett Summers

Brent Anderson

Roman Moore

 160

And now… Michael Harrison

Gwen remembers them all Their faces spring up in her mind's eye.

Cameron Scott, the Marine, was unusually tall with blond hair that was almost white. He was fighting with demons of his own.

Leo Miller, a businessman of Italian descent with dark, short hair, brown eyes, and thick eyebrows. He had caramel skin and a laugh larger than life. Every other word he spoke was a lie.

Palani Kai, a Hawaiian transplant chasing a career as a performer. Finding it hard to break into showbiz, he found himself in Las Vegas. He would do anything for an acting job. He had a smile that could light up a room which hid a soul soaked in shame.

Garrett Summers, a pediatrician, just came to sin city for a medical convention. He had blue eyes and sandy colored wavy hair that never looked out of place. He spoke like a gentleman with all the politeness of good breeding, but he had the swagger of scoundrel. He was married.

Brent Anderson, a minor league baseball player, pitched for the Las Vegas 51s. He was African American but had the most stunning green eyes. He could spin a yarn like no one's business. He could also rack up a debt like no one would believe.

Roman Moore, the local university of Nevada-Reno college kid. He was part Mexican and Native American. He could talk about anything for hours and had more opinions than any one person had any right to. He was funny, intense, and smart. He wasn't such a bad guy, really. She just couldn't stay tied down to any one guy too long without feeling claustrophobic.

All her relationships since Angelo either ended because the guy was a horrible person or because Gwen was. Most of them had been travelers passing through town who had come to her show and caught her eye. All of them had been meaningless flings to keep her tormented soul busy from dwelling on the heartbreaks in her past. Their smiles and embraces poor substitutes for the one she lost. Gwen felt no remorse in using them for her own purposes. After all, she meant as little to them as they did to her. Conversely, now that she knows their eventual fate, that they hadn't lived long after knowing her, Gwen feels a sickness in her gut like black tar coating her intestines.

"And they all died like this?" Gwen asks despite knowing the answer.

The two agents nod in unison.

"Just like Denise Keller," Murphy points out in a flat tone.

"Do you know who I am, then?" Gwen asks in a challenging tone even though she is the one in control.

"Marianne January, A.K.A. Mary James who ran away from St. Paul's Orphanage over nine years ago. Four years later the same Marianne January was found living on the streets of New York and taken to Pennsylvania to live in a group home. Eventually, she was put in a foster home only to disappear several months later at the same time of the mysterious and gruesome death of her foster father," Murphy replies as if talking to a colleague, not the person he came her to arrest.

Mendez pulls out a folded paper from his inside jacket pocket and hands it to Gwen. Slowly she unfolds the mangled paper to see a missing person notice on the inside with an artist rendering of herself at twelve years of age staring back at her.

Gwen slowly shakes her head, exasperated. "I am not now, nor was I ever, Marianne or Mary but have always been Gwenevere. For some reason none of you people can ever get that straight." Gwen crumples up the flyer in her hand into a ball and tosses it over her shoulder angrily.

"Yes, your preference for the name Gwenevere is noted in your file. What's not there is your supposed real last name," Mendez points out.

"It wouldn't be since I don't even know it myself," Gwen replies pragmatically. She takes a deep breath, gives one more glance about her apartment, and turns back to the FBI agents in front of her. "Everything you've heard about me is true except the part where I'm a serial killer who tears apart her ex-lovers. Now here's what's going to happen. I'm going to collect a few of my things and then I'm going to walk out that door and never come back. You'll forget you ever saw me, that we even met, and you'll go on looking for the real killer. You'll see that Michael's friends and family know what happened to him. You won't mention where he was found or mention my name at all. In fact, every time you try to remember me, you'll suddenly lose your train of thought and lose interest."

Before her, Murphy and Mendez stand erect as soldiers would before a drill sergeant, their eyes round in their open stare. Neither shows the vaguest hint of realization that they are now under her complete control. They accept every word she says willingly.

"Yes, ma'am," Agents Murphy and Mendez respond tonelessly.

"Good." Gwen gives them a tired smile. "You can go now, gentlemen." Instantly the two agents turn on their heels and march out of the door. Not bothering to duck under the yellow tape, they break through it. If it weren't for the bleak situation, the site would make Gwen snort.

Gwen lets out a sigh of resignation. Finally, she looks at her lifelong friend beside her. The look on Raven's face says it all. He knows that no words will make this better.

With a flutter, Morna flies out of Gwen's coat pocket and whizzes about the room. Having heard everything and felt and seen everything Gwen had; she doesn't need an update on the situation. *She's looking for clues,* Gwen realizes, watching the fairy's blue blur make its way around the room.

Gwen looks about her once swanky bachelorette pad and her shoulders slump under the reality of it all.

Her eyes are drawn again to the dark blood trail leading to her bedroom. Straightening her posture and lifting her chin, Gwen forces her feet to take her forward.

I need to be alone a moment, Gwen communicates to them both simultaneously, not wanting to see Michael's remains with her friends there to witness her unraveling at the sight. Gwen resolves to take on this new twist in the ever-bumpy road she calls life. She hopes that there will be some justice for the boy caught in the crossfire of her terminal misfortune. Finding herself before the bedroom door, Gwen takes one last steadying breath and turns the knob. The door opens inward with a creak.

The room beyond is dark. Numbly, Gwen flicks the light switch. Blood covers everything. Body parts lie in bits and pieces on the floor, the bed, the carpet, everywhere. The smell of the carnage greets her nose. Gwen covers her mouth to keep from adding the contents of her stomach onto the soiled carpet.

With all the courage she has left, she steps into the room. Flashes of her own haunted memories invade her mind. She's back in the Keller's kitchen six years earlier. Twelve years old, battered, emotionally drained and undone by the death lying about her. Gwen falls to her knees by the bed. Clutching the bloody sheets and comforter in her hands, she buries her face into the fabric and screams. The sound is muffled by the material, yet she still feels most of the tension in her body released through it.

After a long time sitting in this fashion, Gwen finally looks up. What she sees across the room on the nightstand stops her from running out of the room. A clean, immaculate vase filled with dark red roses with black tips sits there. Amongst the fresh blooms, a white card peeks out. Slowly, Gwen rises from the floor and walks around the bed toward the roses.

Gwen has always been more of a wildflowers kind of gal, and Michael knew this. In the five weeks that they had been dating, he had bought her flowers on several occasions. Roses had never been in the bouquets. Hand trembling, Gwen plucks the white card from the sweet fragrant flowers. With trepidation, she flicks it over. This message is scrawled across it in red ink.

Only you can decide who dies next.

Your debt is still unpaid.

"Gwen?" Morna's voice interrupts the hush of the room. Gwen drops the card. It flutters down to the blood-stained carpet. A moment later, Morna stands beside her, now human size. "I'm sorry about Michael," she says with a multitude of emotions conveyed in those four words. She put a hand on each of Gwen's trembling shoulders. "Gwen?"

Unable to speak, Gwen points to the card at her feet. Morna releases her and bends down to pick it up. She brings the card to her blue face and reads, her nose wrinkling up as she sniffs the card between her blue fingers. She gasps and flings the card away from her.

"What is it?" Raven asks, startled. The two girls spin around to stare at him. His silhouette fills the doorway, the light from the kitchen his back lighting.

"A note from the killer," Gwen answers in a weak voice.

"It smells of vampire," Morna adds with deadly certainty. "The whole place does." Gwen and Morna exchange a look.

"That doesn't make sense, Morna. Look at all the blood. A vampire would never kill in this way and waste so much," Gwen insists, the tightness in her chest melting into red hot rage.

"They would if they wanted to make you look guilty," Morna points out solemnly. The truth of her words sinks in. Suddenly Gwen feels decades older. Her mind suddenly recalls the night she crawled out from under the ruins of Bec LaNuff. The dark stranger with the soulless eyes made it possible for her to escape death. She had wanted to give up then, she hadn't wanted anymore pain, but he had said, "We both know you're a fighter; it's not in your nature to roll over and die. You couldn't give up even if you wanted to."

Some part of her can't help wondering if he is behind all this, the hand of fate that keeps dashing all her happiness.

"It looks like it's time we left," Gwen finally announces to her friends. "We don't really have a choice now. I can't keep everyone asleep forever, and I'm not going to wait around here for whoever left that note to kill someone else I love." The moment the words leave her lips, Gwen realizes that it's true. She had loved Michael. Not in the same way she had Angelo, but it had been the beginnings of something real.

Raven and Morna nod in unison. They both turn to leave the room.

"I think maybe we should go our own ways for a while." Gwen's words stop them both in their tracks. They each turn and look at her, but Gwen continues, "I can't ask you two to come with me. If anything, ever happened to either of you, I …."

"Gwen, when are you going to get it through your head that we're not going anywhere?" Raven interrupts her with a firm but loving voice.

"Where you go, we go," Morna adds. Her tone of voice puts an end to the whole discussion.

"All right then," Gwen concedes weakly, knowing full well she can't keep them from following her to the ends of the earth. Raven smiles and returns to the living room. Together, Gwen and Morna leave the bedroom. Gwen avoids looking at the carnage again and closes the door behind her.

Once in the kitchen, Gwen goes directly to the sink. Turning on the faucet she slathers her hands with hand soap before rinsing them off thoroughly in the hot water. Then she splashed water into her face as if doing so would erase the whole horrible thing from existence. *If only that were possible.* Gwen thinks sadly. Once her hands are dry, she bends down and opens the cupboard below. There stashed away amongst the cleaning supplies is her old red duffle bag. The same bag has seen her through all her years of wandering. Inside are her most cherished of belongings and the necessary clothing and supplies to leave in a hurry. Some part of her always knew that her life here would never last.

Grabbing it, she hefts the straps of the bag over her shoulder. Morna and Raven already wait by the door. Morna holds Angelo's old violin case open in her arms. Gwen smiles sardonically as she reaches for Angelo's violin from its display. Her hands stop in midair. Oddly enough, Angelo's Violin has not been disturbed despite the destruction all around it. She is at first relived and then...curious. *How? Why?* Was it just a coincidence that the last remnant she had left of the love of her life was the only thing left intact or had the murder done this on purpose, and if so, why? Gwen shakes herself to dispel the chill creating goosebumps all over her skin. Pushing the thought away Gwen takes the antique violin and places it gently inside the case. Morna closes it, a curious brow quirked at Gwen. She ignores this and steps toward the door.

One chapter ends and a new one begins.

Together the three friends leave the condominium. In their wake they leave their tattered dreams of a normal life, now nothing more than bloody remains.

Chapter Thirteen

Affray

A small figure emerges from the shadows of the nearby rooftop. With her silver-gray eyes, she watches the street down below. Her vision magnified by her rebirth, Lynette has no trouble spotting Gwen and her mangy dog as they exit the building. The witch and the werewolf hop onto their motorcycles and tear off down the street into the Vegas lights.

She smiles wickedly to herself. With a childish laugh, she leaps from the office building soaring over the street. As she descends, she catches a windowsill of the condominium across the way by her fingertips. With ease, Lynette vaults though the window. Glass shatters as she breaks through it. The sound echoes off the empty hallway. The child vampire lands in a crouch amongst the glass shards on the carpet. The eight-year-old girl stands and stuffs her hands into the front pocket of her dark purple hoodie. Her short brown ringlets bounce as she strolls toward the witch's apartment.

They took the yellow police tape with them when they left, the door seeming just like the rest. Lynette whistles a little tune as she turns the door handle. *Locked.*

Abruptly, she kicks the door with the full force of her immortal strength. With a shudder and a tearing of wood, the door flies free of its hinge and into the apartment. Her way clear now, Lynette casually walks inside. The place is a wreck. Even so, she can tell that it was once an expensive and stylish condo. *Witchy may be a bitch but at least she has good taste.* Lynette glances around the ransacked living room before continuing to the kitchen. There she finds the front door splintered in two against the far wall between the dining room table and the open concept kitchen. Smiling at her handiwork Lynette stuffs her hands back into her pocket and turns toward the bedroom. The door is shut. The blood smear in the living room carpet leads to this door. Several bloody handprints are visible amongst the blood splattered door and doorknob.

She wasn't crying when she came back out from finding her lover slain within. Lynette had hoped for some serious water works. The most Gwen did was shake slightly and look very tired and old. It wasn't nearly good enough for Lynette. *You'll get plenty of chances to watch her suffer,* she reminds herself. Reaching toward the bloody doorknob, wicked glee bounces around in her stomach. Then something moves in her peripheral.

With a gasp she spins around to face the front door. A man stands in the doorway, watching her curiously. She doesn't recognize him at first. Then all at once everything clicks into place. He looks worn and haggard, near starved and disheveled. Still, she knows him.

"I thought you were dead?" she chokes out in disbelief, pulling off the hood of her sweater and stepping toward him.

"It's not as though you stuck around to watch the dust settle, little one," he retorts with a dry laugh and a sardonic smirk on his face. His gray-silver eyes weren't the same as they were in Bec LaNuff. His skin is burned, scarred and colorless without any hint of his mortal host's nationality left. His accent is the strongest evidence of who he once was. His hair is gone, all of it. He has no eyebrows, no eye lashes, nothing. He notices her observation, and his smile deepens creating a dimple in his left cheek. "As you can see, I'm not quite my former self just yet." Strolling inside he glances about the living room. "Not my personal taste in décor, but still…."

"What are you doing here?" Lynette asks, taking a few steps backward. "It wasn't my fault! I had nothing to do with what happened to you."

"Shhhh, shhh, little Lynette." He shushes her, putting a finger to his chapped lips. "I'm not here to frighten or to threaten you," he reassures as he tiptoes around the remains of the sofa. He walks toward her, and Lynette's stomach flips.

"Then why are you here?" Lynette asks, her voice betraying just how young she truly is — not just in form but as a vampire. "If you've come for the witch, she isn't here anymore. She and those friends of hers just left." Somehow, she has backed herself into the bedroom door without even noticing.

"I know. I was watching you watch her," he admits as he steps into the dining room. He leans on the back of the end chair at the long table. "No, I'm not here for her, at least not just yet." He looks at her. "I'm here because the talk around town is that you've got yourself a new master." He raises his eyebrows at this in mock surprise. "How do you like being his lackey?"

"It's no worse than the last one I had," Lynette answers coldly. Behind her back, she has a hand on the bedroom doorknob.

"Lazar Toderoau!" He mocks a Russian accent "The Black Russian, The Vampire King and Master of the Thirteenth Tribe of Cain." He laughs shaking his head. "King, indeed. Did you know that pipsqueak's only a hundred forty-four years old? And only eighty-eight since he was reborn to the grave! And they made that infant King?" He gives out a dark laugh much like a bark.

"What do I care how old he is or who the Vampire choose for their King?" Gently, she twists the knob so that all she needs to do is push. "What do you want? Say it already and leave!"

His forehead creases as his brow, or where his brow should've been, raises as he gives her a mock look of surprise. "I remember a time not long ago when you wouldn't have dared to raise your voice to one of your elders, Bethany." He throws her human name at her as if hurtling a dagger into her still heart.

"That's no longer my name," she retorts through gritted teeth. "And I don't owe you any kind of respect. Bec LaNuff would still stand, and all my family would still live if you hadn't lost your mind over that stupid witch!"

The instant he leaps forward, Lynette shoves the door behind her open and bolts. In a blur, she jumps over the blood-stained bed and right out the bedroom window with a crash. She plummets to the ground from the penthouse. Lynette hits the sidewalk on her feet and takes off running. She whizzes around the corner of the building and finds the man she's fleeing before her. Before she can duck under his legs, he strikes at her with his lightning-quick grip. Lynette yelps as he picks her up by a fistful of her brown ringlets. With a wicked smile, he lifts her off the sidewalk. Crawling, thrashing, and hissing, the child immortal looks just like a cat tossed in a bathtub.

"Put me down!" She yells and kicks and punches. With an amused glint in his eyes, he avoids her blows with ease while tightening his grip on her hair. Without warning, he backhands her with his free hand. Light and pain explode behind her retina. It gets him the desired effect. The child spawn is momentarily incapacitated, her body limp but still conscious in his outstretched hand.

"Now, listen to me well, little one." The chill in his whispered voice forms icicles down her spine. "I want you to take me to this

King of yours. Introduce me as a newly made vampire. Call me a friend you've made out here in Sin City."

"No one will believe that! Just look at yourself. You're like a raisin. New vampires heal almost immediately, unlike the old ones. You know this."

"You can tell him that I had an encounter with a witch that didn't end well." He laughs at his own joke. "It's not exactly a lie. That will be explanation enough," he declares.

"Why would I do that for you? I don't owe you a thing!" Lynette hisses. With both hands, she tries to pry his grip from her hair. The pain in her scalp from his tight grip increases by the second, blinding her.

"That's not how I see it." He sighs. "If you don't, I will tell everyone how you ran away like the coward you are instead of fighting along with your maker and your master."

Her attention snaps back to him, terror in her big silver eyes. "How would you know? It's impossible," she declares, stammering.

"I have my ways." he responds coolly. His grip releases and Lynette abruptly hit the cement with a deafening crack. She wails in pain at the break in her tailbone. *Yes, she'll heal in no time, but it still hurts like hell.* "There are certain codes of conduct in a vampire nest." He stands over her, arms folded before him as he lectures the child, "As you were instructed heavily in this code, you know all too well how our tribe rewards cowards."

His threat hangs like a noose in the air above her. She knows he's right. Child size or not, her soul is adult. Her duty was to fight alongside and die with her maker. She failed. Cowed, she looks down at her small hands, resenting for the millionth time that her spirit had been forced into a child's frame. No matter how long she walked the earth she would always be a child. Her strength surpasses man's but never her fellow Vampires. She is limited to the capacity of her physical form, something she must face every single day of her immortal life.

"Fine." She finally looks up at her blackmailer. "But what do I call you? Hmm? I can't exactly walk in there and introduce you as…"

"I no longer answer to that name." He cuts her off with a flip of his pale hand. The hot desert wind sweeps past them, but neither notice. Immortals feel neither cold no heat. The only pain they feel is that which they inflict on each other or done by magic or their greatest enemy the sun. Lynette watches him as his mind turns inward, as if seeing some distant memory. He shivers visibly before he comes back to the present. Making eye contact, he replies, "You may call me Affray."

Chapter Fourteen

Unbreakable Bonds

"We don't stop until we hit Albuquerque," Gwen announces to her friends, who stand in the doorway of her dressing room. They watch her gather her things and erase any trace that she had ever been there. She's already done the same to their dressing rooms and the rest of the theater.

"Come on, Gwen, that's an eight-hour drive," Raven protests, his backpack slung over one shoulder. "It's already late. Let's just drive until Flagstaff."

"We need to put as much distance between us and this place as possible," Gwen insists. She re-checks every drawer in her vanity for missed items. "I won't be able to relax until we have at least one state between us and Nevada."

"I understand but even we have to sleep sometime," Raven retorts.

"Fine, then we'll stop in Winslow," Gwen concedes as she strolls over to her wardrobe and rifles through it. She hesitates when she comes to the end of the closet. There hang her multiple sets of the grand finale outfit. Gwen releases a long, tired sigh. Squaring her shoulders, Gwen gathers the costumes into her arms and off the rod. With the mound of clothes in her arms, she dumps the bundle into a large metal trash can sitting in the center of the room. Adding a few more items she cannot take with her, Gwen whispers, "*Flar Mes Roara*" Instantly, the contents of the trash can catch fire. Knowing the fire will burn itself out, Gwen turns and leaves the room with her red duffle bag. Raven follows, leaving Morna to close the door. The smell of burnt fabric already wafts through the room, yet the magical fire it makes little smoke. No need to worry about tripping the fire alarms or emergency sprinklers.

"Why are we going to Florida, exactly?" Morna questions as the two of them follow Gwen down the hallway.

"I don't know. Maybe I've just gotten used to living in warm climates. You could also say I've got a bad history with snow," Gwen adds as they turn a corner.

"I don't suppose we could just fly to Orlando?" Morna asks, a blonde brow quirked. "It's much more expedient a mode of travel than by motorcycles on the highway." Morna's mouth forms oddly around the word motorcycle as if it were something dirty or naughty to say.

"No thanks. I've flown with you before, unless you meant to fly in an airplane, then..."

"No thanks." Morna mimics Raven's tone of voice. "I will never travel in a hovering metal contraption. That is *not* flying."

"It doesn't matter; we couldn't get through airport security without making a big fuss," Gwen interrupts, glancing at them over her shoulder. "Even if I could hypnotize the whole airport, I can't deactivate all the security cameras unless I went and found each and every one and did it physically." Gwen throws open the backstage door. Her friends follow her. Without the spotlights and crew, the rafters and rigs seem like puppets without masters.

"Which would take way too much time," Raven nods, picking up on her train of thought. "Unless Morna knows a spell that can knock out just the security cameras?" Gwen and Raven turn and look at Morna.

"No. We fae don't dabble in magic that has to do with modern technology. We've never had a need for that sort of thing," the fairy explains as they emerge from the curtains onto the stage. The lights are low, the auditorium empty.

"I don't suppose we can convince you to travel by light, now could we, Raven?" Gwen asks with a mocking smile.

"Ha! I'd rather not show up in some random place naked and weak." He gives out a dark laugh. "That's if I show back up at all."

"Then it's a midnight run by Harley down the interstate." Gwen stands in the middle of the only spotlight and looks up. Closing her eyes, she utters, "*Darkana*" and the spotlight goes out, leaving her standing on the dark stage.

"I prefer to use my wings." Morna leaps from the stage onto the front row of seats. She lands with perfect balance on the back of a dark red folding chair. With the air of strolling down the street, Morna steps from seat back to seat back, row by row. Hopping off the last row, she lands in the aisle in the back of the theater. Morna waits while leaning against a pillar. She watches Gwen and Raven step down from the stage and make their way up the middle aisles of the auditorium. Neither seems in a hurry to leave the theater and this chapter of their lives behind.

Everyone has gone for the night, which means Gwen must be creative with figuring out how to deal with the cast and crew. Her two companions watch as she moves about casting a peculiar spell over every entrance

"Everyone who passes over these thresholds will instantly forget everything they know about the three of us," Gwen explains. "The spell should last a couple days, or at least I hope it does." With this last loose end secure, the trio silently exits the Indulgence theater. These walls have been home to their show "Entranced" for the last year. They leave by the main entrance. Gwen drops her keys off at the box office. They fall into the ticket slot with a clang, echoing as if the final chimes of a bell.

The hallway outside of the theater connects to the casino level of the Indulgence hotel. The three friends pass through the swarm of tourists and greedy locals on their way to the main lobby. Gwen still needs to enchant the entrances of the hotel itself just to make sure none of the hotel's staff remember them either. Luckily, the spell is invisible to any but a magic wielder. To everyone around her, Gwen will just seem like a crazy loon muttering to herself waving her hands about, which won't garnish even a second glance in Vegas. After finishing the side entrances and the employee entrances, they head out the front doors. As they pass under the threshold, Gwen casts her spell one last time.

Thus, occupied Gwen bumps right into someone.

"Watch it there, lassie!" the fifty-year-old redhead before Gwen calls out, catching her by the shoulders before she can tumble backwards.

"Oh!" Startled Gwen takes a step back from the women, shaking her hands off. "Beg your pardon, mam. I didn't see you there," Gwen admits, her cheeks reddening. "My apologies."

"That's quite all right, dearie," she responds, her Irish accent prominent. The lady had dropped her large tote when Gwen hit her. Raven spies it at her feet and picks it up.

"Here, ma'am. I think this is yours." The plump woman smiles at him kindly, her plume of wild read hair bright in the lights of the entrance.

"Why, thank you kindly, youngin'." Many weaves around them with grumbles or glares as they stand right in the middle of one of the sliding doors. Gamblers and travelers either pour in from the

walkway outside or from out the casino within. Raven realizes belatedly that Gwen is staring at the Irish woman strangely.

"Well, we better get out of the way," Raven suggests, taking Gwen by the elbow. Still in a bit of a daze, Gwen lets him lead her away with Morna fast on their heels.

No one says a word until they enter the parking lot outside.

"What was that about?" Raven asks, looking between the two girls suspiciously. The three of them make their way toward the tall parking garage, the Vegas heat present even with the sundown. With the smells of the desert lingers alcohol and cigarette smoke. According to Raven, even neon lights have a scent.

"What didn't you see it?" Gwen asks, amazed. Color slowly returns to her cheeks. "That lady back there was a witch." They nod to the parking attendant in the security booth as they pass into the dimly lit concrete structure.

"She had the wiccan sunburst in her eyes, and magic danced about her in waves," Morna augments. Cars pass them. The screech of tires and the roar of engines echo in the cavernous space.

"Not to mention she had the wiccan aura," Gwen adds, glancing nonchalantly back the way they had come. Thankfully, the woman is not in sight.

"Do you think she noticed that you're a witch, too?" Raven can't help asking, matching Gwen's tone. They turn a corner and slip inside the elevator.

"Of course, she did. We were eye to eye, for goodness sakes," Gwen snorts contemptuously. She reaches out and presses the keypad, and the doors closes.

"Well, what does this mean?" Raven presses. "You don't think she'll bother us, do you?"

The witch and fairy exchange a look. Gwen turns to Raven with a worrisome look in her eyes. Before she can speak, the elevator doors open.

Three teenagers stand right in front of them, a red headed boy beside a tall dark blond boy and his average height sister.

Jonah Crayborn's eyes meet Gwen's. Whatever elation she felt at seeing him in the flesh melts away promptly, with a bitter taste in the back of her throat.

Caught in the moment, no one moves. No one speaks. Jonah swallows hard. He opens his mouth to speak but Raven beats him to it.

"She's not going anywhere with you," Raven declares in a low growl.

"This doesn't concern you, wolf." Leona retorts with a hard set to her shoulders.

"Look, this doesn't have to be difficult. Everyone just remain…"

"You didn't see us. You have no idea who we are," Gwen informs the three wiccan teens in her resonant tone of voice. "You will return to where you come from and never search me out again."

183

Leona tries hard to keep a straight face but can't hold back. Sputtered laughter bursts out of her.

"We're ready for that trick this time," Thayer shrugs apologetically. "You can't transfix us."

"Gwen, just come along quietly. We've convinced Thayer's aunt to help you. Really, it's for the best, you've got to…"

A banshee's screech ends the discussion. The trio before them fall to their knees wailing. To escape the ear-shattering sound, they cover their ears as they writhe on the cement.

Gwen and Raven wait until Morna stops her fairy warrior cry before uncovering their ears. Instantly, the three friends dart out of the elevator and around the bend, leaving their rivals incapacitated. Raven follows behind the two girls, keeping a wary eye out for the others. Ever the protector.

Hurry, they'll be back to themselves again soon, Morna warns. The sound of their running feet echoes off the cement enclosure. Halfway down the aisle, they finally come upon Gwen and Raven's motorcycles, in a shared parking spot.

Gwen and Raven slip on their helmets. Raven hops on and revs the engine. Gwen turns to Morna with her spare helmet in hand. "Come on, Morna. Hop on!"

"No, Gwen, I am of better use in the sky." Morna pushes the helmet back.

"There's no time to transform now, Morna! We have to leave!"

"I will take flight full sized. Worry about yourselves. I'll cover you from above." Morna takes off, running down the aisle toward the square opening in the structure, the night sky visible without. Free of hesitation, the seemingly ordinary human girl jumps up the cement ledge and right off the building.

"Damn fairy! Of all the stupid, crazy..." Gwen mutters as she stows away the other helmet and straddles her green metallic Harley.

"I agree completely!" Raven snorts "We'll skin her alive later," he adds with a conspiratorial smile. Gwen shakes her head ruefully as she starts the ignition and brings her machine to life. Gwen soars out of the parking stall and down the lines of cars. Raven tails her as always. *One to cover her from above, the other to watch her tail.*

Black hair flying behind her, Gwen speeds toward the exit, a long, spindly ramp leading down to the street. Just before they hit the exit ramp, they hear shouts behind them. Gwen glances back to see three teenagers giving chase not far behind Raven.

"*Par Oxy Em!*" Gwen hears Leona's young voice shout. The cement wall right next to Raven explodes. Dust fills the air. Broken chunks of cement crash in a heap to the ground. Between the gaping hole in the wall, part of the ramp and the rubble, the entrance onto the ramp is blocked.

Good. Now they can't follow us that way. Gwen whips her attention back to the front. Laying into her bike, she revs up for greater speed. In a flash they approach the bottom, the security gate in sight.

Like three cyclones of gray smoke, Jonah and his companions materialize between them and the gate. There's no turning back and no time to slam the breaks.

"*Lau Nch Raisa!*" Gwen chants, including Raven as she casts. It's a completely experimental spell. She has no idea if it'll work, but she's out of options. Just as she comes to the bottom of the ramp, Gwen's vehicle abruptly vaults over the three teens. Their shocked faces are priceless as Raven motorcycle soars over them as well.

"*Fro no altae!*" Thayer calls with palms together, reaching toward them. Promptly a blast of freezing water shoots forth. Gwen and Raven find themselves drenched by the air-bound tidal wave. Almost immediately the cold liquid solidifies everywhere it has made contact. Within a matter of seconds, Gwen's entire form is frozen stiff. Gwen can sense that Raven is experiencing the same effects. *That's a nasty trick!*

Their motorcycle's engines sputter. The wheels cease to turn. Gwen realizes too late that her Harley is descending to the ground. The security gate is at the end of her trajectory.

"Get out!" Gwen orders the attendant inside. Seconds before she crashes through the roof of the little booth, the man darts out, rolling across the asphalt. With the shatter of glass and crunching of metal and wood, the motorcycle comes down hard on the booth. Like a fist crushing an empty soda can.

The momentum propels Gwen's ride forward over the debris and into the parking lot. Unable to control the balance of the vehicle,

Gwen and Raven's Harleys fall onto their sides, sliding across the gravel. They both scream and curse as the ground tears at their clothes and into their flesh below. Despite being turned into roadkill, Gwen is startled to see a woman standing in the middle of the road. Her red hair stands out in its wild array, her clothes a broomstick skirt under a flowy blouse, her eyes bright lime green with a golden starburst in the center. *The Irish Witch from the hotel lobby.*

The lady stares down the skidding motorcycles headed straight for her as if playing a game of chicken. *"Haultia emmitula!"* she commands. The two of them come to a halt just inches from her. They both gasp and breathe heavily. Raven grits his teeth to hold in the pain of his damaged body. Gwen is too consumed with fury to feel anything at all.

"Cease this nonsense at once!" the lady before them commands, her Irish accent lending her tone a strict air.

The Crayborn siblings and Thayer dash forward from the parking garage. All three hold onto the power, ready to strike.

Gwen calls on the spell that she had used for the first-time only weeks before. Energy engulfs her, a yellow glow spreading from within and consuming her entire frame. The older witch's eyes widen in amazement. Gwen senses the lady reach for her own power. Before anyone can utter a word, Gwen lets loose her newest defensive. *"Inka captae maegic, enosa un forsaken!"* The light bursts out from her in all directions with a wailing screech. It strikes her assailants, swift and potent. Unable to react, they are all flattened to the ground in a daze. *Where they will stay for at least fifteen minutes.*

"*Gainge raisa,*" Gwen chants, lifting the motorcycles that have them pinned down. The several hundred-pound machines twist as they hover until they are right side up again, and then land on the pavement. Gwen wants to rush to Raven but can't move. They are still encapsulated in the frozen liquid. Gwen thinks up a spell to aid them. "*Haste'sse un war mae.*" With the words passing her lips, a gust of hot wind forms around her and Raven. The enchantment melts away all traces of the curse put on them.

"Raven, get up!" Gwen stumbles to her feet and over to where her friend lies groaning. His eyes closed tight; his tanned face grows pale. Gwen gently rolls him off his injured side, yet still he cries out. "How bad is it?"

"I'm pretty sure I broke something," Raven grunts between gritted teeth. Blood soaks his leg and his middle. Gwen doesn't have to see the wounds to know it's serious.

"Well, you're in luck. I happen to know a little magic."

Raven responds with something between a whimper and a snort. He opens his gold eyes and looks at her. "You should use a little of it on yourself while you're at it." He touches her face and Gwen flinches. With the adrenaline leaving her body, she feels as bad as Raven looks. Healing takes a great amount of energy and from the feel of it, her latest spells do as well. What little strength she has left will barely heal Raven's extensive wounds.

"Gwen." A gust of wind sweeps over them as Morna sets down next to them. With her she brings the smells of blue bells and honey dew melon. "Take what strength you need from me," she whispers, kneeling beside her. With tenderness in her eyes, Morna places a hand on Raven's chest. Morna reaches out for Gwen with the other hand. Gwen takes it, and together they unite their powers. As the energy flows between them, Gwen utters the healing song. As the burn of healing washes over her, Gwen finds herself once more indebted to the power of loyal friends and unbreakable bonds.

Chapter Fifteen

Indefinite Obscurity

Barreling down US-93, Gwen stays as close to the speed limit as her anxious nerves can tolerate. She can't shake the feeling that she's being followed. Despite her best efforts to convince him to split up, Raven trails behind her. The roar of his engine is both comforting and worrisome. So far, they've managed to stay together, keeping impatient motorists from coming between them.

Signaling before she merges into the right lane, Gwen leads the way off US-93 to exit 2 toward NV-172 and on to the Hoover Dam Access Road. Traffic seems to thicken, not lessen as Gwen had hoped. *There goes my brilliant plan to take the road less traveled by.* They continue onto the Hoover Dam with no way to double back.

The wind whips a few black strands of Gwen's hair about, despite her helmet. Gwen feels the loose hairs rather than sees them. Their black shade disappears next to the dark night around her. Without the bright lights of Las Vegas, the dam seems dark and dreary in comparison. The narrow two-way road across the Hoover Dam doesn't allow for speed or maneuvering. Gwen's need for action escalates within her chest like a volcano about to erupt. Gwen glances over her shoulder. Raven is two cars behind her on his black Harley. The machine he rides seems to fit the wolf within. Both animal and machine yearn to let loose.

They pass the forty-five MPH speed limit sign, and Gwen groans. She would pass by the long line of vehicles if the opposite lane weren't just as steadily flowing with cars.

You'd think with all the nighttime disappearances that there would be less people on the roads. Gwen looks up, hoping to get a glimpse of Morna flying above. Nothing but stars and the occasional cloud are visible. When she turns her attention back to the road, she realizes that the line of cars ahead of her has come to a complete stop. Gwen squeezes hard on the brakes, stopping with a screech of tires just inches from the bumper ahead of her.

"That was a little too close." Gwen sighs, putting the kick stand down on her motorcycle. Taking off her helmet, she stands up on tiptoes, craning her neck to see up ahead.

There are no signs of road construction going on. Neither are there police sirens to indicate an accident, Gwen thinks, sending the thought back towards Raven. She feels his understanding and shared annoyance at the delay. The cars in the lane heading toward Vegas come to a halt as well. *Great, we're stuck in the middle of the damn*

Hoover Dam! Isn't that just damn amazing! Gwen feels Raven's mental chuckle and eye roll at her joke.

What's Morna see? Raven sends through their mental connection.

Gwen looks back up to the night sky once more. *Morna, if you're around, can you see what's going on with the traffic? What's holding everything up?*

Black fog, Morna warns, her voice clipped in her thoughts.

Wait, what does that mean? Black fog?

Shouts and screams drown out the sounds of idling cars and annoyed drivers' horns. Gwen spins to look behind her, and then forward again. The screams come from both directions. The others around her notice too, poking their head out of their cars to see what's the matter. The screams grow louder. A man appears out of nowhere, running down the middle of the road, panic and terror written all over his face.

"Wait!" Stepping away from her bike, Gwen grabs the man by the shirt as he runs past her. 'What's going on? What are you running from?" The man tries desperately to wriggle out of her superhuman grasp. He just ignores her. His eyes keep darting back the direction he had just come. "What did you see?" Gwen shakes the man, yelling in his face.

All at once clarity comes to the man's mind. He whispers, "Black fog. Please let me go!"

A woman screams nearby. The man and Gwen look up. Gwen watches with horror as a black fog begins to engulf the cars ahead of her on both sides of the highway. Their headlights disappear as their occupants wail in fear. Cold washes over her. Gwen releases the man in her grasp, unable to take her eyes off the anomaly happening before her. Gwen turns to look back for Raven and gasps. Just a few cars behind him, she sees more black fog creeping toward him. Raven's head snaps back to see the cloud coming. Those it encases scream and disappearing from view.

Raven, something's wrong. Ride the shoulder behind me, we're getting out of here.

But it's up ahead, too! Maybe we should just jump.

What, off the dam? Gwen asks, incredulous.

It's better than driving right into it! he argues. Gwen groans, placing a hand lovingly on the green metallic paint of her beloved Harley.

"Gwen, it's just a motorcycle." A hand grasps hers, pulling it away from the bike. Gwen looks up to see Raven standing on the other side of the bike. Tall, dark, and formidable, she sees fear in his eyes and snaps out of her stupor.

"Alright, let's jump. I'll use the levitation spell to carry us to the shore." Gwen grabs her red duffle and Angelo's violin case off the back of her bike and throws the straps over one shoulder. She joins him on the shoulder. He takes her hand. Together they step up to the wall. "Don't worry, Raven. Floating isn't nearly as scary as flying if you just don't look down," Gwen assures.

Raven gives her a weak chuckle. Gwen looks over her shoulder as the screams of the helpless motorists grows closer on both sides. Quickly, the two friends climb over the edge of the wall. Positioning themselves on the edge, they take each other's hands. "On three?" Raven asks, his nervousness showing behind his golden eyes.

Gwen nods. "One, Two...." Without warning she propels herself forward, bringing the acrophobic Raven along with her. Wind rushes pass them as they plummet toward Lake Mead. Raven's eyes close tight while Gwen begins to chant the levitation spell under her breath. Just before they hit the water, something grabs Gwen by the back of her jacket. Raven lets out a panicked yell as something lifts them upward, away from the lake's surface. Gwen looks up to find Morna flying above them. She clutches the back of both her and Raven's clothes in her talons. She knew Morna could transform her hands and feet into talons at will, but until now Gwen has never seen them.

It's about time you showed up! Gwen gests. Morna gives her a sardonic look but continues flapping her wings, propelling them forward.

"I thought I was very clear that I did not want to fly with you again," Raven shouts up at the fairy.

"You're welcome." Morna smiles down at him. The movement of her wings sends sprays of mist up on her passengers.

Gwen cranes her neck to look over her shoulder at the dam that grows smaller in the distance. The black fog has overtaken the structure completely. Slowly, the lights of the dam itself are encompassed in the impenetrable cloud.

Four streaks of green light shoot out from the blackness over the lake. The lights gain on them.

Morna! Gwen sends the image to the fairy, and she spins to see the oncoming lights. Determination in the set of her jaw, she looks forward, pumping her wings with more force.

"What is it?" Raven shouts over the gusts of wind produced from Morna's efforts.

"Witches," Morna shouts back, breathless.

How long can she keep this up? Raven alone is over two hundred pounds.

Morna, let me go! Gwen communicates mentally her plan to the fairy. With a reassuring smile, Morna releases Gwen.

"*Gainien raisa,*" Gwen shouts, causing her body to levitate easily above the lake. She faces the witches, collecting the power within, searching her mind for a spell that might be the best defense. "*Du-Day Windah!*" Gwen sends her energy into the spell as it rushes from her to the advancing green lights. A giant swell of wind hits their attackers, pushing the four illuminated figures backward while disturbing the surface of the lake. Gwen hears their shouts and cries.

"Get Raven on the shore!" Gwen orders. "I'll meet you there as soon as I can." As Morna flies off, Gwen can hear Raven's voice

protesting, insisting that Morna stay with Gwen. The fairy ignores him.

Her relief at seeing her friends safely away is short lived. Now she has four trained Wiccans to fight and only a handful of spells in her repertoire. Hovering, she moves backwards as she watches the green illuminated beings recover from her spell and dart back toward her. Gwen sends the wind spell forth again.

"*Du-Day Windah!*"

"*Thwart Balk Kay.*" One of the green lights shouts with an Irish accent lingering on the edges of her words.

Gwen watches as her gust of wind pushes outward only to hit an invisible barrier ricocheting backward. Gwen grits her teeth and holds onto her levitation spell with all she's got. Her own spell hits her with the force of a fifty mile an hour winds storm. Despite her best efforts the wind pushes her backward, nearly making her lose control and fall into the lake.

With a battle cry, Gwen sends out power in all directions, not quite sure what's she's doing.

The night sky flashes with light. Thunder rumbles from above and storm clouds gather instantaneously. Lightning cracks from the clouds to strike one of the green forms. A young man yells as the bolt surges through his body. The green light about him dissipates, and he falls limply from the sky. Without the light to disguise him, Gwen watches as Thayer hits the surface of Lake Mead to sinks into its depths. "Thayer!" cries a girl's voice. The smallest of the green lights dives down after him. Her light shows even through the water's dark surface. Suddenly it vanishes.

"*Termi we kallama!*" the being with the Irish voice calls out. Her voice overpowers the night. It bounces off the dam and the canyons around them. Gwen's storm clouds evaporate. The lightning and thunder creep away as if to hide from the witch.

Gwen prepares to release her latest weapon, the *Inka captae* spell, but hesitates. *If I incapacitate them, the remaining two will fall unconscious into the lake as well. I don't owe the Irish witch anything, but Jonah...* The thought of him ending in a watery grave, leaves her feeling cold in the marrow of her bones.

"*Evata Madota!*" A ball of light bursts from Gwen's outstretched palm like a missile toward the two remaining green figures. The female light throws herself in front of the other being before it can hit. She reaches out a hand, catching Gwen's ball of light in her hand. With obvious strain, the woman closes her fists around the light until it seeps out between the cracks of her fingers. The woman mutters something to the light and then it vanishes. Gwen doesn't stick around to see what her adversary will do next. Cursing, Gwen takes off.

With all the speed she possesses, she sends herself flying toward the opposite shore of the lake, hoping she can outrun the two witches or at least seek help from Morna. When the shore comes in view, Gwen sees Morna and Raven arguing on the beach. She darts down toward them. Inches from setting foot on land, the air around her becomes heavy clamping down on her as if an invisible fist. She spins around against her will. There, hovering in her green light, is the Irish witch with the wild red hair. Anger clearly plays across her wrinkled face.

"Gwenevere!" The middle-aged woman shouts in an authoritative voice. "You are here by charged with the unlawful exhibition of magical feats in the presence of Eden Spawn, and with practicing the craft without adept training. I, Thoyen Nicola Blackwool of the Monroe Coven, take you into custody to stand trial before tribunal for your misdeeds."

Gwen struggles to get free of the energy surrounding her, to no avail. She reaches out for the source of power and meets a wall of blackness instead. Gwen tries to scream, to yell, to thrash about. No sound escapes her lips. Not a muscle can she move. She gasps, turning a deadly glare at the redheaded woman floating before her.

"As you have just noticed, you have been temporally restricted from wielding magic." With a satisfied smile, her captor Nicola, turns to the other green light figure beside her. With his face turned down, his dark blond hair glows in the green light about him, his strong shoulders slumped.

Jonah. Somehow this Irish witch got into his head and forced him to remember what had happened that night in the parking lot Gwen rationalizes. *There is no other explanation.* Gwen had thought she was taking every possible precaution when she had visited the Wiccan young man in the dream world. *I'm not hurting anyone,* she told herself dozens of times, *because nothings really happened. We just talk and wander about showing each other places in the real world the other has never seen.* In the dream plane, Gwen thought she was firmly in control of Jonah. She didn't make him do anything he didn't want to, but she kept the truth of herself from him. Now she realizes she is no better than the monster that had enslaved her a few years ago.

"Crayborn, go fetch her friends," the Irish witch commands.

Gwen tries to shout, "Leave my friends out of this!" but she can't find her voice. Her mouth moves but no sounds escape. Gwen tries to get Jonah's attention. He ignores her, nodding to the elder witch before darting off in a blur of green light towards the shore.

"You three will be sorted out in Alcromech. May the Great Mother be merciful to you all." The lady before Gwen chants as if saying a prayer. A sympathetic look crosses behind her lime green eyes. Without another word, Gwen finds herself falling, her arms and legs pinned to her side. Helplessly she plummets into the cold lake, red duffle, violin case, and all. Water overtakes her, emerging her in the lake. Something unseen pulls her downward, sucking her into a whirlpool. Frantic but without escape, Gwen watches the world above fade behind a curtain of dark water. The haunting dream of falling into the watery pit, of being dragged under a body of water returns to her mind. With true mortal fear she screams, air bursting forth from her mouth as water sucks. She sinks into the water's depths to disappear into indefinite obscurity.

Chapter Sixteen

Alcromech

ike water from a whale's blowhole, Gwen finds herself jettisoned back up again by some strange magical force. Bursting out of the water, she emerges perpendicularly instead of horizontally. Soaked and shivering, Gwen gasps for breath, sputtering out liquid. Rubbing water away she opens her eyes. She stands knee deep in a large bubbling river in the heart of a strange forest town. Behind her she hears the roar of a waterfall. The spell that immobilized her has clearly worn off.

Raven, Morna! Frantic, she spins around, looking for her friends. Water, starry night sky, buildings, and people all blur across her vision. Fighting the whirling sensation, she steadies herself. *They're still back at Lake Mead.*

Fortunately, Angelo's violin case is still safely strung across her chest. Out of the corner of her eye she sees a flash of red. Her duffle floats in the water a foot away. Gwen stumbles forward to grab hold

of the strap, pulling it back to her. Feeling steady on her feet again, she turns back to the waterfall to exit the way she had come.

A solid mass bursts forth through the watery veil. Caught off guard, Gwen and the newcomer fall into the stream. Gwen lands on her backside, soaking the seat of her pants. Beside her, she hears a large splash as a woman falls face first into the water. Coughing and cursing in Gaelic, the Irish witch Nicola pushes herself onto her knees. Her icy gaze falls on Gwen.

"What the blast are you trying to do, girl, kill me?" The lady gets to her feet and wades toward Gwen.

"I'm trying to get away from you and the hell out of this place, obviously!" Gwen shouts as she stands, water dripping off her clothes and belongings. *If Angelo's violin gets warped from this, I am going to kill you, old hag!*

Nicola reaches out to grab hold of Gwen. Without a second thought, Gwen rams an elbow into the lady's stomach. Nicola falls back into the stream with a startled yelp. Wasting no time, Gwen darts toward the waterfall again.

Abruptly, Morna shoots out of the cascade of water. Gwen catches the Fae in her arms, managing to keep them both on their feet. With relief in her eyes, Morna looks up to Gwen, catching her breath. Her wings hang limply behind her like a wet blanket. Blonde bangs hang in her yellow eyes.

Gwen gasps as a large, dark shape appears in the waterfall behind her little blue friend. Before Gwen has the chance to react,

Raven breaks through, knocking into the two of them. With a chorus of cries and colorful language, the three friends land in the river.

This time Gwen finds herself completely immersed under the water. Spitting out the river, Gwen pushes herself back up and gets to her knees. Despite coughing violently to eject the fluids from her lungs, she still hears their laughter. Gwen looks up through the black curtain of her dripping wet hair. Nicola stands above her with a stern look on her face and hands on hips. Thayer and Leona unabashedly snicker at them from the shoreline. Unable to contain her mirth any longer, the Irish witch erupts with laughter. Her plump figure shakes with each gasp of air.

Any relief Gwen might have felt at discovering she hadn't killed the two Wiccan youths is instantly eradicated. She has half a mind to strike the two with lightning all over again. Even as the thought forms in her head, she reaches out for her power and finds…. it trapped in a net of darkness, fiercely trying to break through like a chick from its shell. Irritated and grumbling, Gwen rises to her feet. Nicola reaches a hand out to help her up, but Gwen ignores it. Her attention shifts to Morna, who struggles to get out of the water, her wet wings weighing her down.

"Gwen, Morna? You two, okay?" Raven asks, appearing on the other side of Morna to help the fairy up. "I'm so sorry I couldn't stop myself." Guilt colors his tanned cheeks. *It was like I was shot out of a canon,* he thinks, open-minded. Gwen smiles wanly at this. Finally, they get Morna on her feet just as another figure materializes from the magical waterfall.

Gwen looks up and finds Jonah standing before her. His dark blond hair looks almost brown when wet. His damp clothes cling to his every muscle and curve. Gwen would've enjoyed the site if she didn't feel such an overwhelming sense of betrayal. Their eyes meet. Jonah ducks his head, unable to look at her.

"Ah ha, we're all here now. Let's get out of this here creek," Nicola announces to the group. Picking up her broomstick skirt, the witch wades toward the water's edge. Thayer helps the woman up a set of dirt steps up onto the street. A swarm of pedestrians swarm the road behind her.

"What do we do now?" Raven asks, eyeballing the people around them

"What's going on here, Gwen?" Morna asks, visibly shaken by the ordeal. Raven and Morna turn identical looks on Gwen.

"I'm under arrest and going to trial for practicing magic in the show," Gwen answers tersely, twisting her long hair in her hands. Droplets cascade into the river from her fingertips. She tucks her damp hair behind her frigid ears. Jonah has joined the others on the shore. Gwen tries to keep her gaze from him but can't help noticing that he looks completely dry. In fact, all of them do. Shaking off the thought, she continues. "I have no idea what that means for you two or why they brought you along. It doesn't matter. We're getting the hell out of here. Now." Without a backward glance, Gwen wades toward the waterfall. Raven and Morna fall in step behind her.

"I'm afraid that won't be possible, lass," Nicola interjects. The three friends stop.

"You don't know who you're dealing with, so I'll enlighten you," Gwen shoots back smugly, a dark look in her green eyes. "I've been a prisoner before and there's no way I'll go back to that ever again. I don't answer to anyone and that's never going to change."

"We've been living just fine on our own and, honestly, we're not hurting anyone," Raven adds, his shoulders square, his chin raised to match Gwen's stance of defiance. She feels his protective nature growing stronger within him. The wolf is not far from surfacing.

"You can't stop us. No matter how long it takes, we will find a way to escape," Gwen finishes.

"Like I said, child, that is not possible. You're in a Forsaken trading post, you kin?" She states with an Irish accent bright and thick as aged whisky. Nicola makes a sweeping jester to include the whole town.

Gwen and Raven share a dubious expression.

"It means we are trapped," Morna says with a deep sigh. "This place is neutral ground for all the Tribes of Cain." Morna continues addressing her two companions. "Since the vampire rebellion, I assume that the protection wards have been increased to keep the vampire out."

"Which means even if you weren't under my custody for breaking the law, you still couldn't leave, wee ones," Nicola supplies. "Once you entered Alcromech, it became physically impossible for you to leave again unless you exit through the Luficinian roads."

"Please tell me she's bluffing." Gwen turns to Morna, a horrified look on her face.

"What's a Luficinian road?" Raven adds, looking to everyone present in consternation.

"The Luficinian roads are the safe passageways by which all the townships of the Forsaken can be reached. They connect all the trading posts to every Forsaken settlement in the world. I'm afraid, Gwen, that what the witch says is true," Morna replies, crestfallen. She suddenly seems smaller than she ever did before.

"You have to have special approval documents to use any of the Luficinian roads, let alone gain access into any of the Forsaken Townships," Leona informs the three youths who still stand knee deep in the river.

Looking down into the dark water around her knees, Gwen takes this all in.

"And there be no way, be it magical or otherwise, by which ye can get your freedom unless you confront the tribunal and pay for your crimes," Nicola adds firmly, a strong set to her square masculine jaw.

The woman's words ignite a violent surge within Gwen. Balling up her fists, she tries to control the rage. The power begs to break out of her shell,

"That's if they don't execute you," Leona contributes with a snarky air. Although she and her brother share the same eyes, hers hold only distain behind their aqua surface. This tilts Gwen over the edge of self-control.

"*Inka captae maeqic…*" Gwen begins the chant, her intent dark as her onyx hair. As she reaches for the power within, Gwen yet again finds magic beyond her grasp. She can sense it but cannot embrace it and wield it to her desires.

"You see now, don't ya?" the plump Irish witch asks rhetorically. The lady shrugs. "You'll just have to reconcile yourself to the situation, lass." Nicola finishes in a sympathetic voice as she beckons the three friends to join them on the bank.

In a flash, Gwen whizzes to the waterfall. The moment she thrust herself through the watery cascade, the roar of an explosion erupts in her ears. "Gwen!" familiar voices shout in alarm. Something propels her backwards with breathtaking force. Landing with a tremendous splash, she finds herself in the river twenty feet away from the waterfall. Chest heaving and aching from every muscle and sinew, Gwen struggles to breathe. By the time Raven has waded to her, the burning of the blast begins to numb. She looks up at Raven and sees herself for a moment from his eyes through their mental connection. She's shaking like a reed in the wind, her face paler than the moon.

"Are you okay?" He pulls her to her feet with a strong yet gentle arm. With shaky legs, Gwen lets Raven support her. "What in the hell was that?" Raven growls. He shoots the others the feral look of a beast about to tear into flesh. He helps Gwen limp back to Morna. The Fae looks on Gwen with horror and shock on her blue face. Jonah stands at the water's edge, knee deep in the river. His eyes alarmed and his brow knit in concern, his emotions dance like lighting bugs in his buzzing aura.

"Don't fret yourself, lad. She's fine." Nicola dismisses the whole incident with a wave of a hand. "The barrier just stung her, that's all. There's no lasting damage done."

"Are we done with the theatrics now?" Leona asks with a huff and a roll of her eyes. "Let's go already. I want to get to the Black Iris, get some Flaming Crockeye stew before the kitchen closes, and then fall into bed."

That's my sister, ever the ray of sunshine. Gwen hears Jonah's thought as he gulps and climbs back to the bank and onto dry land. Nicola gives the fifteen-year-old Leona a stern look at her whining tone. Leona sobers immediately and bows her head, abashed.

"My apologies, Thoyen Nicola," she mumbles.

"Come along, it's getting late," Nicola orders. "I'll lead the way and Jonah will follow behind you lot. Stay with us at all times, and if you get any funny ideas about giving us the slip, you'll bring nothing but more condemnation upon yourselves."

"We told you; we're not going anywhere with you." Gwen's hard gaze includes all four of the strangers. When her eyes scan over Jonah, he wears an expression of utter dejection. Gwen looks away quickly.

"What, are you going to live in the river?" Leona mocks with a dark laugh.

"That'll be enough out of you girl. Are you the Thoyen here Leona, or am I?" Nicola scowls at the blond teen witch at her elbow.

Her voice firm, her words clipped. People passing by on the street stop or glance their way at Nicola's raised voice. Their eyes linger a moment on the victim of the lecture.

Leona wilts like a daffodil without water and shrinks back to stand behind her brother. Browbeaten she mumbles apologies before ducking her head and clamping her mouth shut.

Relaxing her shoulders Nicola returns her attention to Gwen and her two friends.

"Gwenevere, if you won't come willingly, I can compel you. Along with shielding you from your power, the spell I cast upon you gives me the ability to command you. And like it or not you will obey."

"I don't believe you." Gwen announces, folding her arms beneath her breast. Everything about her stance to her expression issues a challenge to the older witch.

"Fine, you want to do this the hard way…" Nicola shrugs with a long sigh before looking Gwen square in the eyes. "Gwenevere, I order you to come to me at once." The Irish witch commands in all seriousness.

Gwen's laugh of amusement is cut short when she lurches forward. Morna and Raven's cries of alarm echo another, as they watch her horrified. Gwen tries to take back control, but nothing she does will stop her progress. Her legs continue to take large purposeful steps toward the water's edge without her consent. Every hair on her body stands on end and a shiver runs up her spine. *Good Lord, is this what it feels like to people when I entrance them?*

"Wait, just let my friends go. I'll come along quietly if you do."

"No Gwen. We're not leaving without you." Raven declares firmly. Morna shakes her head emphatically.

"Please, just go. There's no need for you two to get drag into my messes anymore." Gwen strains to look over her shoulder to speak to her friend's, despite her body leading her farther away from them with each step. "Stop it!" Gwen turns her glaring green eyes as she shouts at Nicola. "You've made your point now call off the compulsion!"

"Gwenevere, I release you. You may stop now." Nicola says with a nod and a smug gleam in her eyes.

When her body comes to a stop at the bottom of the dirt stairs leading up the shore onto the street, Gwen can't help releasing a sigh of relief. Gwen wets her dry lips and addresses the witches before her with shoulders back and jaw firm.

"Look, unless it's against the law to transform in front of humans I don't see why they can't go on their way. I'm the one you want. Leave them be." Again, Raven and Morna try to protest.

"It is illegal," Leona says in a low voice, avoiding Nicola's eyes.

"I'm afraid they'll have to answer for their misdeeds with their own tribe's judges," Nicola nods, in confirmation. "Besides didn't ye hear the vampire decree girl? All the forsaken must leave the human world for the sake of peace until the vampire mess is resolved. Your friends must go back to the pack, or nest they sprung from as well." relaxing her stiff shoulders Nicola takes a deep breath

before she continues. "Come now, the hour is late and dinners getting cold, and I mean all of you." The witch turns and heads into the foot traffic on the dirt street without a backward glance.

Gwen, Raven, and Morna look at each other. *It looks like we have no choice,* Gwen admits telepathically. *We'll go along for now until I can figure out a way to get us out of this.* Gwen sends reassurance and calm to both her companions through their shared mental connection. She senses their fear and hesitation but their complete trust in her absolves all insecurity.

Raven gently helps the still weak Gwen onto the first dirt step. Morna silently follows behind. As Gwen steps up on the second dirt step she stumbles. Jonah appears before her, his hand clasping hers with a firm grip. He helps her silently up the rest of the stairs. A whirl of emotions dances in his mind, jumbled and confused. Regret, longing, frustration, and misery seem to have him wound up so tight she can almost feel the tension in his muscles. His skin is warm and soft against her palm. A wave of heat surges through her.

Stop it, Gwen. He betrayed you, and you're their prisoner, remember? Gwen emerges onto dry land. Jonah's hand slips out of her grasp as he steps back to help her friends as well. Their eyes never meet, and neither speaks.

Miraculously, Gwen finds herself bone dry. Bewildered she looks up to see Thayer smiling at her, knowingly. Leona stomps off to catch up to Nicola.

"I remember my first time traveling by water," Thayer laughs. "But don't worry, you'll get used to it." He slaps Gwen on the back

companionably. With Thayer's hand on Gwen's back, the Wiccan boy leads Gwen toward the bustling street beyond. Angelo's violin case on her back and her duffle bag at her side bounce with Gwen's every step. Both seem to have dried magically once she stepped ashore along with her attire.

"Wait," Gwen stops abruptly, forcing Thayer to come to a halt. "I'm not going anywhere without my friends." Gwen informs Thayer as she folds her arms a crossed her chest, in a gesture of finality.

"Of course, that's understandable." Before Gwen can say anything, he stumbles on. "I mean if we found ourselves trapped in an unfamiliar place, I wouldn't leave Jonah and Leona's side. At least not until I knew it was safe."

Gwen says nothing instead she watches as the others approach. Both Raven and Morna are now bone dry. Gwen's eyes alight on Jonah and for a moment their eyes meet. With a firm set to her jaw she looks away. Thayer glances between her and Jonah with an inquisitive air.

Does he know? Did Jonah tell them everything, even about the dreams?

"As long as were in this place, I'd like to stay right beside each other at all times," Raven announces. "This place is much too crowded."

"Agreed!" Gwen concedes. Hooking elbows with Morna, who looks about the place as if impressed and terrified at the same time.

"Alright now we can catch up to the others." Thayer steps up beside her to lead them. An awkward silence settles upon the group of teens.

After a while Thayer clears his throat drawing Gwen's attention. "I regret to have to see each other again under such circumstances. But…. how is my favorite Magician?" Thayer asks with a wry yet beaming smile.

"You mean besides getting frozen solid, abducted, nearly drowned, and zapped?" Gwen asks with her own sardonic tone. "Alright, I guess. We're all alive at least." She smiles up weakly at the redheaded young man beside her. Slowly the coil of knots in her stomach loosens a bit. "How's my favorite groupie been since we last met? I'll admit I'm a rather surprised you remember me at all."

"Well, it's never fun to have a bit of your memory erased. I'm doing much better now since my aunt Nicola broke whatever spell you cast on us the night of the show." Before Gwen can open her mouth to speak, Thayer plunges on. "Never mind all of that. I suppose if I were you, I'd have done the same thing." He leads Gwen the others through the colonial village under the starry night sky. A younger Gwen would've been amazed by the collection of strange creatures passing by. Alas her imprisonment in Bec LaNuff robbed her of more than just her innocence. Wonder and awe are things of the past, nothing more than embers growing cold within her scourged core. Gwen glances ahead to see Leona and Nicola in the crowd.

"Do you travel that way often?" Gwen asks, turning her gaze away from them to Thayer's much more pleasing countenance. "By waterfall, I mean." Behind her she hears the roar of the waterfall change in pitch. She glances over her shoulder as more travelers emerge into the river from who knows where. Out of the corner of her eye she can see the others. Jonah's tall personage lingers just behind Raven, like a specter of her accumulating mistakes.

"It's one of the safest ways to travel out in the human world," Thayer replies casually. Returning her focus to the wiccan boy beside her Gwen reaches mentally toward his conscious. His lack of hostility within him, amazes her. The fact that she had struck him with lightning, almost electrocuted and drowning him only moments ago seems to be of little consequence to him. She can't help noticing that his mind is not blocked from her, although she's not sure he wouldn't feel her probing should she try to delve deeper into his memories. Gwen finds no animosity there, just a genuine concern for everyone around him, even her. Surprised by this, she can't help wondering why she can still see auras and read minds even with her power blocked. *I always assumed telepathy came along with the magic, apparently this is not the case.*

Discomfited, Gwen turns her attention to the strange town around her. Alcromech is alive with a hundred different smells. Cedar, unwashed bodies, spices, and herbs of food cooking near blend with the fresh smell of the spring. All together, they mingle into one exotic scent.

"We better pick up the pace. Aunt Nicola insists you be with her when we report to the Tribal Populace Office."

"The what?" Gwen looks at him in consternation.

"It's where they keep track of the citizens of every tribe, especially those who travel through Alcromech. They keep records of where you came from and where you're going."

"Why exactly?"

"For security, I guess," Thayer responds shrugging his broad shoulder, the only aspect of his physique that seems muscular. The rest of his frame is wiry, verging on sickly and malnourished.

Up ahead, Gwen sees Leona and Aunt Nicola emerge out of the melee of people. They enter a tall brown building with a steep pointed roof. A sign hangs over the door in the true tongue, reading Tribal Populace Center.

Before them is the building in question. Once she is close to it Gwen can see that the building isn't built at all but grown from the forest. The exterior walls are tree trunks still rooted in the ground; the roof made of leaves instead of shingles. The Tribal Populace Office doors are wide open. Gwen steps through the archway as she follows Thayer into the foyer.

Inside, the building is lit by enchanted yellow orbs of light floating at intervals near the celling. A long desk made of white aspen bark and gray river stones runs from one end of the room to the other. Gwen assumes that the six creatures standing behind the desk must be the Tribal Populace Agents, Thayer mentioned. Each is of a different Tribe of Cain but dressed alike in an official uniform. An insignia with the initials HCOE is embroidered on their green velvet coat's left breast. *That means High Council of Elders*, Gwen recalls Morna explaining. In front of each officer, The Forsaken await in six separate lines all with luggage in tow. Pleasant chatter fills the building's confines.

Scanning the room, Gwen finds Thayer waving her over at the end of the farthest line. She hadn't even noticed that he had left her side. Leona and Aunt Nicola stand in front of him, both looking at her with identical curious expressions. Gwen makes her way over to them, still connected to her fey friend.

"You'll need to be right beside me, child when we log you in." Aunt Nicola indicates the spot next to her. Disconnecting arms Gwen and Morna squeeze in between her and Leona. Jonah's little sister steps closer to Thayer as if the two of them are lepers or something sinister.

Oh, forget you. I don't know why you dislike us so much, and to be perfectly honest, I don't really care.

"What's happening now, Gwen?" Morna asks, her voice quieter than usual.

"We're being checked into the Tribal Populace Records. I guess they want to know who's coming and going through this place. It's a security thing, Thayer said." The frightened look in the fairies' eyes puts Gwen instantly on alert. "Morna, what's wrong?"

"Did the Wiccan's explain how these people identify you?" Morna asks apprehensively.

"No." Gwen realizes that she hadn't thought that far ahead. "Have you never been to a trading post before Morna?" Gwen asks, surprised.

"No, I have not. Fairies rarely meet with other Forsaken anywhere, especially in a place with a barrier between them and flying freely through the sky. We do not like the idea of having no way out."

Gwen nods, seeing the logic. Peeking around Nicola, Gwen watches the elderly Dwarf couple ahead of them approach the desk. The agent is an Elf who bears no similarities to Emon, Gwen's old tutor and friend, other than the same gold-tinted skin. This Elf has deep brown hair and is medium of height but very thin and stands just as proud and dignified as Emon ever did. After a quick exchange with the agent, the Dwarf couple is given a long, sharp needle fastened to an ornate silver handle.

Morna follows her gaze and together they witness the Dwarves each prick their left ring finger and drip a drop of blood into an ornate bowl with a sculpted Gargoyle resting on the edge. After their blood is deposited, the Gargoyle comes to life. Its eyes glow red as it dips the tip of its tail in the blood and writes words on the ledger set before it. The Tribal Populace agent and the Dwarves watch this occur as though it is the most commonplace thing in the world. Gwen notes that the same process seems to be happening at every agent's station. Once the Gargoyle is done scribbling, the creatures return to inanimate objects once more. The agent then reads the text in the ledger and continues his interview with the couple. After having the Dwarves press their blood fingerprint onto the ledger, the agent rips the forms from the book and hands them to the couple. They thank him before taking their bags and turning to leave.

Morna looks at Gwen, positively petrified. "Gwen, I can't give them my blood." In a hushed voice she explains, "If I could give them a name or something else that would be acceptable, but..." She trails off.

Before Gwen can say a word to the fairy, Nicola nudges Gwen. "We're next," Startled she turns to watch Thayer's Aunt Nicola step up to the desk. *The raised platform that the Dwarves stood on a moment before must have receded into the floor. Somehow the building changes to accommodate the occupants,* Gwen observes.

With the platform gone, Aunt Nicola steps forward to address the Elf agent.

"What? All this nonsense over just one witch! Sounds like rubbish to me," declares a gargoyle in the line next to theirs. About six feet tall, the gargoyle's stone-like wings hang behind him, nearly touching the floor. His only clothing is a loin cloth covering his genitals. The rest of him is the same dark gray and stony texture of every gargoyle Gwen had encountered in Bec LaNuff.

"It's not! I've heard it from more than one source!" His companion, a troll as misshapen and unsymmetrical as they come, stands two feet above the gargoyle. His earth-tone clothes look old and dingy on his oversized body. With the air of a practiced gossip, he continues, "The vampire decree of rebellion and the threat of the war is all because some little lost witch got snatched up by vampires. Then they say she lost control and destroyed Bec LaNuff."

Every hair on Gwen's body stands on end. Astounded, she becomes consumed by the two men and their conversation. She is vaguely aware of Nicola talking with the populace agent beside her but is too distracted to understand anything the two are saying.

"Bah!" the gargoyle exclaims, waving his hand in dismissal. "A witch can't bring down a mountain. Not even they are that powerful. A whole coven of them, maybe, but just one little kid could never. It was an earthquake, that's all."

"An earthquake that happened at the same time and place where she was? That happened just as witches and vampires were battling to the death to save her?"

"Coincidence." The gargoyle shrugs, hefting his satchel over his shoulder as the line moves before them. The troll drags his burlap sack on the wood floor behind him, following his companion. Before approaching the desk to address the populace agent, the gargoyle turns and whispers to the troll. "It's doesn't matter if this witch child took down a vampire stronghold or not. What I call rubbish is this silly rumor claiming that the Vampire would go to war just to kill one witch." With that, the gargoyle turns to the centaur populace agent behind the desk, leaving the troll to mumble to himself in line behind him.

"Morna, did you hear that? Those men's conversation ...." Gwen turns back to Morna, needing to know if she just imagined the exchange. She stops short, finding herself talking to empty space. A gap in the line is the only indication of where the fairy had stood. Behind her, Leona listens to Raven describe what it's like to change into a Wolf, while Jonah and Thayer chatter.

"Where did Morna go?" Gwen asks the others.

Instantly Raven looks up, his eyes full of concern as he starts scanning the room for her. "I don't see her anywhere," he concedes, stepping out of line to stalk back toward the door. Not seeing her in the room, he turns and calls to Gwen. "I'll go look for her outside." Raven dashes out through the archway into the night. "Not by yourself you don't." Thayer proclaims as he chases after him.

"I didn't see her leave. Did you, Leona?" Gwen asks, panic starting to grip her.

"No. But she is a Fairy. Maybe she transformed and flew off?" Leona suggests, with a dispassionate shrug.

"Don't be an idiot! It's impossible for a Fairy to transform into her miniature size without anyone noticing. Obviously, you've never seen it done before! The noise is deafening and the light it produces is blinding. Trust me, she couldn't have transformed right in the middle of a crowded room without anyone noticing," Gwen rattles off impatiently.

"Gwenevere, it's your turn, child. Step forward. I need to introduce you to the agent, and you need to give a drop of blood to the Heritage Basin," Aunt Nicola commands Gwen.

"Morna, has gone missing. I need to find her. Have someone else go first. I'll be right back." Gwen begins to follow Raven and Thayer. Nicola takes her firmly by the arm and yanks Gwen back.

She can feel the heat blazing from her eyes as she glares with fury at the older woman.

"No, you don't, lassie. You can't just go running around Alcromech by yourself. You're only allowed to wander free as long as ye behave. Unless ye let the agent identify you now, I'll have no choice but to put a spell of restraints on ye. Then ya won't be able to take a bat an eyelash let alone piddle without my say so." The older Witch's firm set to her jaw matches the stone-like expression on the younger Witch's face. "And should another witch take possession of ye, they won't be as kind as I have. Nor will they be willing to speak in your defense before the tribunal. You'll be lucky if they don't smite ye on sight."

The older woman sighs, looking a bit haggard, but her tone softens as she goes on "Look, lass. Eventually, either the wiccans or the humans will catch up to ye, if Vampires don't end up killing everyone first." She gives a weak chuckle. "Either way, ya need someone on your side if you're going to survive, child. No one can really go it alone in this world, not for long anyhow."

"I'm not just anyone." Gwen pronounces through gritted teeth.

"I've seen some of what you can do, and that kind of power comes at a price." Nicola nods seeming thoughtful. "Whether ya like it or not, you've got to learn how to use it proper or you'll end up doing someone a terrible harm. Most likely it'll be those you care about most who suffer."

With every word the stone lodged in Gwen's throat slides further into her stomach and grows heavier until at last the Irish witch's monologue is over. Gwen feels utterly buried beneath the burden of her own guilt and the unwanted truth of Nicola's words. She had almost killed her friends once because she hadn't been careful with her gifts. She tore down a mountain and killed hundreds of innocents among the evil when she destroyed Bec LaNuff. She defeated Legion, but had the price of that victory been worth getting her revenge? Gwen's eyes sting from the tears that beg to burst free. Blinking hard she looks down at the woman's hand still squeezing her bicep. Gwen lets her duffle and the violin case drop to her feet on the floor. Unhindered from one of the weights keeping her back, *now to rid myself of the other.*

"Do you mind taking your hands off me?" Gwen's words are polite, her tone drips with venom.

"Are you going to be a good girl, and do as you're told if I do?" Nicola asks in a half patronizing, half kind voice.

Gwen smiles coldly "All I care about are my friends, and one of them has suddenly gone missing in a place foreign to her. Forgive me for rating a person's life over the importance of some test and a permission slip." Gwen sees the anger in Nicola's eyes. Before the lady can respond, Gwen tears her arm free and bolts for the door.

With blood boiling and adrenaline pumping, Gwen charges into the crowd, swarming through the main road of Alcromech. Gwen opens up her mind searching for her friend's presence. All around her she sees auras dance above the heads of the passersby. None look familiar.

Morna! Where did you go, crazy sprite? Whatever it is you're afraid of, we can face it together. You're scaring Raven and me to death with this escape artist trick. Where are you! Gwen shouts mentally.

She hears nothing in reply. Frantic and fed up with being jostled about by the foot traffic on the street, Gwen steps off the road to find a boulder to stand on in front of a small clothing shop. Once upon her perch, Gwen can see better the layout of the gathering post from one end of the main road to the other near the waterfall. The road runs alongside the river. The town continues on the other side of the water as well, the mirror image of her side. Scanning the length of the river, Gwen spots a bridge back near the Tribal Populace Center. Hurrying down, Gwen makes her way to the bridge. As she passes the familiar brown tree-like building she just escaped, she sees Jonah standing outside the door scanning the crowd.

Gwen stops abruptly before him. "I haven't found her yet! Has Raven or Thayer returned?" her words come out between gasping breaths, more from panic than from exertion.

"No, not yet." Jonah's face is set in concern as he steps up to her to whisper, "Gwen, I know you're worried about her, but you really shouldn't have run away from Aunt Nicola like that. She's a Thoyen, Gwen! You don't know what that means so she's willing to be tolerant of your disrespectful manners. Please believe me, you need to be on her good side if you want her help when you face the tribunal. Reject her protection and you'll find yourself stripped of your power or sentenced to death."

Jonah registers Gwen's bewilderment. After taking a calming breath, he brushes a strand of her black hair behind her ear before continuing, "I'm not trying to frighten you. If I could vouch for you and take you into the Coven myself, I would but I'm no one of importance. The tribunal won't take my word for it that you're not dangerous." Sighing in resignation, his shoulders slump. "I get the feeling you had to grow up quick and you've been the grown-up for a long time. Even if cleared of the charges against you, the Coven will look on you as a child. They won't care what you've been through or how gifted you are. You have no family name to fall on, no reputation, and no bloodlines to speak for you. Whether you like it or not, you need help, Gwen. You need friends in the Wiccan Kingdom." He takes both of Gwen's hands in his, clutching them together in a tightly intertwined in a ball of silken fabric and skin between them. "Please, Gwen, come back inside, finish the process, and I promise I'll help you search for Morna afterward."

"How could you lead her to me?" Gwen asks in a half whisper. "After everything that we've…" She quickly drops her arms, to her side, forcing Jonah to let go of her gloved hands.

"I … didn't have a choice." Jonah's voice comes out as a croak at first. "Once she realized I was enchanted, Nicola did everything she could to reverse it and then I couldn't keep anything from her. She convinced me that you were in danger. That unless we took you in custody, something terrible would happen. I … I just…" He takes a deep breath. "I couldn't stand the thought of anything happening to you, especially if I could've prevented it."

Gwen stares up at him as he hovers over her. There is barely enough room between them. A powerful surge of energy seems to pulse from his body to hers. The sensation is both intoxicating and suffocating. His words have a strange effect on her, leaving Gwen wondering if he has some gift for Entrancing as well.

"Fine, I'll go with you." Gwen nods her consent. "I'll do the stupid test, but I'm not going to stand around and do nothing while Morna's missing."

"Of course not," he replies in relief. Jonah's perfect face breaks into a smile. Gently, he takes one of her gloved hands and leads her back into the Populace Center.

Feeling a little shaken up by the calm, but tantalizing, feelings this strange Wiccan boy has on her, Gwen walks on barely feeling her legs.

"There you are, you spoiled little—" One look from Jonah silences Leona, who at the sight of Gwen charged toward them with blonde hair and temper flying. She looks at her brother, confused, but clamps her mouth shut. Throwing her hands in the air, she goes back to sit on a bench along one wall.

Aunt Nicola approaches them next, her face far calmer than Gwen was expecting. The Thoyen looks between her and Jonah, taking note of their joined hands. She meets Jonah's gaze and the two have a quick, silent exchange. Aunt Nicola nods in acceptance and lets Jonah and Gwen pass, waiting to follow behind them. Jonah leads Gwen back up to the agent's desk.

Ah, crap. There's still a line and we lost our spot. I want this over with. I need to get back to looking for Morna. I don't have time to wait in a line! Gwen grumbles to herself.

Fortunately, the Elf agent sees them and waves them up to the front of the line. The other patrons waiting send them annoyed glances as they make their way past. However, no one says a word to them.

"Ah, you've returned!" the Elf says as a greeting, smiling kindly. "Did you find your errant friend? I believe Thoyen Nicola said she is of the Fae, correct?" His long brown hair sways as he emphatically moves his head when he speaks.

"Yes, she's a female Fae. We haven't found her yet," Gwen confesses. Still a bit on edge, she tries her best to be polite to the stranger.

"Ah, well, never fear. We'll put out a bulletin for a missing Fairy and our scouts will keep an eye out for her. But as my grandfather always said, 'Catching a Fae is like trying to hold onto starlight.'" He smiles good-naturedly at Gwen, but she does not find his family saying amusing or comforting.

"Thanks, I'll remember that. What do you need me to do? I'd like to get this over with quickly if you don't mind."

"Of course. Not a problem at all. I've already spoken with your guardian, Thoyen Nicola, and she's related your whole meeting to me. I understand that you are orphaned, correct?" Gwen nods in reply. "Well, that's no matter. As far as your background and bloodlines, that can all be determined here in a Heritage basin. I just need one drop of your blood," the Elf proclaims cheerfully as he hands her the same handled needle he had used before. Gwen gives the thing a disgusted look. "Oh, I should mention that the handle secretes a sterilizing liquid between uses, so it's perfectly safe. It doesn't sting a bit, dear."

"Oh, well, in that case…" Gwen sets the needle down to take off her black gloves. As the black silk fabric reveals her skin, Gwen hears Jonah gasp and turns to see him staring at her left hand. Her gloves discarded onto the counter Gwen looks down at her two bare hands. They are almost identical but for the missing ring finger on her left appendage. Automatically the fleshy stump wiggles and Gwen sighs, meeting Jonah's gaze.

"It's a long and pathetic story. Later, when all this commotion dies down, maybe I'll tell it to you." Gwen smiles a weak smile. His eyes burn with sympathy, as if he somehow knows the whole sordid tale and aches for her suffering. He just nods in understanding.

"Does it matter which finger I poke?" Gwen asks the Populace agent.

"Unfortunately, it's meant to be the left ring finger. You could still prick the remnants of it if you don't mind?" the Elf suggests cheerfully. Meanwhile the Elf's aura dances in a flurry of emotions.

Obviously, the idea of me missing that particular finger is unsettling him for some reason, Gwen observes.

Gwen nods, takes the needle, and pricks the fleshy stump just enough to break the surface and draw blood. Once the blood is pooled into a large bubble, Gwen places her hand above the

Gargoyle-shaped basin and lets the blood droplet fall. Gwen jerks with a gasp when the basin comes to life. Even though she's witnessed this process before, being this close to the enchanted object makes her uneasy. Even so she is mesmerized as the creature uses her blood to scrawl out several lines on the parchment-colored ledger. The language is somewhat familiar to her, but the phrases meanings are lost on her.

When the Gargoyle is done, he returns to his lifeless stone state. The Elf bends over the inscription on the ledger to decipher it. The Elf slowly looks up at Gwen, then back to the ledger. Re-reading it again he looks back up at her and Jonah once more, his pleasant features transformed by a mask of apprehension.

"Well, then. I've been waiting my whole life to find out who I am, don't keep me in suspense!" Gwen demands playfully.

"I'm sorry, sister Witch, but the reading is inconclusive. There are traces in your blood to suggest that you are pure blood and perhaps even of the highest circles of Wicca, but it can determine no specific family line. This is most unusual. In fact, I've never heard of such a thing. The blood does not lie!" The Elf does indeed seem troubled by this and calls over another agent for assistance. The second agent, a Goblin woman, wobbles over. After listening to the Elf's explanation, she bends over the ledger to read the findings herself. Although Goblins are known for having an odd permanent glare, Gwen notices an even odder expression in the agent's eyes as she addresses her.

"Did you take blood from that finger?" she asks, pointing a long boney finger of her own at Gwen's stumpy digit. Gwen nods.

"Hmmm." The Goblin looks thoughtful a moment and then turns to her fellow agent. "I suggest she prick another finger, the right ring finger, perhaps?" she says in her croaking little voice.

"Excellent idea, agent Roucka!" The Elf nods, relieved to have a plausible solution at hand. Smiling at Gwen, he hands her the needle again. "Do you mind trying once more, sister Witch?"

"Sure, why not?" Gwen shrugs taking the needle again and pricking the surface of her right ring fingertip. Again, she drips the blood from the cut into the Gargoyle-shaped basin. Gwen watches calmly this time as the Heritage Basin performs the same process. The Gargoyle uses her blood as ink writing out the new findings underneath the previous reading.

Eagerly the Elf and Goblin lean over the ledger together to read the new set of blood script.

Gwen watches them with rapt attention, her every muscle tight, her every hair taunt with the static of anticipation. Finally, the two agents exchange a disappointed look and turn to face her. Gwen's shoulders slump. It's as though she's been hanging on a cliff her whole life, to finally have someone reach out a hand to rescue her, only to be abandoned again. Still no luck in her lifelong quest for answers. *Why am I even surprised?*

"Not conclusive again?" she asks.

The Elf seems hesitant to answer. The Goblin shakes her head sadly "no" before she moves away, back to her own line to continue her business.

"My apologies, sister, but the new reading is no clearer than the first. But one thing for sure is that you are a pure blood Wiccan!" the Elfin agent adds with a forced smile.

"Is that a good thing?" Gwen asks, looking from the agent to Jonah.

"Yes!" Jonah replies with a little laugh. "It means you have potential to be more powerful in the craft than most Wiccans."

"It also means you have a better chance of forming a marriage with a first circle Wiccan, which gives you more prestige and power amongst your kind," the Elf adds with a bright smile.

"Oh. Lucky me," Gwen replies dryly with a smirk. "Is that all I need to do, then? Can I get my slip and go now?"

"All you have to do is press your fingerprint on the slip. Afterward, I sign it. Then, you'll be all clear to travel to the Monroe Coven. With Thoyen Nicola as your escort, you should have no trouble gaining access into their society." He beams at her brightly. *It seems that Nicola didn't inform the elf of the tribunal in my future. He makes it sound like I'm going to this coven for a holiday.*

Smiling politely back, Gwen presses her still-bleeding fingertip to the paper. Slipping her gloves carefully back onto her hands, Gwen watches with discontent as the Populace agent signs the slip and tears it from the book. As soon as he hands her the slip, Jonah and Gwen say thank you and turn together to leave.

Raven's familiar shape catches her eye. He stands by the door, his demeanor on edge as he waits for Gwen to approach.

"I'll give you two a minute to talk alone." Jonah whispers before weaving his way over to Aunt Nicola and the other Wiccan youths waiting nearby the entrance.

"So, did you find her?" Gwen asks

"No." Raven sighs. "I was hoping you had. Are you all checked in? Can we leave now?" he asks. His tone sounds concerned but she can tell he's torn between his loyalty to her and Morna.

"Yes, everything's all set. They couldn't tell me who I am, of course, but it turns out I'm pure Wiccan." Gwen shrugs. Mentally she adds, *Don't worry, Raven. We'll find Morna. Jonah says he'll help us look for her.*

Unless he knows a special spell for finding slippery little pixies, then I don't see how Mr. Blue Eyes is gonna help out much! Raven grumbles in his mind.

Gwen chuckles inwardly. *No, I don't think he does know such a spell, but at least he's willing to help. Maybe we're getting all worked up for nothing. After all, Morna may look like a teenager but she's something like sixty years old! She took care of herself long before she met us. She's probably the most mature out of the three of us and the most capable. I'm sure she'll find us when she's ready,* Gwen grasps one of his large hands in reassurance. Raven relaxes at her words and sighs, giving her hand a gentle squeeze.

The two friends look up to find the others standing beside them. *I hope they haven't been standing there long. Maybe they don't realize we were having a telepathic conversation.*

Or maybe they assume we are a pair of lunatics silently making faces at one another? Raven supplies. Gwen gives their companions an apologetic look releasing Raven's hand.

"So, what do we do now?" she asks aloud.

"Hunt down a fairy, of course." Raven suggests in a sardonic tone. He begins to move towards the exit but stops short when Nicola steps into his path. Although not a small woman in height or girth, Raven still dwarfs her. However, the look on the middle-aged woman's face lends her a dominating presence strong enough to rival his.

"You still need to be checked in, lad," Nicola informs Raven firmly, hands on hips.

He looks over at the lengthy line before the Populace desk and groans. "Is it really necessary?" he asks the Wiccan woman, sounding more like a pestilent teen than a disgruntled man.

She smiles broadly up at him. "The needle doesn't hurt none, boy. Here, I'll go wait in line with ya." Nicola steps forward and slips her arm into the crook of Raven's. Before she leads him away, she turns back. "Jonah, you go on now and take the others to the boardinghouse. They'll have a few rooms set aside at the Black Iris under me name."

"Yes, Thoyen Nicola," Jonah replies, bowing his head to her respectfully.

 231

"I guess I'll catch up with you at the inn. Keep an eye out for her on your way there. Let me know if you get a sense of her," Raven instructs as Nicola leads him reluctantly away.

"You got it. See you soon." Gwen smiles back at Raven before turning back to Jonah and the others.

"You forgot these." Leona dumps something at Gwen's feet turns on her heal walking out the building without a backward glance. Thayer and Jonah nod to one another before his friend chases after Jonah's little sister.

"Here, you dropped these." With an exasperated look on her face Leona drops Gwen's belonging at her feet.

"Thank you." Gwen replies with tight lips. Gwen finds her red duffle and the violin case on the floor. She had been so preoccupied with finding Morna she hadn't realized that she left her possessions behind. She bends down to grab her duffle and Angelo's violin case. The idea mortifies her. She can always buy new clothes and replace her favorite books, but no other instrument can ever replace Angelo's Violin. As the last piece of the man, she loved left in the world it is utterly priceless to her. With it gone she would feel as though he had never existed at all. Gulping down these dark thoughts Gwen reaches for her luggage.

"No allow me take care of those. *Gainge Raisa."*." Before Gwen can protest Jonah chants and the bags float off the ground in a levitation spell. Her belongings hover in the air between them.

"So, do wiccans do everything with magic when away from humans?" Gwen quirks an eyebrow at him. "Or are you just showing off?"

This gains her a deep throaty laugh from Jonah who turns toward the exit, beckoning her to go before him. With a sweeping gesture of his arm, he adds her luggage and Thayer's to his spell. "We are in forsaken territory after all. There's no need to lug our baggage around." Jonah gives her a playful wink. When he turns to his sister, Leona's face looks as though she's just eaten something sour. "Leona can I…" reason to do things the primitive way." "No thank you. I can take care of my own bags." With that Leona chants the levitation spell and stalks out of the building. Her bags hovering behind her like an odd brown cloud.

Before walking out the door, Gwen quickly scans the room for the gargoyle and the troll she eavesdropped on earlier. Neither is in sight. With a grunt, Gwen forces the whole thing down into the pit of her stomach along with her ever-mounting pile of concerns. *Find Morna first —, the vampires can wait,* she lectures herself. Gwen follows as Jonah leads the way out of the Populace Center. The rest of the luggage trails behind them. On the street the pedestrians produce several cries of alarm as they dodge being pummeled by the floating objects. With their bags in tow, they meld into the traffic crossing the bridge to the other side of Alcromech.

Chapter Seventeen

Reborn unto the Grave

Lynette grits her teeth as she disentangles herself from her latest victim, a handsome teenage boy covered in ink. He had a sick twisted mind and an interest in young girls. He had … but not anymore.

His body falls limp against the settee without her to prop up his lifeless shell. Lying in an awkward position, curved on his back with one arm over his head and the other broken, he stares with big brown eyes at the ceiling.

"Who's the bad boy now?" Lynette snickers at the corpse, which can make no reply.

"Where do you think you're off to, little one?"

With a patient sigh, Lynette turns her attention to her gracious host, the one who calls himself Affray. He stands shirtless in the doorway to the kitchen in an extravagant Bellagio hotel suite. His scars run all along his once-perfect body. He wears only a pair of

black designer slacks. A tailored suit jacket hooked by one finger hangs beside him, as if he were distracted in the middle of dressing. Completely hairless, Affray looks on her with silver eyes and the discernment of a master of lies.

"I've been called back to the catacombs." Lynette leans and wipes the blood from her mouth on her victim's shirt sleeve.

"And, of course, I'm coming along." Affray smiles, slipping his suit jacket over his bare chest.

"I suppose I can't stop you from following me." Lynette turns toward the hotel room door. "I can't guarantee the guards will let you in to see the king, though." Affray stops by the settee and glances down at the dead teenage boy.

"What a waste." He clicks his tongue with disapproval. "You should've turned him. He could've been a wonderful solider. We're supposed to be increasing our numbers, Lynette. Turn the worthy, kill the weak." He quotes from the new mandate put out by Lazar the Vampire King.

"So, did you turn your two guests or were they just breakfast?"

Affray licks his lips and smiles. Lynette shivers. *You're a vampire now, Lynette. Grow some balls,* the child chastises herself.

"Maybe I'll turn the next two," Affray adds as they exist the room, leaving their dead behind. There's no need to leave the "Do Not Disturb" sign on the doorknob. Affray has already paid the hotel management a sizeable sum to leave their room untouched until they vacate the premises. By then there will be no trace of the slaughter that occurred within the Bellagio suit's walls.

Vampires have their own methods of disposal. From what Affray told her, even with modern-day science, no forensic team *would* find a spec of blood. It paid to have an alliance with Elves. Vampires have no scruples in using magic for their own dark purpose. They didn't heed anything The High Council of Elders said about it. *Some laws don't apply to the vampire.* Affray had said once, back when he had worn a handsome face, and still had his dignity.

Ever since the Vampire Decree many of their kind have stopped covering their tracks at all. *Not that it would matter, the humans could never track them down. Without records of any kind, they don't exist in their world. And should anyone happen upon them while in the act of killing or try to catch them, they'd simply become another victim.*

Of course, the human's attribute it all the carnage left behind by our kind to gang wars, or petty terrorism. It would take a vampire savagely murdering a news anchor on live tv for the Eden Spawn to even consider the truth as a possibility. Lynette reasons. *They do love their sweet ignorance, don't they?*

They pass the elevator on their way to the stairwell. The sight of the two of them together makes tourists look at them strangely, and not because of the significant age difference between their immortal shells. Although Lynette can easily pass for Affray's daughter or much younger sister, passersby seem compelled to protect the ten-year-old girl from her hairless and scarred companion. To avoid these Good Samaritan acts, they take the stairs. Once down on the main floor of the hotel and casino, Affray falls back to follow the girl vampire inconspicuously from a safe distance. Outside, they head to the parking garage and the solitude of dark shadows.

Using her supernatural senses, Lynette ascertains that they are alone. Without a backward glance to her companion the girl sprints into a dead run, bounding through the dark recesses of alleyways and behind the many buildings on the Strip. Las Vegas blurs around her in streaks of neon and endless faces. She only slows down to mortal speed when it's necessary to take a crosswalk. Thankfully, their destination is a straight shot down Las Vegas Boulevard from the hotel.

Five minutes after leaving the parking garage, Lynette comes to a halt on the north end of Las Vegas Boulevard. A large rectangular granite sign sits before her below a tall, slanted tree, nestled between two shrubs. It reads Woodlawn Cemetery, city of Las Vegas. A curved drive encircles the sign, and the cemetery lies beyond still in the late-night hour.

With a gust of hot desert wind, Affray appears at Lynette's side, as pale as the alabaster tombstones. Her male companion smiles brightly at the scenery before them and saunters onward. Lynette finds herself following behind the vampire's quick purposeful steps.

He knows the way. Lynette grumbles to herself, and then reason takes shape in her invidious mind. *He's been around several hundred years longer than I. He must've traveled the "Warrens of Death" at one point or another.*

Sure, enough without instruction from her, Affray winds his way through the silent graveyard, stopping before a tombstone shaped like a Victorian coffin. Made of granite, the unusual tombstone is ancient with chips and wear along the edges. "*Mortem Itinere*" is engraved into the flat granite surface in bold, flowery lettering. Lynette, stepping toward the stone, is nonchalantly brushed aside by Affray. Forced to step back, Lynette resentfully watches as her companion pulls up the sleeve of his suit jacket to expose his pale arm. Grunting in pain as his fangs extend, the vampire bites down into his own wrist. His blood oozes out around the puncture holes, dripping red raindrops into the tomb's engraving. He fills only the center of the "M" in Mortem, making the shape of a "V." The blood absorbs into the stone within a minute, as if it had never been there.

Affray bends down, applying pressure to the top of the coffin-stone. With a whoosh of air and a scraping of stone, he forces the lid partially off the base of the headstone. What appeared to be a solid piece of stone now sits in two parts, a deep darkness visible within the coffin.

Without waiting upon ceremony, Affray steps over the edge of the stone and into the empty recesses of the coffin. If she hadn't taken this route before she would've been amazed when the vampire vanished before her, dropping out of sight as if into a deep pit. No sound marks the man's descent. Lynette sighs and follows Affray. She drops herself into the endless darkness. She plummets deep into the earth, her neck craned to watch as the lid to the tombstone slides back in place of its own accord. Her first trip down the rabbit hole had brought to surface her human, child-like fears. It alarmed her to plunge into darkness, falling without anything to grab hold of with no way of knowing what waited for her below. Now she lets the sensation of falling freely in utter darkness sooth her.

After all, this is nothing to the terror of standing before "The Black Russian," she reminds herself, mentally preparing for the encounter ahead of her. At long last, the girl lands in a crouch at the bottom of the pit. She senses Affray waiting for her. She half expected him to run ahead through the Warrens without her.

Maybe he's remembered that I am the one the vampire King summoned, not him. Lynette smiles smugly to herself and breaks into a headlong run. Affray lets out a whoop and tears alongside her. As the minutes turn into hours, she senses that the man is straining to not take the lead, forcing himself to hold back and match her speed.

If Lynette had been a fully-grown woman when she turned, then things would be different. He would be struggling to keep up with her. She fights the urge to gag on the bitter taste in her throat. Instead, she presses even harder. The heavy scent of decay is thick in her nostrils, burning the insides of her lungs, forcing away all memory of fresh night air.

They pass several glowing red symbols etched on the dirt walls of the tunnels, each one a marker for another entrance into the "Warrens of Death" Most send travelers to other cemetery locations. Other entrances indicate prominent vampire colonies. Lynette

ignores them all, her mind blind to any but the insignia of the king. With aching muscles and a sigh of relief, Lynette turns the last bend in the black warren to see a blood red symbol dead ahead of them.

A blood drop is encircled by a six below and a nine above. Shapes like fangs border it on either side. Below the six, a triangle points downward with cross arrows on the tip, and a solid circle on either side of the triangle. The symbol is topped by a three-point crown.

The two vampires slow to a stop before the king's insignia. The glow of the red symbol sheds light on a flat slab of stone resting below it. The same symbol is engraved upon the stone slab.

This time Affray hangs back as young Lynette provides the blood offering. With her bloody wrist she fills in the indented shapes. The moment it is complete, the dirt walls and ground beneath shudder. Disturbing the ground around it, the stone slab slowly rises. Lynette and Affray hop onto the stone as it ascends upward. Rocks and roots scrape against the stone as it picks up speed into a dark conduit. The way above them remains pitch black. Neither speaks. At last, the roof thirty feet above them moves, rock groaning against rock to reveal an opening. Beyond, a dim light shines and a strange cave-like ceiling hang above. *The Catacombs.*

Their stone elevator ascends to the mouth of the opening, delivering them into the monument of the Vampires of old, a cemetery for the royalty of their kind with statues and massive urns instead of graves. When a vampire ceases to exist, they leave nothing to bury.

The first time Lynette entered this room, she was struck by its deadly beauty. The monuments all shone white in the candlelight, in stark contrast to the black marbled floor beneath. One caught her eye in particular, a sculpture of a black swan with wings spread. Besides standing out in comparison to the other stark white monuments, it was also the largest and most exquisitely crafted.

"What are they made of ivory?" Lynette had turned to her escort Dante and asked as she pointed to the black swan. "And onyx?"

Dante had given a low chuckle. "No, the white ones are made of human bones."

"And the black swan?" Lynette inquired.

"Blackened bones and ash." Lynette shivered.

"Whose tombstone is that?"

"The vampire Queen Evaling." After that Dante sent her down into the warrens of death for the first time before sending her off on her new mission, to spy on the witch Gwenevere in Sin City.

Now she barely gives the black swan a sideways glance as she and Affray step off the stone slab and onto the polished marble floor. Affray gives the boneyard a cursory glance as they make their way toward the black stone doors. They each pull a door open to encounter two vampire guards waiting on the other side, one short and bulky with chrome spikes embedded into his shoulders and along his shaven head. The other was a clean-cut, seemingly normal looking, brunette man in a striped t-shirt, faded blue jeans, and sneakers.

"*Selmon, Vernin.*" Lynette nods to each man in turn as she walks past them. "This is…"

"Affray," Selmon interjects.

"Yes, we know," Vernin adds with a smirk as he and his companion step up on either side of Lynette and Affray, ushering them down the corridor of the catacombs.

"How do you know him?" Lynette asks, taken aback, her nub of a nose wrinkling up. "Has the king had someone following me?" She struggles to keep up with the brisk gait of the three adult men around her.

"Naturally," Selmon snickers. He looks to Vernin, and the two vampires exchange a look that makes Lynette feel hot around the ears. Despite his earlier insistence on keeping his past identity a secret, Affray seems oddly at ease with this revelation. He walks along with the same confidence and poise he always has.

"You must think the Black Russian to be a fool if you think he wouldn't spy on his spies," Vernin observes in his indistinct American accent. Selmon chuckles softly, his body shaking and his normally formidable face lighting up in a giant grin.

"It's something I would do," Affray comments with a shrug.

"Huh," Lynette grunts. "I'm sure you would."

The King's underground stronghold seems quieter than her last few visits. Only a few vampires pass them in the corridors. Occasionally a red-clad human servant prostrates before them on the floor as they pass, waiting until they are long gone before moving on to their duties. Lynette watches them from over her shoulder.

Every muscle tense with the overwhelming desire of thirst. She's come a long way since her first hunt, yet still the smell of human flesh and blood drives her to distraction. She might not tear to shreds every human she encounters like she once did, but the urge lingers on.

I doubt the king would spare me if I went around slaughtering his servants without permission. Lynette gulps and forces her attention forward. *Besides, I just had a snack … a few hours ago.* Her stomach grumbles. *Hmm, perhaps we will pick up someone to eat on our way back to the Bellagio,* Lynette thinks to herself. Looking up, she finds her company approaching the King's private council room.

She sees Lazar Taudero standing in the middle of the chamber through the large natural archway. Dressed in an open-collared white shirt, tan slacks with a lavish kimono over it, he passes before a floor to ceiling mirror. The frame is ornate and black like polished lacquer. Approximately a hundred men standing and sitting scatter about the chamber in various forms of dress and era. All of them watch their king as he engages in a heated conversation with a man on the other side of the mirror's reflection. It takes Lynette a moment to realize that that man is someone else entirely, the mirror not reflecting the vampire king. Instead, the glass surface shows the visage of a six-foot two inch tall, slightly tanned man with short black curly hair and deep blue eyes. His posture is as strong as his chiseled features. His fine apparel is as ornate and elegant as the room he stands in. A gold throne sits vacant behind him inlaid with jewels and filigree symbols of his tribe.

"Unless you have something of import to discuss, Lazar, I'm afraid I cannot prolong this … debate any further." The handsome man in the mirror speaks with a dry resonance in his educated tone. "I have my own kingdom to rule, and Wicca lives by both the sun and the moon if you recall. I don't have the luxury you do of being dead to the world fifteen hours out of the day. I'm king twenty-four/seven, as the humans would say." The Wiccan king gives a smug smile at his own jokes and turns as if to leave.

"Just a moment, *Deverick*," Lazar shoots back. "The Tribe of Wicca owes the Vampires a debt. Blood was spilt, a colony destroyed. More than just vampires were murdered in the collapse of Bec LaNuff as you well know. Two years later, still nothing has been done to appease this injustice!" Around the room the other vampires in the council room murmur agreement with their king.

"The term *murder…*" Deverick, The Wiccan King, Lynette presumes, scoffs at the word before continuing, "…is generally prescribed to a violent act by an individual or group upon another individual or group with the intent of ending life. One cannot be murdered by a natural disaster. Any rational being would acknowledge death by an earthquake as an accidental death." He informs the King and the vampires assembled through the looking glass with barely concealed distain.

Several of the vampire council jump to their feet yelling. Others spit on the floor as a general clamor disturbs the room. Lazar turns with raised hands and a scowl. As the assembly quiets, the Black Russian's gray eyes alight on Lynette, Affray, and their escort waiting in the entryway. A dazzling white smile spreads triumphantly across his face, contrasting beautifully against his coffee-colored skin.

"Disaster, you call it. An accident, you claim!" Lazar waves Lynette forward, and the child moves quickly to her King's side. A lump the size of a watermelon lodges in her throat as she faces the Wiccan King through the mirror. "I have here someone who was there at the tragedy. She survived the fall of The Mountain of Blood and can testify that this was no accident!" Lazar Taudero speaks not just to Deverick but to the whole council room with the flare of a Baptist preacher giving a sermon. He puts his hands-on Lynette's small, slender shoulders and squeezes gently as if giving her comfort for her ordeals. The audience of immortals applauds, shouting approval for their king.

"Do you bring a human servant to bear witness before me, Lazar, or is that a Child Spawn I see in your midst?" Deverick inquires with a dark hint in his voice. The vampire council becomes as silent as the grave while the weight of the Wiccan King's words falls heavy on the assembly.

Lazar's momentary triumphant seems diminished before he recovers his brilliant smile and addresses his adversary as well as his underlings.

"Your talent for perception does you credit, Hawthorne." He releases his hold on Lynette and steps toward the mirror. Lynette's

muscles relax when the man's back turns, suddenly grateful to be momentarily out of his clutches. "The one they called Legion, The Vampire Lord of Bec LaNuff, spawned this child, giving her the gift of being reborn unto the grave despite her young age." At the mention of their shared passed Lynette distinctly glances at Affray. His almost white eyes narrow as he meets her gaze. Flushing, she averts her eyes. The floral pattern of Lazars silk robe suddenly the most fascinating thing in the room.

"Unless the law has been changed since we last met in the great hall of Atlantis for the last quarterly meeting of the High Council of Elders, then Legion committed treason in making this child a vampire," the king points out with a tilt of his head.

"You are not Mistaken, King Hawthorne," Lazar admits with a tight jaw and flared nostrils. "However, we are not here to discuss the actions of a dead vampire lord." Forcing a smile, the vampire king paces the room before the mirror. "I simply bring the child here to give her testimony of the destruction of Bec LaNuff. Will you not hear what she has to say?" Lazar puts the question to the other King as a challenge. Although the tightness in his shoulders suggests doubt, Lynette finds herself slowly inching backward away from her king and the handsome yet intimidating man in the mirror. She makes it only a few feet before her back meets something solid. She glances up to see Affray standing behind her, a reassuring expression on his scarred face. She forces herself not to cringe and looks away.

Deverick Hawthorne, king of the Wiccans, sizes Taudero with his eyes before glancing toward someone out of view. An elongated silence hangs in the chamber as an elegantly dressed royal servant appears with a silver tray and chalice. Casually, the king takes the cup and drinks the contents leisurely. When finished, he nods approvingly to his manservant and places the silver chalice back on the tray. Instead of turning back to his captive audience, the king leans closer to the servant and whispers something into the man's ear. The servant, an aging man in his sixties, nods in understanding before hurrying out of view again, presumably to do his masters bidding.

"Well? Damn it, Hawthorne, you cannot ignore this!" Lazar shouts at the man through the mirror. His usual jovial persona of the host of the trivialities gone, Lazar's slight Russian accent slips out with his agitation. "If you will not pay heed to this evidence, then I will take it directly to the HCOE with or without you and justice will be served!"

Lynette senses that the others around her want to break out into cheers once more but stay still, frozen in place on the edge of their seats by the rancor in their liege's demeanor. She can hardly breathe for fear of drawing attention from either of the Forsaken Colossal staring one another down through the enchanted mirror. To her horror the Wiccan king turns his penetrating, blue-eyed gaze on her. The Gold Wiccan circle around his pupils' glows brighter with his scrutiny.

"Very well. Speak, child. I will hear what you believe caused the destruction of the Mount of Blood."

Lazar turns an expectant eye on her. Lynette's throat goes dry. The words get jumbled inside her head. She looks again between the two kings and wishes desperately that she knew how to fake a convincing faint. *Vampires don't faint, stupid! Not unless beaten to a bloody pulp or burnt to death,* she reminds herself bitterly.

"Who, you mean … not what.*"* The words tumble out of her mouth. "A young wild witch came to live under the mountain as Lord Legion's guest."

"What was a witch doing living with vampires and other creatures underground?" Hawthorne interjects. His tone nearly breaks Lynette's resolve to speak.

"Legion saved her life. She had no other home and he offered her a place with him and the forsaken under the mountain." Flashes of memories long suppressed flood her mind, bringing with them the swell of anger she's become all too familiar with. "Despite his generosity and love, she turned traitor and brought her werewolves and the witches of the local coven to wage war on Bec LaNuff. Together they attacked us and killed many until the wild witch went mad and cast a dark spell that tore the mountain apart."

With these last words come the visage of her immortal family, Luca her maker and her siblings Ryan, Lethawyn, and Jezebel. Lynette bows her head to hide the pain and the tears that threaten. Gritting her teeth, she pushes the tears away, replacing them with anger and hatred.

"And what was the name of this wild witch?" Lazar prompts in a sympathetic tone. All around her the chamber seems frozen in space and time, the universe awaiting her next words. When she looks up again, Lynette finds that even Hawthorne's attention is rapt.

"The witch who destroyed Bec LaNuff is Gwenevere," Lynette pronounces as if announcing the Wiccan girl's execution. Triumph builds in her empty breast and Lynette feels as though the weight of the last two years is beginning to leave her. *Justice will at last be done. My family will be avenged!*

"Gwenevere who?" the Wiccan King probes, his brows knit together, his face gone ashen, and a rigid stance replaces his confident posture. His arms cross over his chest as he stares her down.

"Well … sh … she…" Lynette stammers. "She didn't have a last name; she was just known as Gwenevere." Lynette's mind races for something more to give the king, "She was an orphan raised by humans. I swear that's all I know."

"I should've known." Hawthorne's whole demeanor changes, his shoulders relaxing and his arms falling to his sides. He chuckles, shaking his head, "You fool Lazar. You go around making outrageous accusations without even a proper name. Even if this witch did exist, which I doubt she does, not only is what your witness describing impossible for an untrained witch to do, but nearly unheard of even of the most powerful warlords or witches who've ever lived, including myself. And if this person had done this, they're obviously dead, buried under Bec LaNuff like this Legion and everyone else!" Mirth wrinkles the corner of his eyes. "Tear apart a mountain! You must be out of your mind, Lazar, to even entertain this child's delusions. "

"But it's true! She does exist, and she did this, and … and she's not dead at all!" Lynette insists, shouting at Hawthorne. Her little hands ball up into tight fists.

"Really?" King Deverick Hawthorne quirks a dark brow at the little vampire. Condescension drips from his words like blood from a freshly torn artery. "Then where, prey you, is this extraordinary wild orphan witch?" The Wiccan king challenges, his fist placed on his hips.

Lynette hesitates, looking to Lazar her king for reassurance, who nods and gestures for her to continue.

"She's just been taken into the care of the Monroe Coven in Pennsylvania. She's in Alcromech as we speak, awaiting to travel to Monroe with a witch elder named Nicola," Lynette finishes firmly.

"I see." Hawthorne looks thoughtful for a moment. "If this witch is indeed the same who allegedly orchestrated an attack on the peaceful settlement of Bec LaNuff and cast these devastating spells, then my agents will find the truth of this matter."

"And when the truth of these things is discovered, I demand the wild witch be turned over to me for execution," Lazar demands with a wicked glee in his almost colorless eyes.

"Never." This one-word decree takes the smile right off the vampire king's face and the satisfaction out of Lynette's black heart.

"I beg your pardon?" Lazar speaks with clipped words despite his attempts at civility. "Explain yourself, Warlock."

"No witch will ever be given over to vampire law to be judged. Prejudice will always cloud our tribes' thoughts against one another. You know this, Lazar. A vampire tribunal could no sooner try a Wiccan fairly any sooner than a Wiccan tribunal would a vampire."

"No one said anything about a tribunal, Hawthorne," Lazar Taudero shoots back with bitterness and a dark glint in his eyes.

"My point exactly, Taudero." Deverick snorts, shaking his head. Someone speaks from out of view in the Wiccan king's chamber and the man looks away. With gestures and mouthed words, the king communicates with the personage.

Lynette turns her attention to the vampire King standing beside her. The tall, lean, Black man stares at the mirror, nearly shaking with rage. Lynette takes a few steps back, Affray following suit. By the time the king shouts, the two companions are just outside of the chamber.

"Listen to me, King of Wicca! If you do not produce this Wiccan whore to me, I will bleed your tribe dry. I will destroy the cities of man until nothing is left on the face of the earth but rubble and the undead!" The king spews these heated words, his wrath radiating throughout the chamber. His council rouses to anger with him. Someone amongst them starts a chant and soon the Vampire King and all his lords shout in unison.

"Justice or War! Justice or War!"

Deverick Hawthorne the Wiccan King shakes with silent laughter, a smug look on his handsome face. At first no one notices until the man in the mirror can contain himself no more. When his dark chuckle bursts forth from his lean frame, it drowns out the vampire's chants, like waves crashing on the shore drown out the seagull's cries. The room before her goes deathly still. Dozens of gray eyes turn to the mirror with pure hatred. Finally, the Wiccan king's mirth subsides.

"Our kind has gone at one another in seven worldwide conflicts throughout the ages, yet still your kind has learned nothing." Deverick gives his vampire contemporary a smug smile, rolling down his silken shirt sleeves and buttoning his cuffs. "Do what you must, Taudero. Everyone knows this is a fight you cannot win. But then, it's your funeral."

And with that, the raven-haired king stalks out of view. The mirror shimmers and sparks as reflected light fractures in many angles. Lynette cringes, averting her eyes from the pain of the searing light. The chamber ripples with curses, shouts, and hissing. When the light fades, the large, black frame holds what appears to be nothing more than an ordinary mirror.

"Dante!" Her king spins around on his heel, his wild-eyed stare sweeping over everyone in attendance.

"Yes, my liege?" The clicking of boot heels on the marbled floor announces the entrance of the newcomer. "What is thy bidding, my King?" Dante's slender form appears at Lynette's left, his long brown hair brushing the shoulders of his fine gray suit.

"The time has come. The wild witch Gwenevere is in Alcromech," Taudero announces, a firm set to his pointed jaw. "Take a drove to penetrate and capture the witchling. Kill any who gets in your way." Taudero's demeanor transforms from raging mad to cold, collected calm. Dante bows his head curtly in understanding and turns to leave.

"Wait!" Lynette's high voice cuts through the chamber, stopping everyone in their tracks. With every eye including the kings suddenly turned on her, Lynette chuckles nervously before stammering on. "What about our arrangement, my King?" Lazar quirks an inquisitive brow at the seven-year-old. "Remember? You said once Gwenevere was caught that I could have my freedom, that I would be given immunity and protection." Her ribs ache and her skin bubbles as she awaits the Black Russian's reply.

He folds his arms a crossed his chest examining the child vampire as if weighing her. "While the witch yet lives, you are still in my service." Lynette's shoulders slump. "However, you may be of some use in this task. So, I command that you and this new friend of yours go along with Dante. Only when the murderous witch is dead at my feet may you have your freedom."

The vampire king stalks passed them out of the chamber. A swarm of chattering, gesturing council members follow.

"Meet us at the monument. We leave for Alcromech as soon as I have gathered my men," Dante orders Lynette in his Spanish accent before disappearing down the hallway in a blur.

Lynette feels Affray take her by the arm and quickly lead her away from the council chamber and through the corridors of the catacombs. The sound of the council's cries for blood still echoes in Lynette's head. She thirsts for the blood of Gwenevere above all others, wanting the girl's death more than anything. But the thought of war with the witches turns her already cold flesh to ice. It's not until they reach the Vampire cemetery chamber that Lynette fully comes to again.

"Affray?"

"Yes." He pushes the chamber door open, holding it open for her to enter. He gives her a puzzled look.

"Why does the Vampire King want Gwenevere dead so much? Don't get me wrong. I want her dead too, but he seems even angrier than I am, like it's something personal and not just about her destroying a whole nest of vampires."

"Oh. Well. You remember?" Lynette gives him a strange look and shakes her head. "That's right, you wouldn't. You were still in mourning over…"

Don't you dare bring up Luca and my siblings. I will not discuss what happened to them. Lynette shoots him a look that silences him.

"Anyways, the night before Gwenevere and her …. *Lover* was punished, and they were tied up on the cliff; earlier that night Bec LaNuff had an embassy arrive on behalf of King Lazar."

"Really? What for?" Lynette probes.

"To confront Legion about creating a child spawn." Lynette goes stiff but says nothing. "The head of the embassy was the vampire, Queen Evaling."

Lynette gasps, turning instinctively to look at the black swan sculpture behind her. The outstretched wings are majestic in the candlelight. "She died that day. She was buried under Bec LaNuff when it fell, wasn't she?" Lynette whispers. The gnawing in the pit of her stomach tells her the truth before her companion can even speak.

"Yes. And rumor has it, losing his queen is slowly turning Lazar mad."

The shuffling of feet and the scrape of the stone door opening heralds the arrival of Dante and his drove of vampire warriors. She's not surprised to see his tall blonde mate in the group. Dante pushes past his comrades to them. He leads the way back to the tombstone by which they entered the catacombs. Lynette watches him shove the lid off the tomb, exposing the entrance into the Warrens of Death below. He steps aside and gestures for the others to climb inside. One by one, his vampire drove obeys. Dante takes his lover into his arms for a passionate kiss before she too melts into the dark recesses of the tunnel below.

"Come, you two next. I will take the rear," Dante orders with a brisk nod of his head. Affray smiles to Lynette, practically bouncing as he crosses the room, steps into the coffin, and disappears.

Before she follows her companion, Lynette's gaze falls on the black swan. The darkness of the sculpture reflects the color of her

guilt. For the first time since she woke up four years ago without a heartbeat in her chest, heat in her skin, or color in her eyes, Lynette wonders whether it would've been better had she never been reborn unto the grave.

Chapter Eighteen

Dancing Starlight

Where do you think you're going?" Gwen hears Leona's disembodied voice only moments before the girl herself appears out of a mist, barring Gwen's exit. Stopping short, Gwen barely conceals her amazement at Leona's little magic trick, schooling her expression into a smirk instead.

"To look for my friend, Morna. Remember, she's still missing?" Gwen points out crossly to her unwanted roommate.

Upon checking into the Black Iris, Gwen discovered that she would be sharing a room with Leona. She tried to explain that she preferred to share a room with Raven and Morna instead. She promptly received a lecture from the boardinghouses' Matron, Mrs. Subree, about the appropriate accommodations of Wiccans. "Unless married, boys and girls are never allowed to share a room let alone stay on the same floor. Thus, young, single men and the elderly stay on the first floor, married couples stay on the second, and young single girls and single ladies on the third."

How very Amish. Gwen hadn't expected her people to be so old-fashioned. *It's not like I'm here on a pleasure trip,* she reminds herself. Reluctantly she agreed to the accommodations and shuffled off after Leona to their third story room.

After only ten minutes alone with Leona, Gwen decides that the prospect of sharing a room with the cantankerous little blonde Witch, intolerable. This makes finding Morna all the more urgent.

At least then I'll have someone to suffer through my captivity with!

"You're not going out there by yourself." Folding her arms beneath her small bust, Leona squares her jaw and meets Gwen's scowl with a smoldering glare.

"Why the hell not?" Gwen asks.

"Not that I care half-a-moon what happens to you," Leona explains, somehow managing to act as though she's looking down her nose at Gwen while craning her neck to look up at her, "but it's not safe for someone of your circle to be out alone, especially at this hour."

"My circle?" Gwen intones with annoyance. "What, pray tell, is a circle? I don't recall being of any 'circle.'" Gwen does quotations in the air with her fingers.

"Malicious night, don't you know anything?" Leona scoffs. "And you call yourself a Wiccan! You don't know the first thing about what that means, who we are, or what we believe." Leona

throws her arms up in frustration. "You go walking around like you own the whole wide world and we should all be grateful you let us live on the same planet!"

"Look, munchkin, I'm not in the mood for your little temper tantrum. I've got more important things to worry about than your ego." Having had enough, Gwen slows her breathing and croons, "Now move out of the way."

Nothing happens. Leona's eyes don't glaze over. She doesn't go stiff and wait her command. Gwen recollects two things. The wiccan teens were immune to her entrancing when they faced off in the Bellagio parking garage. Also, Nicola had just separated her from her magical abilities before trapping her here in Alcromech. She's been entrancing people to get her way for so long, she momentarily forgot that she couldn't anymore. *Crap. How am I going to get around miss bossy pants here?*

"I'm not going anywhere, and neither are you," Leona informs her coldly.

"But I … Morna needs…" Gwen sways on her feet. She shakes her head as if disorientated, and then suddenly she stumbles backward and collapses to the ground unconscious. The pain of hitting the hardwood floor jars her. The headache that spreads across the back of her skull is agonizing, but Gwen forces herself to stay perfectly still to keep up the charade.

"What in the bleeding darkness?" Leona shrieks, startled. Gwen hears the shuffle of her feet as the girl hurries to her side. "All right, ha-ha, very funny. You can stop pretending now. Hello?

Gwenevere?" She puts her ear against Gwen's chest. Gwen sense her relief when she hears a heartbeat. Suddenly Leona takes Gwen by the shoulders and shakes her hard as if to rouse her. Gwen lets her body go limp. *Maybe she's not pretending?* Leona wonders. *The waterfall sting looked nasty. Maybe it's just taken her this long for her body to go into shock?*

Gwen lets her eyes roll into the back of her head. A moment later she feels rather than sees Leona lift one of her eyelids. Seeing nothing but white, the girl curses and gets to her feet. "I'll be right back, okay?" When Gwen says nothing and still doesn't move, Leona scrambles across the floor stopping at the door. "Don't worry. I'll get help." She reassures before running down the hall.

Gwen waits for the sound of her footsteps to fade before opening her eyes and hopping to her feet. With a self-satisfied little smile, Gwen moves quickly out into the third story hallway.

Notwithstanding her throbbing skull, she sends her mental feelers out into the rest of the Black Iris. Gwen quickly locates Jonah's room on the first floor just below her. In a flash, Gwen travels the two flights of stairs. Stopping before his door, room number seven, signified by seven stars etched into the wooden door. She quickly raps knuckles against the wood.

Gwen hears two sets of footsteps race up the stairs above her. Although muffled by the distance Gwen can still make out what is happening above. "Hurry, Mistress Subree. She just collapsed out of nowhere and..." Gwen hears Leona and the Innkeeper walk down the hall above and then a startled gasp.

"Well? Where is she then?" the head of the boarding house demands impatiently.

"Never mind, Mistress Subree. It seems that my roommate has experienced a miraculous recovery. You're help is no longer needed. Thank you." With gravel in her voice Leona explains. With a huff and a grumble about children playing games, the innkeeper stalks back down the hall. A door slams above accompanied by an indignant shout.

From the other side of room seven's door, Gwen hears muffled talking and footsteps. Thayer flings the door open wide. The red-haired Wiccan teen smiles at her and opens his mouth to speak.

"Thayer! Jonah!" Leona sounds loud in Gwen's ear, as a grey mist appears beside her. "That Vegas showgirl you brought back as a souvenir just played me for a fool! She has gone off on her own like a stup—" the girl herself materializes into a solid form in mid rant. She stops speaking abruptly when she sees Gwen and Thayer staring at her.

"Either you're annoyed or you're angry. I swear I can't remember a single time I've seen you in a good mood," Thayer declares in jest.

Slightly embarrassed but still infuriated, Leona steps right up to Gwen, toe to toe and points a finger in her face.

"How dare you!" she yells. "You don't do something like that to someone. I'm telling Aunt Nicola."

"What are we, five? You're going to tattle-tell on me?" Gwen responds in a mocking tone, gently pushing the younger teen a few feet away from her. "I didn't actually think it would work. It's not my fault that you're so gullible."

"Oh, shut up! What are you doing knocking on their door for?" Gwen notices a hint of possessiveness in Leona's voice.

Hmmm, either she's afraid I'm after Thayer, whom she's clearly enamored with, or she's feeling protective of her big brother.

"Your brother offered to help me find my friend," Gwen informs in a condescending manner. "Also, according to you, it's not safe for me to go wandering around on my own here. So, I've come to get him to join my search party."

"Who cares about your ridiculous Fairy!" Leona yells back. "In case you've forgotten, you're our prisoner! You can't just come and go as you please!"

"By the darkness, what are you yelling about out here?" A shirtless Jonah asks irritably as he joins Thayer at the door. With a t-shirt in hand, Jonah fights a smirk as he looks from Gwen to his sister.

"She's determined to go out and find that crazy pet sprite of hers to the point that she fake-fainted on me," Leona informs her older brother as he slips the garment over his head.

Gwen watches ruefully as he works his arms into the sleeves and slides the fabric over his taunt muscles.

Jonah looks to Gwen for confirmation, catching her looking him over. Cheeks hot, Gwen quickly schools her face into impassiveness and shrugs.

"Okay, so what do you want me to do about it?" Jonah inquires patiently.

"What do I want? I want you to…"

"That was a rhetorical question, Leona, calm yourself. If Gwen apologizes, will that appease so you don't bring Aunt Nicola into this?" he asks his sister.

"That would hardly be penance enough," she huffs, folding her arms across her chest. Jonah gives her a look that only a big brother can give, and Leona reluctantly relaxes her shoulders and sighs. "Fine. If she gives me the sincerest of apologies then I'll forget the whole thing happened, but just this once," she adds.

Jonah and Thayer turn to Gwen with identical expectant faces.

"Seriously?" Gwen shakes her head astounded. "I can't even remember the last time I apologized to anyone for anything. Look, I'm sorry I tricked you, but you were being a pain in the…"

"All right, that will do." Jonah claps his hands together, cutting Gwen's words off. "She said she's sorry. Why don't you stay here and wait for Aunt Nicola and Raven to return?"

She returns his smile with a petulant glare looking anything but pleased.

"You can tell them that we've gone out to look for Morna. Okay, sis?" Jonah looks to Thayer for help; the two boys share a silent exchange.

"Yeah, why don't you guys go on while we wait for Aunt Nicola," Thayer urges Gwen and Jonah. Turning his full attention to

Leona, he adds, "In the common room. Just the two of us, all alone." Thayer flashes a smile and a wink at Leona.

Her breath catches a moment. "Yes, I guess that would be agreeable," Leona concedes, trying to sound indifferent.

"I'll just go get my coat," Jonah tells Gwen before shooting a knowing smile in his sister's direction and disappearing back into the room.

"After you, Leona, *betaphil dauter un darcnaes.*" Thayer seems to coo the last words as he steps into the hallway. Leona swallows hard. Looking awfully flushed, her eyes become giant pools of suppressed longing, fashioned on Thayer. He gestures with his head down the hall as if she's forgotten which way the common room is located.

"Thank you." Biting her lip, Leona almost stumbles over her own feet as she heads toward the front of the boarding house.

"Happy hunting, Gwenevere." Thayer smiles smugly to Gwen before following Leona and disappearing around the bend.

"All right, let's go." Jonah slips out of his room, closing the door behind him. "I know a spell that should help us track down Morna."

"Wow, really? There's a spell for that?" Gwen asks with a little smile. She notes how perfectly proportionate they are to one another. He's neither too tall nor too short. Just a slight tilt of the head from either of them would bring their lips to the same level.

"Yes," Jonah confirms as they walk down the hall. He stops at the foot of the stairs. "But we'll need something that she's touched

 264

or that belongs to her to cast it. If you have a strand of her hair that would be the best," he explains.

"Yeah, like I keep a locket of her hair handy at all times," Gwen mocks as they ascend the stairs together toward her third story bedroom. "She, on the other hand, has a whole nest made of my hair actually…" Jonah raises his brows at this, Gwen snorts "Apparently the scent of wiccans hides fairy scent and repels vampires," Gwen stammers. "It's a fairy thing. Anyhow, I do have her little travel case in my luggage. Fairies travel light, you know?"

"So, I've heard." Jonah pauses a moment in thought. "Is it true that their Fairy garments transform with their skin into any kind of clothing they want?" Jonah aqua eyes alight with fascination.

"Yes, *that* they can do. Pretty cool, huh?"

"My sister would love to be able to do that!" Jonah jokes.

Stepping onto the top floor, Gwen leads the way down the hall to the boarding room that she and Leona share. Thirty stars make a circular pattern on the wooden door before her. Gwen pushes the door open and enters. Jonah lingers in the hallway, nervously glancing down the hall toward the stairs.

"What are you doing?" Gwen stops to look at him, a curious eyebrow cocked. "You can come in."

"Thanks for the invite, but if Mistress Subree catches me on this floor, let alone in your room with you, she'll skin me alive and that's not half as bad as what Aunt Nicola will do to me," he informs with a half laugh.

"Oh, please. I can't believe how prim and proper you all are." Gwen shakes her head. She turns to her bags piled on one of the two narrow beds in the room. Unzipping her red duffle bag, Gwen digs inside. She pulls out a small yellow pouch that contains Morna's few possessions, waving it in the air at Jonah. "Here it is!" she announces.

"Great! Hurry, and bring the whole thing with you. Let's get out of here."

* * * * *

Gwen and Jonah make their way through the thinning foot traffic of Alcromech. They head toward the bridge leading to the other side of the river in a sociable silence. Gwen inhales deeply, the scent of pine mingled with the spices in the air and the smell of meat being roasted back at The Black Iris.

"So, what's this mysterious spell you mentioned earlier?" Gwen inquires as they approach the bridge. The laughing river is the only audible sound now that most of the inhabitants are tucked inside in their beds.

"It's a Silver Stream spell." Jonah smiles at Gwen's dubious expression. "You know that white streak across the sky that airplanes leave behind?"

"You mean jet streams, yes." As they step onto the wooden planks of the bridge, the temperature seems to drop several degrees. Shuddering, Gwen zips up her black leather coat and shoves her free

hand into one of her pockets, the other hand carrying Morna's yellow pouch.

"I don't know if you're aware of this, but people leave a similar streak behind them wherever they go."

"Um, no, Jonah, we don't. I'm fairly sure I would've noticed that before." The boards beneath them creak as they come to the center of the bridge.

Jonah stops to look at her. "You haven't noticed it because it's an invisible stream left behind by our spirits or our auras," he informs her.

The sound of footsteps and voices alerts them to other pedestrians on the bridge. They step off to the side and lean against the railing. Two moderately handsome men approach from the opposite side of the river. Both dressed in human street clothes, and in their late thirties, the men seem to be brothers with identical features. They nod to Jonah and smile at Gwen before moving on. Gwen notes the glow and hum of their auras before returning her attention to Jonah.

"Werewolves." Gwen gestures to the departing men with a nod of her head. "Even if I didn't see their gold eyes, I can tell their species by the color of their auras."

"I guess seeing and interpreting auras is another thing I can add to your list of talents, huh?" Jonah turns to face the river, placing his hands on the railing to look over the edge of the bridge. The water flowing beneath them reflects the dark sky above with white pinpoints of stars and the glow of the moon dancing on the surface.

"Yep. I take it that not everyone can?" Jonah nods. Now alone on the bridge, Gwen settles against the railing, letting her shoulder rest against his. "So, if I can see auras, how come I can't see this, Silver Stream?" Gwen pauses a moment than adds. "Come to think of it how come I can still see auras while under Nicola's restriction spell?"

"To answer the first question, because silver streams are much subtler than our aura and it fades over time. As for still seeing auras without magic…" Jonah thinks for a moment then continues. "Before Dream walking was outlawed, some of the wiccan scholars believed that dream walkers themselves had a strong mental sensitivity that didn't relay on magic. As if their own mental intelligence had a power of its own. I heard a story once of a dream walker who was caught breaking the law. The royal tribunal punished him by stripping his magic away forever. He was left to live the rest of his days as powerless as a human being. However, it was later discovered that while sleeping he was still dream walking, as though nothing had changed"

"Really?" Gwen can't hide her relief. "So, you think maybe dream walking and seeing auras are mental gifts a witch can be born with?"

"Yes. Afterall, only a few Wiccans since the world began have had these kinds of gifts. I've heard of random persons of none-magical tribes with telepathic powers too. By the darkness, even some humans are born with mental abilities."

Unbidden the memory of first meeting Angelo comes to her. How startled she had been to realize that he could hear her every thought. She had supposed she was the only telepath. She realizes she never once thought it odd for a vampire to have this talent.

"Well, let's get started, shall we?" Jonah removes a pouch out of his pocket. "In order to make a silver stream visible we'll cast a water spell."

"What's that in your hand?"

"This is the concoction we need to help us find Morna. Now all we need to make it work is something from that pouch you have there."

With a nervous sigh, Gwen unties the hemp string that binds Morna's pouch together. Inside she finds a smaller bag of herbs, Fairy medicine, a lock of black hair — possibly Gwen's or Ravens, maybe even both — a few gemstones, and sparkling rocks, a small ringlet of dried ivy the size of a ring. Finally, at the bottom she finds what she's seeking. The jewelry box that once belonged to Gwen. The memory of Morna's wilted frame tucked away in the secret compartment flashes in her mind. In this little box, Gwen hid her from Lynette, an evil child Vampire bent on torturing Morna before siphoning the power of her Fairy blood. *At least that vermin is dead now.* Gwen pulls out the jewelry box.

"Will this do? She actually slept in this thing once."

"It's perfect." Jonah takes the jewelry box from her as Gwen reties the pouch and stuffs it into her pocket. "All right then, here we go."

Turning his attention back to the river, Jonah holds the jewelry box in one hand and the magic concoction in the other. "*Allo wae unsilv appre abra ca dab*," Jonah whispers. Gwen watches curiously as he drops the pouch over the edge of the railing into the water.

When it hits the water, the pouch instantly dissolves. It transforms into a silver liquid light ten times brighter than the other reflections in the water. Gwen is mystified as the silvery liquid rises into a watery mist from the river into the air over their heads. Jonah puts the jewelry box into the mist as it flows on the wind. The silvery mist seems to penetrate the jewelry box and come out the other side. Swiftly, the silver mist turns into what looks to Gwen like a cross between liquid metal and light. The Silver Stream then shoots across the bridge, leaving a trail as it whizzes all over the street on the other side of town.

"Hurry!" He quickly hands her the jewelry box. "We better follow it while it lasts. It'll fade away soon." Jonah grabs hold of Gwen's other hand, breaking into a run. She fumbles to put the keepsake away into her coat pocket without dropping it. Her heart pounding with exhilaration and apprehension, Gwen lets him pull her along with him. Their feet sound like thunder across the bridge's wooden planks.

Stepping onto the nearly empty street on the other side, the two chase the silver stream as it seeks for traces of Morna.

The light shoots down the street, startling a Dwarf exiting a building with all the earmarks of a pub. The little man yelps as the light nearly slices through him, knocking him flat on his rump.

"Many apologies, grandfather!" Jonah calls out as they hurry passed the fallen Dwarf.

"Good for nothing Witchlings!" The Dwarf shakes his fist after them.

Up ahead Gwen notices that the silver light has crossed into the river. Once it hits the waterfall, the light bounces back and heads their direction.

"What does that mean?" Gwen stops to catch her breath, forcing Jonah to stop, too.

"The light has picked up Morna's trail from when she first entered Alcromech." He watches the light race in the direction they had just come. "Looks like it's headed to the Populace Center."

With a nod for Jonah to lead the way, they jog back to the place where Morna disappeared in the first place. This time they don't encounter any other pedestrians. As they approach the office, Gwen notices that the doors are shut and the building dark and vacant. Still, the silver light pierces through the door.

"Damnation, the office is closed," Jonah curses.

"Now what?" Gwen asks, perturbed. "Do we break in?"

Just then the light shoots back out the doors. Jonah quickly hops out of the way. The two of them watch in amazement as the light zips back down Main Street again. The light of its previous trip down the road has already evaporated into mist.

"I'm going to go out on a limb here and guess that it's going to show us that she left Alcromech through the waterfall," Gwen says dryly.

"Not possible." Jonah starts to jog after the light. "There's a confining spell over Alcromech. Once we entered, it trapped us within. Morna can't leave this place without going through one of the Lucifinian Roads, which she can't do because she doesn't have a pass," Jonah finishes as he picks up his pace.

With a groan, Gwen hurries to catch up with Jonah. Soon she's jogging alongside him again.

"That slip they gave us at the Tribal Populace Office, that's the pass, right?

"Yep. It works like a magic key," Jonah informs. "Without it, you cannot cross over the borders of the gathering post. In fact, you can't even use it to go on a different road than the one that is designated on the slip."

Halfway down the road, the silver light stops at a rock on the side of the road and curves around to head back toward the Populace Office again. Jonah and Gwen stop at the rock and watch the light flash away with daunted looks on their faces.

"When I went looking for Morna earlier, I got up on this rock to get a better look of the road," Gwen comments. "Could the spell be following my path instead of Morna's?"

"Argh!" Jonah groans running a hand through his dark blonde hair. "Maybe I did the spell wrong. To be honest, I've never used it before," he admits with reddened cheeks.

They turn to follow the already fading light with their eyes. They see it whiz up to the Populace Office and enter the building

yet again before it reappears to shoot down the next street and across the bridge.

"Yep, it looks like it's retracing my steps, all right." Gwen turns to Jonah. "Sorry, I think I ruined your spell by using something of Morna's that once belonged to me." She stuffs her hands into her coat pocket, embarrassed. "So, do you have any other bright ideas?"

"Not at the moment," he confesses. "Maybe Aunt Nicola has the answer."

"It looks like we missed them at The Populace Center," Gwen points out. "I guess they'll be waiting for us at the Black Iris."

"We better head back."

Their eyes meet, and the air seems to electrify between them. All at once, Gwen finds little desire to return to the boardinghouse. Without thinking Gwen links her arm with his. Relief and confusion mix behind his aqua eyes.

Wait. What am I doing? Michael's barely dead and here I am with Jonah like Michael meant nothing. The ache in her soul testifies to the contrary. In consternation, Gwen pulls away. *Jonah must hate me for manipulating him and toying with his memories.*

Jonah places his hand over her arm, keeping her from disentangling their connection. Together, they turn back the way they came.

*For all the darkness, I like her. Ahhh, this is awkward as hell. What am I supposed to say or do now with everything I...*Jonah's thought flow freely like the scents on the wind.

"Can we just put all the past behind us and just be friends?" Gwen exhales, her every muscle relaxing. "If you haven't noticed things aren't exactly going my way and I could...."

"Of course." Jonah interjects. "Gwen, I never meant to get you into any trouble. I ... She ... Aunt Nicola just..." He stammers, flustered.

"Jonah, its fine. I understand, really." Gwen sighs. "I never should've dragged you into my crazy life."

"Gwen." Jonah chortles. "You didn't do anything that I wouldn't have done in your situation." He pauses with a thoughtful look. "I mean, if I could do the things, you can, I would probably erase people's memories too, especially if it meant not being apprehended and facing a tribunal."

"Well, when you say it like that..." Gwen gives him a look and he smiles, shaking his head.

"What I mean is, that ...we're fine. Everything between us is..." Jonah gestures with his free hand between their bodies, his eyes locking on hers. Gwen experiences through his mind's eye the sensation of being so overwhelmed by another individual as to render one not only speechless but without thought as well.

Boy, you give a whole new meaning to the phrase "open book" don't you, Jonah Crayborn? I don't even have to try to peek into your head. Your thoughts might as well be my own.

"Is ... what?" Gwen prompts after an elongated silence, startling Jonah back to the present.

"Is … is … great! It's good. I mean..." Jonah looks away for a moment, avoiding her eyes. *Jonah, you blabbering idiot!* "I'm not angry with you. I just hope you can forgive me for…" His shoulders rise and fall with the enormity of his troubled sigh, and he continues. "I don't know. I just want you to know that I'm here to help you … and your friends, in any way that I can." Having said this releases a heavy burden from his spirit and the flickering of light in his aura settles.

"Thank you, Jonah. I … we, appreciate that." Gwen finishes gulping down the lump in her throat only to find it blocked by the tightness in her chest.

"Come on." With a little smile, Jonah tugs on her arm as he quickens their pace.

Despite spending every night for the last several weeks together in the dream world, they hardly know one another. Now that he's here in the flesh, now that everything in her world has changed, it seems absurd for them to dream walk together any longer. The realization leaves Gwen feeling vulnerable as if a thing of comfort has been torn from her.

They walk peacefully down the empty streets, the buildings on one side, the river trickling by on the other. Together they are as still as the lights in the watery surface, close and yet as distant as the dancing starlight.

Chapter Nineteen

No Circle

Why don't we play a game on our way back?" Gwen suggests. "One asks a question and the other answers it as truthfully as they can." A cold breeze sends her black hair dancing about her face, Gwen traps the wild strands behind her ear.

"All right." Jonah smiles. "But if I'm going to play, I get to ask the first question," he declares.

"Fine, but I can't imagine what on earth you'd have to ask me."

"Well, for starters, what's your last name?"

"I don't know." Gwen shrugs. "I'm an orphan, remember? But the nuns at St. Paul's — that's the Orphanage where Raven and I met — they called me Marianne January," she confides.

"Marianne?" He examines her face. "No offense but you don't look like a Marianne."

"I agree." Gwen laughs softly. *Yet another reason to like you.*

"All right then, how old are you? When's your birthday?"

"I'm about seventeen and I don't know my real birthday. My false birthday is January 12th."

"Is that where the last name January comes from?" Jonah inquires.

"Yes. Now it's my turn." Jonah looks as though he's about to protest, but Gwen continues, "You've asked four questions already. It's my turn," she insists.

"Ask away, then." Jonah concedes as they pass the Populace Office once more. Arms still hooked at the elbow; they turn down the street headed to the bridge.

"Your sister said something about 'my circle' earlier and I was wondering what she was talking about?" Obviously not the question he expected; Jonah looks taken aback a moment. Their footsteps on the wooden bridge creates a hallow resonate sound as they cross. After a long awkward silence, Gwen asks, "Did I say something wrong?"

"No. I'm just thinking how to best answer that." He disentangles his arm from hers and takes a step or two looking about him as if expecting the answer to jump up out of the river. Jonah looks up, his eye catching something on the other side of the shore. Gwen follows his gaze to see the silver light zipping along the shore and curve onto the bridge coming straight for them. "Looks like it found you!" he announces, an edge of fear in his voice.

"Wait, what does that mean?" Gwen asks, her face ashen. "Is it going to hit me? Will it hurt?"

"I don't know. I told you I've never used the Silver Stream spell before." With wide eyes, Gwen looks back and forth between Jonah and the silver light making its way to her. Like a heat seeking missile. Her heart starts to race as if she were running a marathon.

"Isn't there something I can do to stop it?" she demands.

"Just stand very still," Jonah suggests, uncertainty lacing his words.

Gwen takes a deep breath and braces herself for the impact. The light is nearly upon them, its silver glow almost blinding as it approaches. Gwen clamps her eyes shut and turns her face to avoid the searing light. An instant later it pierces her body. Like lighting surging through her, the Silver Stream absorbs into her flesh. The sensation sends liquid dynamite through her veins from her toes up into her crown.

An eternity becomes a second and in her mind's eye she sees a hyper sped-up version of her entire life. She relives it all in rewind until she hits a physical shroud covering the first five years of her memory. Gwen opens her eyes wide, feeling rejuvenated physically yet alarmed.

I've always suspected but now I'm certain someone has put a barrier in my mind. Some kind of spell hides my early childhood from me. She had hoped it was just a metaphorical block, something she could undue with time. Now it seems someone else will have to lift the block for her. *But why were those years blocked at all? Was it to protect me or to protect someone else? Someone for some reason doesn't want me to know who I really am or ever to return home.* The guardian of her dream world springs to mind. *Could he have done this?*

"Hello?" Jonah, laughing softly, pokes her in the shoulder as if to see if she' still alive. "Is anyone home?"

Resolving to puzzle out her mental block later, she focuses on Jonah and the here and now. *The past can wait; after all it's been waiting twelve years already,* she reminds herself.

"What was that?" She looks at her companion, perplexed.

"Did your life flash before your eyes?" Jonah asks expectantly, a half-grin on his face and a wicked gleam in his aqua eyes.

"You knew that was going to happen!" Gwen slugs him in the arm half playfully. "You butthead!"

"Ouch!" Jonah shakes his arm and massages the shoulder. "That really hurt." He laughs.

"Good!" She smiles back. "Why'd you lie and say, 'I don't know what'll happen, I've never done it before'?" Gwen asks, mocking his voice.

"Just thought it would be fun to watch you freak out. I mean, you try so hard to seem tough all the time. I figured it might be fun to mess with you." Jonah chuckles.

Gwen raises her fist again as if for another punch, suppressing a smile while trying to look menacing.

"I'm sorry." Jonah puts his hands up in surrender.

"Just don't you do that to me ever again," Gwen warns.

"Promise," Jonah says, grinning while visibly crossing his fingers. "Besides, I didn't lie. I haven't ever done that spell before, but I've seen it used a few times. I knew it wouldn't hurt you."

Gwen shakes her head at him and rolls her eyes before she resumes their trek across the bridge. Jonah quickly falls into step beside her, shoving his hands into his coat pockets.

"So, back to my question." Gwen nudges him in the side with her elbow.

"Right. What is a circle?" They step off the bridge onto the shore and Jonah stops to look at her. "With Wiccans everything comes down to blood, including our class system."

"Okay, but why blood?" Gwen asks. *What does that have to do with circles?*

"Because the purer a Wiccan's blood, the stronger in the craft they are or can become. Pure bloods, as in a Wiccan born of two pure Wiccans, make up the first circle or upper class." Jonah looks to see if she understands. She nods and gestures for him to continue. "The second circle is made up of Wiccans with one Wiccan parent and a parent from another Tribe of Cain."

"All right," Gwen replies, perplexed. "Hmmm."

A wisp of wind flitters over the river carrying past them the smells of the woodland town and sounds of night creatures. Brushing her long black hair out of her yellow-green eyes, Gwen notices that the Black Iris is just a few buildings up the shore.

Instinctively they both start walking down the street toward the boardinghouse at a leisurely pace.

"So, if a Wiccan had a baby with a … Giant, perhaps? Their kid would be considered second circle?"

"Exactly, and because the blood is a little diluted by the blood of another tribe, they're less powerful in the craft and thus a second-class citizen," Jonah clarifies.

"Huh." Gwen thinks a moment. "What about the other three magical tribes? Surely a child born of a mermaid and a Wiccan would be first circle not second. They carry the power in their blood, too, right?"

"Yes, and no." Jonah seems uncertain. "Although Elves, Fairies, and Merfolk are also gifted with magic, their talents are limited."

"Right, Morna told me all about it when we first met," Gwen recalls the conversation long ago one night in Bec LaNuff after she had rescued the Fairy. "Elves control the land, Fairies the air, and Mermaids the sea." Gwen counts off the tribes on her fingers. "Wiccans are the only ones who control all the elements."

"Exactly!" Jonah smiles brightly. *I'm impressed she knows so much for a wild Witch, far more than I expected.* "So, because of this, a part Wiccan, part mermaid child would still be less powerful than a pure Wiccan."

"Hmmm, and the third circle must be a human wiccan half-breed, correct?" They walk up the steps of the Black Iris onto the huge wrap-around porch. A few lights shine in the windows but

otherwise the boardinghouse is still. The smell of late supper still lingers in the air.

"Of course." Jonah avoids her eyes. He turns to walk along the railing of the porch, letting one hand glide along its ridges. He turns his eyes upward to the starry sky. *And this makes me virtually worthless, powerless, bottom of the heap,* he adds mentally.

Gwen sees a barrage of images float through his mind, which puzzles her greatly. The images of a couple seem to dominate his thoughts. By their appearance and his emotions toward them, Gwen surmises they must be his parents.

"Does being part human make a wiccan less powerful in the craft then?" she asks, pretending she doesn't already know. Gwen joins him by the railing, leaning her back against it so she can watch his face partially lit with moonlight.

His thoughts are so easy to read; I almost forget he isn't saying them aloud. I better be careful around him. I like knowing what he's thinking. One slip and he'll resent me not telling him earlier. He'll shut me out. I'm sure Wiccans have a spell for that.

"Yes," Jonah sighs. Running a hand through his ash blond hair, he turns to lean against the railing beside her, folding his arms over his chest. "Third-circle Wiccans are very weak. No amount of training or practice will ever make you as good as the other circles," he admits, swallowing a lump in his throat as he goes on, "We are the working class, the servants, and the foot soldiers in times of war. We're the expendable ones."

"Jonah, are you third circle? You and Leona?" Gwen asks in a soft whisper, almost not wanting an answer at all.

"Yes." He finally looks up at her, emotion tight in the lines of his eyes. "I come from a long line of Wiccan men who prefer humans. My mother was human, my grandmother, and my great-grandmother. So, you see, my blood's very diluted." He stands up straight as if accepting the truth. She senses his relief in having admitted it to her. "It doesn't bother me that much, the being less powerful in the craft, I mean. But Leona … let's just say she won't stop until she's proven everyone wrong about third circle Wiccans. She's going to single handedly change the entire system. Someday we'll be equals, she says." Jonah shrugs.

"I like the sound of that." Gwen smiles weakly, suddenly at a loss for something better to say. "So, do you serve someone, then? Or work for somebody?"

"Ha, yes, I do." Seeming more at ease now, Jonah turns to stand before her, his demeanor changing to that of an authority teaching a novice. "I better explain that to you now since it's only going to get crazier around here before we leave to go to the Coven. I'm going to give you a crash course in Wiccan culture."

"Like Wiccan 101?"

"Exactly." He clears his throat. "I am sworn to the house of Barnabas Blackwool," he announces officially.

Gwen looks at Jonah shocked as the realization fully sinks in. *Wait, isn't Blackwool Thayer's last name?*

"You serve Thayer's family?"

"Yes," he says calmly, no emotion in his face.

"But he's your best friend," Gwen declares as if the idea were preposterous. Her voice raises in volume as she speaks. "What does that mean exactly? What do you do as his servant?" Suddenly needing to move from the irritation gathering in her gut, Gwen begins to pace the porch.

"Shhh." Jonah looks to the front door as if expecting someone to pop out. "Don't wake everyone up. Mistress Subree will skin us alive!" he warns in a hushed voice.

"Fine, but only if you answer my question," she bargains.

"I always walk two steps behind him. I don't speak unless spoken to when we're in public. I do all the menial things throughout the day for him like open the door or get him food, all done with magic, of course. I run his errands, I tend the house, I assist in spells, I convey messages between the Blackwool house and the other houses, and so on."

"You're a slave, then?"

"By choice," Jonah proclaims defensively. "Look, a third circle without oaths of fealty to a house of the second or first circle is like a homeless bum. He has no shelter, no food, no way to provide his own livelihood. We're not allowed to operate our own trade or to get goods without a name to call on for credit. A Wiccan without a house to serve is easy pickings for all the rest. He's the carcass the other's circles pick apart. The whores, and the blood sacrifices for dark magic." Jonah takes a steadying breath. "Believe me, I'm pretty well off where I am. The Blackwools have always been good friends with the Crayborns. In public we must obey the rules, but in private we're treated like equals. We're family."

"If marrying or mating with humans makes your lives this bad, why on earth would any Wiccan do it?" Gwen asks, still horrified by all this new information.

"Because the heart can't help who it loves," he quotes, all the anger gone out of him now. *And I never understood what my father meant by that ... until now.* His eyes hold hers in meaningful look.

A shiver runs along her skin from head to toe. *Is he saying what I think he's saying? No, Gwen, he didn't say it, he thought it. Besides no one falls in love after knowing someone just a couple of weeks. Technically, this is only your third real-life conversation with him.* Gwen breaks eye contact, continuing her pattern of walking back and forth along the porch rail.

"But it's not all bad. A third circle can marry into a second circle family," Jonah submits.

"And does this change the status of the third in the relationship or for their kids?"

"The third circle wiccan becomes *Sodae itee,* first or second circle by association."

"Which means…?" She pauses in her pacing a moment to look Jonah square in the eyes.

"That they're accepted not as first or…" Without skipping a beat, Jonah continues. "Seen as near equals to seconds. The same goes for their children."

"But they'll never be considered first circle?"

Jonah shakes his head and sighs.

"Does this kind of marriage happen often?" Gwen continues pacing the porch.

"Often enough. In fact, Leona and Thayer have been betrothed since birth."

"What?" Gwen stops pacing again and steps up to him. "Wait. So is Thayer first or second circle?" she asks, folding her arms under her breasts.

"He's second." Gwen goes to speak but Jonah raises a hand, cutting her off. "And before you ask, it's his mother who's not Wiccan. She's of the Merfolk."

"She's a Mermaid?" Gwen's eyebrows shoot up in astonishment. Jonah nods.

"On land, her tailfin transforms into legs. In water she goes back to a Mermaid. On land, she's extremely sensitive to heat and has to drink four times as much water as the rest of us are supposed to consume in a day."

"Wow!" Gwen thinks a moment. "Does that mean Thayer changes into a Merman every time he takes a bath or gets caught in a rainstorm?" Gwen jibes.

"No," Jonah answers with a throaty chuckle. "He does have gills, though, and can breathe underwater without the aid of a spell or magic device. But he doesn't grow fins."

"Really?" Gwen digests this latest information for a bit, not quite sure what else to say but not wanting to end their conversation

just yet. "So, you're happy, then, with this arrangement? I mean, you being sworn to Thayer's family and all?"

"Yes," Jonah answers honestly, a little smile playing at the corner of his mouth. "I'm well taken care of, and I get to live under the same roof as my best friend." He shrugs. "I can't complain."

"So, no regrets at all?" she probes, not certain why.

"Nope." He swallows hard, his eyes searching her face. Gwen sees the image of a teenage girl appear before her eyes, floating up out of Jonah's memory. With auburn hair in a long main of wild curls, lime-green eyes, and a face full of freckles. She is a wisp of a girl so thin and small she seems almost inhuman, more like a leaf than a person. It takes Gwen a moment for recollection to click in place.

Wait. She looks just like the mermaid that attacked us in his dreams the second time we dream walked together.

The mystery girl conjures up a multitude of mixed feelings within him that Gwen can't wrap her brain around: Tenderness, bitterness, anger, resentment, friendship, joy, and love. The last constricts around Gwen's heart like a vice. *Who is that?*

The Black Iris front door creeks open and Leona pokes her blonde head out. She scans the scene before her, seeing the two of them. She fixes Gwen with a suspicious look but turns her attention to her brother as she slips quietly outside.

"What by the moon are you two doing out here? Is this what you call Fairy hunting?" she asks with the air of a mother hen scolding her chicks. Gwen tries awfully hard not to laugh at her.

 287

"No, Leona." Jonah sighs. "The spell didn't work, and we couldn't track her down. We were just coming back now," he explains as patiently as he can.

"Well, it's late, Jonah, and we've got a busy day tomorrow." Leona glances at Gwen for emphasis. "Some people shouldn't be out at this time of night."

"You're quite right, little sister. We should all get to bed." Jonah ushers the two girls inside, entering the boarding house last and shutting the door quietly behind them.

Inside, the light from the orbs in the front entry shed a dim glow on the registry table and the tables and chairs in the room, giving the room an eerie quality. No one else is present so the three quietly tiptoe through to the hallway beyond. Leona hugs her brother at the foot of the stairs and turns to go up to their third story chamber. Jonah waits for Gwen to begin ascending before turning to go down the hall to his own room.

"Jonah?" Gwen stops halfway up the steps, looking over the railing to the hallway below.

"Yes?" A moment later Jonah appears beneath her, craning his neck to see her. "What is it?" he whispers.

"Where are Thayer's gills?" Gwen whispers back with a smirk and a light in her eyes.

Jonah smiles broadly, the dim light casting his features in contrasting shadows. "Hidden under his cheekbones and along his rib cage. Was that all?"

 288

"What circle am I? According to that test I'm pure blood, but I don't have a house since I don't have a name. So, what does that mean?"

"Oh." Jonah's mouth tightens, his smile disappearing. His eyes cloud over as if dreading his own answer. "It means you're nameless, houseless. It means you have no circle."

Chapter Twenty

Home

The colorful meadow of her dreams beckons, the same as always yet different. The wind rustles through the trees and dances across the surface of the flowers swaying the hem of Gwen's sunny yellow dress. The feel of the grass is cool and invigorating under her bare feet and against her bare legs. Sunlight kissing her skin. The aroma of the meadow lingers through her nose and in her lungs. Gwen feels at peace. She lets her hand hang down. Here she wears no gloves, and all her digits are present. Her fingertips caress the petals of the flowers that meet her knees just below the edge of her yellow baby-doll dress. Gwen notices that she's also wearing a green cloak, hood hanging down her back. The long train of her velvet cloak weighs down the flowers as it drags behind. Her apparel is eerily like the clothing she wore the day she was found as a child lost in the woods.

That was almost twelve years ago, Gwen realizes. *My blue-eyed guardian angel should have made an appearance by now.* Gwen scans the clearing. Yet everything seems still, herself the only living creature present. She's not sure what to do without her usual dream guide. After all, she's never been in this place without him.

Gwen lets her mind reach out into the world. Embracing the essence of all around her, she finds herself emerged in the life-force of the forest. Closing her eyes, she lets nature's energy surge through her. She basks in its strength and beauty. Unexpectedly, the melody of the forest playing in her mind changes key. Something is out there affecting her environment. Something dark and foreboding lingers nearby.

Gwen's eyes flutter open abruptly, shocked by the hostile presence. Gwen gasps. For the briefest moment she sees a figure standing amongst the trees at the edge of the meadow, watching her. Turning to go, the figure melts into the woods.

"Hey, wait! Who's there? Come back!" Gwen shouts after the mysterious stranger. She takes off running in pursuit. Her cloak hinders her process, so she hastily unhooks the clasps and abandons it. Dashing forward, Gwen finds herself at the edge of the meadow. Despite the warning tingles of dread up and down her spine, she plunges into the woods.

Within the forest the sunlight seems to have vanished, leaving her walking in near darkness. The soothing scents of the meadow are replaced with moss and decay. Her breaths become labored. Gwen stumbles over tree trunks, dodging tree limbs as she hurries after the personage. Gwen can still sense them going deeper into the wilderness. It seems as though she's been wandering forever. For some time, she only feels the strange presence before her, but can't catch sight of them. Possessed with an overwhelming need to know the identity of her watcher, Gwen trudges onward.

One thing's for sure, it's not the boy who has always governed my dreams, nor is it, Jonah. She imagines the Wiccan boy, along with all her other companions, sleeping soundly in their beds back at the Black Iris boardinghouse. *This is someone entirely different, someone I've never met before, not in the dream world or in the waking.*

Gwen emerges from a grove of trees to find a small creek before her. On the other side stands a modest white and yellow cottage grown of the earth, trees, and plants that surround it.

It looks vacant, Gwen notes, seeing the front door hanging open, the shutters of the windows agape, the interior dark and still within.

Something about this little house nestled in the heart of the woods strikes a familiar chord in some dark corner of her mind. Gwen tries to summon the memory to the surface, to force full recognition to take hold. Alas, her efforts are in vain, making her mind sore from the exertion and herself dizzy. Carefully Gwen makes her way to the creek and kneels beside it. Catching her reflection in the creek's surface, she scoops a handful of water and splashes it over her face and neck. The fresh water does the trick. She can think clearly again, her equilibrium restored.

Gwen rises slowly to her feet and crosses the shallow creek to the other side. The icy water sends pleasant shivers up her bare legs. Once on dry land again, Gwen hesitantly approaches the forest cottage. She sends her mental feelers out to explore the space within. There is no one inside.

Still a little unnerved by the mysterious person in the woods and the sudden appearance of this strangely familiar house, Gwen steps up to the front door and enters.

Sheesh! It's pitch black in here! Almost as if she had uttered a spell, several orbs of light appear near the ceiling all about the room, illuminating the darkness. The magic glow sheds light on a little common room with a seating area on one side and a kitchen with a large hearth on the other side. Nearby, a dining room table and chairs rests just before the large open window. The furnishing is also grown, not built like the house. The cupboards to the floor are all different shades of green and yellow. Only the stone hearth is made of a deep earth red, drawing Gwen's eye as it stands out in the room against the white aspen walls. Crossing the room, she stands before the hearth wishing for a warm fire to heat up the sad emptiness of the place. Smoke starts to arise from the wood in the fireplace. Completely without her doing, a fire sparks and begins to burn.

"I didn't do that," Gwen confesses aloud to the empty cottage.

Whirling around, Gwen looks on the abandoned dwelling with renewed interest. *What if the house can sense my will and provide what I desire?* Gwen steps up to the yellow kitchen cupboards and flings a few open. Nothing is inside. Gwen shuts them, and then

allows herself to think on a favorite food. Opening the same cupboard again, Gwen finds a sprig of purple grapes waiting within. Laughing, she takes the fruit out. Returning to her examination of the house, Gwen idly plucks grapes off the stem and tosses them into her mouth. They taste exquisite. Munching on her snack, Gwen turns to the door leading into the next room. She looks in the dark opening and suddenly orbs of light appear again to light her way. Gwen steps into a bedroom. Along the wall to her left, a set of wooden stairs leads up into what looks like a loft.

I'll go upstairs next, she tells herself, turning her attention back to the bedroom before her.

A large bed sits against the north wall between two large windows, with deep-red blankets and yellow sheets and pillows. Tossing the now-bare stems of the grapes aside, Gwen makes a mad dash for the bed and throws herself face first onto it. She sinks slightly into the soft folds of the mattress below. Gwen inhales deeply. Lilly of the Valley and honeysuckle linger on the covers. With a little laugh, Gwen turns onto her back. Smiling up at the ceiling, Gwen notices the painted mural of a beautiful blue sky above.

Again, recognition tugs at her. Slowly Gwen gets up, standing on the bed to get a closer look at the painting above her. As tall as she is, she can easily touch the ceiling with her fingertips. Gwen traces the swirls of the clouds and the birds that fly by.

Who painted this? Who slept here? Where is the owner of the house now? Gwen steps down from the bed onto the handwoven rug

below. With an air of wonder Gwen examines the handful of objects occupying the rock-like nightstand beside the bed. A white candle sits in an old-fashioned gold candle stick holder with a looped handle. Clearwater pearls strung in a curious necklace amongst rose-shaped rubies and emerald leaves lay across a pair of books stacked on top each other. In a cup, looking for all the world like a real tulip bud, a collection of paint brushes and quills reside.

Gently, Gwen picks up the unique necklace. Holding it up to the light to see the sparkle of the gems sends lights dancing about the room. For just a moment she considers wearing the necklace, even taking it with her.

Remember, Gwen, none of this is real. It's just a dream. If anything, it's a reflection of a real place in the real world but you're not actually here. You're not actually holding this necklace at all.

Gwen sets the necklace on the tabletop and picks up the books. Each book has a symbol engraved upon it in gold leaf. The meaning escapes her, but she's certain they're of the true tongue in origin. The texture of their covers reminds Gwen of flower petals but seems sturdier, more like leather. She sniffs the cover of the larger book.

Yep, it smells like a rose. She sniffs the other, sunflower. Putting the rose-scented book down Gwen flips through the pages of the smaller sunflower-scented one. The pages have an earthy organic feel, like old parchment. Words are scribbled across the pages in green ink in the true tongue. It's plain to see that it is someone's journal. She knows she shouldn't pry into other people's lives but feels compelled to read some of it. She notices that it's only a fourth of the way full and turns to the last entry in the book.

October 31st the Eleventh Year of the Reign of House Hawthorne
My beloved little wildling,

Today you are five years old! When you wake, I will take you to the Fairy Glen over the mountains to meet the wind Fairies of the East. It's time you met our people's most trusted ally. Perhaps someday you will have a Fairy kin of your own. I had one once as a child named Breeza. She was as blue as the sky and wild as a bird. She's passed on now, but her people still know me, and they will welcome us as honored guests into their halls.

I'm glad to see you're turning out more like me than your father every day. Not that I think ill of him, it's just that he belongs to the Wiccan world. He doesn't belong to the earth like we do. I hope this all makes sense to you someday when you're grown, and I am gone. I can't explain why we live the way we do, all alone so far away from the world, but I hope you know that your mother loves you very much. Oh, so very much. As long as we stay hidden, we'll be safe. Someday when you are grown the world may be safer. Maybe then you can go into the Wiccan world and be one with your own kind if you wish. There's a chance you may be just like me and abhor the traditions and customs of our people. If so, you can always come back here. This place will always be your home. I think I hear you stirring up above. You must be awake. I must be gone. We have a grand adventure ahead of us today on this, your birthday. I love you, dear.

Love,

Your mother, Julie

Gwen sits there a long moment staring at the name signed at the end of the page. She feels hollow inside, a shell of the child she once was. She feels stupid for envying this mother and child and the special relationship they seem to share. With misty eyes, she shuts the book and places it down on the table. Noticing a little knob on the stone table, she opens the drawer. The inside is almost bare, the only contents a lock of braided hair with two different-colored strands woven together.

Her heart skips a beat and then starts to drum against her ribs. Her breath goes still in her lungs. With a shaky hand, Gwen touches the black and gold braid. Gwen's other hand closes around her gold locket. Mentally looking on the identical braid hidden within. She's forgotten how to breathe; it takes her several tries before her lungs resume their work. Even so, her knees threaten to buckle beneath her. Suddenly, scared out of her wits, Gwen shuts the drawer and turns to bolt from the room. She gets to the door but hesitates at the foot of the stairs leading above.

Something is beckoning her up into the loft. Some part of her needs to see the little girl's room. With a steadying breath, her hand tightly clasping her locket, Gwen crosses the landing and slowly ascends the stairs. Every step makes her heart a little heavier with dread. Once at the top Gwen scans the child-size dwelling.

A little girl's aspen wood bed sits in the corner, made up with a green blanket decorated in yellow sunflowers. A child-size aspen table and two chairs sit before a large circle window, letting in the bright sunlight. A fireplace takes up the far wall near the bed, the same deep red stone as the fireplace below in the kitchen. Gwen forces herself to cross to the center of the room.

This isn't possible, she tells herself. Shutting her eyes tight, Gwen wills herself to wake up, to leave this shadow of her past for the present and the reality to which she's become accustomed. Slowly she opens her eyes finding herself still in the center of her childhood room.

"But how?" Gwen asks the walls. "This place should be a pile of ash now, just rubble. I can't possibly be standing here," she tells the fireplace as if it'll sprout a face and speak back to her, explaining the whole strange story.

In her previous expeditions into the dream world, she has always visited real places. She learned that from her guardian and from trespassing into Jonah's dreams. *Could she also visit places from the past? Could her dreams also show her glimpses of the future as well?*

Gwen can't be certain, but she believes that she is standing in her house, the home she lost so long ago.

* * * * *

The shadows of memories play across her mind. Gwen sees a translucent version of her five-year-old self sitting at the table reading a book to a Fairy doll.

"Nevermore quoth the Raven, nevermore." Little Gwen reads in the true tongue. Smiling at the doll, she makes a face and caws like a bird. Laughing at herself the girl goes on reading.

The girl evaporates as the vision vanishes before her eyes leaving Gwen staring, aghast. Although the child is gone, the Fairy doll and the book remain on the tabletop. Timidly, Gwen reaches down and takes the little black leather book in her hand. This book is manmade, not like the floral-scented journals below. Curious, Gwen puts this new book to her nose and inhales deeply. Burnt cedar and chamomile, the combined scents linger, conjuring up vague images from her forgotten past.

Gwen notices that the cover has no title or symbol, so she thumbs through the pages. It's all handwritten in the true tongue with a strong, clean, and masculine hand. She turns back to the title page at the front of the book.

A Collection of my Favorite Poetry and Wild Tales from Around the World. For my little Black Star with love from D.H.

Again, something tugs on her memory and Gwen turns to see a tall, dark-haired man sitting beside an even younger version of herself on the bed. Gwen can't see the man's face as his back is to hers and he faces the child. He holds out both his hands, each balled up in a fist.

"Choose one," he commands the little dark-haired girl, looking to be maybe four years old.

"What do you mean?" Gwen watches her own child face squint up, perplexed, as she looks at the man's fist and up into his face with obvious confusion.

"It's a game that humans play," he explains patiently. "I have hidden something in one of my hands and now it is up to you to decide which one has the prize within." The man's voice caresses warm feelings inside her heart and pulls at the dark emptiness in her memories.

"And if I choose the right one, I get to keep the prize, right?" Little Gwen asks, seeming to get the concept now. He nods in reply. "Well, doesn't seem like much of a game. You've only got two hands. I've got half a chance of winning or losing either way." She shrugs.

The man laughs deep in his chest "You'll never know if you don't try," he coaches.

Little Gwen puts on a "thinking" face and taps one finger against her lips in concentration as she seriously ponders her choice. Finally satisfied, she makes an elaborate show of flourishing her hand in the air before she places a finger on the man's left fist.

With an equally elaborate flourish, the man opens his palm before her nose. It is empty. Four-year-old Gwen visibly slumps in disappointment. With another small laugh the man opens his other hand to show that it too is empty.

"What! You tricked me. There's no prize at all!" Gwen grumbles, crosses her arms over her chest and huffs, "I don't like this game."

"Come now, Black Star, there is a prize. You're just not looking in the right place." The man snaps his fingers. Little Gwen gasps and looks down at her own hand to see a black stone ring with a symbol in filigree appear on her ring finger.

She looks up at him through her curtain of straight black hair and smiles broadly. "That was a good trick."

"Thank you. It's called a Black Star Diopside," he informs her, indicating the oval stone on the ring.

"Black star like me!" little Gwen proclaims in awe.

"Yes, it reminds me of you."

"Oh, is that why you call me Black star? Cause that's not my name, you know." Little Gwen points out matter-of-factly.

"Yes, I know that's not your name. I call you Black Star for a lot of reasons. But mostly because you remind me of my mother and this was her favorite gemstone," he tells her as he touches the large oval-shaped stone of the silver set ring. "See? It has a four-pointed star in it and it's black just like your hair." He reaches out to stroke a lock of it from her face and tucks it behind her ear. Smiling, she climbs into his lap and wraps her arms around his neck.

"Thank you. I love it," she tells him.

"I love you," he whispers into her dark hair and the vision vanishes before her eyes again, leaving grown-up Gwen alone in the empty room.

Gwen finds her legs giving way beneath her and in an instant is sitting on the floor, lost in a tumult of emotions.

She hadn't remembered much about her father, but the tiny fragments she had of him had always given her the impression that he was a cold and distant man. Someone who visited them rarely and never showed her kindness. The man she had just seen and the child she had once been, were far more companionable than she had ever imagined. *Had we been close once and then something happened to tear us apart? It must've been something so terrible that it had made me doubt him, so much that I had been unsure if he were even my father at all.*

Gwen looks down at her hands and wonders where that Black Star Diopside ring went. *In both visions I had my gold locket on,* Gwen realizes. "And I still have it. What happened to that ring?"

"Gwen!" A man shouts from without the walls of the home. Startled, Gwen jumps to her feet and races across the room to look out the round window. Sometime during her visions, the sun had gone down and now Gwen looks out into a starry night, the eerie forest, and the creek below her. At the water's edge stands the blond boy from her dreams, now a man in his twenties in up-scale, regal dress. He looks up at her with panic in his eyes. "You fool! What are you doing here? Get out! Get out before she finds you!" he screams.

His words bring a chill to her very bones and suddenly Gwen remembers all his past warnings. *Run, Gwen, Run and don't return until I call for you.* He hadn't summoned her here. She had followed a stranger to this place, a place she now realizes is forbidden. Suddenly frightened, Gwen turns to run to the stairs and stops abruptly. There, standing at the top of the stairs, is a woman. With platinum, almost white-blonde hair and violet eyes, the woman stands in stark contrast to the black dress and cloak she wears. She stares at Gwen with an empty expression as though she is looking through her and not at her.

Gwen is frozen in place, unable to move forward or back rooted to the spot by sheer terror.

The woman tilts her head. Her lips twist into the tiniest hint of a smile. "Dead. They're all dead. No one lives here anymore, don't you know? Burnt, all burnt. No one lives here anymore, don't you know?" The woman speaks in a ghostly voice seeming only half-aware of what she is saying as she slowly steps closer to Gwen.

One step, two steps, three, then four.

Yet Gwen can't move and inside she screams at herself, *wake up, wake up from this nightmare!*

"Mine. All Mine. It's not yours anymore, don't you know?" The woman screams at Gwen suddenly in a wild rage.

Five steps, six steps, and then seven.

The woman is right in Gwen's face as she wails, "He's mine, it's all mine!" And with the screech of her voice, the window behind Gwen shatters into tiny, minute pieces. A huge gust of wind rushes into the room, knocking Gwen down onto her knees with the impact. Gwen yells as she falls.

The woman now hovers over her. The wind blows her cloak back to show its violet lining within, her blonde hair whipping about her face as wild as the hatred in her eyes. Gwen notices a large, oddly shaped red crystal hanging about the woman's neck. The woman drops to the floor to look Gwen in the eye.

"Dead. You're dead. No one wants you anymore, don't you know!" she whispers in a cold tone as she encloses the red crystal in her fists. "Only the daughter of the dead can you be and burn with your mother in hell!" With this, she squeezes the crystal tight.

Gwen throws back her head and howls in pain as every vessel in her heart restricts, her chest aching as though it will collapse inward with the strain. Simultaneously, the room around her catches fire. But the woman is nowhere in sight.

The rafters, the table, the bed, even the floor around her, are ablaze. The heat sets her skin to blistering and her lungs to aching.

"Wake up, Gwen. Why can't you just wake up?" she demands of herself. Yet no one answers, and still, she finds herself trapped between one world and the next. Unable to fully control her body, Gwen huddles up into a ball, willing the pain to cease yet forcing herself to accept the inevitable until she remembers her guardian angel.

"Please, help me! I can't do this on my own!" she calls out to him, hoping that he's still waiting outside, that he's still here in the dream world. The roar of the fire fills her ears as the flames engulf her. Then, with a creek, the floor gives way beneath her. The whole upstairs loft crashes through the ceiling into the bedroom below, the flames and debris crushing her mother's things beneath her.

No more journals with her mother's loving words. No more painted ceiling with her mother's brush strokes. No more lock of their intertwining hair. No more home.

Jonah was right, Gwen thinks. *The dream world is more dangerous than I ever knew. I was a fool to play with things I didn't truly understand.*

Ash and smoke fill her lungs as she is ensnared by the blaze, cradled in the charred remains of her childhood home.

Chapter Twenty-One

Mother

"Gwen!" All at once Gwen opens her eyes, startled to find her guardian sitting next to her as she lies amongst the flowers in the meadow. "It's okay, Gwen. It's over. You're safe now." Unbelieving, Gwen takes several steadying breaths as she sits up looking around, in shock. She is more at peace but in her gut, she knows her childhood home is now gone, its smoldering remains hidden somewhere deep in the forest beyond. "See? You're back in our safe place," he explains.

"Our safe place?" Gwen looks up at him in confusion.

"Yes. I can only protect you here, Gwen. Please, don't ever go wandering into the woods again. That is her domain."

"Whose domain? Who was that woman? Was that my home?" Gwen demands, slumping down into the wildflowers, exhausted. "Were those my mother's things? Was that my father? Will you for

once give me some answers?" She shouts into the clear blue sky, digging her fingers into her dark hair as if holding her throbbing scalp together.

The young man looks down at his hands folded in his lap as if looking for the answers she seeks there in his empty palms. After a few moments he finally looks back at Gwen. His brilliant blue eyes full of pain.

"Look, I'm sorry I yelled at you, I'm just—" Gwen trails off, not sure what to say, her head still reeling from her encounter with the violet-eyed woman.

"No, Gwen, it's okay. I wish I could just tell you everything you want to hear. However, it's … a lot more complicated than that." Their eyes meet, and Gwen is struck by how much he still resembles the boy she first met when she was five here in this very field.

He has the largest eyes she's ever seen on a man, big blue pools of innocence and hope. With the same long nose and full feminine lips now set in a long face with high-boned cheeks, her guardian is the perfect mix between man and boy. The image of a cherub turned guardian angel if ever she saw one. Twelve years and hundreds of dreams later, she is almost an adult, and he must be in his twenties by now. *Yet, I still don't know… what is your name?*

He smiles sadly at her. "Sorry, I can't even tell you the answer to that question." Squinting, he investigates the horizon, toward the direction where she had once seen the White Kingdom. Now she knows that that Kingdom is a real place and that it is the realm of the Wiccans. "The dream world isn't the best place to exchange information. You never know who is watching and listening." He looks back at her again with his great big, blue doe-eyes. She sees fear and love shining through them. "This meadow is my domain. I have the power to control what comes and goes into this place. Yet you have power here, too. Remember the times you've seen glimpses of the future? Remember seeing the mountain that chased you?"

"Yes." Gwen sits upright, suddenly fully alert. "That was the future?"

He nods. "That was Bec LaNuff. That was the forces trying to warn you of what lay ahead of you," he explains. "You made that vision appear. You were guiding yourself then."

"Hmmm. It would've been better if I'd just told myself to stay the hell out of the Poconos Mountains," Gwen scoffs. "I think the subtlety went right over my head with that one." Memories of her imprisonment in Bec LaNuff surface. Gwen fights them down with bitterness. When she looks back up at her companion, he is sitting right next to her. Their shoulders almost touch he is so near. It's been a long time since he's been this close to her without vanishing.

"We can't always understand the visions when they come, but fate does try to help us along the way, if it can." He watches her with his childlike eyes, a sympathetic look.

"Who are you? What are you? Why do you bother with meeting me here like this?" Gwen asks, forcing herself to keep her hands folded in her lap instead of reaching out to take his hand lest he vanish again. "Wouldn't it be easier just to find me in person?" In the first dream he had hugged her. He hasn't touched her since. *I wonder why?*

He shakes his head with a resigned sigh. "I'm sorry, I can't…"

"Tell me? Yeah, I know. It was worth a try anyway." Gwen sighs, dismissing the whole subject with a wave of her hand. "You seem to know an awful lot about me, and I can't help wondering how that is when I barely know anything about myself." A gentle breeze picks up and the meadow seems to dance all around them. The rustling of the leaves is like the soft crash of waves on a shore.

"I promise, Gwen, someday it'll all make sense. Until then, be careful where you go in your dreams."

"Got it." Gwen remembers something from her dreams with Jonah. "Is there any reason I should be worried about walking through doors in dreams? And do mirrors mean anything?"

"Crossing through doorways in your own dreams — no, but should you cross over into someone else's dreams again, then yes. And mirrors can be dangerous in the dream world, too. They can represent the future and show us truths about ourselves but also, they can be used to spy on another's dreams without detection. You did Jonah a favor when you broke that mirror at the bottom of the lake." Gwen gives him a surprised look. "Yes, I know about your little visits into Jonah Crayborn's dreams."

"Wait, but how?"

"If you haven't guessed yet, I'm a Dreamwalker, too. I'm always watching over you while you sleep to keep you safe from her."

"And why is this your job?" Gwen asks, her chest filling with tenderness for this nameless boy that she can't quite explain.

"Because it's all I live for. Because I'm the only one who knows you're still alive."

"And without you, I would've died that night when she burned the place down? I'm right, aren't I?"

He looks at her bewildered. "How did you know that?" he demands, fear creeping into his voice.

"I saw a gypsy once and she told me about the night my mother died," Gwen explains. "The whole thing wasn't entirely clear, but she did mention that a blond, blue-eyed boy had rescued me from the fire. Obviously, that was you." She slowly reaches out her hand to take one of his. He notices and scoots away from her.

"Yes. That was me," he confesses reluctantly. Suddenly, not so eager to meet her gaze, he plucks a flower from the field and begins to pull the petals off the stem.

"So, you know exactly what happened that night and I'll bet you could tell me who I am, who my parents were, and all sorts of details about my past."

"Yes," he answers as he tosses the remainder of the flower away.

"And yet you won't tell me because you're trying to protect me, and the only way to do that is to leave me ignorant of myself?" Gwen asks calmly.

"Yes." The boy shrugs, his blond locks bouncing with the gesture. "You're simply not ready to know the truth, Gwen. Not yet."

"Fine. I can wait if I must." Gwen presses her lips together in grim acceptance. "Is there by any chance anything I need to know before I get back to the real world? Something you *can* tell me, perhaps?" she presses.

"As a matter of fact, there is. I assume you've heard about the Vampires declaring war?"

"Yes, we saw the announcement on TV." Gwen nods in affirmation. "And we're going with Jonah to his Coven to wait things out, so to speak," Gwen adds with a bitter tone.

"What's a TV?" the boy asks, raising one quizzical blond brow at her.

"Never mind, it's not important."

"There's something you're not telling me." His angelic face takes on a stern protective air, his blond brows furrowing.

"Well…" Her gut fills with apprehension and annoyance at the very idea of admitting the truth of her current predicament. She forces it down, reluctantly. "Where do I start? I'll give you the abridged version," Gwen says sarcastically as she gets up to her feet. "Someone's murdering my boyfriends and framing me for it. So, I'm wanted by the police yet again!" Gwen throws up her hands in mock exasperation and then begins to pace through the flowers in a line before her listener. "While trying to get away from all that, it

turns out I'm also wanted by the Wiccans for practicing magic in front of humans."

"Wait, explain?" He gives her a look that says volumes.

"Hey, don't judge. A girl has to make a living. Trust me, there are worst things I could've been doing." Gwen gives him a meaningful look.

"Point taken, continue." He waves her on with an uncomfortable look on his handsome face. *He doesn't seem to like the idea of me doing those other things. Hmmm, he's not a normal guy, that's for sure.*

"Anyhow, now I've been apprehended by Jonah, his little sister, his best friend and some Thoyen Nicola lady. They're taking me to their coven to be held on trial for my misdeeds." Her companion opens his mouth to speak but Gwen plows on. "*And* it so happens that their coven is the same blasted group of witches that tried to rescue me," Gwen uses finger quotes in the air, "from Bec LaNuff a few years ago and refused to save the only man I've ever loved." Gwen gulps, all the sarcasm suddenly drained from her after admitting it all aloud. She looks down to notice that she's worn a path in the wildflowers with her pacing. Remorse for the crushed flowers forms before she remembers she's in a dream. "So, yeah, I get to deal with looking at those heartless bastards' faces on top of everything else."

Suddenly feeling weak, Gwen collapses back to the ground to sit face to face with the young man. He gives her a sympathetic look but says nothing. Neither of them speaks for a long awkward moment.

"Do you have any idea who would want to frame you for murder?" he asks.

"Nope," Gwen shakes her head. "Although I'm pretty sure it's a vampire."

"Huh, well, that's a start at least." He squints up his face as if thinking. "Well, it so happens I've heard of Thoyen Nicola Blackwool. She's got a reputation for being fair minded and a defender of the friendless." Gwen looks at him, surprised. "I think you may find a champion in her. She may uphold the law, but I think she'll take your unusual situation in consideration and fight for a lenient punishment on your behalf."

"Really?" Gwen's doubts wrestle with one another in her gut. "You're not going to help me scheme a way out of her custody? You're saying I should just go along with it and stand trial?" she asks, disbelieving, a rock forming in her stomach, crushing her doubt, and leaving her with utter disappointment.

"Well, considering the circumstances, a Coven isn't the worst place for you to hide from this vampire that's killing off your lovers." His mouth seems to use the word lover as if the idea were distasteful. "Also, you're a minor unschooled witch completely clueless of our laws and customs." Gwen gives him a stale look. "Don't give me that look. I'm not demeaning you — it's the honest truth as they see it."

"Point taken. Continue," Gwen grumbles.

"This means they can't hold you, a child, to the full measure of the law when you didn't even know you were breaking any laws to begin with. Especially with someone trustworthy like Nicola Blackwool on your side, you'll be exonerated if not mildly punished and the whole thing will blow over."

"That's what you think. I'm not so sure," Gwen admits, although his words dispel some of the dread weighing her down.

"After tonight that woman you encountered here will wonder if you're really alive, or if the girl she saw in the cabin was you at all and not just some strange illusion. Either way, she will be on the lookout for you. A coven can provide you protection from her as long as you stay out of other people's dreams and don't traverse out of this meadow when you are dreaming," the blond youth adds in a chiding tone.

"Sorry. I knew I shouldn't have followed her into the woods."

"There's nothing to be done about it now," he comforts. Gwen senses he wants to hug her or pat her shoulder, but he keeps to himself. "Just be careful while you're in the Coven. Keep the Gypsy's fortune-telling to yourself. Try not to expose all your gifts to the Thirteen Elders all at once. You never know, one of them could be in league with her." He says *her* with a tilt of his head toward the woods. "And whatever you do, don't tell anyone you're a Dreamwalker or speak a word about any of your twisted visions," he counsels.

With a sigh, Gwen ponders this a moment. Still sitting in the grass, Gwen plucks a few blades of it and rips it to pieces in her hands. She senses him watching her, and wonders if he's thinking what she's thinking. When she looks up, her green eyes lock on his blue eyes and for the briefest of moments she gets the hint of a memory.

It is a memory from the lost years of her early childhood, before her mother's death and before her time at Saint Paul's. The two of them sit just like this in the meadow as children. He taught her to make whistles out of the grass and leaves. She made him a necklace of flowers in exchange for the crown of flowers he had made for her. They were happy. *But things were simpler then.*

"You seem to know a lot about..." Gwen tries to think of an appropriate name for the terrifying woman in the woods but all she can think of are her unnatural violet eyes. Gwen shivers involuntarily, "...her." Gwen finishes, hesitant to ask the question she's dying to ask. "Why? Why do you know so much about my mother's killer?"

His shoulders slump and his eyes cast down to his hands. With the air of a sinner in a confessional he replies, "Because..." He gulps. "She is my mother."

Chapter Twenty-Two

Maker

How much longer must we wait?" Lynette grumbles under her breath while perching on a rock just under the cover of the pine trees lining the river. The other members of the vampire drove wait in different attitudes all around her in the middle of the woods. The moon shines intermittently tonight, occasionally hidden behind thick cloud cover. "We've been here almost the entire night. It'll be dawn soon. Where is this associate of yours coming from, Dante, the underworld?"

"Something like that." The Spanish vampire glances up from filing his elongated nails at Lynette. At his feet, his lover sprawls on the cold wet grass despite her fine black suit. "Don't fuss, little Lynette. She'll be here before the sun comes up. I expect her any moment."

"She? Who is she? If vampires are blocked from getting into

Alcromech or any trading post, then who or what is this woman we're waiting for?" Lynette demands in a petulant tone, hopping off her rock. "How can she do what we can't and how is she going to stand a chance against that witch Gwenevere?"

"You will see, little one." Dante croons in his dark accent as he leans down to offer a hand to Peyton. As soon as she is on her feet, the tall blonde vampire wraps herself around him like a scarf.

Lynette groans at this and walks to the water's edge. Selecting a small boulder, she hefts it up over her head and launches it into the air. It makes a tall arch before falling. It hits the other side of the river's bank with a crack as it crushes a small tree. It's limbs splinter, leaving jagged edges pointing around the rock. Lynette snickers.

"Not bad." Affray appears at her side. Light from the river reflecting the moon bounces off his bald scalp. In this lighting, his scars are accentuated by the contrast. "Let's see if you can match this."

In a flash he is next to a boulder bigger than himself. He hefts the rock with ease and poise, vaulting it expertly. It arches twice as high as her throw. When it lands, Affray's boulder smashes a tree ten feet farther in land than hers. It then rolls on to cripple several more trees and shrubs before it finally settles. Affray turns to Lynette with a toothy smile of pride.

"Show off," Lynette grumbles, turning to walk back to the rest of the drove within the tree line. A loud splash and a flicker of movement catches her eye. Lynette spins around to face the intruder.

The river ripples as something long slithers onto the bank. It emits a screeching sound as if a flock of birds dying a tormented death. The creature slowly emerges onto dry land. A tangle of long blond hair hangs around its head, obscuring its face. Slowly it twists as its arms reach forth, digging into the dirt. It howls in agony. What looks to be a long tail fin warps and shudders. Flesh rips and bones crack. At last, the thing pushes itself upward to stand on its newly developed legs.

A woman's silhouette stands before them on the bank. Despite the darkness, it's clear the woman is stark naked. With a flip of the head, her silvery blonde hair falls behind her, revealing an ethereal face with large round blue eyes. They scan the tree line expectantly.

"You didn't tell me it was her!" Peyton hisses into Dante's ear, her hold on him suddenly more like a vice than an embrace. She shoots a dark look in the other woman's direction as she saunters toward them.

"I didn't think it merited mentioning," Dente replies coolly. "What does it matter? We need someone who can get inside."

"What the hell are you?" Lynette blurts out incredulously. Her skin feels hot and itchy as she tries to avert her gaze from the naked woman's frame. There are things she'd rather not see, especially if they're things her immortal child body will never obtain.

She glances Lynette's way and then makes a double take. A look of bewilderment crosses her surreal features. "I could ask you the same thing! Dante, is that a baby vampire I, see?" She turns her astonished gaze on the Spanish vampire. He nods, slowly disentangling himself from his amore to walk toward the newcomer.

"I love it! Is it yours? Can I, have it?" the silvery blonde prattles on, a childlike gleam in her eyes.

"What? No, you can't. I'm not a kitten or a…."

"Calm down, Lynette, she didn't mean it," Dante interrupts. "This is Brielle of the merfolk. She's going to help us with our little witch problem."

"She is? How? I thought no one could get into this Alcromech place." Lynette folds her arms, glaring at the mermaid. Even with Dante standing a foot away and all the others present, Brielle seems completely comfortable with her nakedness. Abruptly Peyton appears at Dante's side draping an arm around his neck. She stares the other woman down with fire and ice behind her gray eyes.

"We're the only tribe excluded from the gathering posts." Peyton addresses Lynette without ever taking her eyes off her competition. "But a member from another tribe can come and go as they please."

"Brielle is going to snatch this Gwenevere for us." Dante finishes with a patient sigh, Lynette imagines is for Peyton's benefit.

"Huh, yeah, that's if she can go head-to-head with a witch," Lynette chirps, gaining her a look of approval from Peyton.

"Never fear, baby. I've got my fair share of witch's eyes in my collection." Brielle smiles proudly, and a quiver of hatred runs through Lynette. *Witch eyes? I like the sound of that!*

"You can't kill this one, Brielle," Dante warns, still ignoring Peyton, who hasn't removed from her place of possession. "She's important to my King."

"Of course," Brielle concedes with a flippant wave of the hand.

"How will you find her though? There's got to be lots of Witches in Alcromech now." The realization dampens Lynette's vengeful euphoria.

"Brielle can glean Gwenevere's likeness from your memories," Dante explains.

"If all goes well, I won't even need to lay an eye or hand on her." Brielle tilts her head with an exaggerated thoughtful look and adds, "but in case it doesn't work..." The Mermaid flashes Lynette a bright smile. "Just hold very still, baby. This can sting a little." Before she can react, Brielle draws Lynette closer to her. With nowhere else to look, Lynette becomes trapped in the woman's gaze. A humming vibrates from the Mer-woman's hands seeps into Lynette's skull. Her vision spins. Brielle's large eyes blur before Lynette's field of vision. The world becomes a whirl of vibrant painful colors as memories of Gwen filter up from the past behind her eyes.

* * * * *

Lynette comes to a while later, finding herself on the ground in a heap. Her skull is splitting. Every thought seems to hurt as she tries to process what just transpired. Groaning in agony, she closes her

eyes and slowly gets to her feet. When she ventures a look around, she realizes that she is alone. Suddenly alert, she twirls around, looking through the lines of trees for any of her vampire companions. Nothing. No one. Even the nude mermaid seems to have vanished. Half panicked, Lynette walks toward the river hoping to find someone there.

At the water's edge she makes out the dark silhouette of a man. He turns at the sound of her approaching steps. Affray's hairless scalp catches the moonlight, giving him a kind of silvery halo. Lynette joins him at the edge of the river and glances about expectantly.

"They've all gone hunting." He supplies before she can open her mouth. "I volunteered to wait for you to wake up. We can go join them if you like?"

"Wait, what happened with the mermaid? Did she get what she needed from me? Is she sneaking into the trading post now?" Lynette asks, flustered.

Affray nods. He stuffs his hands into his jean pockets and turns back toward the woods. He motions for her to follow him with a jerk of his head. Lynette falls in step beside him. She struggles to match his adult gait with her short, child-size legs.

"Brielle set some kind of trap for Gwenevere. Something that exploits a loophole in the trading post's protection spells. She assured that we'll have Gwenevere by tomorrow evening, unharmed." He supplies this information so matter-of-factly she could almost forget that the man standing beside her had once cared for the witch.

Lynette tries to avoid thinking of her time in Bec LaNuff these days. It only reminds her of the family that she lost in the last battle and the mountain fortress caved in and killed most of the inhabitants. She had thought she was the only vampire to survive. That is until Affray showed up. Yet still she can't help wondering what the reunion between Affray and Gwen will be like.

Would the witch even recognize the man? After all that had transpired between them, how would she feel to find out that he is still alive? Not that I care how she feels, but what about Affray? He's the closest thing I have left of my family. How would he feel about seeing Gwen again?

Lynette puzzles over these thoughts as they move through the woods in a pregnant silence. *Maybe he's thinking the same things?*

Crickets chirp all around them, adding awkwardness to the companion's lack of words. Lynette tries to focus her mind on something other than Gwen. Her thirst, the delicious way blood slithers down your throat after a kill … but her mind keeps snapping right back to the same idea. Gwen and Affray's first meeting after the destruction of Bec LaNuff.

What had been their last words to one another? Lynette tries to imagine their last moments together. She wasn't there. So far Affray has been tight-lipped about his former lover. Left with only her own assumptions, the images fly through her head, playing out their own story. By the time she's worked through her own elaborate version of the event, Lynette finds herself brimming with the need to know the truth. Cautiously, she glances at her companion as they walk swiftly through the trees.

"You never told me what happened," Lynette begins. "Back in Bec LaNuff, I mean."

Affray ignores her, keeping his face forward. He follows the mental sensation left behind by the others. Now that they are both sworn to the king, they share a bond with the rest of his vampire subjects. Lynette watches expectantly, looking for any acknowledgement of her query. Affray might as well be taking a private stroll through the woods for all the attention he gives her. Lynette shakes her head irritated at her own stupidity.

Switching mental gears, she allows herself to seek out the distant hum of Dante and the vampire drove.

It had been the same for Lynette with Luca her maker and her sisters Jezebel, Lethawyn, and Ryan. She could feel them in her mind even from far away. They were each like humming vibrations inside her head. Each had its own note, each with a different frequency and volume. Luca was always the loudest. She figured that was because he was her maker and responsible for her transition into a vampire.

Gwenevere is the real one to blame for her change. Luca had simply done as his maker had commanded him. Because Legion had been Luca's maker, Lynette was even bonded to the lord of the mountain as well. His hum in her brain had been more distant though, like music in another room.

Those hums were a pleasant companion always with her. She had found comfort in their presences and felt safe hearing them in her brain ... until she couldn't anymore. That's how she knew for sure that none of them survived the collapse of the mountain. Ryan had died not long before. The feeling of her abrupt absence was almost like an explosion set off in her skull. Lynette felt Ryan's pain before she died. Someone had been torturing her. The thought sends her into a fury even now. *How dare someone touch one of my sisters!* After Gwen's surprise escape, her maker and siblings had all gone off in pairs to search for her along with many of the rest of Legion's loyal servants. Always inseparable, Lethawyn and Jezebel went together. Luca had taken the young Ryan with him. Lynette had begged to go with them but was flatly denied.

"It isn't safe for one such as you, my child," Luca had stated. *"Your job is to stay inside and help defend the fortress from the witches should they come back seeking revenge for Gwenevere's imprisonment."*

So, Lynette had stayed. When only three of the four came back she hadn't needed Luca to tell her what had happened to Ryan. She already knew. However, Luca did tell her who was responsible for her sister's untimely demise: Raven and his pack.

Once the witch is handed over to the King, I'll take care of her friends. The wolf and the fairy will pay for their part in the destruction of my family.

Affray stops abruptly beside her; body tense his gaze scanning the forest to their right. Then Lynette hears it too, the laughter of

children. Without a backward glance, Affray moves quietly yet swiftly towards the voices in the trees. Lynette catches up to him, apprehension bubbling in her belly.

Together the vampires peer through a cluster of trees. Before them two little boys, perhaps seven or eight years old, dressed in coats and rainboots kneel amongst a circle of rocks. Their attention is rapt upon a metal cage nestled between two large stones. A creature stirs within the metal encasement. The boys burst into excited peals of laughter. One of the boys undoes the clasp of the cage door. Slowly he pulls a large lizard out and displays it before his friend. The other boy looks on the captive reptile with awe.

What are you two doing out at this time of night, idiots? Lynette chastises inwardly. *It's this kind of stupidity that got me turned into a child spawn. If I hadn't snuck out at midnight to meet Vanessa at the park, I'd wouldn't be this thing now. I'd be...twelve.* The realization sinks in. *I'd be twelve years old now, still living with my mother, father, and my two brothers.* Longing and melancholy threaten, but she pushes her emotions far down into the deep.

"It seems these two scamps have laid a trap and caught themselves a new toy." Affray whispers more to himself than to Lynette. "And now they have found themselves in a trap of their own." A cold smile creeps a crossed his lips.

"Wait." Lynette catches the man by his shirtsleeve, forcing him to turn his gaze from his would be treat. "Not them. Come on we'll find food elsewhere."

Affray fixes a calculating gaze upon her child face. He looks in her eyes a long moment as though seeing there a weakness to exploit. "Why not these tender morsels here? Why waist such a perfect opportunity?" Suspicion lingers on the edge of his silken voice. "You don't eat children, do you?"

Lynette swallows hard, the truth shards of glass tearing up her mouth and throat. There was nothing for it, she couldn't deny it now. "No, I don't" She answered in a soft voice.

Admitting it aloud was like saying she was afraid of the dark. Vampires had neither scruples nor fears. *I'm not a real vampire though, I never really was.*

Affrays silver eyed scrutiny lingers on her a long moment. Then all at once he turned on his heal and walks back the way they had come. Before Lynette runs to his side, she quickly glanced back at the two boys, still giggling over their scaley new friend. She pushed the two from her mind along with all thoughts of her former life.

The two vampires continue their trek. Surprisingly, Affray doesn't bring up her dietary choices again. Even though she knows he has never had any such inhibitions. If anything, he prefers the blood of the young and innocence.

"I suppose you're owed some kind of explanation," Affray sighs. She looks up at the man walking beside her expectantly. Too afraid he'll stop talking if she interrupts, she keeps her mouth shut and listens. "After everything she and I were to each other, I wouldn't blame you for being confused at my willingness to hand Gwenevere over to the Vampire King." He glances down at the vampire stuck in an eight-year-old's body and smiles wanly. A dimple tries to form beneath his tapestry of scars and burns. "I won't share the details of what transpired on the day the mountain fell but I will say this. Just as everyone predicted, she was the undoing of me. That's why I'm willing to let her go. That's why I'm going to give her over to Lazar and turn a blind eye to her punishment. She killed a lot of Forsaken that day. Even I can't stand in the way of the retribution demanded of such an act. It may kill me to watch her perish, but alas it is out of my hands."

His confession both surprises her and confirms her suspicions. He was right. Everyone thought him a fool for falling for the child Gwenevere. Their very union tore the mountain fortress apart. Still, he had loved her in his way. Lynette once believed he would never let the witch go no matter what she cost him. In the end, it turned out to be everything. Despite her better judgement, Lynette ventures another inquiry.

"And the scars?" She lets the question hang a moment, waiting to see how he reacts. When he just gives her a blank stare she continues. "Was that from her? Did she…"

"More or less. Yes, she caused these scars. I would've laid the world at her feet and in turn her foolish actions doomed me. I'll heal in time, of course, but the scars within never will. Such is the case with many a tragic love affair in the end." His original accent shows itself slightly as he finishes. He looks up towards the trees and points ahead. "We're here. The others are just beyond that streetlight."

She recognizes that he's changing the subject. Clearly, he's done talking for now. Reluctantly Lynette looks up and finds that they have come to the edge of the woods into a small housing development. She senses them, too. Together they walk through a dark street toward the streetlight. They turn toward the first house on the right, the first house where people had been living. Judging by the rhythm of the heart beats she hears within the green siding house; they won't be living much longer.

The smell of fresh blood wafts to her nostrils even before Affray pushes open the yellow front door. Her thirst kicks in and her stomach growls. Instantly she starts salivating and the adrenaline rush that always accompanies her killer instincts sweeps over her. In the dimly lit foyer, they find a trail of blood smeared across the floor into the kitchen. A limp body resides in the middle of the linoleum floor. The open refrigerator light illuminates the dead stare of a man in his forties.

Affray walks over and investigates the still warm corpse, bending over him he checks the pulse. Shaking his head, he straightens, turning back to Lynette. "This one is bone dry. Chances are we'll have to check the neighbors for an untapped blood supply."

Lynette nods and heads towards the stairs leading upward. She can still hear one heartbeat above and senses that some of the other vampires are up there too. When she reaches the landing, she sees three open doorways. Through each one she sees a vampire hunched over a nearly dead human — Mother in the master bedroom, teenage daughter in one room and the last, a young boy maybe a year or so older than she.

The vampire in the master bedroom finishes with the mother, straightens up, and goes into the bathroom to clean up. Peyton steps out of the master bedroom a moment later and regards the child vampire with a quizzical brow.

"Feeling better, little one? We all thought maybe you mightn't wake up at all after the mermaid was done with you," she says in a condescending air but somehow manages to make the word mermaid sound vile and loathsome at the same time.

"Yes, I am. Although I am hungry."

"Aww, too bad we finished off this lot already or you could have had a little sip, baby." The vampire puts a hand on her hip and tosses her long blond hair over her shoulder. Her tone digs underneath Lynette's skin and burns her within. Lynette grits her teeth, but before she can spit out the verbal venom forming in her mouth, Affray steps between them.

"Not a problem. I've located some dinner nearby." He says this to Peyton before turning his back on her in dismissal. He waves to Lynette to follow him. "We'll see you back at the river," Affray adds absently as they descend the stairs. Lynette tries not to giggle as she senses Peyton's annoyance and heated glare directed at their backs.

She must admit that it is odd how different Affray is from his former self. Lynette had mixed feelings about him before because of his association with the witch. But now that he's free of her he seems to be a whole other person. A person she finds herself growing fond of. The realization is startling at first but now she's used to the idea. It's not like she can be choosy about her friends, and truly no one is perfect. Sure, he once loved the woman who ruined her life. He seems to have seen the error of his ways. She finds herself willing to forgive him for his past mistakes and accept him as family.

Lynette happily follows him down the street a few houses and into a brightly lit, white, ranch style home. With an aching belly, they cross the threshold and Lynette sees the occupancies of the home sitting stiffly in a row on the living room couch. Affray obviously zipped on over here first and compelled them into obedience before fetching Lynette. The realization makes her feel tingly, knowing that he had put that kind of effort into making sure she was fed. Trying to hide the strange mix of emotions playing within, Lynette puts on a show of nonchalance. She observes the feast before them.

This house wasn't occupied by a family but by a group of roommates — four college-age young men. Lynette turns a toothy smile on her friend and beams.

"This fits my usual taste, but what about you?"

"Oh, don't worry about me." Affray gestures towards the upstairs and Lynette listens closely to hear the heart beats of two personages above. "It looks like a couple of the frat boys had their girlfriends staying over." He smiles with self-satisfaction and heads up the stairs.

Once he's out of sight, Lynette hears screams from above. She smiles. Affray prefers his food scared and fighting for dear life. Lynette couldn't blame him. She kind of likes it that way, too.

Focusing all her attention on the four men awaiting her, she notes that Affray's compulsion over them is fading. Soon the young men will have their wits about them again. Although Lynette has managed a little compulsion now and then, her abilities are nowhere near Affray's level of talent. No two vampires are exactly alike. Yet neither of them is as impressive as the Witch Gwenevere with her entrancing spell. Upstairs the screams go momentarily silent. The men before her shake themselves and look about, confused, as if waking from a strange dream. One by one they come to realize her presence in the room.

"Hey, who the hell are you?" the oldest and biggest of the bunch asks as he rises to his feet in a threatening stance. He seems on the alert but unsure. After all, it's only a little girl standing before him not the man who knocked on their front door only moments before. He was genuinely confused since he couldn't remember what happened after. Some part of him was aware that danger was near.

"Human instincts to survive are strong," Luca had told her once. *"But the drive to feed will give you the strength to overpower them even though you are not as strong. Give into your thirst completely and it will take care of the rest. Your greatest weapon is the element of surprise, Lynette. Use it and you'll never go hungry."* It had been good advice as she had at first been terrified to attack her prey.

"We're going to play a game," Lynette informs the college boys standing before her with a sweet little smile. "You're going to tell me the worst thing you've ever done and I'm going to decide how you will die based off your answer."

The young man glares at her before turning to his friends, still sitting confused on the couch beside him. "Someone, get this kid out of here."

A crash shakes the ceiling above them. A young woman screams in fear. Her begging and pleading with Affray for her life is heard muffled from above. This sends all the young men into an absolute frenzy. The main guy turns toward the stairs as if to run to his girlfriend's rescue. One of the others follows him. The other two hurry toward her with angry looks in their eyes.

"Stop!" Lynette whizzes a head of the men at the foot of the stairs, blocking their path. Her sudden inhuman movement shocks the four young men. Stunned they turn their eyes on her all frozen in place, by disbelief and fear. Their horrified looks give her a sense of wicked glee. "Don't worry about the girls," Lynette instructs as she takes a step down the stairs, coming closer to her prey. "They won't be alive much longer, unless my friend decides to turn them into vampires, then…" She shrugs. "They'll most likely be Affray's new pets and won't care about any of you anymore. So, you might as well stay right here with me and have some fun before you die."

"What are you?" One of them asks, glancing at his companions who share the same ashen expression.

"A vampire obviously. Didn't you hear anything I just said?" Lynette scoffs.

Again, a woman screams from upstairs. This emboldens the largest of the men, the one closest to her to take action. He lunges toward her, his large hands prone to snatch. Like a spring Lynette vaults into the air. Even before he can register his surprise the large man's forward momentum tips him forward. His hands catch the stair Lynette was just perched on, saving his face from a nasty collision. Behind him, his roommate's shouts of dismay, catches his attention. He flips himself onto his back witnessing the young girl's descent. Soaring over the four of them she lands in the entryway.

The man closest to her acts swiftly, punching Lynette in the jaw mercilessly. The impact sends the child spawn flying backwards. Her back hits the front door. It jolts her, but immortal as she is, she feels no pain. She pushes off the door like a bouncy ball, ricocheting toward her attacker. He delivers a series of punches, Lynette either deflects or dodges. Two of his friends quickly join him in his assault. Lynette's brown curls bounce and sway around her field of vision as she maneuvers with inhuman speed. Twisting and uncoiling herself to strike one assailant while avoiding another. The constant onslaught would've worn out a mere mortal, but the child vampire keeps up with the fully-grown men's pace. Footsteps running up the stairs catches her notice.

The other one is getting away. Affray will never let me live this down if one slips by me.

The realization gives her a boost of adrenaline. With a guttural cry, Lynette kicks the legs out from under one man. Before he hits the floor, she lunges forward, narrowly missing a kick to the stomach from her first attacker. With her forward momentum she delivers a powerful thrust to the third man's nose, breaking it with a bloody crunch. The second man falls onto the floor wailing in pain clutching his injured face. Spinning around on her heel, she grabs the shirt front of the third man with her claws. Hurtling him a crossed the living room before the man can react. His cry of alarm ends abruptly as he collides with the flat screen television on the far wall. Breaking glass, and shattered bones accompany the chorus of curses from the other men lying at her feet. The college boy and the appliance crash to the floor in a mess of blood, circuits, and drywall. Although he might look it, the man isn't dead just yet.

The last man standing hits the upstairs landing and throws open the bedroom door. A second later small hands grasp around him around the middle. Finding himself flung off his feet and backward, he plummets down the stairs. He rolls to a stop at the bottom of the steps. His roomies providing cushioning for his fall.

With a leap the child spawn lands on the bottom step soundlessly as if a feather floating earthward on the wind. The moans and wails of the injured men before her subside as they one by one turn their gaze to look upon the child standing over them.

When Lynette turns her colorless gaze on the remaining three roommates, their faces look as white as her own. Each one motionless as a wax statue. Their thumping heart beats louder than

Lynette's own thoughts. Lynette gives them a wicked sneer leaning toward them. "Now who wants to spill their guts first?"

Her double meaning seems to have the desired effect. Eyes go wide and suddenly all three young men begin to confess their most horrible of deeds. Each one mortified and amazed at the words pouring out of their mouths.

Suddenly Lynette gets a wonderful awful little thought.

"What if instead of killing the worst of you, I turn him instead and kill the others?" She asks the question aloud, not caring for their thoughts on the matter one bit. Notwithstanding the obvious rhetorical nature of the question the men all begin to answer her with various pleas and supplications of mercy. "Silence!" the eight-year-old vampire commands and the young men obey. Their anger, their hate, their fear all revealed in their eyes whilst they find themselves helpless. "Yes." Lynette nods to herself, her chin rising and her shoulders square. "The vampire King mandated that we needed to turn more humans to grow our army, and I need a new family." She smiles at them as she looks between the four petrified men, with giddy anticipation. "But first I'm hungry…"

With that Lynette leaps upon the nearest man. Before he can even register the movement, she yanks him by the hair, bringing his head toward her level. The others scream and shout in horror as she tears into his neck with her razor-sharp fangs. As the blood oozes down her throat, and screams fill her ears, she formulates a new mission for her future. One that gives her freedom, protection, and power as the master of her own family. This time she would be the leader. She would be obeyed and respected, love and feared. This time she would be the maker.

Chapter Twenty-Three

Revelations

By the light of day Alcromech looks like a fairytale village, Gwen observes from the rooftop of the Black Iris. With her violin at her side, Gwen watches the rising sun cast its golden rays on the world around her. The water dividing the gathering post, glistens like a river of translucent fairy dust.

Few of the inhabitants are out at this hour. Only the hum of nature lingering in the air. Careful not to lose her footing on the slanted roof, Gwen faces the rising sun. She takes in a deep breath of clean mountain air. Exhaling she sets Angelo's violin under her chin and begins to play.

Her passionate melody glides across wind, filling the morning with its sweet voice. Gwen closes her eyes as she continues to play, letting her fingers do their work while she lets her mind work out her troubles.

The dream still haunts her even by the light of day. She had learned so much, yet still she feels no closer to knowing her own identity. Nor was the mystery surrounding the boy who guards her dream world, solved. She can't fathom why he has chosen to be her protector. *Especially now that I know his mother killed mine and tried to kill me as well. She's the one he's been hiding me from, the reason he's always told me to stay away from this world.* Gwen continues to play, her song growing in vigor.

Even without the mysteries of her past, she has plenty to worry about here in the present. Last night when she awoke from her nightmares, she slipped out of her room to sneak down to see Raven. Instead of sharing a room with Jonah and Thayer, he had managed to convince the Mistress of the House to let him stay in a storage room with some blankets and a pillow for a bed. Gwen crept easily to the back of the boarding house and knocked on his door. She needed to talk about her dream, and she had realized, belatedly, that she hadn't seen Raven since before she went to bed.

He took the heritage test at the Tribal Populace Office yesterday, too. Maybe his test worked. Maybe he has gotten some answers. Gwen had been so caught up in trying to find Morna. When that had failed, she had been swept up in the excitement of getting to know more about her own kind and spending alone time with Jonah that she completely forgot about Raven. The guilt had been half her motivation for knocking on his door in the middle of the night. Although she could feel his mind wide awake within the storeroom he never came to the door. Even when she whispered his name and sang a silly song through the keyhole, he did not reply. He had laughed at the song in his mind, but it did nothing to dispel the shroud of melancholy he was under. At last, he never spoke to her, not even mentally. Shut out both physically and figuratively, Gwen had finally gone to bed feeling even more culpable.

Tossing and turning the rest of the night, she frequently arose from her bed to stand at the open window. Mentally, Gwen shouted Morna's name into the night along with several colorful expletives about naughty little sprites. Alas, this hadn't made her Fae friend reappear. Eventually, she went back to bed to wrestle with anxiety once more. Finally, the dawn crept up from behind the mountains, the sky growing light. Careful not to wake Leona. who lay fast asleep, Gwen had quickly slipped out of bed. Grabbing Angelo's violin, she headed to the roof for her morning routine, and some much-needed musical meditation.

Now as the last notes of her song play out on the strings, Gwen contemplates all the information she has gleaned from Jonah the night before. Jonah had dropped a few bombs on her. First, he announced that he was a servant in his friend's home and a lower-class citizen in the Wiccan society. Then, he all but declared he loved her in his mind. Of course, he isn't aware she could hear his thoughts, but still his words and body language had suggested as much. Then the image of the redheaded girl in his memories had made him so conflicted. A strange sensation stirs within her even now. She sees a whirl of green and red in her mind, with heat and anger in her belly. Then, lastly, he had made it clear to Gwen that she was in no way safe in the Wiccan world. *I'm nameless, I have no circle.* To be without a family name or house of her own, even as a servant she was like a bum, dirt of the earth to her own people.

I've been there and done that before. No big deal. History repeating itself as always.

Her song finally done, Gwen takes a deep breath and releases the last note of the violin's string. She opens her eyes to see a black bird circling above her. It caws down at her in greeting.

"Long time no see," she calls up to the raven companionably. "It is you, isn't it?" The bird answers with a cry. *Is that a yes or a, no?* "I hope you're here as a sign of good fortune, because I've had all the bad luck and ill omens I can handle for a lifetime." The raven caws at her twice more before flying off into the distance, the sensation of comfort and wellbeing leaving with his presence. "One of these days I've got to figure out what the hell is up with that bird." She mumbles to herself.

The sound of whistling jolts her. Startled, she almost loses her footing on the slanted roof. Once recovered, Gwen spots Raven below her hanging halfway out of the attic window. He holds onto the windowsill to keep from falling down the deep, sloping roof.

"Well, good morning." Gwen stows the violin and bow away in their leather case and clamps it shut. With the case in one hand, she gingerly picks her way over the roof toward him. "Did you hear me playing or am I just that predictable that you knew right where to find me?"

"It's dawn. Where else would you be but out on a rooftop or balcony playing?" Raven shrugs, his black hair hanging loosely around his shoulders. Sleep still lingers in his golden eyes. Gwen slides slowly down on her bum to the edge of the window. She hands him the violin case and he sets it inside. He then takes her hand, pulling her back into the boardinghouse. Her gold locket slips out of its hiding place beneath her shirt, gleaming in the sunlight. "Predictable doesn't cut it. This playing to the sun thing has become a regular habit with you."

"It's just my little way of remembering him, that's all," Gwen replies with a quiet smile as she nonchalantly stows her locket away inside the neckline of her black tank top.

Raven's eyes meet hers. A tumult of emotions whirls within his eyes. An indescribable kind of tension impregnates the air between them, leaving Gwen itching to slip behind his mental barriers and find the cause of it. *You promised, Gwen, remember? You won't cross into his inner thoughts without an invitation ever again. A lot has changed over the past several years. Neither of us are children anymore,* she scolds herself.

"What do you wildings think you're doing?" a loud booming voice demands as the sound of stomping feet shakes the floor. Startled, Gwen and Raven step away from the window. Emerging from the door into the attic, a very spherical woman stalks toward them. Mistress Subree, the proprietor of the establishment, has pink and yellow eyes that set off her rosy cheeks yet contrast her chestnut-brown hair done up in a bun. With impressive speed for a woman of her girth, she crosses the room to confront the two of them. "No one is allowed up here, or on the roof, you miscreants!" the innkeeper announces indignantly.

"Our apologies, Mistress, we didn't know," Gwen chirps with forced sincerity and humility. Retrieving her violin case with one hand, Gwen grabs Raven's sleeve with the other and leads him quickly passed the fuming matron and out of the attic. Gwen tries to contain the mirth bubbling inside of her. She glances at Raven as they hurry down the stairs.

"You miscreants!" he mocks Mistress Subree's voice.

Gwen erupts into a peel of laughter. "Wildings!"

Raven smiles.

On their way downstairs Gwen stops by her room. Quietly she slips inside a moment depositing the violin case on her bed. Leona is still sound asleep. She snores softly, her dark blonde hair splayed across her pillowcase. Gwen slips back outside suppressing a giggle. Together she and Raven descend downstairs to the first floor.

Breathless and laughing, they enter the empty common room. They pass a very ornate floor-to-ceiling mirror. Next to the stairs is the front desk that takes up the whole wall. For a Wiccan boardinghouse, the registry desk looks basically the same as any human hotel. Keys hang on hooks; cubbies line the back wall for mail and packages sent to the guest of the establishment. *They even have a registry book like an old-fashioned hotel,* Gwen notes to herself. No one sits behind the desk as the two youths pass by. Across from the staircase is the front door on a wall of tall windows. The early morning sunshine filling the room with warmth and light. In front of the windows reside benches and several round wooden tables. They seem to grow right out of the floor. Chairs made of bent twigs, nothing binding them together but its desire to take that shape encircle them. Gwen notices that the glass in the windows seems somehow wild instead of manmade, with swirling patterns in the surface of the glass, reflecting on the polished wood floors. On the far wall a large hearth with a strange glowing fire that changes colors burns within. No wood fuels the flames. It just hovers in the hearth like something out of dark dream, a predator waiting to strike any that come near it. Gwen glances towards the buffet table by the kitchen door, nothing. *Breakfast isn't served just yet.* She remarks to her friend mentally.

"So, are you going to tell me what happened at the Populace Office last night? I'm dying to find out your real last name!" Gwen asks as she drops down in a chair. She swings her legs up onto the tabletop to rest, leaning back to give Raven an expectant look.

"Well…" Raven hesitates a moment, looking around as if to be sure no one else is coming. He takes the chair opposite her, spinning it around he sits in it backward. "My last name is Mahiigan," he announces in his deep molasses voice. Gwen's eyebrows raise at this, but she says nothing. She gestures for him to continue. "And the test…" Raven clears his throat and continues, "…said that my father was a Werewolf, and my mother is human," he replies hesitantly.

"Was? That means he's no longer living?" Gwen inquires.

"Yes. He passed away before I was born," Raven admits as though the words cost him dearly, but he goes on. "His name was Jacy Mahiigan, and he was a Native American, a descendant of the Mohawk tribe."

"So, you're part Native American? That would explain a lot." Gwen lets her legs slide off the table. Sitting up, she leans closer to him and squints up at him. "Come to think of it, I can see it in your face." She smiles.

"Really?" Raven seems calmer now and tries to smile back "Well, that's only the one half of the family tree. Wait till you hear about my mother." Restlessly, Raven gets up and starts pacing back and forth before the front desk, deep in thought.

"Don't leave me in suspense. Let's hear it." Gwen watches him curiously, trying to read his body language as an alternative to reading his mind. *He's nervous and a little upset, perhaps even angry.* "What's your mom's name?"

"Her name is Chandrankanta Hebbar." Gwen's eyebrows shoot up into her hairline at this and Raven laughs before going on. "She's from India. Apparently, her family immigrated awhile back so technically she's an Indian American, too."

Gwen busts up laughing. With a big grin on her face she announces, "So you're a double Indian!" She laughs again, her voice bouncing off the walls of the common room.

"I thought you would like that," Raven admits, a smile playing at the corner of his mouth.

"Oh, I don't like it. I love it! I can't imagine a cooler combination than that."

"Thank you. I think."

"So, this mother of yours, Chan-na-drak-something, is still alive?" Gwen asks folding her legs beneath the chair.

"Yes, as far as anyone here knows anyway. The Populace Agent said that my father's family might have more information on her." Raven walks over to a bench resting against the window to sit. "Maybe even an address." He looks down at his hands for a moment.

"You don't seem to be happy about this." Gwen slides off her chair and crosses the room to stand before him. "Raven?" When he does not look up, she grips his chin with her thumb and index finger. Gently she raises his face to look at her. She sees a tumult of emotions twirling within his golden eyes. She gives him a sympathetic smile. "You were hoping she was dead, too, weren't you? Is that what's troubling you?"

"It sounds kind of awful but, yes." He lets out a long sigh, leaning back against the wall of glass behind him. "The nuns always said they thought it was my mother who dropped me off at the orphanage. They said she looked like me, same skin, same features, but not the yellow eyes." Gwen nods at this, getting the reference. "I kind of hoped they were mistaken and perhaps she had died in childbirth. That she hadn't been the one to give me away." Closing his eyes tight, he hunches over, cupping his face in his large hands.

"What do I do? Should I find her? Would she even care to know who I have become or that I'm still alive? Did she ever care about me at all?"

The sun-drenched bench feels warm through the fabric of her jeans as Gwen sits down beside him. She reaches a handout and rubs his back in a circular motion.

"I know after all this time it still hurts, and it's a wound that will never heal. The rot just spreads darker and deeper." Gwen feels her heartbeat quicken as her own misery begins to engulf her. "I understand what you've gone through better than anyone," she adds in a dark whisper.

"Gwen, your mother didn't abandon you. She died." Raven gets up from the bench and stands, looking down at Gwen.

"She was taken from me." Gwen looks up at him with wrath smoldering in her green eyes. "And my father wasn't there when we needed him." Gwen grips the bench tightly as she closes her eyes and envisions the dream, and the woman with the violet eyes and the house in the middle of the woods. "And she paid the price, we both did. None of it would've happened if he'd been there when she—"

"But Gwen…" Raven grabs her by the shoulders, making her stand up from the bench and look at him. "If it hadn't happened, you would've never come to St. Paul's, we never would've met. I can't image my life without you in it." Gwen is overcome by the feeling in his voice. She is speechless. "At least you know your mother loved you."

"You don't know that your mother didn't." Gwen brushes a strand of his long black hair that had fallen into his eyes, back behind his ear. Placing her hand on his cheek, she continues, "And even if she didn't, or doesn't; does it really matter now? I love you. Morna loves—"

"Gwen." He cuts her off. Something like hope flashes behind his eyes and Raven pulls her in close to him. "It doesn't matter as long as I have you. Do you think that we could be more…?"

The sound of shoes slapping on the floor, and two male voices breaks into their reverie. Startled, Gwen and Raven look up to see Jonah and Thayer walk into the common room and stop abruptly at the sight of them. Thayer takes one look at the two of them embracing and turns his gaze toward his friend. Jonah stares at them as if he's as seeing them for the first time in his life.

"Hey, there you are!" Quickly Gwen steps away from Raven, his arms falling away from her without resistance. She smiles nervously at everyone and bounces across the room toward Jonah and Thayer with a bright toothy smile on her face. "So, what do you have in store for us today?"

"Ah, have you decided you like captivity? Decided to befriend the enemy?" Thayer jokes, a playful light in his lime green eyes.

"Yeah, sure, whatever. Keep your friends close but your enemies closer I always say." Gwen jokes back with a wave of her hand. "I'm stuck here. I might as well make the best of it, until I find a chance to slip away."

"Yeah, that's not likely but I admire your spirit. Anyhow, we have to get a few things before we meet up with the other Wiccans in Alcromech. We'll be traveling all together to the different Covens in a week." Thayer hesitates a moment to see if Jonah will say anything but clearly Jonah is still processing something. He looks at Gwen, blank-faced. "You'll need to get some appropriate Wiccan clothing."

At this Gwen notices that they've changed from their human street clothes and are now attired in what she assumed Thayer means by appropriate Wiccan clothes. Their pants have a leathery texture to them but have no seams or stitching anywhere. *I bet they make Wiccan clothes with magic, hence no need for needle and thread,* Gwen observes to herself. Although their pants appear to be made of the same material, that is where the similarity in their clothing ends.

"I see. Nice clothes."

"You like?" Thayer does a slow spin to show off his outfit. Thayer's pants are black, and his shirt is black with green swirling designs that look like a ram's head. Silver buttons trail up the front, leading up to a Mandarin collar. Over that Thayer wears a long flowing green jacket of an almost transparent cloth with a symbol magically embossed in full color: a ram's head. The symbol is on both shoulders and upon the front left side of his chest.

"Yes, I do. It's a cross between something modern and something medieval."

"Yes, my sister will take you shopping," Jonah adds suddenly as if just realizing what they are discussing. He shakes his head as if to dispel a haze. "I mean, Leona will take you shopping. You will go shopping with her for clothes. Right?" He corrects himself, flustered.

"Okay, if she ever wakes up, that is," Gwen replies, wanting desperately to invade Jonah's private thoughts but half-afraid of what she will discover.

"Leona's always been a late riser," Thayer replies. "It takes the bed catching on fire before she'll get up." He smirks.

"Huh." Gwen responds as she studies Jonah's attire. *His clothes are clearly of a lower quality than Thayer's,* she notes. His pants are brown, his shirt cream-colored with a distressed, old look about it. It too buttons up the front, his collar simple and curved about his neck. On each shoulder the symbol of a crane standing over an egg is etched in orange and white. Over his shirt he wears a brown, leathery vest which matches his pants.

"Hey, Jonah, do a spin. Show her the back of the vest," Thayer jovially instructs, noticing Gwen's appraisal.

Jonah does as commanded and turns around. There, a symbol identical to the one on the back of Thayer's jacket, is embossed but with fewer colors. He spins back around to face her, a look halfway between pride and shame on his face.

"I wear my own crest on my shirt, but the vest is a symbol of the house I serve under," Jonah explains. His eyes meet Gwen's, and she knows he can see the displeasure in her eyes. The word slave sticks in her mind like a dam in her the flow of her thoughts.

"So, the Crayborn crest is a Crane, huh?" Gwen steps up to Jonah; reaching out a hand she traces the lines of the symbol on his shoulder with her index finger. "It's an elegant and proud bird," she comments, her voice a little rough as she adds, looking into his perfect aqua eyes, "It's beautiful."

"Yeah, yeah, your clothes are pretty neat." Raven's voice speaks from just behind her left shoulder, startling Gwen. She drops her hand from Jonah's shoulder. She turns to look at Raven. Their eyes meet only briefly but it is enough to know that he is disgruntle. His brow furrowed; he glares at Jonah. "Well, don't let us keep you," he adds. "Don't you have errands to run?"

Thayer squints at him, perturbed. Jonah opens his mouth to speak.

"Hello, children. Breakfast served yet?" Aunt Nicola steps out of the hall and into the room. Jonah clamps his mouth shut and bows his head in difference. She crosses the room to stand next to her nephew.

"Afraid not, Aunt." The ginger head boy response.

Nicola's clothes are a notch more extravagant, then the wiccan boys. She is adorned in a massive multi-layered, rainbow-colored cloak of shimmering material. Underneath she wears a white high neck dress that fits her curvy frame in a way that flatters without seeming clingy. Its fabric rivals the finest silk. The same ram heads design stitched upon the back. She wears white boots that come up just above her ankle. *Those are very distinctly witchy-looking boots.* Both Blackwools wear a gold-chained necklace with a large medallion of their family crest on it, and gold rings with a completely different symbol over a gemstone on their right ring fingers. The sight of the rings reminds her of the vision she had of her father in her dreams last night.

"Just curious. What do your rings symbolize? Their symbol is different from your necklace and clothes?" Gwen asks, directing her question to Aunt Nicola.

"Oh, that!" Thayer steps closer to Gwen and extends his hand to show her his ring more closely as he speaks, "We wear the medallion of our father's family, and we wear the ring of our mother's family." Upon closer inspection, Gwen notices that the symbol is of a starfish set over an opal stone.

"So, the starfish is for your Mermaid mother's family?" Gwen asks.

Aunt Nicola looks taken aback a moment while Thayer just smiles and looks at Jonah, who smirks back and shrugs his shoulders in response.

"Yes, that's right, child. My little brother married himself a maiden of the sea," Aunt Nicola confirms. "Although there were plenty of good Wiccan woman to be had, he would have no other than Glendene."

Outwardly Thayer glances at his aunt, a look of annoyance in his eyes, his lips pursed tightly. The look pulls Gwen inside his thoughts before she can stop herself.

That's my mother your slighting, Aunt. Nothing's wrong with having a Mer for a mum, he thinks defensively. *Just hold your tongue. She'll preach to you the importance of bloodlines again,* Thayer instructs himself. Gwen listens in on his thoughts, staying as quiet in her own mind as possible so that he does not notice her intrusion.

I wonder if telepathy is a common gift among Wiccans. Thayer's lack of mental barriers suggest that her talent is as rare as she is. Although, Emon the elf who tutored her in Bec LaNuff had not been surprised to learn she had the gift. Her first great love, Angelo, a Vampire, had been telepathic as well. *Perhaps telepathy isn't very common, but it certainly isn't exclusive to my kind.*

"I understand I need to get myself some of these fancy clothes, too?" Gwen changes the subject.

"Why, of course. We can't present you to the Thirteen Elders of the Coven looking like some ... well, like a normal teenage human girl," Nicola finishes. Gwen hears the insults in the lady's mind, words like Eden spawn and mortal born, thought with a distasteful air.

Realizing that she is still in telepath mode Gwen shuts off the connection, retreating to her own thoughts. *Careful, Gwen, one slip and everyone will know. Remember what your guardian angel said?*

"What, they don't like tank tops and blue jeans?" Gwen jests, looking down at her own clothing. "I think I look pretty good in them." Jonah and Thayer start to speak, but their words die out. When Gwen looks at Aunt Nicola again, she does not look amused.

A shuffling of feat announces the entrance of a serving girl. The sound and the aroma wafting from the platter of sausage links, and bacon draws the groups attention. Another servant, a tall skinny, dark haired young man follows behind her. Then another serving girl after him. Each caring their own platter of breakfast comestibles.

The youths all move as if to rush towards the buffet table to ravage the breakfast dishes even whilst in the servant's arms. In a flash of rainbow colors, Nicola cuts off the lot of them. Calmly she leads them toward one of the tables. Naturally, Thayer and Jonah fall instep behind her. Their deference for the older witch evident in their every muscle.

An incredulous look passes between Gwen and Raven, along with a flurry of memories from their long sordid history with authority figures. Rolling her eyes in the other's direction, Raven responds with a silent chuckle. Trying to school his face, he ushers her after the others.

When they approach the table Gwen remains standing. Raven takes this cue from her and waits beside her. He folds his arms over his chest patiently. The moment the servants retreat into the kitchen, Raven and Gwen move with one mind toward the food. Gwen retrieves the two of them plates from a serving table. Quickly the two runaways pile their plates and begin eating as they walk toward the fireplace, side by side.

"Ahem!" Nicola's voice draws their attention. The two stop and glance at their table. The middle-aged Witch gives them a stern look.

Then she gives a curt nod to the two young men beside her. Thayer and Jonah bounce out of their chairs as if released from a frigid spell.

Thayer makes himself a plate and returns to the table to dig into his food. His aunt shoots him a disapproving look. Reveling in the ecstasy of his meal, Thayer is incognizant.

Meanwhile Jonah dishes up food and brings a plate to Nicola. He waits, by her side watching her adamantly. She scans her plate giving him a formal nod of approval. With that Jonah returns to the buffet to get his own breakfast. Returning to the table Jonah eats in a passive manner.

Nicola returns her cold gaze on Raven and Gwen once more. She makes a curt nod of her head to the vacant chairs at their table. Her meaning is clear, yet Gwen ignores it and leads Raven over to stand before the hearth. The warmth from the magical floating fire soothing to the bones. The two woman's eyes meet again. This time Nicola points at them, then the empty chairs.

"Come sit with us children." Her voice cherry and bright. Her eyes cold with indignation.

Unflinching Gwen stuffs a piece of bacon into her mouth chewing slowly.

Nicola's smile melts into a stiff line, her jaw set like stone. In the same instant her aura ignites, forming around her auburn crown. A lightning storm of vibrant colors.

Am I really the only one that can see that? Gwen asks herself. The pleasant chatter of additional guest entering the common room dispels some of the air of feminine contention. A tension Gwen hadn't realized was present alleviates her stomach.

Is something wrong? She feels Raven open his mind to her just before sending the thought. *Don't get me wrong, I don't want to share a table with the lot of them either but… that is not the only reason you're standing in protest, is it?*

Gwen sighs and turns her back on the others to gaze into the fire. She feels the double sensation of two sets of penetrating eyes on her skin. One set, Raven's as he awaits her response. The second, Nicola boring holds into the back of her head. Oddly, the heat of the fire pales in comparison to the latter.

That boy Jonah, you know the blond one? Raven acknowledges his understanding through their bond, Gwen forces herself on. *Well, last night was not the first time I've seen him sense that run in we had with them after the show.*

What does that mean, Gwen? Confusion turns Raven's eyebrows into one dark line.

We've been…dreaming together. She admits mentally.

Raven's eyebrows disappear into his hair line and his eyes go wide. *Explain. Please.*

So, you know how I've been having all those dreams in the meadow and the white kingdom with the blond-haired boy…

Are you saying Jonah is the boy from your dreams you've been seeing since your childhood? Raven interjects mentally in disbelief.

"No, no." Gwen says aloud. She takes a deep breath before continuing. "No, that boy is someone else altogether." In a quick procession of images, Gwen relays last night's dream through their mental connection.

"Oh. Wow." Raven shakes his head as if to dispel the images from his mind. "Well, I have a hundred questions about this "Dream Guardian" of yours, but that can wait." He stares into the fire thoughtfully a moment. "What does this have to do with Jonah?"

"When I fell asleep on the night, we first met Jonah, I dreamt of him. Only it wasn't just a dream. He was there in my head, or I should say I was in his head." Gwen glances over at the others before continuing. "I had unknowingly entered his dreams and was controlling the dream itself. Jonah realized it and told me I was a Dreamwalker."

"Is this common with witches?" Raven asks.

"I don't know. But I gather it's frowned upon."

Hmmm...and this kept happening? Gwen nods.

The first time was an accident, but I kept doing it because...

Because you like him. Raven interjects.

I do. Gwen gives a weak laugh. *Or at least I did until he sent his crazy aunt after me.*

How did he know who you were or where to find us? I thought you said you had erased us from all their memories.

Apparently, Aunt Nicola could sense that something was wrong and used a counter spell to bring those memories back.

Raven glances up and a strange look crosses his face. *Jonah is coming this way.*

Gwen straightens up as she watches her former dream boy approach.

"Gwen, Raven. Follow me please." Jonah speaks formally turning on his heel.

The two friends follow, depositing their empty plates into a bin at the end of the buffet table. Gwen's sees a flash of light in the corner of her eye. Glancing over her shoulder she witnesses as another flash of light emits from the dirty dish bin. Their two plates, now sparkling clean, float out of the bin. They land softly on the pile of dishes stacked at the end of the buffet table. *Now that is a neat trick.*

Abruptly Gwen collides with Raven, not realizing that he had stopped walking. Gwen waves off Raven's concerned looks with a blush in her cheeks. He relaxes and his shoulders returning his attention to the others.

To her surprise, they had met up with Thayer and his aunt back at the receptionist desk. *I didn't hear them get up from their table. You need to be on full alert here Gwen.* She chastises herself. *You don't have the luxury of exploring this strange new place.*

"Can you lads give us a moment alone? I need to have a word with Gwenevere."

"Of course, aunt." Jonah and Thayer seem to reply in unison. Raven opens his mouth to object, but the older witch's heated glower silences him. Gwen gives him a reassuring smile and with that he follows the other teen boys to wait by the front door.

"Look, child. The Forsaken do things a certain way. There is little tolerance for subordinance here. You are not in the unruly world of humans any longer. Ye better reconcile yourself to it." Nicola takes a breath. Most of her agitation escapes as she exhales. "Just do what I say to do. Keep your sarcastic remarks to yourself and dress how I tell you. Then we'll get along just fine, lassie."

With a stiff jaw and yellow pallor, Gwen opens her mouth to speak. Nicola turns on her heal, darting towards the group of young men. Effectively dismissing Gwen out right.

"Now you, young wolf, need to come with me" Nicola waves a finger at Raven in authority. "There are others of your kind here and you must find some from your father's pack to join with on your journey. Go on, boy, and fetch your belongings so we can get on with it." She shoos him away with a gesture.

"I'm leaving right now?" Raven looks alarmed. "Can't I say goodbye to Gwen? We haven't found Morna yet. I can't leave without at least knowing she's safe." He turns to Gwen for help.

"Jonah says she can't leave Alcromech, plus I know she would want to see us before we leave." Gwen joins the others, her gaze never once falling on Nicola. "She's going to turn up soon, I'm certain." Gwen attempts to assuage him, despite the unsettling feeling resting in her own stomach.

"Even so, we can't wait around here for the Fairy to show herself. You sir are a Were, not a Witch. So, we be moving ye on over to wolf lodging straight away. You can visit your witch and the fairy whenever she pops back up later." Raven goes to protests but

Nicola cuts him off. "In a week, the trading post will shut down completely and all travelers need be to their destination by then. Ye needs to have made arrangement with your kind to go and meet your real pack, ye kin, lad?" Nicola registers the distress in Raven's face. "You're very devoted to this girl and that Fairy, aren't you, boy?"

"Yes. Gwen's been my only family for over twelve years, and Morna, well ... she saved my life more than once." He hesitates a moment, looking back to Gwen. "I don't suppose I can stay with Gwen and come with you to your Coven, can I? Perhaps as a special circumstance?"

"No, boy, it's not possible." Aunt Nicola shakes her head. Raven looks visibly crestfallen at this. Aunt Nicola moves away from the Wiccan boys to take Raven by the arm and lead him away. "I promise you'll have a chance to say a proper goodbye to your wee woman here before ye depart."

Raven looks over his shoulder at Gwen as Nicola pushes him gently toward the stairs. Reluctantly, he peels his gaze away. Disappearing down the hallway.

"Now off with you two. I sent you off with a list of supplies and yet you're still here, gawking at the lassie. Move it along, boys, we haven't time to waste today!" This jolts Thayer and Jonah into action. They both give Gwen a quick bow before they pass her on their way to the door. Jonah opens the door with a spell for Thayer and the redheaded teen exits the boardinghouse with a strut befitting his station. Before Jonah follows his friend and master, he looks back to Gwen. The misery and longing on his face, unmistakable.

"Ahem." Aunt Nicola clears her throat. Jonah jumps and hurries out of the Black Iris to catch up with Thayer, who waits for him on the steps beyond.

Gwen can't help but sigh when he leaves. Turns around she finds herself face to face with Aunt Nicola, who watches her with a curious look.

"Don't think I don't see what's happening betwixt the two of you." She nods toward the door. "All while the other one pines after you like a lovesick pup." The middle-aged woman shakes her auburn head in disgust.

"What on earth are you talking about? What other one?"

"I can see the stars in your eyes, girl." Aunt Nicola crosses the gap between them taking Gwen's hand in hers. Gwen bulks at the contact but forces herself not to pull away from the older woman. "He's a fine lad for sure. I'm terribly fond of Jonah myself. Although you're a wild thing, and I don't just mean you being untrained in the craft, child, I like you. You've got a loyal and courageous heart. I can see it. But you can't make that boy break with his parents' wishes and turn him away from his betrothed. It would only hurt you both in the end."

"His what?" Gwen is cold in her core and still as a statue. Her mind tries to compute all the lady's words but finds her heart won't, can't understand them.

"Oh, you didn't know. He hasn't told you?" Sympathy shows through Aunt Nicola's eyes with understanding as well as surprise and displeasure. "It's not like Jonah to keep the truth from one or to tell a right-out lie. Perhaps he genuinely cares for you, child?" Nicola sighs heavily. "None the less, he'll do what's expected of him."

"Who is she?" Gwen asks, the numbness inside beginning to thaw into a white-hot wrath. She finds herself gripping Aunt Nicola's hand tightly.

"Isla Blackwool, Thayer's younger sister." Aunt Nicola looks down at their joined hands, visibly in pain from the strain of Gwen's grip. "And Thayer is betrothed to Leona. The Crayborns and Blackwools have long been close. It was the great wish of Jonah's parents that their children would become part of our family and with marriage raise their social standings."

"I see." Gwen releases Aunt Nicola's hand and takes a step back. "So, it's an arranged marriage of convenience. He doesn't love her, right?" Gwen looks to the other woman for reassurance, not sure why it would matter if he's lost to her anyway. Still, some part of her needed the answer to be "No."

"I don't know, child. They've grown up under the same roof. Have always known they would be bound as husband and wife." Gwen can see sincere sympathy in her eyes. "You're a striking beauty, and you do seem to get on well with one another. But I'm sorry, dear, it just cannot be."

Before Gwen can respond, Raven comes stomping into the room with his duffle bag slung over his shoulder, dressed head to toe in black with a black leather jacket completing the stereotypical biker look. He takes one look at the two women and goes still, sensing distress. "What's wrong? Gwen, are you okay?" He drops his bag by her feet and takes her by the shoulders to look down into her face. "Did something happen to Morna?"

"Oh, no, it's nothing really. We were just talking about..." Gwen looks to Aunt Nicola for help.

"How things will be inside the Coven. Nothing dire has befallen your Fairy, lad," she reassures in her Irish lilt.

"Oh. Well, good." Raven relaxes visibly but his large hands still cling to Gwen's shoulders. He curls her in under one arm, hugging her to his side. "Well, should we go, then? Are we still waiting for Leona?"

"Aye. I nearly forgot that little snippet is still snoozing." Aunt Nicola slaps her hands together for emphasis. "I'll get her and be out directly. If you like, you can go on without us. We'll meet you on the other side of the river, by the Tribunal Populace Center," Aunt Nicola instructs before bounding across the room and up the stairs to hunt down her absent niece.

A moment later, Madam Subree appears at the bottom of the steps, and upon seeing the two of them standing there, gives them a sour look. "You be checking out today?" she asks as she slides behind the registry counter.

"No, ma'am. Our whole group is staying another week at least," Gwen replies with forced politeness, her chest still tight and her mind reeling from her conversation with Aunt Nicola.

"Hmph. I don't like it. You two smell of trouble." She points at them with a bouncing finger then taps the side of her nose. "I can smell the troublemakers and you two reek of it."

Gwen looks up at Raven, who returns her look of bewilderment. Simultaneously, Gwen smells his shirt while he smells her hair, sniffing in an exaggerated manner.

"Sheesh! Gwen, you smell like a stale grandma." He pretends to recoil from her in disgust.

"Yuck! She's right. You smell like bad Indian food!" Gwen proclaims, and Raven rolls his eyes at her as Gwen laughs at her own stupid joke.

"Come on, let's get out of here. We need to talk." Again, he puts an arm around her shoulder and together they walk out of the boardinghouse with the mistress of the place glaring at their backs. As they take their steps side by side, Gwen tries to keep her mind in the present and listen to Raven instead of dwelling on certain painful revelations.

Chapter Twenty-Four

Friend or Foe

"Gwen? Gwen?" With a jolt she rousers herself, finding Raven's hand pressing gently on her shoulder. The sounds and sights of the world around her breakthrough as if reviving Gwen from a trance. People chattering in the true tongue mingles with the laughter of a pack of children playing. All hailing from various tribes, the children dart between the shops, giggling and shouting, as they play some form of tag.

Raven's shadow envelopes her, like a protective barrier between her and the world. He lets his hand fall from Gwen's shoulder, yet his brow remains furrowed. They wait outside the Tribal Populace office. A growing stream of supernatural beings weave around them, the two friends the solid rock in the tide of uncertainty. "You, okay? Have you heard anything I've said?"

"Of course," Gwen shrugs. "You were talking about how we're growing up. You mentioned my birthday. "You're not a kid anymore." You said and there was something about letting go of the past, moving on and redefining relationships." Gwen pauses to read his expression. *Uncertain, hopeful, disappointed, and annoyed? Hmmmmm.* "That was the gist of it, right?"

"Close enough." Raven mutters in a beleaguered breath. He looks away a moment as if looking for inspiration from an unknown source. When he returns his gaze on her once more, an alien look plays at his features. Deep rooted emotions writhe within, trapped behind his quiet demeanor and his large golden-iridescent eyes.

What is agitating you so much? Gwen percolates privately. Unwilling to ask aloud or dig for answers within Raven's psyche. He seems both excited and frightened. *Perhaps it's just the fact that we'll be separating for a time and he's worried about me and concerned for Morna. Yet excited to meet his father's family?*

"Look Gwen there's something I need to tell you. Something I should've said a long time ago but-" He starts to stammer before taking a deep breath. He straightens his posture, as if bracing himself for impact. "Gwen I Lo…."

"Here we are at last," Aunt Nicola calls out. Gwen starts a little turning to watch them approach. Leona trails closely behind her adopted aunt with a sleepy yet annoyed grimace.

Raven gives a deep low grown, closing his eyes and cursing under his breath in English.

"Perfect timing." Raven notes in a polite air, all be it through a forced grin.

"Good morning, Leona." Gwen supplies.

"Good morning to you," the short blonde Witch answers back civilly. She looks Gwen up and down with a look halfway between distain and envy. "We've got some shopping to do," Leona informs her with a sigh. Gwen in turn looks over Leona's attire.

Beneath a feminine version of the brown wiccan servant vest, she wears a short dress/tunic in cream with the Crayborn family crest embossed on the shoulders of her three-quarter length sleeves. Underneath her tunic she wears brown leathery leggings, with a brown version of the same Witch boots Nicola wears. Like Jonah, Leona wears no jewelry. Her long blonde hair is done in a simple long braid slung over one of her slender shoulders.

"Yes, yes, away with you two." Aunt Nicola spins Gwen and Leona around and gently pushes them down the street. "Now, Raven, you come with me. We have some Werewolves that are looking to make your acquaintance."

Reluctantly, Raven lets the older woman hook an arm though his and lead him down a side street and onward to another part of town. Gwen watches them go with some jealousy. *I'd much rather go meet up with Werewolves than go clothes shopping with Leona any day.*

"Come on, the dressmaker shops are this way." Leona waves a hand toward the other end of the Main Street of the township. As she turns to go, Gwen sees Thayer's family crest on the back of her vest just like Jonah's clothing. She confidently walks onward, the Blackwool crest on her back like a talisman. *Maybe because she knows it'll be her family crest someday. Then she'll dress like Thayer, wearing his family's medallion and her father's ring.*

"Dressmakers?" Gwen bulks. "Please tell me that I'm not required to always wear a dress in the Coven. I was hoping pants might be involved at least some of the time." Stuffing her hands into her jean's pockets Gwen falls in step beside the shorter girl.

"You will wear dresses mostly, but leggings are allowed beneath your frocks. On special occasions you will be permitted to wear pants." Leona eyeballs Gwen's jeans and sneakers with obvious envy. "However, there are only two kinds of shoes permitted for Wiccan woman to wear and neither one is a sneaker."

"Well, I'm not getting rid of my Converse. I'll just stow them away until all this Vampire nonsense is over."

"Nonsense, you call it?" Leona shakes her head with an exasperated sigh. "One can only hope it'll end soon, but if you knew anything about Vampires, you'd know that they will never back down. If they can't win a fight they'll die trying."

"I know quite a bit about Vampires, actually. Probably more than you ever will know," she adds and can't help smirking when Leona gives her a glare in response.

"I doubt it!" the little Witch grumbles.

They pass several shops of various kinds as well as a fresh food market. Gwen enjoys the heat of the morning sun on her bare shoulders, relishing what she realizes may be her last time in human clothes for the unforeseeable future. On the streets the pedestrian traffic is beginning to thicken as more of the Trading Posts inhabitants and visitors come out to get provisions for their journeys. Gwen's black razor-back tank top, blue jeans, and black converse sneakers gain her several disapproving glances from women and the elderly. Meanwhile, her hourglass figure and long, flowing black hair gains her approving looks from every passing young man. One such man, an Elf with long dark hair and wild eyebrows, is so distracted by Gwen that he nearly stumbles over a Goblin pushing a cart of vegetables from the market. Gwen smiles wickedly to herself, hearing the Goblin and the Elf arguing behind her.

Leona stays quiet. She doesn't even look in Gwen's direction. Keeping her eyes forward, she leads Gwen to a cute little shop with a white gingerbread-house storefront. The sign above the door reads, "Allianne's Adornments: Dressmaker, Jeweler, and Shoemaker."

"There are several dressmakers in Alcromech, but Allianne is the best," Leona informs her. Pushing the stained glass, wooden door open, she steps inside and holds the door for Gwen.

Gwen enters the clothing store and pauses a moment to take it all in. To her right a beautiful middle-aged Witch with orange eyes sits behind a glass display case full of a large variety of unique jewelry and accessories. They glitter and shine in the glow of the magic floating orbs placed all around the shop.

"Merry meet, Madam." Gwen smiles at the shopkeeper, Allianne herself she assumes.

"Merry meet, Child." The lady smiles back, her mahogany brown hair falling in waves about her tan Latina face. The lady goes back to rearranging some jewelry in the case, leaving Gwen to look about the shop.

Before her she beholds hundreds of racks of clothing in rows upon endless rows, making the back of the store seem miles away. To her left several walls are lined with tall shelves packed with shoes and footwear of familiar and exotic designs.

"Done gawking yet?" Leona asks from the middle of the store. Several chairs, lounges, and couches make a seating area underneath a chandelier of glowing orbs of light in multiple sizes. "We don't have all day, so I suggest we get started." Gwen walks over to join the younger girl. "We're going to need to take all her measurements, Mistress Allianne," Leona calls out to the shop keeper, who makes her way over in a flash of light. Suddenly standing next to Leona, the two women observe Gwen.

"If I had to guess I would say her dress size is Elm." Allianne rubs her chin, eyeballing Gwen's physique. The lady reaches her hand into her other sleeve and pulls out a long strip of measuring tape that seems somehow connected to the sleeve itself. "Stand very still, sister." The woman suddenly zips around Gwen at lightning speed, wrapping her measuring tape around Gwen's waist one second, then measuring her shoulders, her length, her bust, her inseam all in less than half a minute. Done measuring, the woman appears before Gwen again beside Leona. "Yes, she's an Elm, all right. Please sit down, sister, and let me look at your feet," the lady instructs. Gwen takes a seat in an exceptionally soft, oversized, chartreuse armchair. Allianne measures her foot, smiling up at Gwen. "What clothing does my lady require today?" When Gwen just shrugs, the dressmaker turns to Leona for answers.

"She's no lady. She's a nobody." The dressmaker looks aghast at this, but Leona stops her from speaking "However, she's under the protection of House Blackwool, Thoyen Nicola Blackwool."

"Well, then, it would be my honor to serve Thoyen Nicola's ward!" This news seems to rekindle the dressmaker's enthusiasm for serving them.

"We need everything on this list, Mistress Allianne." Retrieving a scroll out of her vest pocket, Leona hands it to the dressmaker. She unravels it at once, scans it, and nods. Leona takes a seat on a plush-pink velvet lounge opposite Gwen, crossing her legs as if settling in to wait.

"Yes, of course, right away." And like that, the dressmaker bolts away in a flash of black skirts. Gwen gets dizzy trying to keep track of the woman as she zips from one end of the store to the other collecting items. Periodically she dumps these items into one of the cubicles lining one wall. *Dressing rooms,* Gwen surmises.

"Jonah told me he gave you a breakdown of the Wiccan class system last night."

"Yes." Gwen tears herself from her fascinated study of Madam Alliance's actions to look at Leona. "And?"

"And I was just curious if you understood where you fit into it all?"

"Yes, I'm no circle," Gwen admits flatly. "But, as Thoyen Nicola's ward, what does that make me?" Gwen asks.

"Technically, second circle by association," Leona says stiffly, her nostrils flaring. "But not *Sodae itee*. One must marry above your circle for that distinction."

"Why? Shouldn't I be considered third circle like you and be like a servant to Aunt Nicola?"

"Because you're a pure blood. Even without a name, that counts for something. But only if someone in the second or first circle is willing to take you on as their ward and vouch for you."

"Hmmm, I see."

Just then the dressmaker approaches, not the least bit out of breath. "Your items are ready for you to inspect and try on, Mistress Gwen," Allianne informs her as she bows slightly.

"Thank you very much, Madam Allianne. How do you know my name?" Gwen asks as she rises from the armchair.

"It's part of the enchantment on my shop. I instantly know the name of everyone who walks over my threshold."

"That's a useful trick." Gwen's comment makes the dressmaker smile. Crow's feet crinkle at the corners of her orange eyes.

"Please, come with me." Gwen and Leona follow the dressmaker to the assigned cubicle. Gwen steps inside the stall surprised that, like the store itself, it is bigger within than it appears without. Leona closes the door to the cubicle, giving Gwen the privacy, she needs to undress. Hung up all around her in the ornate dressing room is her new clothing.

"Leona, why are they all black? The dresses, the leggings, the jackets, cloaks, and even the shoes, all black! Don't Witches like colors?" Gwen works her feet out of her sneakers without bending over to unlace them and scoots them aside. She carefully lifts the chain of her locket until the locket pops out of her shirt and then up over her head. She coils it up and stuffs it into one of the back pockets of her blue jeans.

On the other side of the door, she hears Leona snicker a moment before replying. "We only wear lots of colors during festivals and Wiccan holidays, like Sam Haines. Other than that, we wear the colors of our house on our cloaks with the family crest. The rest of our clothing is the color of our circle."

"So, brown is third circle, I'm assuming, and black is second?" Gwen asks as she unzips her jeans and slides them off.

"Very good, you're at least paying some attention to some things going on around you."

Gwen rolls her eyes at this while folding her jeans and placing them on a chair. "So, what is the first circle color, then?" Gwen's voice is muffled as she pulls her tank top over her head.

"White," Leona answers.

Gwen drops her shirt on top of her pants. Standing there in matching royal blue bra and panties she notices a pile of old-fashioned-looking lady's undergarments on a table. "Do I have to wear this ancient underwear? I mean, no one's going to lift my skirt to check or anything, are they?"

 372

"No, no one's going to do that." Leona chuckles. "I suppose it doesn't matter really what you wear under your clothes except that Aunt Nicola is buying them for you."

"Good. In that case, we'll leave it here and save Aunt Nicola some money, although I have plenty of money of my own. I don't need Aunt Nicola's charity." Gwen ignores the undergarments and finds herself some black silky leggings and sits down to pull them on.

She not your aunt, you twit! Gwen hears Leona think; aloud she says, "The Forsaken don't take human currency." Leona scoffs.

"What about gold and precious gems?"

"That they do take; however, as a prisoner in custody awaiting tribunal, all your assets are as good as frozen."

"Wait, what?" Gwen hops to her feet, pulling her stockings on. "How? I don't live in your world. All my assets are in the human world, remember?" The notion irritates her something awful. *I worked hard for my money and what I didn't earn was left to me by Angelo. If they think they can take everything away from me, they don't know who their dealing with!*

"That doesn't matter. No matter where you hide your piggy bank, they'll find it. But don't worry, they won't touch it unless you're sentenced to death or imprisoned for life." *That's only if you're lucky.*

"Oh, gee, what a comfort that is," Gwen grumbles as she goes back to trying on clothes.

"You do need to try everything on so that Mistress Allianne can fit them to you if they need any adjustments," Leona informs. "While you're busy doing that, I'm just going to step out and visit a few other shops. Wait here for me to return. Don't go wandering about by yourself." The younger teen instructs as if she were her mother.

"All right," Gwen replies as she steps into a long black form-fitting dress. She marvels when the buttons in the back button up all by themselves. She observes herself in the mirror and grimaces at her reflection.

"Promise me you'll stay put!" Leona demands through the door.

"Okay, I promise. Don't worry, I'll be a good girl," Gwen concedes, pulling on a short black jacket to go over her dress. Not liking the way, it constricts her arms, Gwen shakes her head at her reflection and peels the thing off. Gwen can feel Leona's hesitance to leave, her energy buzzing with uncertainty and anxiety. *If she gets lost or runs off on my watch, Aunt Nicola will never let me forget it.*

"I'll be fine, just go do your errands. I'm a big girl, Leona, I've been taking care of myself since I was eight years old." Gwen slips on some Witch boots and opens the dressing room door. Leona watches her with skepticism in her eyes. "You don't need to worry. Just go." Gwen waves her away. With a curt nod of her head, Leona hurries out the door in a flash.

"Ah, that dress suits you, lady Gwen." Mistress Allianne appears by Gwen's side suddenly.

"Yes, I like it, too. Except it's a little tight in the legs, makes it hard to walk. I don't suppose there is time to put a slit in the skirt, perhaps?" Gwen asks.

"It takes no time at all." Smiling, the dressmaker utters a chant and gestures with her hand. Along one side of her skirt, the fabric splits of its own volition, rising to her knee and folding the extra fabric in on itself, making its own finished edge.

"That's amazing!" Gwen laughs. "Can we make it come up to mid-thigh and add another identical one on the other side?"

"Whatever you like, lady," the dressmaker concedes, and as before, makes the dress alter itself with her magic chants while waving her index finger. When done, Gwen observes herself in the mirror, the dress making her look like a sexy Morticia Addams.

"Hmm, this neckline doesn't work for me." Gwen turns to the dressmaker and reconsiders her last comment. "No offense, Mistress Allianne."

"None taken, lady Gwen. What I make is largely generic in style and meant to be altered to the individual customer's taste. Just ask and I will make all the alterations you desire."

"Well, in that case, I'd like to remove the collar of the dress and lower the neckline."

"How much lower?" Mistress Allianne asks with a smile playing at the corner of her full lips and a wicked gleam in her orange eyes.

"How low can I go?" Gwen asks with a quirk of her brow.

The dressmaker laughs. "I knew when you walked in the door that you weren't going to be the typical customer."

"I know what I like," Gwen admits. Glancing at the contents of her dressing room she adds, "And we've got a lot of work to do."

"What style of neckline would you like?" Allianne asks.

"A scoop neck, I think," Gwen answers, standing before a long, oval, antique mirror next to the dressing rooms. Again, Allianne utters a spell and swishes her fingers around. The fabric of Gwen's dress transforms around her high collar to fold in on itself and rescind down the front of the bodice. When done, Gwen inspects herself in the mirror, noting just how much of her large breasts are now visible. She turns around to look at the dressmaker. "Is this too much?"

"Where did you get that?" Allianne stares at her, pale-faced. Slowly, she points a shaky hand at Gwen's chest. Gwen looks instinctively down to see that half of the strange scar over her heart is visible.

"I've had it since I was a child. I don't remember how I got it," Gwen answers slowly.

Allianne nods at this and takes a step close to Gwen. The two of them standing eye to eye in height, she looks into Gwen eyes and chants, "The Dark Star Will Rise Again."

"What?" Gwen is startled by the words. "What is that supposed to mean?" she asks, alarmed, a dark wave washing over her body.

"Nothing, lady." Allianne seems to come back to herself from somewhere far way. She smiles brightly. "It's just an old saying where I come from. You just made me think of it, that's all." She takes Gwen by the shoulders and spins her gently back around to face the mirror. "I think maybe we should raise the neckline just a bit to cover up that scar." She looks at Gwen's reflection straight in the eye with a serious look and adds, "You shouldn't let anyone see it."

Gwen swallows the lump in her throat and nods her consent. In an instant, the neckline is altered and her scar out of sight. Soon the dress is done, and they move on to all the other alterations. Gwen keeps a calm face and tries to joke as they continue the work. However, on the inside she is a raging sea of emotions.

In the dream last night, my father called me Black Star.

* * * * *

An hour later Leona finally returns to collect Gwen. Her alterations hadn't taken nearly as long as she had thought. Leona takes one look at Gwen's dress and her jaw drops. "What in the name of Lucifer are you wearing?"

"A dress," Gwen answers, looking down at the dress she had been wearing when Leona left. Along with the twin thigh-high slits and plunging neckline displaying an impressive amount of Gwen's cleavage, Gwen had replaced the middle section of her silky dress with a black see-through lacey material, her navel and tight stomach visible beneath. The same lacey material replaced the long sleeves from the shoulders, flaring out at the wrists giving the dress an ultra-

sexy, Gothic princess feel. Around her neck Gwen wears her gold locket, which hangs enticingly just above her cleavage.

"That's not how it's supposed to look," Leona says, bewildered.

"I disagree. It looks better like this. Trust me, it's much more comfortable to wear now than it was before." Gwen smiles. "Now, how on earth am I getting all that to the Coven?" Gwen gestures to a rack which holds her new all-black wardrobe. "It can't possibly all fit into my bags with my human clothes and all my books."

"There's a spell for that. The dressmaker can handle it." Leona dismisses the clothes but pauses a moment as she looks Gwen over again. "Aunt Nicola is going to tear my ear off for this. I knew I shouldn't have left you alone," she groans. "Come on, everyone should be waiting for us."

Retrieving her Converse and the pile of clothes she had walked in wearing, Gwen moves to follow Leona. "Well, we're off, Mistress Allianne. It was a pleasure to meet you!" Gwen exclaims with a radiant smile for the dressmaker behind the counter. Gwen reaches one hand over the counter and takes the lady's hand and shakes it emphatically, earning her a chuckle from the dressmaker. Her smile dims a bit when the lady's eyes alight on Gwen's locket. She must snap her attention back to Gwen as if torn from another world. "Leona says you can send my things to the Coven for me?"

"Why, yes, Lady Gwen. You're off to the Monroe Coven, correct?" Something passes behind her eyes that Gwen can't decipher. She resists the growing temptation to slip into the woman's mind.

"Yes, but how did you…"

"I just know." Allianne smiles, her white teeth contrasting nicely with her mocha skin. "Just leave it to me; they'll be waiting for you when you arrive at Thoyen Nicola's dwelling."

"Thank you very much. I appreciate it."

"Wait just a moment, please," the dressmaker calls as she zips around the counter reappearing right in front of Gwen. Mistress Allianne looks in Gwen's eyes as if searching for something, her face ablaze with something like recognition. "You just remind me of someone I used to know. It's probably just a coincidence but you've got something of her about you, only you're darker."

"And who was that?" Gwen asks, her heart thumping in her chest as her breath catches.

"Annajulia Rosenblaze." The dressmaker whispers the name like a prayer.

Leona gasps. Gwen turns to look at her, confused. "You know that name?"

"Everyone knows the Rosenblaze family!" Leona announces as if Gwen is a simpleton.

"I don't know that name. I'm not from around here, remember?" Gwen reminds Leona irritably in a whisper.

"The Queen's maiden name is Rosenblaze. They're one of the highest families of the first circle," Leona informs her matter-of-factly.

Just then, the front door opens, and a tall handsome man with short, black, spikey, hair and piercing apple-green eyes walks in. He

is dressed in a white suit with a purple cloak over it. The crest embossed on his shoulders and left breast are that of a crow perched atop a tilted scale with a large silver star that outweighs a golden sun.

He looks over the three women, smiling brightly to Leona with a nod in greeting.

"Merry meet, Professor Leven," Leona calls out before the man moves on to rifle through some suits on a rack.

"I must attend to this customer, excuse me." Before the dressmaker leaves, she stops and takes Gwen's empty hand and places a small round object into her palm, closing her fingers around it. "Please, take this as a gift. Should you ever need help, lady, should you ever need a friend, kiss the mirror, and speak my name and I will appear in the glass."

Before Gwen can respond to this the dressmaker zips away to attend to the gentlemen.

"What was that about?" Gwen opens her hand to look at the dressmaker's gift. It is a gold compact as big as her palm inlaid with birds and flowers and imbued with jewels. Leona glances down at it.

"It's a summoning glass," she informs Gwen, seeming a bit tense. "We should go."

Nodding absently, Gwen follows Leona. Gwen smiles back at Mistress Allianne once more before stepping out of the shop. *Who was this Annajulia woman and why would the dressmaker want to help me just because I remind her of this old acquaintance? And*

what does The Dark Star will rise again mean? Gwen can't help but wonder as she picks up her pace to catch up to Leona, who is already halfway down the street, her blonde braid bouncing wildly behind her. Gwen looks over her shoulder one last time at the shop and sees Allianne standing at the door watching her. *Who are you woman? Are you a friend or foe?*

Chapter Twenty-Five

Wild Tales

The rainbow shawl dances behind the Irish Witch as Thoyen Nicola leads Raven deeper into the small township of Alcromech. The colors are dizzying in their movements but not enough to distract him from his anxious thoughts. He clenches and unclenches his fists, apprehension rising from his gut with every step.

Get hold of yourself. It's not like this is the first time you've ever met someone of your own kind, he reminds himself. Memories of his former pack flutter through his mind, leaving him both comforted and bereft. It's been a long time since he's spoken to any of them. At first, he was too crestfallen over Gwen's failed rescue attempt to care much about anything or anyone. The pack had been kind enough to give him his space. Later, when Gwen turned up alive, he hadn't given one thought to returning to his old pack. In one way or another, he knew his path in life would always run parallel to Gwen's. Maybe even someday their two paths would converge into one. Raven sighs. He holds on to that thought to steady himself as they enter a more densely populated part of town.

The narrow streets teem with a more convivial crowd than the main thoroughfare. Buildings appear less well-kept, drenched with a feral perfume as is its inhabitants. Ruggedly clothed and crude of manners, Raven can't help but think of the creatures milling between the earthen buildings as a "rough crowd." With the forest jutting right up against the structures, this part of town looks, smells, and feels wilder than civilized. Despite himself, Raven smiles.

He watches with a growing sense of respect as every pedestrian ahead of them makes way for his escort to pass. Every Wiccan they approach makes a sign of a "w" with their fingers before their forehead as they bow their heads to Nicola Blackwool.

Some Wiccan sign of respect, no doubt, Raven figures.

Despite this, most of the populace continues with their boisterous conversations and loud, drunken singing. Up ahead Raven spies a peculiar building. Instead of tree-grown like the others, this is made from a mound of earth, like unto a shop dug out of the center of a hill. The road ends just before it in a large circular patch of dirt — no cobblestones here. Makeshift tables and chairs made of rocks and tree stumps scatter about it. Burly looking men and women roam between these tables and into the large, double, stained-glass doors of the hill-encompassed building.

Into this throng Raven follows Thoyen Nicola as she enters the establishment. He can't help smirking at the sign above the door of a moon behind the words *"Caprete Lunamiera,"* meaning "Captured Moonlight" in the true tongue. Within the shop's double doors, Raven finds himself confined in a small dirt tunnel entryway. The colored glass diffuses the sunlight into muted colors, giving off a dim eerie glow to the room. Behind a wooden stump-like podium stands a lumberjack of a man beside a gnarled wooden door. His long, wild, red hair stuffed into a tiny beanie while his enormous beard spills over the front of his flannel shirt down to his stomach. He makes Thoyen Nicola look childlike in comparison. In the confined space Nicola's herbal scent mingles with the odors of dirt, wood, sweat, and liquor.

"Well, hello, High Witch." The ginger lumberjack swipes off his beanie and gives her an exaggerated flourish and a bow. If it weren't for the heavy scent of alcohol on the man, Raven would call the gesture a mocking one.

"Hello yourself, lad." Aunt Nicola keeps a serious face and cool tone to her voice. The man straightens from his bow with some difficulty and smiles roughly at the two of them.

"What can I do you for, m'lady?"

"This wolf has an appointment with the Caddo Twins," Nicola informs him.

"Does he now?" Mr. lumberjack leans dramatically to one side to look around the Witch at Raven, a measured look in his smirk. "Hmph," he says to Raven before returning to his upright position.

"That he does, boy." Nicola folds her arms before her chest with an impatient sigh.

"That be all well and good, ma'am, but we don't allow outsiders inside. High Witch or not, you'll have to stay out in the skein." He gestures to the outside, the sounds of the drunken melee still audible from within.

"Of course, that won't be a bother. Just be a good lad and show this youngin' which of 'em beasts inside be the ones he's lookin' for," Nicola demands, turning to Raven she nudges him forward.

"Will do, Witch." The ginger begins to peel off his hat again as if to bow but Nicola swipes the hat from him and tosses it back in his face.

"Oh, forget it, stupid oaf. Get on with it before I do your job for ye!"

This seems to sober the lumberjack a bit. He hurries and plants the hat back on his head. Turning to the wooden door, he pushes it open and stands aside to let Raven step through. The doorway and opening beyond is pitch-black. Raven pauses, turning hesitantly back to his Witch escort.

"What exactly is this place?"

"It's a Werewolf Inn. The Black Iris is for Witches; Captured Moonlight is for your kind."

"Oh." Raven should be comforted by this explanation but somehow, he isn't. "What should I..."

"Just go speak with the Caddo Twins and they'll tell you everything you need to know and do. I'll wait for ye until you're done." Raven's face must show his uncertainty, for the Irish Witch flashes him an amused smile and pats him on the back affectionately. "Don't cha worry yourself, boy, they won't bite unless ye bite them first." Before turning away, she sets her gaze on the lumberjack. "And you. e a dearie and have a mug of Wolfbane sent out for me parched throat." With that, the lady turns and heads to the stained-glass doors, giving him a shooing gesture before she exits.

"You going in or not, Wolf? I ain't a doorstop," the ginger man beside him demands, his golden eyes looking blurry and intoxicated again. Without responding, Raven blows out a breath and enters the darkness before him. A moment later the lumberjack follows behind him. The wooden door closes with an ancient creak and casts the passageway into a deeper shade of black. Raven hesitates as he is struck by the overpowering smells and the complete darkness of the den within. The pungent odor of wild things, strong drink, dirt, and mold fill him with an animal's yearning.

"Let me show you the way, pal." To Raven's relief the other man steps around him and takes the lead. He hears his shuffling steps ahead of him on the dirt floor but sees nothing. A grunt and a long creak alerts him to the opening of another door. A wave of laughter and talking greets him from the next black room.

"This way. The Caddos are sitting in the far corner stall." As the man speaks, Raven's sight shifts from human to animal. Everything in the room about him appears in a silvery glow as their internal energy penetrates their surfaces, revealing themselves to his wolf eyes. "Can you see where you're going yet?"

"Yes, I can now," Raven answers with relief. "Which direction is their stall again?"

"West corner, farthest from the bar." His escort points it out. Raven nods to the man before turning in that direction.

With his adjusted sight Raven takes in the common room of the Captured Moonlight. Men, women, and children sit about tables and chairs like the ones outside the building, similarly dressed to the Werewolves he saw on his way in. The floor beneath him is hard-packed dirt, the roof above him roots and grass growing out of sod. To his left is a long bar that seems to double as a receptionist desk with several female employees working behind it. A hunched over old gentlemen with skin winkled like tree bark mans the bar. He rubs down the butcher-block surface with one hand and refills drinks with the other. Patrons sit on tall logs before the bar, ordering refreshments or questioning one of the several barmaids about available lodging. The girls aiding the elderly bartender seem to all have the same look about them.

Maybe they're all sisters? May even be the geezer's daughters or granddaughters? One of the young ladies in question crosses his path. She expertly balances a large wooden tray of jugs, plates, and glasses. Raven stops abruptly to let her pass him. Her gold eyes sparkle as she smiles at him before hurrying on with her duties. Raven watches her leave, her red hair bouncing along behind her. *I wonder if the doorman is their brother.*

Coming back to himself Raven makes his way through the many bodies coming and going and rounds the tables to his destination. As he approaches the corner booth, he sees that it is vacant. Puzzled, he looks about for two men that might resemble twins. However, he sees no two men who look alike. Turning back to the booth, Raven takes a few steps closer and hears snoring. Peering under the table Raven finds a man lying asleep on the booth's wooden bench, dressed in human street clothes: blue jeans, basketball shoes, a t-shirt, and a blue zippered hoodie. The man snores peacefully under the cover of a Pittsburgh Pirate's baseball cap.

Raven hesitates to wake the man and begins to quietly back away when he feels a hard slap on his shoulder. Startled, Raven turns to find a man in his twenties standing beside him. A head shorter than he, the young man has the trademark golden Werewolf eyes.

"You must be Raven!" The new stranger states as he grasps Raven's right hand and gives him a vigorous shake. "Pleasure to meet you, brother. Come, let's have a seat and wake up Thunder." This man has his hair shaven around the lower half of his head but shaggy on top in a light brown turf. He releases Raven and scoots himself onto the other bench at the booth. Without hesitation, he smacks the sleeping man's feet off the bench, making his body slide sideways off the seat. The napping man jerks awake with a shout. He grabs the edge of the table to keep himself from tumbling completely to the floor. Once recovered, he hauls himself back into his seat, glaring at his rude booth guest.

The first man's body shakes with silent laughter at his twin's expression. With a grumble, the once-sleeping twin leans down and retrieves his baseball cap from under the table.

"Do you mind? That's the first chance I've gotten to sleep since yesterday!" He slaps the cap back on his head. His complexion is cream-colored like his brother's. Raven also notices that his hairstyle is identical.

"That's what happens when you spend all night hiding up in a tree." The hatless twin slaps his brother on the back good-naturedly before returning his attention to Raven.

"Don't just stand there! Take a seat. I'll buy you a drink." He slaps the table beside him sociably. At this, the other brother notices Raven for the first time. "This is Raven Matthews. The lost wolf Gideon was telling us about," the first twin informs the second. He gives Raven a quick appraisal before nodding a curt greeting.

"Nice to meet you both." Raven scoots into the booth beside the hatless twin. *He's at least friendly,* Raven reasons. He extends his hand across the table. The other twin grabs it and gives him an equally firm handshake to his brother's.

"Welcome to the fold, lost brother," he responds, settling back onto his bench. "We're the Caddo twins. This is Lightning."

"And he's Thunder," finishes the twin beside Raven. He flashes a big smile. Raven sits quietly a moment looking between the two of them waiting for the punchline to the joke, but neither says a word.

"Oh, you're serious? Those are your real names, not just nicknames or something?"

"Yes. Our parents have quite the sense of humor." Lighting's face splits into a huge grin, his mirth spreading to his eyes. Thunder sighs and nods impatiently.

"We're descendants of the Caddo Indian Tribe. And we're twins, so … it's befitting," Thunder adds.

"I don't think he's heard the Caddo legend of the Werewolf Twins, brother," Lightning informs his twin. "He looks confused."

"Nope, I can't say that I know that one," Raven admits. Just then laughter erupts from a table at the other end of the room.

"Where we're going, you'll hear it and every other wolf myth or legend ever told nightly around the fire," Thunder replies. "You'll be inundated with lore, whether you like it or not," he adds with a sideways smirk and a laugh.

"Where are we going?" Raven leans his elbows on the table, eager.

"To Akwesasne to meet with the Fenris Lykaios," Lightning replies with a smile.

"Akwesasne is the Mohawk Indian Reservation in Franklin County, New York. It's better known as St. Regis," Thunder clarifies. "And the Fenris Lykaios are the Werewolves Council. They're holding a massive pow-wow there next week to discuss the Vampire crisis," he finishes dryly.

Lightning shakes his head, his bright smile replaced by a scowl. "There's nothing to discuss. If even one bloodsucker steps out of line, we should tear 'em to shreds." He pounds his fist on the tabletop for emphasis.

"I'm with you, brother, but these things aren't up to the likes of us." Thunder shrugs. A loud crash jerks their attention to the other side of the room. They see two men lying on the broken remains of a wooden table. The two drunken men look alike, both of Native American descent. Despite looking like brothers, the two men wrestle with one another struggling to get the better of his opponent. Around them several of the other patrons cheer them on, either in favor of one man or the other winning the fight. The two men get to their feet and start throwing punches at one another. One manages to hit the other square in the jaw and this sends the man flying back into the bar. He crashes into a few glasses sitting on the bar. They shatter and send liquid flying. The alcohol hits one of the redheaded barmaids in the face and she shouts in indignation.

The old man bar tender returns from the back storeroom to see this all happening. Slamming down the crate he holds in his arms on the bar, he turns on the two drunken patrons. With a voice like a roar he shouts, "Take it outside now. Brawl out in the open, you idiots."

Terrified of the old man, the two drunks stumble toward the door, making their apologies along the way. "And I'm charging the damages to your rooms!" he informs them as they go. Then the old bartender/inn keeper turns his angry glare on the rest of the bar with a look of warning. All the patrons who had been cheering on the drunken brawl quiet down and return to their tables and stools, carefully avoiding the old man's gaze.

Raven returns his gaze back to his companions. The twins look at each other with a shrug. "That's Orson and Brutus. They're always fighting," Thunder informs Raven.

"You know them?" Raven asks pointing his thumb in the direction of the door.

"Yep, that's the Aleut brothers. They're part of another pack, part of the Aleut tribe. Their people come from the Aleutian Islands in Alaska," Lightning explains, "but we see them regularly at the Lutucus Natrea Tomahawk."

"What's that?" Raven asks, confused.

The twins look at one another with a smirk. "Werewolf fight club," they reply in unison.

"What, you never heard of it?" Thunder asks, disbelieving.

"Well, I just assumed if you were part of the fight club, you'd adhere to the first rule of fight club," Raven responds smugly, barely concealing a smile. "Even if I did know about it, we're not supposed to talk about it."

It takes the twins a moment to get the movie reference and then they simultaneously burst into laughter.

"You're funny, brother," Lighting informs Raven, smacking him on the back once more.

"Anyways, your father's people will be in Akwesasne at the werewolf council as well," Lighting informs Raven, waving a barmaid over to their table as he speaks. "They'll get you squared away and reunited with your proper pack."

Raven nods in understanding. A tendril of his apprehension melts out of his stiff shoulders at the thought of meeting his real family. Aunt Nicola informed him that she had learned quite a few of them were still living.

"Good morning, brothers. What will you have?" the same barmaid that Raven passed earlier asks as she scrubs down their table with a cloth.

"Two pints of Black Alpha draft, two roasted chickens, and for my friend here…" Lightning clasps Raven on the shoulder and looks at him expectantly.

"A mug of Wolfbane," Raven adds uncertainly.

The maid and the twins all look at him oddly.

"No, lad, that's a woman's drink! You need something that'll keep the hair on your chest," Lightning insists.

"Just bring another Black Alpha for him as well," Thunder instructs the barmaid with a wink as he tosses a coin in her direction.

"I'll have that right out." She collects the coin of the tabletop, not sparing a glance for Thunder or his twin. However, she flashes Raven a smile and tosses her red hair over her shoulder before walking away.

Raven forces himself not to blush. He turns back to the twins to find the two of them staring at him with an identical look of respect.

"Looks like we've got ourselves a real ladies' man here, brother," Lightning comments to Thunder with a sideways glance.

"Hmmm, I bet you got a dozen ladies chasing your tail," Thunder adds with a smug smile. "You got yourself a woman, Raven?"

"I ... well, uh ... it's more like two," Raven replies, thinking fast. Almost everyone thinks Raven's dating both Gwen and Morna. Of course, it isn't true, but he's learned a few things from his former pack about Werewolf men: they're likely to drink alcohol with breakfast or for any reason at all, they're extremely competitive, and they don't respect modesty or humility. If he wants to fit in amongst his kind, he must be strong, confident, and most importantly, an alpha. It doesn't matter that he's never thought of himself as any of these things. He must fake it enough to get by. Of course, if either of his two best friends heard him claim to be dating them both simultaneously, they might likely skin his hide to teach him a lesson.

What harm can a little lie do? After all, it's not like the twins will ever meet the girls.

"Ahhhh!" Lightning slaps him on the back yet again, smiling broadly as his brother bangs the table with both fists in approval. "That a boy, that a boy! Why have just one, right?"

"Are they Were, or are you the kind that dates anyone you please?" Thunder asks, scooting in closer to hear the juicy details.

"One's a black-haired Witch and the other's a blonde Fairy and ... they're best friends," Raven fibs, ignoring the guilt twisting in his stomach.

The twins give him an impressed look. Just then, their barmaid returns carrying their drinks on a wooden tray. Thankful for the distraction, Raven takes his drink. The brothers claim their drinks, simultaneously taking a large swig. As soon as the barmaid leaves, they both turn back to Raven.

"All right, let's hear more about these ladies of yours!" Lightning demands loudly. "How did you snag a Witch and a Fairy without either of them knowing about it?"

"I can't imagine they'd agree to share the same man." Thunder thinks about it a moment then adds, "Well, I hear Fairies can be rather kinky, actually, but a Witch…"

"Now that's a story for another time, boys. But enough about me." Raven settles back against the bench and takes a swell of his draft before continuing. "What's this about you sleeping all last night in a tree, Thunder? That sounds like an interesting story." Raven raises his thick brows at him, feeling more comfortable in the role he's playing.

Lightning erupts into a loud guffaw as Thunder's face turns red and his expression sheepish.

"He was trying to woo a lady Elf that works at the Populace Center and…" Lighting begins.

"And she said she couldn't be seen," Thunder continues with an annoyed look at his brother. "Bringing a man back to her room at the *Silvre Trium*."

"That's the Elf Inn," Lightning interjects.

Thunder sighs, "She said it wasn't befitting a HCOE official, but that I could climb the tree next to the inn and she'd let me in her bedroom window and…"

"The Elf never came to unlock the window!" Lightning finishes for his twin, erupting into another peel of laughter, slapping his knee, and nearly spilling his drink in his other hand.

Raven can't help grinning. Thunder just shakes his head and dismisses the two of them with a wave of his hand, his face a deeper shade of red than before.

"Forget you two. I'm going back to bed," Thunder announces, lying back down on the other bench and pulling his baseball cap over his face. "Wake me when the roasted chicken arrives."

Lightning looks at Raven and together they start laughing again.

"Let us have a toast to women in all their many shapes and sizes!" Lightning suggests after their laughter finally subsides.

"I'll drink to that," Raven replies as they both lift their glasses and bang them against another's. When they begin to drink a gulp turns into a guzzle. Without a word, Raven, and Lightning race to be the first to down their tankard. Raven slams his glass back down on the table just a blink before Lightning does. This earns him another slap on the back as the two yell in triumph.

"Stop braying, you mangy dogs! I'm trying to sleep over here, remember?"

"You might as well forget about sleep, Thunder. The maid's bound to be back soon with the grub," Lightning informs his twin with a quick punch to the heel of Thunder's shoe. This results in Thunder kicking back at his brother. The Caddo twins soon have a playful skirmish ensuing right there in the booth. Raven sits back and watches from the safety of the far edge of the bench with a smile on his face.

If the rest of the Werewolves in Akwesasne are like these two, then there's absolutely no reason to be worried about meeting my kin, Raven realizes.

The twins eventually settle down and Thunder tries to resume his nap once again. Raven turns to see their pretty redheaded barmaid returning with the two roasted chickens for the twins. Her golden eyes meet his and again she beams a smile at him. Raven returns it with an awkward grin and a small nod. She seems to take this as encouragement and makes an effort to stand ridiculously close to him as she places the twins' food trays before them on the table. Raven can't help inhaling her scent: lemon, sugar, and barley. He should be aroused by her closeness and her pretty smile but all they do is remind him of another woman with gold eyes, and an even prettier smile.

Morna, where on earth have you flown away to and why?

"I'll be right back with another round of drinks," she says. When the maid leaves, she looks over her shoulder at Raven with a look that seems to say, *Come, and get it if you want it.*

He'd rather not think too much on Morna just now or he knows he'll drive himself mad. Raven sighs as he watches the Caddo's rip into their meals, feeling a tinge of guilt still lingering from his elaborate over-exaggeration of his relationship with his two female companions. He is certain he's not the first man to ever make up a story to impress his fellow men. Still, it felt rather beneath him.

For all I know the whole Elf story was made up, too, he reasons to himself as he impatiently taps his empty tankard on the table. *And I'm sure in Akwesasne there'll be no shortage of wild tales.*

Chapter Twenty-Six

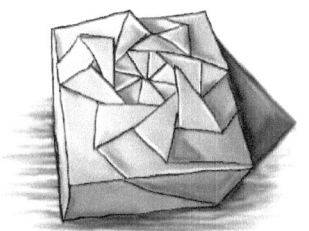

Lurking in the Shadows

$\mathcal{T}$he pleasant smell of sweetmeats and the sounds of friendly chatter greet them as Gwen follows Leona into the Black Iris common room. A few of the tables are occupied by the boardinghouse's other guests. On the far end of the room, Leona spots Nicola and the others sitting at a round table right before the large hearth. Gwen's shoulders slouch as she notices that Raven is not with them.

"There you are lassies!" Aunt Nicola calls to them as they approach, stopping the conversation amongst the group. Jonah and Thayer turn in their chairs and look at her. Instinctively their eyes sweep over her body and her newly acquired attire. Their eyes register surprise before they each avert their gaze quickly back to Gwen's face. Jonah swallows hard before mumbling a greeting. For the briefest moment, Jonah's and Gwen's eyes meet and something like electric ice shoots through her veins. Gwen looks swiftly to the others, forcing a calm face.

"Is Raven not joining us?" Gwen asks Nicola hopeful.

"No, not just now, anyhow. He'll be stopping by this evening I expect." Nicola coughs as she makes a quick appraisal of Gwen's new dress. "Well, I must say that is a singular dress you're wearing, child," the middle-aged Irish Witch comments, tight lines appearing around her lime-green eyes. "I didn't take you for a girl that likes … dresses."

"I usually don't." Gwen folds her arms across her chest. The pose emphasizes her deep neckline and full cleavage. "Although I don't wear them often when I do, I like to stand out," Gwen finishes with a smug little smile. Nicola's eyes narrow slightly at this comment.

"Well, no one could accuse you of ever being plain, lass," she replies with an obligatory smile before she shifts her eyes to give Leona a pointed look. Leona bows her head, her cheeks burning red. Gwen suspects if Leona were a turtle, she would crawl back into her shell to avoid the elder witch's glare. "Come take mid-day meal with us," Nicola orders cheerfully, indicating the two empty chairs at the round wooden table. Of course, either seat puts Gwen next to Jonah.

Leona quickly plops herself into the chair between her brother and Thayer. Gwen has no choice but to take the seat between her disapproving guardian/captor and her closest Wiccan ally/two-timing, lying, engaged former crush. Jonah rises from his seat to pull out her chair for her. Gwen manages to mutter a thank you without looking at him.

Breathe, Jonah, breathe! It's just a dress, she's just a girl. His thoughts float out of his befuddled mind, from behind his red cheeks and his painfully averted gaze that still seems to keep wandering back to Gwen's amply exposed cleavage. If Gwen weren't positively livid with him, she would be laughing at him.

Curse you, Jonah, you're not allowed to be adorable. Why didn't you once think of your fiancée when we first met? I wouldn't have made such a fool of myself if I'd had even a hint that you were spoken for. What am I supposed to do now? Huh? For a moment Gwen considers inserting these thoughts into his mind and confronting him here and now. With a defeated sigh, she lets the idea go.

Large, heaping plates full of sweat meats, and vegetables arrive at their table brought by third circle Wiccan servants all clad in brown. Thankfully as they eat, Nicola launches into a massive monologue about the rules of being her ward/ prisoner and the way things will proceed. This leaves little space for conversations and gives Gwen ample excuse to not interact with Jonah the entire meal.

Amongst all the witch's preaching about customs and decorum, Gwen manages to gather the ground rules of her amicable imprisonment. She is to be always chaperoned, most often by Leona. *Goody!*

She is not allowed to visit Raven at the werewolf inn, but he is permitted to visit her at the boarding house, or they may go about town if they stay on the main roads of Alcromech, *with* a chaperone of course.

Using magic in any form is strictly forbidden until after Gwen's tribunal. Even though the protective barrier of Alcromech keeps anyone from doing harm to one another, Gwen is still not allowed to use magic for even the most menial of tasks.

Gwen is not allowed out of the Black Iris after dark, no matter what.

If she breaks any of these rules, there will be dire consequences, yet Thoyen Nicola is vague about the particulars.

"You act as though you plan for us to be in Alcromech for a while," Gwen comments. "I don't know about you, but I'd like this whole tribunal business over and done with as soon as possible. I've got my permission slip thing; I thought that was all we needed?" Gwen adds, taking a bite of her food.

"When we leave is entirely up to the elders of the Monroe Coven," Nicola clarifies. "The slip *thing* gives you access to use the Luficinian Roads, but it won't get you access into the Coven unless the elders permit it," Nicola replies. "That won't happen until the other of the thirteen elders agrees to acknowledge my claim to take you on as my ward and deem it safe for your entrance. This could take a few days or more as it must be a unanimous vote." Gwen can tell by the tone of her voice that this fact irritates Nicola, but she's trying to be patient and understanding with the process.

"What happens if they don't all agree?" Gwen probes. "Does the whole tribunal get canceled and I get to go on with my life?"

Nicola snorts. "No. Sorry, lass, but there's no chance of that." Gwen's shoulders slump. "Ne, instead another Witch or Warlock

from another Coven would have to take you on as their ward. They would be responsible for your detainment and would need to procure a Coven that would agree to hold your tribunal."

"Why not just take me straight to the King?" Gwen quirks a dark brow. "Or some kind of court? If being a wild witch and practicing magic before humans are such dire offenses, shouldn't my tribunal be held before someone more official than just a pack of elders in a random coven to which I don't even belong?"

This produces a snort from Thayer and Jonah and a glare from Leona.

"Believe me, dearie, a random pack of elders is as official as you want this tribunal to get. Having the king and his elders pass judgement on ye would have far worse outcome if they ruled unfavorably on ye." The seriousness in Nicola's voice sends a shiver down Gwen's spine, erasing all desire to discuss the matter further.

"Oh, I see. Just curious." Gwen gulps hard. The rest of the meal is eaten in near silence, the somber mood hanging around them as a thick black cloud.

By the time lunch is over Gwen can't wait to get away from the Irish witch and her teenage Wiccan crew.

"I'm tired. If it's no trouble, I'd like to go take a nap in my room," Gwen asks Thoyen Nicola with as much forced politeness as her naturally sarcastic voice can muster.

"That'll be no trouble at all if it is agreeable with Leona."

"No, that would be great. I need to catch up on my studies for alchemy anyway." Leona agrees, seeming surprised by her luck. "I half expected you to want to go wander around Alcromech all day."

With that, Leona and Gwen make their exit. An itching feeling between her shoulder blades tells Gwen that Jonah's gaze follows her as she leaves. With tight lips, she forces herself not to look back.

Leona almost skips past the registry desk and on down the hall. *Apparently, Leona really likes studying Alchemy,* Gwen muses.

"You, girl!" The boardinghouse's patroness calls out to Gwen abruptly, jolting her to a stop. With her mind elsewhere, Gwen completely missed the presence of Mistress Sabre behind the registry counter.

"Yes?" Gwen answers uncertainly not particularly in the mood to converse with the large, surly woman at this precise moment.

"A package was left for you while you were out." She proclaims. Without a backward glance at Gwen, the hefty woman reaches into one of the cubbies behind the registration desk. She retrieves a small square box. Without any consideration for its contents, Mistress Sabre slaps it down on the counter before Gwen.

The package is wrapped in shiny gold and white paper. It is twisted and folded up over the top in an origami fashion to resemble a multi-pointed flower. A small white tag hangs from a string under the flower closure. Gwen pinches the tag between her thumb and forefinger to read the scrawling handwriting.

"For Gwenevere," she reads aloud. The note says nothing else, the other side of the tag blank. "Wait. Who left this package?" When

Gwen looks up, Mistress Sabre has already shuffled on down to the other end of the counter. Ordering about a Wiccan servant, the lady gives Gwen an annoyed grimace.

"I wasn't here when it was delivered. No one was," Mistress Sabre adds with a disapproving sneer at the girl servant standing beside her. Little older than twelve, the dark-haired girl ducks her head and hurries away to a backroom. "Someone was supposed to be manning the desk after breakfast. Yet somehow none of the bloody servants who were on duty this morning, made it to their posts on time." She yells half in response to Gwen and half in the direction of the back room. Gwen imagines this is where the other servants of the Black Iris must be cowering from their mistress.

"Oh, I don't suppose you've heard of surveillance cameras here in Alcromech?" Gwen asks with a wry tone, picking up the box and looking it over for more writing.

"What are you prattling on about?" Mistress Sabre asks, irritated. "Just take your box and be on your way, girl. It's none of my business who it came from. Open it. That's the way to find out." The proprietor of The Black Iris dismisses Gwen with a wave of her large arm.

Rolling her eyes, Gwen hesitates before turning to go. Looking over her shoulder, she glances back into the common room at Jonah and the others. They still sits at their table talking amongst themselves. *Would he have...? Or Raven?* Trying to summon up every possible sender in her mind, she heads up to her room.

Halfway up the stairs, Gwen hears footsteps above her and looks up to find Leona at the top.

"Are you coming or what?" she demands with hands on hips, her long blonde braid flipping over her shoulder as she fixes Gwen with an annoyed scowl. With a huff, she turns and stomps on down the hall.

Gwen sighs as she follows her roommate. *I'm not sure how long I can stand waiting around in this place. Especially with someone several years younger than me and half my size trying to order me about. The elders in the Monroe Coven better make up their minds fast and move things along soon. I can't be held responsible for what I might end up doing to Leona if they don't.*

By the time Gwen enters their bedroom, Leona has already dumped a stack of old leather-bound books upon her coverlets. The blonde teen sits cross-legged on her bed, hunched over an open book in her lap. Her forehead creased in concentration as she reads.

Gwen is not tired at all; she just said that to get away from the others. She had hoped Leona would have something better to do than sit around and watch her nap and that the excuse would afford her some much-needed alone time.

So much for that plan. Gwen sighs. *Oh, well, I do have a mystery gift to open. I might as well amuse myself with that. First things first, I'm getting out of these boots before I lose a toe.*

Gwen sets the box in question down on the bed beside her. After wrestling with the laces, Gwen manages to wiggle her feet out of the Victorian-style boots. Once both her feet are free, she spreads her

toes with a sigh. Stuffing the boots under the bed, Gwen settles down on the covers.

Picking up the gold and white box, Gwen examines the ornate origami flower until she discovers a means to undo it. With quick fingers Gwen tugs at two separate petals of the paper flower at the same time. The paper spreads, falling apart into four separate sides exposing a small box seeming to be made of shell. Inside the box resides a strange yet exotic violet flower, something between a lily and an orchid. It has long filaments supporting multiple pods surrounding the stigma in the center.

"Why on earth would someone send me just one odd-looking flower?" Gwen asks, only half aware she spoke the question aloud.

"Hmmm?" Leona asks, glancing over at her from her books. Gwen brings the strange box closer to her face to get a better look. "Wait! Gwen, don't!"

Before Leona's words register in Gwen's ears, all four pods suddenly spring open, releasing thousands of tiny spores right into her face. The spores blind her, clogging her nostrils and her mouth simultaneously and overpowering her with their sickly-sweet aroma.

Coughing and gagging, Gwen cannot help but inhale the spores into her lungs. She drops the box reflexively, trying to rub the burning spores out of her eyes as she pushes frantically off the bed. She rushes to the window, desperate for fresh air. By the time she fumbles to open the latch her face feels numb, her lungs sore. Her sight blurs and shifts. The colors and shapes of things around her rearrange before her eyes. The sounds in the room seem hollow and distant, as if coming to her from down a long tunnel.

Someone shouts her name. Something grabs her by the shoulder and shakes her vigorously. Then Gwen feels propelled forward, her bare feet moving beneath her as if leading her somewhere all their own. Her legs, her arms, and her whole body seem vague and empty as if they are not really hers at all.

She is whisked away by this near empty vessel down corridors, stairs, and doors, until sunlight shines around her. Even so, the fresh air and sunlight do nothing to dispel the spores in her lungs or clear the swirling images. Water rushes, birds chirp in the trees, and people talk nearby. These sounds seem both miles away and right inside her skull. Her mind throbs and a high-pitched ringing overwhelms her.

Under foot she can vaguely feel dirt and rocks, then wooden blanks. The sound of a watery current surrounds her yet seems foreign as if she is hearing it for the first time. Her throat still aching, she coughs and chokes, yet she is unable to form words. Her lips are numb and immoveable.

Feet thunder on the wooden planks behind her. Many voices both female and male call out a name. She is not certain if they are calling for her or someone else. Just at this moment, she does not recall having a name at all.

Onward and onward, she is propelled by a force greater than anything she's yet encountered. Some vague corner of her mind knows something is terribly wrong, that she's under some kind of

curse. However, that voice is tiny and distant, unheard amongst the tumult of other voices. Forming complete thoughts seems something nonsensical now.

Hands grope at her. Someone tries to block her path and take hold of her. This does nothing to detain her determined feet. Barely seeing the outline of their faces, the colors twists and blends them into nothingness before her. She pushes against the person. The sheer will of her need to move forward forces the large solid mass aside. More entities try to stop her, shouting.

"Gwen! Gwen Stop!"

"Aunt, do something!" another voice pleads terrified.

"You heard your sister, boy!" An older woman speaks. "The girls inhaled the poisonous spores of a Coerisa Phantasmagoria flower! She can't fathom us. She's completely beyond her own wits. Her body not in her own power!"

"Who would do this, and why? How do we stop her?" a young man demands as the people around her make more attempts with their arms and bodies to stop her forward progression. All they can do is postpone her. The force compelling her is unrelenting. Their hands fall away like the stars trying to grasp the sun.

"Someone needs information from the girl or needs the lass herself badly enough to do such a thing," the older woman explains. "It's a rather clever way to get around the wards of Alcromech. Technically no harm has been done to the lass so there's nothing the protective barrier can do, and it wasn't a person who did it to her but a thing."

"But where is she going?" a teenage girl asks, frantic.

"Out of the trading post, of course." The older lady replies with cold certainty.

"But she can't. The wards won't allow it. She's a prisoner; the detainment spell is keeping her here and blocking her way out," another young man notes with concern.

"Aye, lad, it is. Which means…" the older lady councils, "…if we can't find a way to get her out from under the flowers curse, she might do herself a terrible harm trying to get through the barrier."

Gwen hears all this without comprehension. The wood planks have been replaced by a dirt path beneath her bare feet. She pushes through thick foot traffic. Swirling masses of bodies on all sides press in both directions. Even with this obstacle, she is undeterred.

"Thayer lad, form a protection circle around Gwenevere. Try a dampening spell." The older female voice commands.

"But that will only buy us a little time. Where are you going?" A teenage girl interjects

"To find something that can absorb the spores. It's the only way to stop her." The older woman replies, her voice becoming distant as she shuffles away. The swishing of her skirt fading into the thronging foot traffic. Voices start to chant about Gwen. Their meaning lost on her befuddled mind Before she knows it Gwen steps off the dirt road and into gurgling water. Her skirts soaking up the moisture turn heavy about her legs. The sensation of the cold jolts her almost to clarity.

Wait? Am I in the river? What am I doing in the river? What am I doing? What is happening?

Gwen tries to shake off the odd images before her eyes. She tries to force her body to answer to her call. Nothing changes. Stumbling over herself, she wades further into the water. Voices call after her again. This time she knows to whom they belong.

Jonah? Nicola, Leona, and Thayer? Why don't you do something? I can't stop! I can't stop! Gwen tries to move her lips, to force out more than a croak or a groan out of her swollen mouth but to no avail. Soon their voices are drowned out by the increasing roar of the water.

The waterfall! The realization sends Gwen into a state of panic. *If I'm forced to try to go through the waterfall, the barrier will just shoot me back inside like it did yesterday. It'll hurt like hell but ... might the sting of the barrier break the curse I'm under?* The thought gives her momentary hope. Gwen ceases fighting the effects of the flower. Allowing her body to push forward, Gwen reaches out her hands as she approaches the waterfall entrance of Alcromech. Cold, unforgiving water crashes down upon her as she steps fully beneath its tremendous downpour.

The barrier does exactly as it had before. Gwen is hurtled through the air backward, landing twenty feet away from the waterfall. The burn of the barrier stings like an enormous jellyfish. The pain of it is instantly replaced by the sensation of drowning as Gwen is submerged into the river's depths. Gasping for air and fighting to keep from being pulled further under by her skirts, Gwen pushes back to the surface. Sputtering out water, Gwen emerges drenched and mostly coherent. Her version has improved but isn't completely repaired. The world still attempts to spin around her.

"Gwen!"

She turns to see Jonah and the others wading through the water toward her. Relieved that she can recognize them now, she moves in their direction only to find her feet will not obey. To her horror, Gwen finds her body is still compelled by the effects of the cursed flower.

"Jonah!" Not able to focus on the details of his face, Gwen still reaches her arms toward him. "I can't stop!" she mutters out of numb cold lips, her voice still hoarse from the spores and choking on water.

"I'm coming, Gwen. We'll help you, I promise," he calls back to her, nearly within reach now. He takes her outstretched hands in his, determination in his aqua eyes. He tries to hold her in place, but Gwen's unrelenting body just drags Jonah along with her toward the waterfall.

Soon Nicola and others surround her on all sides.

"Join hands, quickly. I think I know the spell to break this." In an urgent voice, she speaks to Gwen, "Here child." Nicola quickly hands Gwen a thin damp cloth. Beneath the nearly translucent folds, there seem to be crushed flowers within. "Ye needs hold this over ye mouth and nose, it'll absorb the spores of the flower in ye lungs. It will help with our spell." Gwen holds it to her face as best she can as her body continues to move forward.

"Repeat after me!" Nicola orders the Wiccan youths. Forming a circle around her, they wade awkwardly through the water with her, chanting.

"Re lentae, Re versae, Coerisa Phantasmagoria, Re lentae, Re versae! Purifinica, purifinica, Resto rum!"

Gwen feels the spell their joined hands and words create. She senses the power of it trying to unravel the flower's effect on her. Throwing her own will into the energy of the counter spell, she fights with all she's got to resist the urge to step into the waterfall again. It looms before her only a few feet away now. Thayer enters it backward, still joined by the hand to Leona, and Nicola, on either side of her while Jonah is directly behind Gwen, in a circle about her. Gwen steps beneath the water and…

With even more force than before, Gwen and Jonah are ejected with a boom and a huge spray of water. Searing pain engulfs Gwen's flesh as she soars through the air. This time she is prepared and takes a deep breath before landing in the river. She hears Jonah land beside her with a loud splash. A few moments later, she bursts out of the water gasping for breath and struggling to keep her head above the surface.

Arms grasp her about the waist, pulling her to her feet. Pushing her long, dripping, wet, black hair out of her eyes, Gwen smiles appreciatively at Jonah. His face is clear to her now.

"I've got you." His eyes scan her face, hopeful. "Are you all right, Gwen? Is it over?"

Gwen pants exhaustedly and then nods, the motion making her nearly lose her balance. She clings to his arms to steady herself and looks up into his enormous eyes. He smiles with obvious relief, the tension going out of his shoulders and the muscles of his arms. Suddenly nothing matters more than him.

"Are you crazy? Why did you grab a hold of me at the last second? You could have been hurt! The barrier would not have done anything to you if you would just…"

"I had to try at least!" he defends himself, laughing ruefully. "I don't care what happens to me. I just can't stand the idea of something happening to you." He steps in closer, their faces inches from each other's.

"Jonah, I…"

"Are you yourself again lass?" Nicola's loud booming voice breaks the reverie of the moment.

The two quickly step back from one another and turn to see the others wade nearer, waist deep in the water themselves.

"I think so," Gwen calls back.

"Come on, let me help you back to the shore," Jonah offers, placing Gwen's arm over his shoulder and scooping her up in one deft motion. With a little yelp of surprise, Gwen finds herself clinging to Jonah's neck, cradled in his arms. He carries her to the water's edge, water dripping from her long skirts.

"I'd protest but this blasted dress is awfully heavy when soaking wet," Gwen confides despite her horse voice. The warmth

of his solid frame feels pleasant through their wet clothing, and Gwen struggles not to shiver.

Jonah chuckles. His perfect teeth gleam white in the light reflected off the river. "I am only glad we could help. If anything happened to you…" Jonah lets his words fall away, with a blush on his cheeks that leaves Gwen pondering what he might have said next. Gwen lets her head rest on his shoulder, her face nestled into his neck. She cannot help but inhale him. Beeswax, rosewood, and musk, the smell of his skin help clear away the scent of the cursed flower. Gwen sighs.

All too soon they meet up with the others by the edge of the river. A crowd has formed on its bank. Several the citizens and travels of Alcromech murmur among themselves, watching them as they climb onto the shore. Among them, Gwen spies the gentlemen who had been in Allianne's dress shop earlier.

"Bring her over to me, Jonah!" Professor Leven's voice rises above the rest. He stands next to Nicola, the two exchanging whispers as Jonah sets Gwen back on her feet before them. Gwen releases her hold on Jonah's neck with reluctance, feeling him step away from her as if feeling life leave her body. "Are you all right, Lady Gwenevere?" the professor asks eagerly as he strips off his long coat and drapes it about her shoulders for warmth.

"I'm fine now," Gwen pants. "Thanks, um…"

"Professor Vincent Leven, at your service, dear." The tall dark-haired man gives her the slightest bow.

"Go on about your business, the lot you. The girl's unharmed. There's no need to be hanging about!" Nicola commands the crowd of gawking creatures watching. With scowls and murmurs, their audience disperses.

Gwen turns to watch them go, but the movement sends her head reeling and she teeters on her feet. Before she can fall, Professor Leven quickly takes her by the elbow. Nicola takes her other arm, and the others follow behind as they help her walk down the road. Weak and exhausted, Gwen does not protest the help, although at any other moment she would find the gesture condescending at best.

"Do you remember anything? Do you understand what just happened to you?" the professor questions, concern visible in the crease between his dark brows.

"I got a package with a strange-looking flower inside. It sprayed me with…" Gwen shakes her head to remember more clearly but even the conversation at lunch seems hazy now. It's almost as if the flower has erased part of it from her mind. "Something that made me sick or dizzy. I was in my room with Leona at the Black Iris." Gwen looks around at the shops of Alcromech; some of the onlookers from the river still trail along after them as if hoping to hear some of their conversations. Gwen tries to glare them away but feels the muscles in her face aren't quite up to the task and decides to ignore them instead.

"Who sent the box with the flower?" the professor demands, half asking Gwen, half Leona, who walks just behind them.

"It didn't say," Gwen answers weakly, seeing the scribbled handwriting in her head and wondering if she had seen that handwriting before. Just then, a memory of another note handwritten comes to mind. It had been written on a white card amongst a bouquet of roses left at the scene of Michael's gruesome murder only days before.

Only you can decide who dies next.

Your debt is still unpaid.

Those two lines scream to her now. But were they written in the same scrawl? Gwen can't answer her own question; her mind is too befuddled. Could the strange flower have come from the same person? It made sense and yet didn't at all. The last note sounded as if the sender planned to kill someone else that she loved. This new mystery gift, although also a flower, had been intended to get her out of the safety of the trading post but not to kill her or anyone else. It hadn't any ominous threat included like the last note either.

"Do you know of anyone who would do something like this?" the professor asks as they turn before the populace center to cross the bridge. "Do you have any enemies? Someone who would want to lure you out of Alcromech at this time? Is there someone who would want to hurt you in any way?"

"I'm not sure," Gwen supplies after a moment's pause. *I haven't told any of them yet about Michael's murder. Do I share that info now? I'm not sure being suspected of murdering my boyfriend would help my case at the tribunal much. On the other hand, if they've been following me before they showed up to take me into custody, they may already know.*

Gwen glances at Nicola on her right, wondering if the lady will notice if she should slip into her thoughts. Just then the older witch looks into Gwen's face and for a moment Gwen can't help wondering if the lady can read her mind.

"Is there something you want to tell us, lass?" Instead of accusation, Gwen sees only genuine concern in the Irish witch's eyes.

"Something like this happened to me the other day, only it was someone else who suffered, not me." Gwen swallows the lump of apprehension in her throat and continues in a faint voice. "A strange note with flowers was left then, too ... only I'm not sure this isn't something completely different."

"What do you mean, child?" Nicola's face has gone ashen, and her muscles stiff. The hand gripping Gwen's arm tightens its grasp.

"I believe that I may have two separate persons stalking me for completely different reasons," Gwen confesses in a hushed voice, the realization sending a cold numbness through her already soaking wet frame.

"Do you have the note from the last time?" Professor Leven speaks up. Gwen turns to him apprehensively and shakes her head in the negative.

"Why?" she asks, confused.

"Because there's a little spell we can do on the note that will tell us about some info on anyone who touched that card or maybe

even identify the person who wrote the words," he explains, glancing at Nicola over Gwen's head. The two exchange a knowing look.

"Professor, the Coerisa Phantasmagoria flower is still in our room. I didn't dare touch it. The note should still be there, too," Leona supplies from over Gwen's shoulder. The man beside Gwen nods.

"Good, then we might just get some answers." By now they've crossed the bridge and made their way up the stairs of the Black Iris. Gwen allows the professor to help her inside and to a chair at one of the tables in the common room.

"I'll go get the note!" Leona offers and hurries out of the room.

"Don't touch the flower or the box, girl! Just bring the note," Aunt Nicola calls after her adopted niece before returning to Gwen's table.

"Jonah, young Master Blackwool, why don't one of you get lady Gwenevere a drink while the other goes and informs Madam Sabre of the presence of the poisonous flower in the boarding house? Someone will need to quarantine it from doing further harm." The professor's words send the two young men scrambling off in different directions.

Without needing to communicate which will do which task, Jonah hurries to the kitchen while Thayer races down the corridor, calling out for Madam Sabre. This leaves Gwen alone with the two adult Wiccans who both stand before, neither deeming to take a seat at the table beside her.

"Gwenevere, let me formally introduce you to Professor Vincent Leven." Nicola indicates the thirty-something man beside her with a respectful bow of the head. "He's a teacher at the Monroe Institute and another member of the Thirteen Elders of Monroe."

"Pleasure to meet you, Professor." Gwen bows her head to him slightly, gripping the arms of her chair to help keep the room from spinning around her. "So, you're another elder of the Monroe coven. Doesn't that mean you're a Thoyen, too? They're the same thing, right?"

"Yes, they are, Lady Gwenevere." He smiles broadly at her, as a teacher would a clever pupil. "I'm sorry we had to meet under such circumstances."

"You were supposed to meet tonight at dinner when we discussed the matter of your tribunal," Nicola adds. "I was hoping to get Professor Leven here to vote on our side. With his sympathy for the situation, it might help sway the rest of the Thoyens to grant your entry into the coven. Two Thoyens speaking on your behalf is far better than just one."

"Well, you've got my vote for sure now." Professor Leven puts his hands on his hips and examines Gwen as if trying to solve a puzzle. "It's one thing to hold an untrained, underage witch accountable for breaking the law, but when the youth in question had no knowledge of the law in the first place and is being hunted by dark powers, it changes the situation entirely."

"I agree, Vincent. I think the child is in more need of asylum than a tribunal. That's why I've decided to take the case on myself.

She's survived this long on her own, so obviously she's not as great a danger to herself and others as one might imagine a wild witch would be, however…"

"She is guilty of some serious crimes, true." The young Professor finishes Nicola's thought. "I think considering this new development, it's clear that she needs a coven not only to train her but to protect her. There are all sorts of undesirable creatures that would do any number of evils if they had a chance to get a young witch under their control."

You don't know how right you are. Gwen snorts inwardly. On the outside she tries to keep her face calm as the two adults discuss her as if she isn't even present.

"I'm glad ye see it my way, Vincent." Nicola sighs with relief. "Especially now, after all this, we need to get her out of Alcromech and into the safety of Monroe immediately!"

Just then Jonah comes bounding into the room with a silver chalice in hand.

"Here you are, Lady Gwenevere." He places it before Gwen on the table, out of breath. "Is there anything else I can get you?" he asks formally, taking on the air of the servant that society has deemed him to be. His mind reels with a thousand unspeakable feelings that Gwen is only privy too because of Jonah's open and unabashed mind.

I can't leave her side, I can't. I must be with her. How can I marry Isla when I love another? If anything, ever happens to Gwen, it'll kill me. Not being with her will kill me. Surely everyone will understand. *Won't they? Do they really expect me to marry the girl my parents picked out for me, to marry a friend? What would Father say if he was here? What would Mother think?*

"No." Gwen answers quietly. "I'm fine, thank you." Their eyes lock on each other and suddenly Gwen can't fight the need to tell him everything. Everything she's ever thought, felt, or done, right here, right now.

"I think it's best I skip dinner with you all tonight. I'd have a better chance of convincing the rest of the council in person." Professor Leven speaks up, completely oblivious to the tension hanging in the air between the two teenagers.

The professor's voice jerks Jonah's attention away from Gwen. Their broken eye contact abruptly ended as the broken dream of their would-be affair. Both relieved and disappointed that the moment has passed, Gwen shuts Jonah's thoughts firmly out of her head. *I will not take what belongs to someone else. The first opportunity I get, I'm getting the hell away from here and all of them, especially him. All I can ever give him is pain.*

"That's an excellent idea, Professor." Nicola and the professor clasp hands and make the Wiccan sign of respect for a Thoyen over their foreheads with their other hand.

"Give the professor back his coat now, child. He needs to be off, and we need to get you upstairs and out of those wet clothes."

Nicola helps Gwen to her feet as Gwen peels Professor Leven's long white coat off her shivering shoulders and hands it back to him. He smiles at her with a nod.

"Till we meet again, Lady Gwenevere." He bows to each of them in turn before turning on his heel and making his exit with a purposeful stride.

"I'll go find Thayer," Jonah offers, speaking to his aunt but his eyes brush across Gwen with a silent plea.

"That's a fine idea, lad. Thank you."

Without glancing at him, Gwen turns with Aunt Nicola, and they leave the common room. Gwen can't control her shivering body. Taking this for fear, Nicola holds Gwen close to her as they climb the stairs up to her room.

"Now don't you fret, lass. We'll protect you; we'll get you out of here and to the safety of the coven. But first I think it's time you told me your story, dearie. I mean the whole story. And I warn you, girl, I'll know if ye be lying. For your own good as well as ours, ye need to tell me the absolute truth. We need to know what be lurking in the shadows."

Chapter Twenty-Seven

Lost Spirit

Darkness cloaks him as he watches over the Black Iris boarding house. His eyes fall on one of the upper windows on the third floor, waiting for the lady of the hour to appear. The rest of the Black Iris seems dead as the grave to Raven — nothing but the muttering and snoring of sleeping witches. Despite the pleasant quiet of the woods behind the boarding house, Raven feels a heaviness in the night air. The shadows seem darker, every sound more ominous.

Someone tried to harm Gwen. The thought nearly sends him into an animal rage every time it crosses his mind. He can't tell anymore who he's most angry with. The ones who sent Gwen the cursed flower, the incompetent witches who were nearly powerless to protect her, or himself for not being with Gwen when the whole thing happened.

Raven clenches his fists with a growl. He sends several quick punches into the tree trunk beside him. Ignoring the scraping of bark against his knuckles, he pummels his unforeseen adversary. The tree groans and cracks, splitting in the middle. The sound seems loud in the still night. Raven steps back with an exhausted, anguished sigh. He stares down at his shaking hands. Blood drips into the dirt off his split knuckles as his hands throb. For a moment, the pain soothes the dark places in his soul.

Wood creaks nearby. Perking up, Raven looks up at the boarding house. Gwen slowly climbs out of her bedroom window on the third floor, her long black hair pulled back into a ponytail trailing down her back. Despite being all dressed in black, Raven's wolf eyes see her in the silvery glow of the moon. Luckily, the room she shares with Leona faces the back of the Wiccan lodging, leaving her exit only visible to him. In a few deft maneuvers, Gwen scales the side of the building and lands on the ground like a cat. *Gwen has always been extremely agile and strong.* She scans the tree line with her emerald eyes. He waves her over. Giving him a mischievous smile, she jogs a crossed the opening to meet him in the cover of the woods.

"Did you have any trouble getting away this time? The Caddo twins didn't try to tag along again, did they?" Gwen asks in a hushed voice as she stuffs her hands into the pockets of her black leather jacket. Her eyes are bright with excitement, her pale skin iridescent to his night eyes. *Beautiful.* Raven shakes the thought away, forcing himself to focus on the task at hand.

 425

"No. They're getting suspicious, though. "Raven runs a hand through his long black hair which hangs loosely around his shoulders. "This is the third night I've turned down their invitation to go running with the wolves. I had to tell them I was spending the night with a girl to get them off my case," Raven admits, realizing belatedly how that might sound to Gwen.

"Oh! Is there some pretty she-wolf about which I should know?" Gwen teases with a sideways smirk as they make their way deeper into the woods that run along the edge of Alcromech.

They've already searched the perimeter of the trading post to the north, and west of the Black Iris. No weakness in the trading post's magical wards have they found, nor have they found any signs of Morna. Tonight, they search the east end of Alcromech. If they find nothing still, then they're out of options for their escape. Try as she might, Gwen still can't access her magic. Raven won't hear any more talk of escaping on his own. With Morna still missing and Gwen's powers temporally suppressed, the idea is too absurd. *No, they either leave altogether or not at all.*

"No, of course not," Raven blurts out too quickly, gaining an incredulous look from Gwen. "I mean yes, there are some pretty girl wolves around but I'm not, I wouldn't…"

"Relax, Raven!" Gwen chuckles with a wicked smile. "It's okay, you don't have to give me every detail of your love life. I figure you'll spill the beans when someone special comes along, but until then…" Gwen shrugs and then ducks under a low tree branch.

Gwen peaks over the branch at him to add, "There's no need to be embarrassed if you have a fling."

"I'm not because there is no one."

"Uh huh, then why are your ears turning red?" Gwen inquires with a quirked brow. Turning, she picks her way through the muddy path between the trees. The smells of the musky woods thick about them do nothing to hide Gwen's scent from his supernatural sense — wild berries and wildflowers with a tinge of smoke, which he's always found odd since Gwen doesn't smoke. She's always had a hint of charred wood about her.

"I'm serious, Gwen. If I were in love with someone, you'd be the first to know," Raven insists, trekking through the mud after her.

"Well, not everything has to be about love, you know; sometimes it's just about companionship or for fun really."

"Okay. I'll keep that in mind, thanks," Raven answers with an exasperated sigh. "Can we just focus on finding Morna and getting the hell out of this place, please?" The smell of water has been growing stronger and now Raven can hear the river somewhere off to the left of them.

Gwen shakes her head and chortles to herself.

"Someday, Raven, someday you're going to have to let your guard down and let someone love you." Gwen informs him over her shoulder, "And learn to love someone back." Her attention gets caught up in climbing over several fallen trees.

The comment makes Raven lose his step, almost stumbling over a tree trunk. He gulps down hard on the ball of feelings lodged in his throat. "What makes you think I haven't already...." When he looks up again, Gwen has made it into a clearing twenty feet ahead of him.

"We're here!" she announces, turning to gesture for him to follow. "I can feel the power in the magical wards; I can hear it humming." Mystified, Gwen cautiously steps towards the edge of the clearing. With a hand outstretched, she searches for the invisible wall.

Just tell her already. Raven hears the voice in his head shout at him. The voice is the alpha male buried inside the wolf. He isn't afraid to go after what he wants. *Yeah, but Raven is,* he reminds himself disparagingly. *What's there to be afraid of?* asks the wolf. *Everything! What if I pour my heart and soul out to her and Gwen doesn't feel the same way? What if our friendship can't recover from it?* he inquires of the wolf. *That's nonsense; she'd never turn on us. Even if not our mate, bonded like litter mates are we. Lover or sister, Gwen will always love us.*

The voice speaks sense, and the thought comforts him, but still, he's not quite emboldened enough to say the words to Gwen just yet. *First, we find Morna and a way out of this mess, and then I'll do it. I swear.* This seems to satisfy the wolf ... for now.

Raven joins Gwen in the clearing. Looking at the woods on the other side, he detects nothing out of the ordinary. Even his wolf night vision sees nothing to indicate that an invisible force field is before his eyes.

"Are you sure it's here?" Raven looks to the left and right of them. "I still can't see anything." Collecting a small twig from the ground, Raven chucks it towards the trees. It soars through the air a moment before abruptly hitting an unseen wall. It falls to the ground with a thud.

"Well, that answers that question." Gwen steps up to stand just before the twig. Putting both her hands up palms out, she places them firmly on the force field. It ripples at her touch. The trees beyond the clearing seem to shift momentarily as if emerged in clear water. The effect is rather disorientating. "Now let's see if there are any weaknesses, shall we?" Closing her eyes Gwen chants under her breath the same group of words repeatedly.

"Revale ey Fau lete, bray ke bindae, Revale ey Fau lete bray ke bindae!" As she does this, she walks slowly sideways along the unseen force.

"How do you know what to say?" Raven can't help asking as he watches her in wonder. "I mean, where do the ideas for spells come from when you've never been trained how to use magic?" He paces in the clearing, his hands shoved into his jean pockets. "I guess I've always wondered how you do it. Nicola and the others seem to act as though you're a kid playing with matches. But for all I can tell, you're a natural with all of this."

Gwen stops in her tracks. Her shoulders slump and she exhales in frustration. "Well, thank you, Raven." Taking a break from chanting, Gwen opens her eyes and looks at him. "It does come naturally to me, I suppose. I've watched Leona read a dozen books in the last few days about various subjects pertaining to the practice of witchcraft. It seems like classic magic is supposed to be complex, yet somehow what I do seems simpler. Maybe I've just stumbled upon a condensed version of magic. No herbs, candles, or sacrifices required." Gwen jests, Raven gives her a little chuckle. "I don't know. I guess I just think of words in the true tongue that would best communicate what I want to occur, and I put them together like lyrics in a song. Then I chant them over and over while I focus all my energy and my every thought into my spell. I say the words until I know without a doubt that the spell will work. I put my faith into the words, and somehow it makes my intent, my desire come true."

"Hmmm … I guess that makes sense."

"Yeah, well, it helps if I can actually access the magical forces of the universe first." Gwen sighs deeply. "Right now, I'm like a candle without a wick!" She throws her hands up in defeat and walks to the edge of the clearing, toward the sound of the river.

"Still can't do magic, huh."

Gwen shakes her head but doesn't turn around to look at him. She just keeps walking deeper into the woods, keeping just to the left of Alcromech's magical barrier.

Raven jogs after her. When he catches up to her, he falls in step beside her despondent trudge. Crickets chirp in the night and fireflies dance amongst the bushes. The river's gurgling grows louder with it the scent of wet dirt, water, and fish. Gwen stares out into the dark night, her eyes listless and distant. Her long black ponytail bounces against her black jacket as she moves. The cool night breeze sends her bangs fluttering across her face in tendrils. Gwen's mouth is set in determination, despite the feeling of despair that hangs about her.

"Don't worry, Gwen. We'll find a way to get out of here."

"What good would that do?" Gwen replies after a long silence. "Unless Nicola lifts the restriction spell upon me before we escape, I'll just be returning to the outside world completely helpless. And unless *Morna* decides to stop playing the world's longest game of hide and seek, we'll be minus our fairy to boot!" Gwen nearly shouts Morna's name, spinning around as she speaks as if saying it to the trees. She waits a moment, waiting for the little blue fairy to pop out from behind a bush right that moment.

Raven can't help scanning the trees for their friend as well. But the moment drags on, and Gwen's words are answered only by silence. Together they turn and resume walking toward the river. Within minutes they emerge from the trees onto the riverbank. They find themselves now several miles downriver from the Black Iris. On the opposite end of the trading post from the waterfall, this part of the river is quiet and peaceful. Fewer buildings line the river here, but none are within hearing distance of where they stand.

"Why do you think she left?" Raven asks as he bends down and collects several pebbles from the bank. Handing a few to Gwen, they skip the stones across the surface of the water. "What's Morna up to? Why stay hidden all this time?"

"I wish I knew. She was afraid of something, that I do know. I also know that, thanks to the magical barrier, no one can get out of Alcromech without taking the Luficinian roads."

"And Morna can't because she didn't take the heritage test or get the travel slip thing, right?"

"Exactly! So, she's stuck, unless she comes out of hiding." Gwen adds in exasperation.

"And she's not doing that because…?"

"I don't know, Raven," Gwen half shouts in frustration. Out of pebbles, she stuffs her hands into her pockets and kicks a large rock into the black water. It sinks with a plop, bubbles escaping to the surface as it plummets. "She's hiding something. She has been all along, you know that, right?"

"Yeah, I guess I did," Raven admits, tossing his last pebble across the river's surface. Without anything to distract him, he finds himself staring down at his empty hands. "But what is she hiding? And why would she hide anything from us? She should know she can trust us by now, shouldn't she?" Raven can't keep the pain out of his voice and see's Gwen's face react to it with betrayal in her own eyes. She reaches out a hand and places it on his back.

"You'd think." Gwen tries to laugh it off, but the attempt is forced. Her voice falters. Her weak attempt at a smile melts away even before it forms. "Whatever she's hiding, it has to be something pretty big to make us worry like this."

"So, what are we going to do?" Raven asks after a beat. "I can't stand the idea of us going down separate paths, literally out of this place, and I can't follow you to the coven."

Gwen lets her hand fall away from him and takes a few steps upriver. Her back to him, she looks at the trading post a moment before speaking. "We can't fight them. We can't escape. We can't leave Morna behind. We can't do anything!" Gwen's voice almost breaks as she bows her head, shoulders slumped. She looks all at once ridiculously small and childlike, vulnerable, something she hasn't been ever since they reunited after her escape from Bec La Nuff. She was a prisoner once before. She was stripped of her power and at the mercy of others then, just like she is now.

The thought fills him with a strange mixture of melancholy and rage. The wolf rumbles in his gut, begging for an enemy to tear apart in her defense. Yet killing someone wouldn't help them out of their predicament. Both Raven and the wolf know this. Raven closes his eyes and fights his animal instincts down with all his might. The creature within quiets but remains just beneath the surface; simmering in his restless need to enact vengeance in the name of his beloved.

Gwen's startled scream pierces through the still night. Raven's eyes fly open, and he gasps. Gwen lays on the riverbank, her face contorted in fear and panic. She claws at the wet dirt, trying to find a handhold as something wraps around her legs, attempting to drag her beneath the water's surface.

"Raven! Help!" She calls for him and he sprints forward. He manages to grab hold of her hand just as she loses her grip and slips farther into the river. Now up-close Raven can see that the thing coiled around Gwen's legs is scaly and shimmering.

With all his might, he pulls Gwen back toward the bank. Her unseen assailant below the river's surface pulls against him. Finding himself in a tug o' war for Gwen's life, Raven calls for the strength of the wolf. The animal inside him gives him power. Raven pulls Gwen to him overcoming her attacker. Gwen's panicked screams quickly turn into angry shouts. Gwen tries to balk, to kick her way free, as Raven pulls her away. Water splashes wildly about them drenching them as the thing clinging to Gwen struggles to regain its hold on its prey. During the struggle, something small rolls out of Gwen's inside jacket pocket onto the wet dirt.

Suddenly the head and shoulder of a woman burst forth from the water's surface. Her features are overcast, and she says not a word. Her arms reach out toward Gwen and transforms before their eyes into long, willowy tentacles. Shouting, Gwen flips onto her back and starts kicking the scaly coil off her legs. She uses her one free hand to deflect the woman's attacking tentacles. Grunting and straining, Raven continues to pull Gwen to safety. The woman's mutated limbs wrap themselves around Gwen's upper body and yank hard. With a jerk, Gwen's hand is torn from his grasp.

"Gwen!"

Gwen's shouts are silenced as the tentacles pin her arms to her side and wrap around her head, covering her mouth and eyes. Unable to breathe, Gwen thrashes wildly as the strange creature submerges into the river, pulling Gwen below with her.

* * * * *

It all happened in a matter of minutes. One moment she was standing on the bank of the river, Raven standing just a few feet behind. Alcromech asleep around them in the stillness of the night. Then all at once, Gwen found herself fighting for her life against a creature she had never encountered before.

Mermaid... The thought hit her right away and brought back the image of the woman from her last dream walk with Jonah. She didn't have long to dwell on the fact, however. As soon as she realized she was in real danger, Raven was at her side. Grabbing her hand, he attempted to pull her out of the monster's clutches. Only the lady below the river proved stronger than Raven alone. She employed all her magical limbs into enmeshing Gwen in her deadly embrace. The moment Raven lost hold of her hand there was nothing Gwen could do to fight, to escape. That's when the world became liquid, dark, and endless. Dragged beneath the river's surface, magicless, helpless, and losing oxygen, Gwen truly panics.

She pushes and shoves against the barrier standing between her and the magic on which she has always relied. It is her only real weapon in the world of the forsaken. Yet nothing she can do makes the restriction spell weaken.

Damn you, Nicola! Damn you, Jonah! You've doomed me. They could've released her from the restriction spell after the whole mess with the cursed flower. They did not. Instead, they left her powerless as a doe in a hunter's scope. They knew she was being targeted yet they did nothing to really protect her. *And now I'm going to die.*

The world spins around her. *Oh no, I'm almost out of air.* She struggles to glance upward toward the water's surface. The little light from the moon barely illuminates it from the rest of the dark fluid around her. She forces her body to move toward that spot of light. At the same moment, the creature unwinds its tentacle-like arms from around her. They transform back into regular feminine limbs. With the tentacles no longer obstructing her mouth, Gwen struggles not to take a breath.

Before Gwen can take advantage of this opportunity, the woman paddles her arms through the water. Still entangled in the mermaid's scaly tail, Gwen is dragged along behind her. Desperately trying to paddle herself, Gwen tries to swim back towards Raven. The watery creature possesses superior strength to her own. Helpless, Gwen finds herself swiftly propelled in the opposite direction of her only friend. *Where is she taking me? Where is the Man in Black with the soulless eyes when I need him?* Delirium starts to take hold of her. *Hello out there? I can't fulfill your evil plans if I'm dead, now, can I?* Gwen neither hears nor sees any sign of her lifelong apparition.

Gwen chokes, her eyelids flutter, and darkness encroaches upon her vision. It swallows up the bit of light flashing up above her as she and her captor move through the water like a Jet Ski.

This is it? Is this how I die? As the light fades from view, she finds herself slipping into what feels like a heavy sleep. … *The final sleep.*

Suddenly, a bright light overwhelms the darkness, eradicates it from her sight. The brightness revives her. It brings her back from the brink of consciousness. The light comes nearer. The vague shape of a small young woman hovers at its center. The girl's features are lost in the light. A golden braid of hair is evident and billowy shapes float out from behind her. *Are those wings?*

Arms wrap around Gwen's waist. The feeling of the new personage wrapped about her gives Gwen comfort, not terror. She opens her mouth, and a large bubble emanates, floating over Gwen's entire head. Inside the bubble, Gwen feels her face completely dry and gasps. *Air!* Sweet oxygen fills her lungs as she sucks in desperately. With the air comes greater clarity. *Morna, you beautiful creature, you!*

Gwen feels only briefest sensation of joy and recognition from the girl before the mental connection is closed, leaving Gwen wondering if she might be mistaken.

The being of light tucks her head beneath Gwen's chin. She presses Gwen to her chest and tugs with incredible force. Instantly the mermaid's progress forward halts. Realizing her captive is being stolen, the water maiden whirls back to confront them.

Her rescuer releases Gwen to face the woman. With Gwen's legs still caught and unable to swim to the surface, she is forced to watch how this skirmish will play out.

The sea maiden's hair splays out around her head in tendrils of gold, her face cast in harsh shadows and blueish-silver tints. *Definitely not the same mermaid from Jonah's dreams. This is a grown woman, not the teenage girl with hair like fire.*

An ugly sneer contorts the woman's otherwise attractive face as she lungs toward the illuminating being with wings. The woman's arms transform again into tentacles.

Unfazed, the small woman flicks the encroaching limbs aside effortlessly. Her arms remain at the ready to deflect the sea creature's further attacks. The mermaid does not give up easily. She attempts to encircle the glowing teen in her appendages. Instead, she finds her prey has slipped from her grasp with a speed that defies moving through water. Suddenly the blue, glowing girl appears behind the mermaid. With hands outstretched as if holding an invisible ball, a small orb of white light forms. By the time the watery woman has spun around to face the other woman, the glowing orb has overtaken her. The mermaid jolts in shock. Turning, she attempts to flee from the orb of light with Gwen still entangled in her tail. The lady does not get far.

When the orb's light encompasses them, Gwen and the mermaid are left paralyzed, like flies stuck in ointment. Gwen's every muscle stiffens. Even the look of terror is captured on the mermaid assassin's face. With all three of them encircled in the white orb's light, the mythical sphere ascends. The sensation resembles that of an elevator only without the jolting or the sense of gravity.

Within moments, the orb breaks through the water's surface. The dark, moonlit night sky is high above them. The trading post's main streets are empty at this late hour. Still frozen in animation, the orb floats them through the air to the river's bank. Once the orb touches the ground, it bursts as a bubble, releasing everything within from its spell. With the river water, Gwen, and the mermaid crash to the ground. Water splashes about them, spilling into the river or absorbing into the soil. Gwen lands hard on her hip, her legs still trapped in the mermaid's vice-like tail. Likewise, the mermaid is also jarred by the impact of the fall, responding with shouts of pain. Only the woman bathed in light lands softly on her feet.

Gwen turns to see the glowing girl's light diminish and fade into her skin. Morna stands before her, blue skin, golden braid over one shoulder, and wings sopping wet. Gwen fights the urge to run to her friend and scoop her up into her arms. *Raven will be overjoyed to know she's okay,* Gwen realizes. She quickly scans the riverbank and the road nearby. No sign of him anywhere

On dry land, the mermaid's tail and tentacles reshape, returning to human arms and legs. Finally, free Gwen scurries away from the mermaid. Without her scales and mermaid appendages covering her, the woman lies on the bank naked. She tosses her long, wet, blonde hair out of her eyes to glare at them both. She glances suspiciously between the witch and the fairy. Indecision is evident in the tense hunch of her shoulders.

"Start talking, Mer." Morna speaks. Her eyes narrow as she stares down the woman at her feet, her demeanor dark as the fairy paces in front of her captive. "Who are you? Why are you hunting Gwenevere? Who sent you?"

"Do what you will." The Mermaid snorts in distain. "You'll get nothing from me."

"Perhaps you won't talk to her, but I've been known to be pretty persuasive." Nicola's voice startles Gwen and the mermaid. Simultaneously they turn to see Nicola followed by Raven briskly jogging towards them. Both look out of breath. Nicola wears a long white night gown underneath a warm woolen cloak. She has slippers on her feet. Her hair is thrown up into a hasty bun. Tendrils of red hair spill about her ears.

"Gwen!" Raven practically slides on the bank to skid at her side. Kneeling in the mud, he takes her by the shoulders, quickly surveying her for any sign of injury "What did she do to you? Are you okay?" Gwen cannot help shivering. Raven wastes no time peeling off his coat and draping it over her shoulders.

"I'm fine, Raven," Gwen assures. Mentally Gwen adds, *Morna got to me just in time. A few seconds longer and I would've drowned. How did Morna know where I was or get to me so fast? Where did she come from?*

She saw the whole thing. Raven opens his mind to her, showing her his memory. In it she sees the mermaid attack her from his eyes.

Just before the mermaid dragged her under water, Gwen sees a tiny Morna roll out of her inside jacket pocket into the wet dirt on the bank. As soon as Gwen disappeared into the river, Morna got to her feet in a panic. With a blinding light and a deafening roar, she instantly transformed into her human-size self.

Before Raven even had a chance to register that the long lost Morna had finally returned, the fairy spun on him with urgency and command in her voice. "Raven, hurry, get Nicola! Meet me upriver!" Uttering a spell, her light shone even brighter as she dove into the water.

The whole exchange takes only a moment and then the two friends return their attention to the present.

"The lass is fine, Raven. Mer-folks have the ability to secrete a solution from their scales that temporarily leaves their captives dormant. Frozen between life and death. Although the magical wards never would allow anyone to do harm to another within its barriers, one can still cast non-deadly spells." With hands on hips Nicola advances on the vulnerable Mer-woman with a look that would terrify the most loathsome beast. The blond mermaid shivers involuntarily. "I suspect her aim was never to kill Gwen but to capture her and deliver her to someone else."

Nicola pauses as if to give the Mer-woman a chance to confess or contradict but the lady stays silent. "Of course, the fool couldn't have kin that Gwenevere here, is under a spell and incapable of leaving the trading post."

The look of utter confusion turns to outrage in the Mer's eyes tell that Nicola's suspicions are correct. Suddenly the mermaid lunges towards the water's edge, only to be jerked back by unseen hands. With a banshee like screech the mermaid falls on her back onto the wet sand, chest heaving and eyes wild. Her evil eyes fix on Morna, who clearly still holds the woman in her magical grasp.

"All that matters now is finding out who sent her," Morna pronounces. Still pacing along the bank, Gwen notices that her friend seems to be avoiding looking at her and Raven. *What is her deal? She makes us worry all this time only to save me at the last possible moment and then treats us like strangers.*

I know, it all seems so odd. Something's up with her. Can you get inside her head? Will she talk to you mentally? Raven suggests through Gwen and his shared mental thread of thought.

Gwen tries to send the thread of thought toward Morna, sending feelings of love, concern, and gratitude into her mental words. She finds a blank wall over her friend's mind. All attempts to mentally knock on the barrier as if asking for permission to enter are ignored. Gwen watches Morna the whole time. The fairy tenses the moment Gwen's mind tries to touch her own, but she keeps her eyes averted. She looks at the sky, the river, the soil under her blue toes, even at Nicola, but never at her so-called friends.

Gwen turns to look at Raven, whose eyes are big with expectation and hope. She nods sadly in the negative. Raven's face falls and he releases a pained sigh as he punches a fist into the dirt.

"I have ways of discovering these things," Nicola announces as she pushes up the sleeves of her cloak, flourishes her hands before her, and chants, *"Mem orate, curvate, extrac tae! Otum provot, mem orate retri voe extrac tae!"*

The mermaid stiffens, throwing her head back and arching her back as if in incredible pain. With eyes brimming with hatred, the captured sea maiden visibly tries to resist Nicola's spell. She utters a spell of her own in her defense.

Gwen watches the two women with wonder. Her ability to use magic might be temporarily out of order, but her talent to detect magic and discern the mechanisms within a spell are still very much intact.

What is she doing? Raven asks.

Trying to extract her memories. The mermaid has a spell on her mind keeping Nicola from making her confess aloud in a truth spell. So, she's trying to bypass that spell with a memory extraction. If successful, it will take her memories and put them into Nicola's mind.

After several minutes of straining, Nicola's hands fall, and she gives a huff and walks away. The mermaid collapses to the river edge, unconscious in exhaustion from fighting Nicola's will. Nicola steps up to Gwen and Raven. Tired lines appear in her forehead and around the eyes.

"I'll handle this one. Gwen, why don't you let Raven here take you back to the Black Iris and get back in bed. You've had quite the ordeal."

"I want to…" Gwen protests but Nicola silences her with a curt gesture of the hand.

"There's nothing you can do to help me, lass. You're under my care and I mean to do a better job of protecting you from here on, you kin?" Gwen reluctantly clamps her mouth shut and nods. Raven helps Gwen to her feet. "And take that wee fairy with you too, Gwenevere. I'll be needing a word with her shortly, so you better keep a better eye on her this time," Nicola instructs. Raven and Gwen automatically agree. Nicola returns to the mermaid's limp, prostrate body.

Focusing their complete attention on the fairy, the two friends shuffle over to Morna.

Gwen opens her mouth to speak to her small blue friend, but Morna bows her head and turns without a word. She leads the way back toward the boarding house, letting them trail silently behind her. Morna's long, iridescent wings hang limply down her back, her shoulder's slumped, her head downcast as if depleted of her essence. She seems for all the world like a shadow of their vacant friend. Merely an empty vessel for a lost spirit.

Chapter Twenty-Eight

Liberation

*B*y the time they enter the dark boarding house, Gwen is brimming with questions. Stopping before the register desk, Morna turns to face them at last. Her face is contoured by the moonlight shining through the glass door and windows. Gwen senses no relief in her heart-shaped face, just apprehension. Wringing her hands, the fairy's glance bounces around the empty dining room and back to Gwen without lingering long. Morna doesn't look at Raven at all. Unease hangs around Raven like a fog. He glances between the two girls and clears his throat.

"Well, I'm gonna get back to the Captured Moonlight. Everyone will be wondering where I am," Raven announces to the room nervously with a forced, casual smile. Before turning to leave he hesitates at Morna's side. He moves as if to put his arm around her and then chooses instead to give her a slight pat on the shoulder. "I'm glad you're back, Morna." He gives Gwen a quick hug, saying goodbye. Gwen listens to his retreating tread. The door shuts as he makes his exit out of the Black Iris, leaving the witch and fairy alone.

Gwen folds her arms across her chest and tilts her head, boring holes into Morna's skull with her expectant gaze. Morna barely looks at her. When she does, her large yellow eyes seem so hopeless and childlike it almost curbs Gwen's anger. Almost. Gwen taps a foot as she waits for Morna to finally open up her mouth and say something. Anything.

"You naughty little bug!" Gwen blurts out. "What were you doing in my jacket? We've been looking for you everywhere, you..." Gwen's face changes as realization dawns. "That's why Jonah's spell didn't work that night. You were in my jacket all along! How did you get in there without anyone seeing you? And how did you live there for so long? Even fairies must eat." Gwen's agitation shows itself in the form of expressive hand gestures.

"Keep your voice down!" Suddenly, Morna steps up to Gwen's face, her wings still dripping water behind her. She places a finger over her lips and shushes Gwen. Together they look toward the stairs and pause to listen for movement. No one stirs.

"Well? Are you going to explain yourself?" Gwen demands in her normal voice with her hands on her hips.

"I slipped out of the Populace Center quickly before anyone saw me and changed size behind the building. I waited until you came out looking for me and slipped into your inside coat pocket," Morna confesses sheepishly.

"Well, that explains how you disappeared, but not why," Gwen concedes, still a little miffed.

"No one can know that I'm here," Morna explains in her hummingbird tone. "I can't go back to my kind, Gwen. And if anyone here knew who I really was, they'd catch me and send me back to my mother for the reward."

"What reward?" Gwen's hands drop from her hips suddenly. Morna turns away. "Morna? What kind of trouble are you in? What did you do?"

"I ran away. This you already know." Morna's shoulders droop. "What you don't know is that I was supposed to marry a prince and this marriage would've brought with it a treaty between my nest and another rival nest. I agreed to the marriage before I met you. Before I met…"

Gwen doesn't need to be a mind reader to know whose name she's reluctant to say.

"When you were trapped in Bec LaNuff, Angelo and Raven were looking for help storming the fortress. I went to my people first before going to the witches. I went to my own mother and told her all about you." Morna's voice wavers for a moment before she takes a deep breath and continues. "How you had saved my life. How important you were to me. However, she did not see the advantage in helping a witch, especially when Vampires were involved. My emotions in the matter had no sway over her." Morna turns to look at Gwen, her eyes misty, her face caught in turmoil. "When it became obvious, they wouldn't help, I renounced my claim as heir to the throne and forsook my bonds to my nest and all my Fairy kin."

"Wait, what? Your claim as heir? To the Throne?" Gwen sputters incredulously, bewildered. "You're a Fairy princess?" Shocked, Gwen wanders over to a table and drops down into a chair. Morna quickly follows, kneeling before her. She takes Gwen's hand in hers.

"I'm sorry I couldn't tell you. I was afraid of being found and I thought…" Morna bows her head as if the right words are hiding under the table.

"Thought what, Morna?" Gwen scoops her friend's chin with her free hand, forcing her to look up to face her. "That I would turn you in? That I would send you away?"

"No … I mean, maybe. I just…" She shakes her blonde head, water droplets spraying on the floor. She sighs, her blue shoulders slumping. "I liked being just like one of you. I liked being a normal person, and as you've already I guessed, I like…"

"Raven?" Gwen interrupts, finishing the sentence for her little Fae friend.

"Yes. My feelings for him began when I healed him. You remember at Bec LaNuff during the battle when we came to rescue you from…?"

"I remember." Gwen stops her from saying her former capture's name. Gwen pulls Morna up to her feet and indicates with a nod for her to take the chair next to hers. Morna sits after arranging her wings over the back of the chair. "I remember we went in to help the Werewolves fight the Vampires and we found Raven … I couldn't heal him because I still wore the serpent ring, *His* ring." Gwen pauses, rubbing below the knuckle of her left ring finger through the fabric of her gloved hand. All her gloves have stuffing in the tip of that particular finger to hide the fact that it's missing. "I asked you to heal Raven for me and then I left you two alone to go kill him. I should've never have left you…"

"It's fine, Gwen. We made it out," Morna reassures, reaching out she places her hand on Gwen's knee.

"Yes, but you might not have." Gwen balls her hands into fists as she stares off into space, as if seeing the destruction of Bec LaNuff all over again. "I almost killed us all, and a lot of people did die because of me. All because I was blinded by rage. I would've done anything to end his life."

"Because he was a monster. Gwen, you never meant to take the mountain down. You never wanted to hurt any of those people. You must cease to bury yourself in guilt and accept that there is nothing you can do to undo the past."

"Is that what you're doing?" Gwen fixes Morna in her gaze. "By hiding and not trusting us with the truth? Is that how you're accepting things and leaving the past in the past?"

Morna swallows hard as if trying to get down Gwen's harsh words. She glances away guiltily. Gwen sighs, relaxing her tensed posture. She leans in and surprises her friend with a hug. Instantly Morna wraps her arms around Gwen, burying her head into her shoulder.

"So, the question now is what happens next?" With a little laugh, Gwen pulls back to look at Morna. "What kind of reward is your mother offering for your return, anyways? Free fairy wings, mystical gems, a million dollars…?

Morna giggles. "No. The reward is a spell. Any spell in the fairy spectrum, which can be quite the prize when you consider the possibilities."

"It could also be incredibly dangerous if the wrong person were to cash in on that reward." Gwen's forehead furrows between her brows thoughtfully.

"We best not let anyone find you then, lass." Gwen and Morna jump to their feet turning toward the doorway. There Nicola stands, nightgown and all, looking weary and haggard. "Didn't mean to startle you ladies, but it's late and we all should be off to bed."

"What happened to the mermaid?" Gwen asks.

"She's been turned over to the HCOE officials. They will sort her out and get to the bottom of this whole mess. We should know soon who's after you, Gwenevere, and what they want. However, in the morning we will send Morna on her way."

"What do you mean by that, Thoyen Nicola?" Morna asks nervously.

"I mean that I will help you slip out of Alcromech undetected, back the way you came in."

"But why would you help her? She's running from her own kind, she's not a witch, and she's certainly not your problem. Why wouldn't you just turn her into the officials, too?" Gwen asks incredulously.

"I realize that under the circumstances in which we met I might seem like the kind of person who adheres strictly to the law." Nicola sucks a haggard breath between her teeth. "However, I am not without a heart," Nicola admits. She shuffles into the room to join them in the moonlit dining area. "I once found myself betrothed to a stranger, too. I didn't particularly like having my life decided for me. I don't see why your friend should have someone else do the same thing to her. Not to mention, she'll most likely be subject to some punishment for betraying her tribe. That is if she should be returned to them."

Morna and Nicola exchange looks that communicate the severity of the punishment the fairy might be dealt.

"So, you will help me? I can't thank you enough, but..." Morna looks to Gwen. "I have nowhere to go, and I can't abandon my friends."

"It won't be forever, Luv, just until this business with the vampires is worked out." Nicola looks off into space as if seeing the future materialized before her. "Then maybe you and your friends can be reunited." Nicola tries to sound hopeful but something in her tired eyes shows how terrifying the future might be even for one like

her. "Until then, there's an old hermit's cabin just outside of the Monroe Coven. You can stay there.

"Yes, Gwen and I know this place." Morna chirps hopeful. "It was a long time ago, it's probably not the same Hermits cabin I took Gwen to after she escaped Be…" Morna suddenly claps her mouth shut, realizing her near slip. Gwen squeezes the fairy's shoulder in assurance.

"It's okay Morna, Thoyen Nicola knows all about Bec LaNuff." Morna gives Gwen an amazing look. "It was necessary to tell her everything after the attack the other day. You probably overheard all that commotion with the freaky flower that nearly poisoned me with its spores zombifying me."

"What?" Morna's eyebrows rise toward her hair line and her face goes from royal blue to pale blue. "By the stars, no! I'm sorry Gwen, I had myself under an immobilization spell. I could neither hear, see, or feel much."

That explains how you could live in my pocket without moving once and why you never responded when I called for you. Gwen thinks to herself.

"I was meant to stay in that state until you arrived in the coven. I only woke up when I did because of the jolt of your struggle with the mermaid. I had no idea you were in danger, or I never would've done something so thoughtless. By the all the seasons Gwen please forgive me!" Morna rushes to Gwen gathering her in a damp hug. Her arms cling to her as if frightened Gwen might fly away into the wind if the fairy should release her. Gwen wraps her arms around her, planting a kiss on the top of Morna's wet blond head.

"There's nothing to forgive. No one knew any of this was gonna happen." Gwen assures her friend. *Well… we did know someone was after me but not that they would follow me here or what they could do.* Gwen reasons in her head.

"What happened? Are you okay now? Was this mermaid the same one who used the flower on you before?" Morna Steps back from Gwen, leaving one arm still wrapped around her friend, just in case.

"I'm okay Morna, thanks to Nicola and the others. They lifted the curse. If they hadn't been there, I don't know what would've happened." Gwen smiles weakly at Nicola.

"Thank you, Nicola. I'm forever in your debt. You can ask anything of me, and I'll do it." Morna declares her voice touched with utter respect.

"There's no need for that child. I would've done it for anyone. Besides, I took Gwen on as my ward, she's my responsibility now. However, at this point we have no idea if the mermaid is connected to the other attack. Nicola stifles a yarn. "For now, lassies, if you don't mind, I'd like to get back to my bed and so should ye." Nicola starts to head toward the stairs but abruptly stops to look at them. "Morna, you ought to change back to your regular size and sleep somewhere concealed tonight. Leona *is* the type to stay strictly within the law. I fear keeping this kind of secret would trouble her moral sensibilities."

"Ah, probably best we don't tell any of the others either then?" Gwen asks. Nicola nods with a conspirator wink and heads off to bed. "Well, you heard the lady," Gwen quips with a weak laugh.

Morna nods. Taking a deep breath, she steps a few feet backwards to allow space for the transformation. Then she closes her eyes. Her skin glows from within. Slowly the light grows into a shimmering light, making the air around her quiver. The sound like cracking eggs and a whoosh of air heralds the end of Morna's transformation. When the process is over, Morna floats in mid-air, only four inches tall. With wings now dry, she flutters over to Gwen and lands on her shoulder.

Gwen carefully makes her way across the room and up the stairs, mindful of her small passenger.

"I'm sorry I wasn't honest with you, Gwen. I panicked and then … I stayed hidden out of shame and fear. I hope you can forgive me." Morna's small voice chirps in Gwen's left ear.

"Of course." Gwen smiles. "Although you're going to have to make this up to Raven." she points out.

"What do you recommend I do?" Morna asks in trepidation.

"Hmm … I say a big wet kiss ought to do it!"

Morna sends Gwen the mental equivalence of an eye roll. With a smirk and a wicked gleam in her eyes, Gwen barely suppresses a chuckle as she pushes open her bedroom door and slips inside.

* * * * *

The following morning, Raven shows up at the Black Iris at dawn. He bounds through the doors just as Gwen follows Nicola down the stairs into the common room. Cider and freshly brewed coffee fill the air so thickly, Gwen imagines she could take in a deep breath and taste it. Gwen hears pots and pans banging, brooms swishing, and footsteps prattling from the kitchen. *The Black Iris's morning staff must already be busy with breakfast preparations.* One of the kitchen girls scurries out with a tray of pastries and muffins. Their smell whiffs in tendrils behind her, dominating the room. She places it on the sideboard next to the coffee and cider in the dining room.

Before the girl turns to leave, Gwen and Raven simultaneously make a beeline for the tray. Finding herself nearly smooshed between the two. The kitchen girl ducks out of the way and runs for the kitchen, bewildered. The two friends snatch several pastries and a few muffins. Freeing up one of his hands, Raven stuffs his muffins into a coat pocket. He grabs himself a mug of coffee. Gwen follows suit, stowing pilfered pastries into her pocket and getting a cider. They meet up with Nicola, who waits for them at the door. She gives them a bemused smirk as she pushes the door open.

"Follow me, children."

The two obey, slipping out of the boarding house after the middle-aged witch. She doesn't wear her multi-colored Thoyen shawl today. Instead, she is dressed like one of the servants, in brown. *Trying to keep from drawing attention to their activities,*

Gwen surmises. The sun creeps over the forest, lending the trading post a magical light. Few roam the streets at this hour, but servants.

Where is Morna? What happened last night? Raven asks mentally whilst his mouth is full of blueberry muffin. He opens his mind to Gwen as they trail behind Nicola across the wooden bridge.

Completing the mental connection, Gwen shows him the events of last night after he left. He sees the whole thing in his head as if a movie projected from Gwen's brain into his.

So now Morna is stowed away in my coat pocket and we're on our way to the waterfall to send her back out into the world, Gwen adds to bring him up to date.

Gwen finished her pastry. Careful to select a portion without frosting, Gwen tears off a piece of the extra pastry in her pocket and offers it to Morna. The fairy pops out of the right inside jacket pocket just long enough to take the food. Morna gobbles it up greedily.

Wait, I thought no one could get out of the trading post unless they left through the Lucifinian roads? Raven interjects as he takes a swig of coffee.

That's what I thought, too, but apparently Nicola knows a way.

Assuming, that this works, and we get her out, are you sure Morna will be safe at the hermit's cabin? Raven asks as they make their way through the streets of Alcromech. The shops lining the street silently watch over them like sentinels.

I think so. If it's anything like the place Morna sent me when she helped me escape from Bec LaNuff the first time, then it won't be anything fancy but it's isolated and no one from the outside world knows it's there. It's not within the Coven's boundaries but it's close enough that Nicola says I can visit her from time to time.

Gwen senses that this quiets Raven's reservations. If only she could be as confident. Gwen drinks from her cup, letting the cider warm her inside out. Gwen senses Morna inside her pocket finishing her nibble of pastry. The fairy sends feelings of comfort and peace through their bond.

Before long they find themselves back at the beginning of Alcromech, standing next to head of the river and the waterfall. Nicola casually glances about as if sensing through her mental abilities whether they are unobserved. Seeming satisfied, she turns her gaze on Gwen. "It's time."

Gwen nods. Gingerly she reaches into her inside coat pocket. Cradled within her palm, Gwen retrieves Morna, holding her out before Nicola and Raven. In her miniature size, Morna stands in the center of Gwen's hand, wings fluttering. She glances between her friends and then to Nicola with trepidation.

"Go on and make your goodbyes. She needs to stay small for the spell to work and it's less conspicuous." Nicola instructs with a small smile. "Sorry you won't get to hug it out."

"That's fine. We'll have plenty of time to hug when we see one another again," Morna chirps. She turns a sad smile to her two friends. "I'm sorry I waisted so much time hiding. We could've been together these past weeks."

"It's okay. We'll make up for it later," Raven assures. "At least you'll be near Gwen. Promise you'll keep an eye out for each other, for me?" Raven looks between the two women.

"Of course," Gwen and Morna answer simultaneously.

"And you, take care of yourself, okay?" Morna insists as she flies up to hover before Raven's face. "Don't lose yourself to the wolf while you are off with your tribe. Leave some of the man we love to come back to us when this is all over."

"Yeah, promise you won't let the Caddo twins turn you into their triplet. We like you the way you are already," Gwen adds with a smirk.

Raven smiles. "I will, I mean I won't." Raven chuckles. "I promise I won't change too much."

Morna flies to his cheek and snuggles up to it. She's careful to avoid his stubble. Raven puts his hand to his cheek, cradling her there against his skin a moment. When his hand falls away, Morna swoops over to Gwen to rest on her shoulder.

"Everything is going to work out with the tribunal and the coven, I know it, just as long as you keep your temper. Just promise you'll come to visit me the moment you get a chance."

"And every single free moment I have," Gwen adds, smiling sadly.

"I love you both," Morna declares with a weak voice. Gwen and Raven mutter I love you back. Then Morna walks over to Gwen's cheek and gives it a little peck. Turning, the fairy flies over to

Nicola, who stands a little way off trying to give them their space. "I'm ready to go, Thoyen Nicola."

"Good. It's getting late and we don't have a moment to lose." Nicola holds out her hand and Morna lands in the center. Taking a deep breath, the Irish witch squares her shoulders and closes her eyes. She holds her other hand above Morna and begins to chant. *"Invisque, no ambre aire! Li otta fin otta barre!"* She continues the spell until Morna begins to glow white with a throbbing light pulsating around her. Morna holds out her arms and marvels.

"What have you done to her?" Gwen asks, half curious, half fearful.

"I've made her invisible or undetectable to the trading post's barrier spell. It can only work on something as small as she. Although I've only seen it done on objects, not living things, I'm confident the spell will do the trick."

Gwen and Raven exchange worried glances. "Well, what happens if it doesn't work?" Raven asks, his face showing his unease.

"The same thing it did to Gwen when she tried to leave under the influence of the cursed flower," Nicola answers with a sigh. "She won't be harmed permanently but the barrier will sting her and send her right back inside it's ward." Before Gwen or Raven can object, she continues. "But that won't happen." Gwen and Raven nod.

"Goodbye, Morna. I'll see you on the other side soon." Gwen smiles, forcing her voice to sound cheerful.

"Goodbye, Morna. We'll all be back together before you know it," Raven adds, putting an arm around Gwen, hugging her to his shoulder.

Words escaping her, Morna swallows back her tears and waves goodbye instead.

"It's time you be off, little one," Nicola announces.

Morna nods understanding. She zips out of Nicola's hand toward the waterfall, her pulsating white light fading as the distance between them widens. Gwen and Raven watch her go with twin pangs of heartache. They both hold their breath as they watch her small light approach the roaring waterfall. One moment she hovers before the large cascades of water. The next, the light shoots through it and is gone. Nicola waits with them a few moments, all staring at the waterfall expectantly. At last Nicola breaks the silence.

"She's passed through the barrier," she announces, her shoulders relaxing as the tension leaves her.

Gwen reaches out her mind towards Morna and feels nothing. With a sigh of relief, Gwen turns to Raven. "It's true. I can't feel her anymore. At least she's not in Alcromech."

"But how will we know when she's safely arrived at the hermit's cabin? Is there some way she can communicate with you from there?"

"We'll know." Nicola takes Gwen by the elbow and leads the two youths back up the road, leaving the waterfall behind. "There is a summoning glass at the cabin. We can contact her from my own summoning glass in my home without anyone in the coven knowing."

As they walk back to the boarding house, Raven asks Nicola questions about the cabin and the Monroe Coven. Gwen zones out until their voices are little more than a hum in the back of her brain.

Be careful, Morna. I'll be by your side as soon as I can be. Somehow, we'll all get through this mess and be together once again. Gwen sends the thought out into the world, unable to send it directly to the one she seeks. Hoping that just sending positive energy her friend's way will help safeguard her from danger. As they step onto the creaking bridge, Gwen's eyes turn toward the head of the river and the waterfall. Visible in the distance, its roar nothing more than a soft rumble now. Gwen feels the distance between her and Morna like a black hole growing within her chest. Swallowing her emotions down into her belly, Gwen closes her eyes and focus her energy elsewhere.

I will see her again, she assures herself. *First, I have to convince a tribunal that I'm neither crazy nor deadly. Then I must get them to absolve me from unwittingly committing crimes against Wicca. Right. How hard can that be?*

Gwen tries to be glib but some part of her is terrified of what lies ahead of her. Her freedom and her very life hang in the balance. *At least Morna has her freedom.*

Ironically, Gwen feels just as much captive now amongst her own kind as she ever did as Legion's slave. Although Nicola's sympathy to Morna's plight gives Gwen hope. *Perhaps Wiccans are more understanding than I thought? Perhaps the Elders in the Monroe Coven will be lenient? I've faced worse odds,* Gwen reminds herself. *And I managed to come out alive every time. One way or another I will find liberation.*

Chapter Twenty-Nine

Hope for Peace

"**O**w!" Leona yelps. "You're standing on my foot!" she declares to Thayer in an annoyed whisper.

"Sorry, darling." Thayer makes a show of mock contrition as he shuffles his weight, unpinning Leona's foot while planting a quick peck on her cheek. Leona's face flushes. Thayer beams with pride as if embarrassing his betrothed is his whole purpose in life. Gwen snorts. Jonah rolls his eyes while fighting a smirk of his own.

"Shhh!" Aunt Nicola looks over her shoulder at the group of teens with a scowl. Once everyone seems still, she returns her attention back to the front of the room.

Sandwiched between Raven and Jonah just behind Nicola, Gwen can barely make out the floor-to-ceiling mirror on the far wall.

Everyone in the room stares at it expectantly.

The room feels stuffy and cramped as the occupants of the Black Iris gather in the common room, with barely any elbow room to speak off.

Ten minutes earlier, Gwen had been having lunch with Raven outside on a bench by the side of the river. A handful of pedestrians walked about in the midday sun. Since being moved to the werewolf inn, Captured Moonlight, Raven had been at the Black Iris and near Gwen as often as his new werewolf cohorts will allow. In the middle of their meal, a strange voice filled the air as if speaking from the blue sky itself. Startled, everyone stopped what they were doing and look up into the sky to listen.

"An announcement is being conducted in ten minutes!" the disembodied voice echoed outdoors, the sound bouncing off buildings and even overpowering the sound of the river gurgling. "An emergency missive from the High Council of Elders is being conducted in ten minutes! Everyone gives haste to your nearest looking glass!"

Leona, their chaperone for the day, who had been standing ten feet away, rushed to their bench.

"Come quickly inside. We'll watch the announcement from the Black Iris common room," Leona had instructed. Confused, Gwen and Raven obliged, abandoning lunch to follow everyone else inside.

In a matter of minutes, the common room was packed from door to registry desk. Late comers had to stand on the stairs or climb on chairs and tabletops to see over the mass of waiting bodies.

"Does anyone mind explaining why we're all staring at a mirror?" Gwen whispers, to no one in particular. So far, she's spent as little time as possible with Jonah since the incident at the waterfall. They shared an intimate moment that day as he carried her out of the river after breaking the flowers curse, a moment that convinced her she was hopelessly in love with Jonah. The feeling had consumed her so completely that she was all but ready to declare her love to the mountain tops and take the consequences that came with it … until she saw the turmoil within Jonah's heart. Then everything changed. Suddenly she remembered that she was just as cursed and poisonous as the flower that had incapacitated her and taken over her mind. That's when she made the decision to bury her feelings for Jonah and do the right thing for everyone.

After she was attacked by the mermaid, she had to fight the automatic desire to run to Jonah and tell him everything. Even worse was fighting the desire to slip into his dreams and dream walk with him. Some part of her knew she couldn't hide her feelings from him if she were inside his head. She also wasn't sure she wouldn't be tempted to seduce him in the dream world. That would complicate things far more than just having a few very steamy dreams.

How do you convince a man you're not in love with him in the waking world if you've already made love to him in his mind?

So, she has kept the mermaid attack and Morna's reappearance a secret as Nicola instructed. She's even managed to avoid being near him or looking him directly in the eyes until now. Even with layers of fabric between them, his body heat sends a sizzle through her where their arms press against another. With difficulty, Gwen pushes the thought away, like trying to shove an elephant out of an elevator.

"Witches prefer water scrying and looking glasses for passing communications." Jonah leans over her, putting his lips to her ear. "All the magical tribes do. The rest have their own channels," Jonah explains in a muffled voice. Gwen flinches at the wave of heat his breath on her ears and neck sends throughout her frame. When the sensation subsides, she nods her head in understanding, although only half of her listened to a word he just said.

A hush falls over the crowd as the surface of the mirror ripples and shimmers. A new image replaces the room's reflection. Gwen stands on her tiptoes to get a better view. Instead of the waiting crowd in the common room, the mirror reflects a semi-circle of twelve men and women standing in a line on the marble steps of a grand building. *A representative from every tribe but the vampire,* Gwen observes. Humanoid and creature alike, the group stands tall and proud united behind one man. He is tall, black-haired, and blue-eyed, with sun bursts around his pupils. Gwen can only assume the leader is the King of Wicca. He wears a refined suit of white with a deep blue velvet robe over it.

"Since the declaration of rebellion was sent forth by the thirteenth tribe of Cain, the High Council of Elders has diligently endeavored to negotiate reconciliation with our wayward tribesmen." The man addresses the unseen masses.

"That's Deverick Hawthorne. He's the Wiccan King." Jonah leans in and whispers to her as if hearing her unspoken question. Gwen only nods and watches the man before her, mesmerized as he continues speaking.

"Many of you have seen firsthand the slaughter and disappearances taking place out in the human world. These actions fly in the face of our rules of conduct to stay out of the public eye and remain hidden until the Morning Star sounds the bugle heralding the end of the reign of men." He speaks with confidence and refinement. His voice is neither too deep nor high. His eyes pass over the unseen masses with both gentleness but resolve. "It is the belief of the Council that it is only a matter of time until this unruly behavior exposes not only the Vampires but all the Forsaken. If these circumstances weren't dire enough, it has come to our attention that members of the Vampire tribe are orchestrating attacks on an individual within the safe confines of one of the trading posts."

This news produces a series of exclamations and outcries from the audience around them. The nervous muttering dies out quickly as their King continues.

"Despite the protective wards placed on all the Forsaken trading posts, the responsible party has managed to make several attempts to harm and abduct a person. The victim of these attacks will remain anonymous but is a subject of my own tribe. However, one of the agents working on behalf of the vampire in this matter has been apprehended."

The King of Wicca waves a hand in a flourish and the image in the mirror ripples. When the ripple ceases, the image within the mirror is of a new location. A woman is tied up to a pole in the center of a cobblestone town square underwater, yet she is in the middle of a giant pocket of air. Her blonde head hangs down, her face shielded by her curtain of hair. Her body is clothed by a thin white shift that ends at her mid-calf. It is splattered with blood. Her feet are bare — her arms and shoulders too. She hangs limply off the metal pole, looking already half mangled, bruised, and bloodied. A green-tinted palace looms in the background, ancient and authoritative above her. Mermaid villagers mill around her just outside the pocket of air, whispering or shouting expletives at the prisoner. Their insults penetrate through the water into her dry air made prison.

Gwen goes cold inside as recognition dawns. The mermaid's condition has disintegrated so much in the last three days since she attacked her, that Gwen almost didn't place her at first.

What have they done to her? Gwen can't help wondering. Part of her feels a twisted kind of satisfaction. Her better part's knees almost buckle from guilts crushing weight. *No matter what I do, or where I go, someone always gets hurt because of me.*

"The prisoner is Brielle of the Eastern Waters, of the Mermaid Tribe." Again, people gasp and mutter in surprise around her, but Gwen ignores them to hear what the king will say next. The mirror's

image ripples back to that of the elders waiting behind the Wiccan King. "Although Mermaids have lived in peace with the Wiccan tribe for generations, we take this attack on one of Wicca as an act of war. If the Vampires are willing to manipulate other tribes and use them as pawns in their childish rebellion, then they have taken things too far and endanger all treaties and all peace between the rest of the twelve tribes. With safety paramount in the HCOE's mission, we are officially declaring that all trading posts will be shut down entirely to prevent any further attacks of this nature. All forsaken are ordered to hasten to the Lucifinian roads and to their respective covens, nest, packs, townships, and kingdoms tonight by the stroke of twelve."

Again, the Wiccan citizens about her whisper and react to this news with anxious voices and frightened looks.

"This will keep the tribes divided in the physical but is necessary to keep the Vampire from dividing us politically. It will also limit their ability to cause further damage to our delicate alliance." When the Wiccan King finishes, a sad look passes behind his eyes.

Another man steps forward from the semi-circle of the High Council of Elders. He appears to be older than the Wiccan King by twenty years. With his trident of greenish metal in one hand, he uses it as a walking stick to steady his weakening stride. As he comes forward, the Wiccan King and he bow heads to each other in respect. Then he takes the other man's place in the center of the circle before the mirror. Gwen watches with a strange mix of emotions as the wiccan King melts back into the line of elders. For some reason, she can't tear her eyes from him. *It's not like I've seen him before, have I?* Reluctantly she forces her attention to the elderly man instead.

His greying hair twists in tendrils down his shoulders and back, matching his beard that hangs just above his beltline. He has sea green eyes. His skin is of a deep tannish color, making him seem a mix of Caucasian and Pacific-islander. He wears knee length pants and a sleeveless tunic in teal made of a kind of material that reminds Gwen of Morna's fairy garb, only shimmering like scales. The golden, braided belt that rests on his waist seems to be his only ornamentation. His arms, legs, and feet are completely bare, making him seem less formal than the other elders. Despite this he still commands the audience before him with just as much air of authority as did the previous king.

"I, Abdiel Northsea, King of the Merpeople, have interrogated the prisoner along with my fellow elders. She has been deprived of water and salt for three days to the point of dehydration and starvation. Still, she will not give up the names of her Vampire compatriots and refuses to divulge their intentions with the Wiccan she had been sent to abduct."

The Mer King pauses to take in a breath, as if the words he is about to speak pain him to utter. "For the crimes of treason, Brielle Easternwaters much be punished. We of the HCOE have also decided that an example must be made of her, so that others will not be so easily swayed to sympathize and align with the Vampires in this conflict."

The room about Gwen hangs heavy with anticipation, the air thick with the accumulated tension felt by all those watching.

"For this purpose, I declare that Brielle Easternwaters shall be burned with hellfire until dead." Gwen gasps. The room goes still. No one breathes; no one moves. His announcement sends a chill through Gwen's body that makes goosebumps appear on her arms.

No. No! Gwen shakes involuntarily. *I must stop this! I must stop this!* Gwen reaches towards Nicola, placing a hand on her shoulder. The witch glances back at her. Her eyes reflect Gwen's feelings, but she shakes her head at Gwen and places a finger over her lips.

Gwen's heart sinks. *I can't watch this.* Gwen turns and pushes her way towards the Black Iris's front door. The audience of captivated wiccans reluctantly moves before her, giving her annoyed looks as she presses passed them. Suddenly she feels a hand on her shoulder. She spins around to shove the person away only to find herself gathered into Jonah's arms. She instantly relaxes and presses her face into his chest, wrapping her arms around him as if holding on for dear life. Heat and desire mixes with her overwhelming sense of guilt and despair, and suddenly all she wants is for Jonah to whisk her away far from reality. Raven stands just behind him, his face white and his expression sympathetic.

When will people stop dying because of me, Raven? When will it end? She sends the thought to him, opening a mental connection to him into his mind. He stares at her, sympathetic and lost for words both verbal and mental.

Gwen forces herself to look back at the mirror. Raven and Jonah follow her gaze and watch with her as the Mer King finally continues speaking.

"As her King, I will carry out this sentence." Abdiel says the words with a shaking voice. He turns and mutters an incantation, creating a portal in the air beside him. As he steps toward the portal, the Wiccan King steps in his way. Startled, the Mer king looks at his contemporary, confused. The two men either share a mental exchange or communicate with their eyes, because the older man gives a nod of understanding. Grasping the younger king by the arm in a salute of respect, he then takes his place back in the line of elders as the Wiccan King turns toward the mirror to address the masses again.

"As it was one of my subjects who was wronged, I have requested and have been granted the right to carry out the execution." This news sends a new sensation through the room. As the Wiccan citizens around, her watch their king walk through the portal. The mirror ripples again to show him step through another portal into Brielle's air bubble prison, in the Mermaid Kingdom. Gwen perks up, looking about the room. She senses and hears the thoughts of the people around them. An overwhelming sense of pride seems to fill the room as his subjects watch him calmly approach the doomed mermaid. Brielle looks at him, her hair falling away from her face enough for Gwen to see her eyes. Fear fills them to the brim, making them seem larger than normal. The King gives her a brief nod, and something mentally seems to transpire between them. Brielle's shoulders relax and her faces changes. She nods back to him in understanding. With a groan, she straightens up to stand tall before him. She closes her eyes, ready to accept her sentence.

"For the crime of treason and in violation of the treaty of Wind, Earth, and Sea agreed upon by our ancestors, Brielle Easternwaters, you are commended to death by Hellfire. Go into the darkness from whence you came to burn in the Master's fire forever more!" His words and his tone said two different things. He was sending her into eternal torment, but his voice was easing her fear and saying he was sorry for what he had to do. Gwen suddenly felt the same sense of pride and love her fellow Wiccans seemed to have for this man whom they called King.

The feeling took away her guilt, took away her pain, and left her in awe of the man who would take this burden from a fellow King so selflessly and yet comfort the condemned in her darkest hour. Riveted by this extraordinary man, Gwen keeps her eyes focused on him.

"Enfla mae, curseae dorm ante hellfire!" The King utters the spell with a gesture of both of his hands and suddenly green flames burst forth all over Brielle's body. At first the mermaid resists crying out, keeping her eyes shut tight and gritting her teeth as the cursed fire grows ever stronger. The flames triple in size, burning away her white shift, her hair, and eyelashes. When the fire grows larger and hotter still and the mermaid's skin blisters and boils beneath it, Brielle can resist no longer. She opens her mouth and lets out an anguished cry that pierces Gwen into the core of her soul. Gwen

clings to Jonah still, watching from her peripheral. Brielle crumbles into a pile of tissue and bone. Her screams finally die out as the fire disintegrates every inch of her completely out of existence. Gwen's gaze stays still on the Wiccan King. One tear seems to slide on his cheek, which he doesn't wipe away. He watches the mermaid's whole horrible death with an unflinching yet distant stare. When the mermaid Brielle Easternwaters is no more, the green incandescent Hellfire extinguishers themselves. The room takes a collective sigh of relief.

Deverick Hawthorn, King of Wicca, turns back to the portal and slips through. When the mirror image ripples again, he exits the portal on the other side to stand before the other elders. His back is turned to the mirror, and he faces the others. Before Deverick can turn and take his place at the center of the circle again, another elder steps forward in his place.

This time it is a blue woman of small stature, dressed in deep blue in a knee length dress of a familiar leafy material with wings fluttering behind her. Gwen gasps. The resemblance is uncanny. Only a few variations distinguish the mother from her daughter. Deverick returns to stand with the others as the Fairy Queen addresses the unseen audience beyond the mirror.

"Let this stand as a testament to all the thirteen tribes of Cain of what justice will be served to those who cross the elders. And to the Vampire King we issue this warning: give up this foolish rebellion or we shall wipe your tribe from the face of the earth!" The fairy woman's voice even resembles her daughter's, but where Morna is sweet and kind, this woman impresses upon Gwen a cold, dominating manner.

Her words send a feeling of dread through Gwen. *The Elders are fools. If they think the Vampires will take this calmly, then they have sorely underestimated their foe. They haven't squashed the Vampire rebellion; they've just killed their reconciliations. They've ruined any chance of peace with the vampire, any chance to bring them back into the Forsaken fold. Brielle's death will not be the last Forsaken casualty.* Gwen knows this with absolute certainty. This is only the beginning in what will be a brutal conflict. The chance that life would return to the way it was just died along with the tattered hope of peace.

Chapter Thirty

Less Than Nothing

he mirror ripples one last time to settle back into its original reflection. The shocked faces of the occupants of the Black Iris stare back at themselves. Slowly everyone begins to turn to each other speaking amongst themselves. Some hurry off to their rooms with an air of purpose.

When Nicola turns around, her nephew and niece begin speaking over top of one another, anxiously seeking answers. Nicola placates them, but her attention seems drawn elsewhere. Gwen watches the witch from across the room scanning the common area with her eyes. When her gaze falls on them still standing by the door, the woman's face changes from concern to displeasure. That's when Gwen realizes that she still clings to Jonah, circled in his embrace.

Embarrassed, Gwen blushes but, before she can untangle herself from Jonah's arms, Thayer and Leona follow their aunt's gaze and see them in the same pose. The look of utter rage in his little sister's eyes burns Gwen with guilt. Pushing Jonah away unceremoniously, she hurries wordlessly past him and Raven. Ignoring Nicola and the others, she bolts towards the stairs hoping to retreat to her room. Once there, she plans to grab her violin and slip up onto the roof for some much-needed musical therapy. Instead, Gwen finds herself abruptly stopped at the foot of the stairs when Leona appears in her path.

"That was all because of you, wasn't it?" Leona demands loudly. Several of the Wiccans nearby look toward them, curious. Gwen tries to shush her, but this only enrages the teenage witch further. "It was! What is it with you? You just go around ruining everything and leaving devastation in your wake?"

"That's not fair. You know nothing about me; you have no idea what I've been through. I was attacked by that creature. I didn't ask for it. I didn't even know there were vampires after me until just now," Gwen rebukes in a hushed whisper, trying to keep the rest of the room from listening in on their conversation.

"Yeah. that's right, nothing is ever your fault. I suppose you just wound up in my brother's arms by accident just now as well, huh?"

"I was upset. He was comforting me. It wasn't what it looked like," Gwen responds through gritted teeth. "If you want to get mad at someone, get mad at your brother. I'm not the one going around misleading people. He was flirting with me. He had plenty of opportunity to mention that he was betrothed but he didn't!" the words just keeping pouring out of Gwen. Like molten lava, spewing from the torrent of emotions erupting from within. "I mean, we were practically dream dating since you all came to my show. He took me to your childhood home and everything. He confided in me about your parent's death. He could've mentioned it then or after we saw a manifestation of his fiancée in the dream world, but no! And yet I'm the bad guy here?"

"Wait, what? Have you been Dreamwalking with my brother?" Leona's stunned face, jolts Gwen into realizing she has exposed too much. Gwen clamps her mouth shut, her face going ashen. Before Gwen has a chance to formulate a reply, Nicola steps up, taking each girl by the elbow.

"This is neither the place nor the time for this sort of thing, lassies. I suggest you take this conversation upstairs while you hurry and pack up your things." They both look at her, startled, but allow the older woman to push them toward the stairs. Once Nicola releases them, Leona bolts in front of Gwen, cutting her off. She stomps up the steps.

Leona bursts through the door, stalking into their shared room. Throwing open the closet doors, she chants a simple lavation spell. A large blue suitcase floats from the closet onto her bed. By the time Gwen enters the room, Leona is whizzing about collecting her things and stowing them away into her suitcase. Once done, she slows to human speed, closes the flap of the suitcase, and zips it up.

Gwen walks over to her bed. Underneath she retrieves her red duffle bag and her other luggage — all her belongings still packed since Gwen has never been in the habit of fully unpacking. *You never know when you might need to leave in a hurry.* Quickly, Gwen peers inside to make sure everything is there before zipping the bag closed.

"Well, I'm all ready to go," Gwen announces as she takes her bag and drops it by her violin case by the door earlier that morning. Gwen spins around to face her fifteen-year-old roommate, staring back at her with open hostility. Yet something in her face and stance suggests that some of the heat in her fire has died out. Leona utters her spell again, sending her luggage floating over to the door where it lands next to the door frame.

"So, you've been Dreamwalking with my brother, huh?" She sits down on her bed and crosses her arms and legs, giving Gwen an expectant look.

"Yes." Gwen sighs, letting her own indignation drain out of her a little. "Before you all captured me, I would visit Jonah. It wasn't his fault at all. It was entirely my doing." Gwen walks over to her own bed and sits down opposite Leona. "You can tell Aunt Nicola that if you want, but unlike the rest of you I'm not scared of her."

"She's not..."

"My aunt?" Gwen finishes for Leona. "Yeah, I'm aware. But I understand she'll be your aunt-in-law someday."

"Did my brother tell you that?"

"Yes, he did," Gwen replies shortly.

"But he didn't tell you about Isla?"

"Thayer's little sister?" Gwen keeps her face impassive. "No, he didn't mention her, but *Aunt* Nicola did." Gwen puts emphasis on the word aunt. "Apparently, she's Jonah's intended, something your parents and the Blackwools cooked up when you were all kids. So, I was told."

"That's right." Leona watches her as if trying to read Gwen's expression. "I don't suppose something like family honor and duty would mean much to someone like you."

"Someone like me?" Gwen laughs. "Wow!" She leans forward, her hands gripping the edge of the bed. "You know nothing about me, yet you assume so much. Look, I have never intentionally stolen another woman's man and I never will. However, if a guy makes a play for me but neglects to tell me he has a woman in his life…" Gwen shrugs her shoulders. "That's not exactly my fault now, is it?"

"No." Leona's demeanor softens a bit. "I suppose that's not something I can fault you for."

"I think we got off on the wrong foot here." Gwen relaxes her shoulders, letting the tension inside her melt away. "I realize you're just worried about your brother. If I had a brother I'd probably be concerned, too, if some strange girl showed up out of the blue and I didn't know the first thing about her." Leona seems taken aback by this, her mouth working as if the words won't take shape. "I swear to you, as of today, I have no interest in engaging in a romantic relationship with your brother, I only desire his friendship."

"So, you don't love him. You were just messing around with him? It wasn't serious?"

Gwen hesitates before she speaks "I thought I was falling in love with him but…" Gwen exhales and looks away suddenly at a loss for words. After a moment she looks back at Leona and sees her looking at her curiously. "I don't want to complicate his life, okay? I could lie and tell you that it didn't mean anything, that I feel nothing for him but … I can't. But the last thing I want is to make him miserable and honestly, I don't see how anything between us could ever happen without hurting him in some way."

"Good. But it wasn't just Jonah I was worried about. Isla is my best friend, has been my whole life." Leona grimaces in thought. "And I don't really know if my brother loves her or not, but I know that she loves him."

Gwen sneaks a peek inside the girl's mind and sees a slew of memories of Leona and Isla Blackwool growing up together. She sees their friendship, their bond making them closer than sisters, not master and servant. Leona is entirely unaware of Gwen's intrusion since her mind was already reviewing these thoughts. Gwen shuts the mental connection without Leona being the wiser.

Gwen knows now with absolute certainty that Isla is the girl she had seen in Jonah's thoughts, the one who had given him such mixed feelings. The one whose face had made her see green and red.

"Their marriage, as well as Thayer's and mine, will make everyone incredibly happy. It's what my parents wanted."

"Then I wish you all the happiness in the world," Gwen replies sincerely. "I don't understand why Jonah didn't just tell me about his betrothal himself."

"I have a feeling that men lose brain cells when you're around," Leona answers quickly. "I've never known my brother to go weak in the knees, or weak in the head for that matter, over a girl. Honestly, I thought he was immune to female wiles, but..." Leona's eyes scan Gwen's ideal female anatomy till they make eye contact. "You're no ordinary girl now, are you?"

"Not that I can tell," Gwen answers nonchalantly. "Honestly, I've never met a man who wasn't interested in me in one way or another."

"Humph. I'd bet anything that you're a glimmer," Leona nods, as if confirming her own suspicions. "The Elders will be able to tell you once they conduct their examination."

"Wait, they're going to examine me? For what? Why?" Gwen asks, naturally displaying discomfort by the idea.

"To identify you, to help you find out who your parents were and, most importantly, to learn of your capabilities." Leona stands, seemingly calmer now that Gwen's no longer a threat to her little family. "They won't let you stay in their community if they find anything they don't like," she adds, smirking smugly. She moves toward the door to retrieve her suitcase.

"Great, sounds like a blast," Gwen replies, rising off the bed.

With her bag in hand, Leona scoffs and then exits the room without a backward glance at Gwen.

"Well, here goes nothing," Gwen says aloud to the room before she, too, collects her bag and slings the strap of her violin case over her shoulder. She gives one last glance at the little room and notices her black leather jacket hanging on a peg on the wall next to the door where she had hung it last night. Gwen steps over and retrieves it off the hook. *Well, the good news is, I'll be seeing Morna tonight.* Gwen takes some comfort in this, soothing the hollow feeling in her gut. After folding the jacket, she unzips her duffle and stuffs it inside.

Gwen finds Leona waiting by the front door in the common room. The Black Iris seems alive with bustling activity. Mistress Subree hustles about behind the register desk, ordering her staff as they help a handful of customers check out. A few maids push past her with cleaning supplies or linens. A steady stream of Wiccans is taking their leave of the boarding house. Gwen glances around, noting that no one else from their group is in sight.

"Where is everyone?" Gwen asks when she approaches Leona.

"Nicola left a note at the desk for us. Everyone went on ahead to the Lucifinian crossroads and we're supposed to meet them there. Raven will be there, too, it said." Leona grabs her blue suitcase and turns to the door.

"Wait, why didn't they just wait for us? Why is everyone in such a hurry? We've got until midnight. I mean, what's the rush?" Gwen throws the shoulder strap of her red duffle over her head to join the violin case and follows Leona out of the Black Iris. "I thought I couldn't go to the Coven without all the Thoyens' permission anyway. Wasn't that the whole reason we were hanging around here all this time?"

"I don't know why we must leave right this second. Maybe Aunt Nicola is anxious to get on with the journey. As for getting you into the coven, Professor Leven figured something out." Leona shrugs.

As they step onto the wooden bridge and cross over the river, Gwen glances back at the Black Iris. Her whole stay here in Alcromech lasted a couple of weeks, yet so much seems to have changed in that short amount of time. With a sigh she leaves it behind, hoping that life in the Coven fairs easier than it did here.

* * * * *

"Looks like I'll be here awhile," Jonah grumbles to himself. He stands at the back of a lengthy line of servants waiting to deposit their masters' luggage at the transference gate. Behind him hovers his Master Thayer's and Aunt Nicola's baggage as well as his own. With a sigh he lets the biggest trunk float down to the ground. Taking a seat on it, he ignores the disapproving glares of his fellow servants.

On the outskirts of the trading post lies the Alcromech Crossroads. *The outdoor facility is much like a human train station,* Jonah muses. The admittance office behind him parallels a platform made of red rock before a line of archways of thirteen twisted tree

trunks grown together to make the gateways. Thirteen gateways in all, one for every Tribe of Cain. They lead to the Lucifinian roads — a network of secret protected paths to all the townships and Covens of their hidden world. Next to each gateway is a transference gate, a portal designed only to convey luggage to the township at the end of the adjoining gateway. *Baggage Claim.* This is one of Jonah's many responsibilities as a servant to the Blackwool household.

It never rains in a Forsaken trading post. All trading posts are controlled by an enchantment that conceals the township from the outside world, keeps strangers out, the forsaken in, and keeps the climate at the perfect temperature. Even so, Jonah still fidgets with his tunic, wishing he could exchange it for a plain white t-shirt. It's almost as though he can feel the heat of the midday sun in the sky. *Get used to it, buddy. You're stuck wearing Wiccan clothes until the Vampire conflict is over,* he reminds himself.

The thought does nothing to ease his mood. It isn't just his formal attire that bothers him. His mind keeps replaying the moment he had with Gwen during the public announcement earlier. He could feel her unease as she stood beside him. He knew the moment that she began to panic. She had reached out to Aunt Nicola in alarm and then bolted as if she couldn't handle watching the mermaid's death. He doesn't pretend to understand why the whole thing bothered her so much, but he had gone after her instinctively. When she turned into his arms, he wrapped himself around her without thinking of it. It hadn't been sexual; it had been protective. Gwen was in distress, and he didn't hesitate to offer whatever she needed of him. It felt good to hold her again, especially since she has been avoiding him ever since her incident with the flower. It took everything in him to let her go after carrying her out of the water to the bank that day. For her to withdraw from him afterward, tore him up inside.

What about the other day, when I walked in on Gwen and Raven embracing in the common room of the Black Iris? Up until that day I would've sworn Gwen and the Werewolf were just friends, maybe even like brother and sister. But now … I thought he and the Fairy were involved. Did I read the signals all wrong? Is Gwen retreating from me because she is really involved with Raven and hadn't meant to lead me on, and now she's trying to let me know how she feels without hurting me?

"Ho there, Blackwool's man!" The baggage clerk, a Troll with shaggy hair dressed in an HCOE uniform, calls from behind a desk at the head of the line. "You're next. Bring your master's luggage up to the gate!" Jonah looks up astonished to find that the line moved without his notice. A gap is before him at the Transference gate. Glancing over his shoulder, he finds a line of servants grumbling and shuffling their feet impatiently behind him. Hopping up from his seat, Jonah scans platform thirteen quickly but still finds no sign of his sister, or Gwen. Aunt Nicola and Raven stand beside the entrance to the platform waiting for the two girls to arrive. Thayer waits with the other Wiccans travelers before the thirteenth twisted tree gateway — the Wiccans' own designated Lucifinian road.

"My whole party hasn't arrived yet," Jonah addresses the Troll clerk stepping up to his desk, the luggage floating along behind him as if tethered to him on an invisible string. "May I give you what I have and check in the rest when they arrive?"

"You know the rules, boy!" the shaggy-mane Troll retorts. "The luggage for each household must be deposited together. Otherwise, you get every which one's things mixed up with someone else's."

"I guess that means I have to go to the back of the line, then?" Jonah asks, exasperated.

"That's what it means." The troll shrugs indifferently, shifting his gaze to the servant in line behind him. "Next up!" he shouts.

Jonah winces, giving the Troll a glare before he makes his way to the back of the baggage line. At the end of the line, he sees a familiar face, Rory Mellanor, servant to House Leven. His uncle is the captain of the King's Royal Guard. Like Jonah, Rory's mother had been human, only she still lives while both of Jonah's parents died over ten years ago.

"Jonah! I thought I heard your voice." Rory is a stocky young man of twenty-four with black curly hair and big orange eyes set in a round face with rosy cheeks. He reaches out and grabs Jonah by the elbow. "Where did you just come from?"

"Las Vegas." Jonah returns the gesture, clasping Rory by his elbow. "My sister was curious. She had never been before."

"Is that right?" The two young men release each other, Jonah taking his place behind Rory and House Leven's luggage. Rory shifts to look at him, the Leven's belongings moving with him to float beside him so as not to obscure his view. "What's this crazy rumor I hear of Thoyen Nicola taking on a wild witch as her ward?" Rory asks, an excited gleam in his tangerine eyes.

"You heard about that?!" Jonah shakes his head, amazed. "Sheesh! News flies fast."

"So, it's true?" Rory exclaims, nearly bouncing with curiosity. "What's her name? How'd you find her?"

"Well..." Jonah runs his hand through his dark blond hair, trying to decide how much he should disclose, when he spots Professor Vincent Leven stalking across platform thirteen toward them. The history and culture professor is a tall man about Jonah's height with black spikey hair, light-tan skin, and striking features. As a pure blood, he is attired in a white suit. Over that he wears a deep purple cloak, purple being one of the Leven family colors. A toppled scale and a crow emblem on his shoulder. "Looks like Professor Leven needs you," Jonah informs his friend.

"Rory!" the thirty-year-old man calls out, his lime green eyes bright from excursion.

"Yes, Lord Leven?" The smile on Rory's face disappears; serious as a priest, he straightens his posture and turns to address his master. "What is your bidding, sir?"

"You forgot to pick up Zellah's present from the jewelers!" he informs his chubby servant. "Luckily for the both of us, I happened to stop by Allianne's shop on the way here."

"I'm terribly s-s-sorry... s-s-sir, it w-won't h-h-happen again! I p-p-promise!" Rory's eyes are wide with terror.

"Oh, stop that! It's fine. Just make sure you don't forget next time." Professor Leven teases, slapping his servant on the shoulder companionably, "I don't know why we keep you around. What do you suppose would've happened if I returned to the Coven without a gift for my intended for our binding day, hmm?"

"I-I…" Rory swallows hard. "I don't know, my lord. I assume Lady Zellah Bloodsworn wouldn't be too pleased?"

"No, she wouldn't be pleased." Vincent Leven agrees, laughing.

"Mistress Bloodsworn scares me a little, sir," Rory admits with a nervous laugh of his own. It seemed to Jonah that Rory doesn't realize how lucky he is to have such a fair-minded master. Rory is needlessly nervous around Vincent Leven, who never would raise a voice or hand to him. Meanwhile other Wiccan servants find themselves beaten and starved on a regular basis.

"You're wise to fear her, boy. The truth is she scares me a bit, too. Just be grateful you're not the one marrying her." The Professor laughs again in a way that says he's not really joking.

Maybe it's good that Rory is so cautious not to offend his master. The Professor's intended bride is not a kind soul and has a reputation for tormenting her servants to the point of insanity. Jonah can't help feeling sorry for his friend, after all.

Professor Leven pulls a long, thin jewelry box out of his cloak pocket and holds it to Rory. "Hold on to this for me, will you, Rory?"

"Yes, sir, of course." Jonah watches as his friend takes the box and stows it inside his master's nearest bag.

"Professor, I didn't realize you were back from the Coven." Jonah had waited patiently for the master-servant banter to subside before addressing the older man. He didn't want to come off as disrespectful should anyone else be watching.

"Why, hello there, young Crayborn. Yes, I just got back yesterday, which is ironic now that we're all being forced to leave." His face changes from light joking to seriousness all at once. Stepping closer to Jonah and lowering his voice, he continues. "Speaking of, how is Gwenevere holding up? I was distressed to get the missive from Nicola about the mermaid attack. I hope our young lady isn't too shaken up from the whole thing."

Taken aback, it takes Jonah a full three seconds to realize the meaning behind the professor's words, the pieces of the puzzle snapping into place inside his head. "She's doing all right. Of course, the execution upset her. I don't think she or Aunt Nicola were warned about that by the elders ahead of the broadcast."

"Well, of course not." Vincent Leven shakes his head exasperation. "It would've been considerate, but the HCOE doesn't explain itself to anyone. Hawthorn handled the whole thing well though, I thought."

Both Jonah and Rory bob their heads in agreement.

"We have a fine and noble King. The same can't be said for all the tribes." Rory offers, his pride obvious in his voice.

"That is very true, young Rory. Very true," Professor Leven agrees.

"Professor, were you able to convince the Thoyens to allow Gwen into the Coven? Will they accept Aunt Nicola's decision to take responsibility for Gwen and let her hold her tribunal in Monroe?"

This piques Rory's interest, and he perks up, looking between the two other men expectantly.

"No. They flatly refused to take her. However, now that the HCOE has shut down all the trading posts, they won't have a choice." The professor smiles with satisfaction.

"Really? I guess you're right." Jonah lets his shoulder relax, not realizing they had been tensed to begin with. "The HCOE's decree supersedes the Thoyens' authority. Gwen must go somewhere."

"Exactly. After Thoyen Nicola contacted me letting me know about the mermaid attack, I tried to appeal to the other Thoyens again, but they wouldn't budge. After that I sent a special request to the King."

"You did?" Rory exclaims, excitement practically bubbling out of him. "Have you heard back from him?"

"Yes, I did and…"

"Gwen's here," Jonah announces, impulsively, not meaning to say it aloud. The other two men turn to follow his gaze.

Stepping through the arch of the crossroad's platform behind his sister is Gwen, dressed all in black, a dark angle if ever he's seen one. His walking fantasy carries her luggage looking about as if confused, her long black hair swishing in the breeze.

"That's Thoyen Nicola's Ward, Rory," Jonah absently tells his friend. They watch as Aunt Nicola waves Gwen and Leona over. Leona obeys but Gwen stays put as Raven makes his way to her.

The Werewolf moves as a man determined and focused on one thing. His long black ponytail trails down his back between his broad shoulders. Gwen receives him with a full hug and a warm smile. When they separate from each other Gwen shivers visibly, rubbing her arms. Quickly, Raven peels off his black coat and drapes it over Gwen's shoulders. She laughs at him. Smiling, he collects her in his arms and the two look into each other's eyes, talking earnestly. Watching them, Jonah all of sudden hates Raven like he's never hated a man in his life. Guilt quickly follows.

"You don't say? Does she have a last name?" Jonah looks up at Rory, who looks at Gwen, mystified, as if she were some dangerous yet exotic beast.

"She goes by Gwenevere since she's a wild Witch. She has no family name."

Rory nods understanding. "She's gorgeous," he blurts out involuntarily. "Is that big guy she's talking to her boyfriend?" Rory looks thoughtful. "They look good together."

"They're not a couple." Jonah insists quickly, trying to ignore the ugly feeling twisting inside his gut. "They're just good friends. They're only hugging like that because he's a werewolf and they're having to part ways for a while. They've known each other a long time. He's like a brother to her, really." When Jonah looks at the

Professor and his friend, he sees identical looks of sympathy in their eyes.

"Of course," Professor Leven supplies with a forced smile.

"So, she'll be staying with Thoyen Nicola in our little Coven, then?" Rory asks changing the subject as any good friend would.

"Yes, she doesn't really have anywhere else to go," Jonah admits.

"Well, we'll just have to make her stay as comfortable as possible." The Professor smiles. "Won't we, Rory?"

"Yes, sir, we will do that." Rory smiles brightly.

"Well, I better go speak to Thoyen Nicola. See you both in Monroe." With that the Professor hurries across the platform toward Nicola and the others.

"Oh, the lines moving," Rory announces, shuffling forward with his levitating luggage behind him.

With a sigh, Jonah moves forward, grateful when Rory starts a conversation with the servant in front of him, giving Jonah the chance to clear his own head.

Jonah glances over his shoulder at Gwen and Raven still talking ridiculously close to one another.

This one doesn't belong to you, Jonah. She belongs to…. someone else. The voice of reason finishes for him. Other men call it conscience, but he's always heard it as his father's voice. In life he had always been a practical man. Falling in love with his mother was the only impulsive thing Alva Crayborn had ever done. *You have a woman, too, remember?*

Just then Leona hurries across the platform with the rest of the luggage trailing behind her in midair. She scans the line and makes a beeline toward him.

"There you are!" his little sister exclaims, seeming a little out of breath and tense. "Here's all of the rest." Leona releases her control over the levitation spell on hers and Gwen's things as soon as she feels Jonah form his own spell. Uttering the words, he makes her cargo shift over to combine with his own. "Merry meet, Rory," Leona addresses the other servant in the tradition Wiccan greeting.

"Merry meet, Leona," the boy replies.

"Next up!" shouts the Troll at the transference gate. Rory, suddenly snapping out of his haze, hurries forward as the line moves.

"What took you so long?" Jonah asks Leona absently as he, too, moves forward with the line. He can't stop himself from watching as the professor approaches Aunt Nicola, Raven, and Gwen. Raven steps back from Gwen to shake hands with the older man.

"Gwen and I got talking and lost track of time." Leona notes her brother's expression and follows his gaze, her eyebrows knitting together in a look of concern. She suddenly turns to him. "Jonah?"

"What?" He tears his eyes away from the object of his fascination to look his sister in the eyes — aqua around a sunburst of gold, just like his.

"She knows," Leona whispers solemnly.

"Who knows what, Leona?" he asks, something rotten twisting in his gut.

"Gwen knows about Isla," she replies, worry in her face.

"Did you...?"

"No," she answers quickly, folding her arms over her chest. "But it doesn't really matter because it should've been you. I expected more from you, brother."

"Hey, what is that supposed to mean?" he asks defensively. "Nothing happened, okay? I didn't do anything wrong!"

"No, but you didn't do the right thing either. Isla deserves better than that. Hell, even Gwen does! You should've told me about the Dreamwalking, too," she adds in a low whisper. Before Jonah can stop her, Leona turns and walks away, leaving him feeling more wretched than he knew was possible. He suddenly realizes that he's never disappointed her before. Jonah doesn't like the way it feels one bit. Until today Jonah never knew he could feel guilty, embarrassed, jealous, and hateful all at once.

"Next up!" yells the Troll clerk. Jonah and the line move forward. Consumed in his own thoughts, Jonah tries to figure out what he'll say to Gwen if she ever speaks to him again.

There's nothing to say. Jonah spins around, looking about wildly for the source of the voice. It sounded just like Gwen, or maybe he had imagined it did. Jonah finds her in the crowd on the other side of platform thirteen, staring right back at him. *Yes, that was me just now.* Gwen speaks in his head although her lips don't move, and her face stays impassive.

How did you...? Are you a telepath? Jonah thinks, gazing back at her, bewildered.

Yes. I usually try to stay out of people's minds but honestly, Jonah, you project your thoughts. You practically scream them! You make it exceedingly difficult for me to keep out of your head.

So, you've heard everything I've thought? he asks, stunned. *Do you know everything?*

No, but I've heard a lot and I know a lot about you because of my gift.

Gwen, I'm sorry I didn't—

Tell me you were engaged? Gwen finishes for him. *Don't be. It's not like anything happened between us. It wasn't anything at all.* Her words cut him like a knife, unable to think clearly enough to reply, but Gwen continues. *In fact, it was less than nothing.*

Chapter Thirty-One

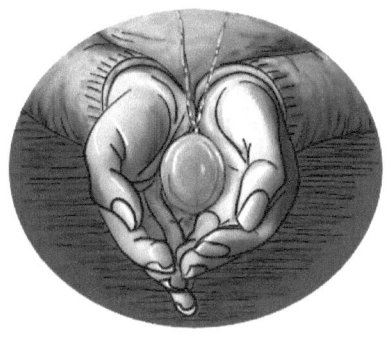

Hidden Paths

t's time I found my own gateway," Raven says, breaking Gwen from her mental conversation with Jonah. "It looks like my escorts are here." He indicates with a nudge of his head toward the entrance to the platform. Gwen looks past him where two identical young men wait. Gwen recognizes them as the twin Werewolf brothers who passed her and Jonah on the bridge the first night. The brothers nod at her with big silly grins but stay where they are, as if not wanting to traverse on Wiccan territory.

"Already?" She turns to look up at her tall, dark-skinned friend. "What gateway is yours?"

"Number seven," Raven answers with a sigh. "I'd much rather go with you. You know that, right?"

"Of course. And I wish you were," Gwen grumbles, shoulders

slumping. "But I guess rules are rules and it can't be helped." She forces herself not to glance in Jonah's direction but instead at the gateway and the tunnel of trees beyond the twisted tree entrance. "It seems the universe is forcing us to go separate ways once again." She shifts her gaze to look into Raven's wild golden eyes. "But it's only for a little while." She smiles weakly.

"I certainly hope so." Raven steps forward, putting his hands on her shoulders, his leather jacket rustling under pressure. "Please try to be careful with those people. I know they're your kind, and the Blackwools and Crayborns seem decent enough for Witches, but…"

"You're thinking of the Wiccan family that attacked us in New York, aren't you?" she interrupts him.

"Yes. I can't help but worry that some of these Witches will react the same way to you. They might fear you." Raven squeezes her shoulders, and Gwen puts a hand over one of his, seeing the concern in his face. "Even amongst your own, Gwen, you don't quite seem to be normal. We both know all too well how people react to something they don't understand."

Gwen nods solemnly. "I'll try my best to fit in and stay out of trouble," she promises with a reassuring smile. "I'll have Morna with me to help out."

"Like that's much comfort. Gwen, you've got a talent for standing out and you attract trouble without even trying," Raven snorts. "And Morna … she's a whole other breed of trouble all her own."

"Oh, like you're the poster child for good behavior?" Gwen retorts with a chuckle. "You just worry about getting to know your father's people and learning what you can about this mother of yours," Gwen instructs. "If anything goes wrong, I'll find a way to contact you, okay?" Gwen gets up on her tiptoes to give him a quick peck on the cheek, his stubble prickly against her skin.

"Okay." Raven tilts his head to plant a kiss on her forehead. She wraps her arms around him in a bear hug, pressing her face into his chest. "Please, tell Morna that I … wish her well." He speaks softly into Gwen's hair.

"I will," Gwen whispers back.

They linger in this embrace a long moment before Gwen steps back to look at him. "All right let's not drag this out. You might as well get going," she says with a husky voice, folding her arms beneath her breasts.

"Take good care of yourself, Gwen." Raven cups the side of her face in his large dark hand. She smirks and presses her face into it. "You'll always be in my thoughts." She senses that he wants to say more but holds back. She takes his hand from her face and closes his fist, kissing his knuckles before letting him go. With a sigh, Raven stuffs his hands into his pockets and turns.

"Raven!" Gwen calls to him when he's about to step through the platform entrance. With an expectant look, he turns back to her. "Your coat!" She peels it off her shoulders and hurries toward him. "We wouldn't want you to get cold on the Mohawk Indian reservation. I imagine it gets pretty cold in that part of New York, being so close to the Canadian border and all," Gwen prattles on nervously.

"Yeah, I guess you're right." Reluctantly, he takes his coat from her, suddenly wishing he could just throw her over his shoulder and take her with him.

Gwen smiles. *I wouldn't mind that either but honestly if I were going to run off with you, I'd use my own feet. I don't much like being manhandled, thank you very much.* She thinks in his head, making Raven smile shyly, his cheeks going slightly rosy.

Goodbye, Gwen. I love you; he blurts out mentally.

"I love you, too. Take care, big guy." Gwen winks comically.

Gwen watches him head toward the twin Werewolf brothers. The one wearing a Pittsburg Pirates cap gives Raven an "okay" sign. His brother shrugs his shoulders and mouths something indistinguishable to Raven while his twin makes a wing-flapping motion with his arms in a most comical fashion. Gwen can tell even from this distance that Raven's face is blushing. He shakes his head at them and mumbles something in response. The three of them turn and wave to Gwen before they walk away. One twin throws an arm over both Raven's shoulder and his brother's as they go. The sound of their laughter floats to Gwen, leaving a bitter-sweet taste in her mouth before she turns away.

Don't look back, Gwen, she warns herself. *It'll just make it hurt worse.* Instead, she weaves her way through the gathering crowd of Wiccans on platform thirteen to find her party. She spots Nicola ahead. To her dismay, Jonah has joined the group standing next to

Thayer and his sister. Gwen's step falters only a moment before she throws her shoulders back, raises her chin, and stalks forward. *I sure hope it's a short trip to the Coven; otherwise, this is going to be a painfully awkward journey!*

"So, did you get to say goodbye to your young Wolf?" Aunt Nicola asks as Gwen joins them.

"Yes, I did." Gwen pushes down the wave of loneliness Raven's absence is already bringing on. "I wanted to ask, Thoyen Nicola, if there is some way, I might contact Raven at the reservation? You know, some spell for communicating over long distances? I imagine you lot don't use cell phones," Gwen adds with a smirk.

"No human devices or technology is allowed in any Forsaken settlements," Leona informs in a huff as if mortified Gwen would even suggest it. Gwen tries not to laugh at her.

"One could always communicate by scrying through water," Aunt Nicola supplies thoughtfully.

"Hmmm, is this something you can teach me?" Gwen asks, shifting her body to look directly at Nicola and to remove Jonah from her field of vision.

"Of course, it's part of the training you'll receive at the institute." Aunt Nicola adjusts her multi-colored cape before continuing. "Every fledgling Magician learns the basics of our culture and history at the institute while apprenticing a sage spellbinder. As your guardian, I will undertake the bulk of your tutelage."

"I look forward to that," Gwen lies with a too-bright smile. *You'll find I know a lot more than you think I do and learn faster than most. And I have a Fairy secret weapon handy for help with difficult spells.*

"I've got good news for ye, lassie," Nicola chirps. "Professor Leven got special permission from the King to allow me the right to claim you as my ward and to hold your tribunal in the Monroe Coven," Nicola announces this, punctuating the news with a clap of her hands. "Isn't that great?"

"Yeah, that's a relief." Gwen forces a smile. *So, what that means is that the Thoyens of Monroe didn't want me and now I'm being forced upon them by the King. Great, that's going to make me awfully popular.* Gwen grumbles to herself. "So, why are we standing around? When do we go through the gateway?" she asks with a sigh.

"Why, whenever Thoyen Nicola is ready," Professor Leven answers, appearing at Gwen's side.

"She's the senior member of the Wiccans traveling today," Professor Leven explains to Gwen. "Would you do the honor of leading us through the gate?" he asks Aunt Nicola politely, looking over Gwen to address the older Witch beside her.

"Why, of course, Vincent." Nicola smiles good-naturedly at the younger man. "Come along, wee ones, let's go home!" She proclaims with a gleam in her eyes. Quickly, the youths fall in line behind their Elder. Uncertain where she should go in the pecking order, Gwen begins to follow Nicola. Abruptly she is cut off by Thayer and almost bumps right into Jonah.

"Excuse me, sorry … um … you should stay between me and Leona," Jonah mumbles, clearly flustered, his cheeks bright red.

"No need for that, Jonah." Vincent Leven steps up to Gwen's elbow, threading an arm through hers without ceremony. "I'd be delighted to escort our guest to our Coven." He smiles down at Gwen. "It'll give me a chance to get to know more about my newest pupil."

"Gwen, I was hoping you might walk with me, so we might get a chance to talk. There are things I need to say to you," Jonah says in a low voice, pleading in his aqua blue eyes.

"There's nothing to talk about," Gwen assures with a gentle voice. Mentally she adds, *please, Jonah just let me be.* "Professor Leven maybe you can answer my questions while we walk. There's still so much about life in a Coven that I'm not sure I'm prepared for," Gwen admits, dismissing Jonah by turning her attention to Vincent.

"Fine, whatever," Jonah says though tight lips. Balling up his fist, he turns his back on them to catch up with Thayer.

"I'll walk along with you, too," Leona chimes in, popping up on the other side of Vincent, hooking herself to his free arm. "By the way, how was your sabbatical, Professor? Where did you go to this time? Did you bring back any fascinating souvenirs from your travels amongst the Eden spawn?" Leona hops alongside him, looking up into the man's face in admiration. *Clearly Professor Leven is well liked by his students.*

"It was a splendid trip. One of my most exciting, actually!" Vincent beams a brilliant smile back at Leona with familiarity. "I went to Peru this time and visited with the local Witch Doctors in the area. It's always surprising how little of the true craft is practiced amongst humans. Even the more in-tune spiritually are barely skimming the surface of the supernatural, yet they dare call themselves Witches," he chuckles.

Although Gwen wants to learn more on this subject, she finds her attention distracted from them by the proceedings around her. About thirty Wiccans are gathered on the platform. Thoyen Nicola emerges from the crowd and approaches the gateway. The conversations die out as they all turn to watch her. The stocky redheaded Witch approaches the twisted tree archway, stopping just outside the opening. She raises her eyes to the heavens and her hands into the air palms up.

"Goddess and Great Mother," Nicola quotes in reverence to the sky. "Bless us, your children, on this journey that the secret roads might ever be protection from those who would do us harm and grant us entrance into thy Covens as your rightful descendants of thy sacred bloodlines. Bring us peace and harmony in our rituals and rites and ever guide us toward balanced lives. Blessed be!" As she finishes the prayer, the congregation of traveling Wiccans echoes the words, "Blessed be," with an enthusiastic reverence.

Thoyen Nicola steps off the red rock platform over the threshold of the Lucifinian road, passing beneath the twisted tree gateway. With shoulders back and confidence in her stride, the redheaded woman walks on down the tunnel of trees. The rest of them follow behind her like a marching band in a parade. Multi-colored cloaks flutter behind them in the wind, with colorful family crests amongst a sea of brown-clad servants following their masters.

Still jointly attached to the professor with Leona, Gwen and her companions pass under the gateway near the head of the procession behind Nicola, Thayer, and Jonah.

Hmmm, I half-expected that we'd be teleported through space as though the gateway was a wormhole, Gwen notes, a bit disappointed.

Above her, the trees twist together in an arch all the way down the path to complete the feeling of being in a tunnel. No sunlight penetrates between the tightly woven branches, yet the tunnel is brightly lit by floating orbs of light at intervals along the tunnel's canopy. *It's awfully quiet in here. Not like being in the forest at all.* Glancing down, Gwen notes the hard, dark, dirt path beneath them: no plants, rocks, insect, or animals interrupt its surface. She sniffs and finds she can't detect the trees or leaves. The only smells are from the travelers, not the surroundings. A chill runs up her spine and Gwen shivers involuntarily. Suddenly Gwen wishes she hadn't given Raven his coat back or that she had kept her own jacket handy instead of stuffing it into her duffle.

"Are you alright?" Professor Leven asks, concern visible in his handsome face. "There's really nothing to be afraid of. The Lucifinian roads are perfectly safe; no Vampire can assault you here," he adds, good-naturedly.

"I'm fine." Gwen smiles weakly up at the man linked to her arm. Leona looks around their shared escort to give Gwen a suspicious glare. "It's not Vampires I'm bothered by, it's the road itself. It's so … unnatural and otherworldly. It feels confining," Gwen admits, ignoring the other girl.

"Are you claustrophobic by chance, Lady Gwenevere?" Vincent Leven asks seeming intrigued by the very notion.

"No. Not at all." Gwen laughs, dismissing the idea with a sweep of her free hand. "I just don't trust closed roads with no way out, or forests without the sounds of animals. The whole thing feels suspicious to me."

"I suppose it would be to someone not accustomed to traveling this way." He pauses a moment in thought. "I recall the first time my father took me and my younger sister on the Lucifinian roads when I was eight. It was the longest walk of my life. I thought the road would never end and that we'd never see the sun again. We'd just wander forever and ever never finding a way out." He laughs at the memory. "Now, I barely notice how quiet it is, and the road seems to be shorter every time I traverse it."

"How did your sister react to the road that first time?" Leona asks, her aqua eyes alight with curiosity and wonder of her teacher.

"She didn't like it one bit and demanded my father carry her the whole way. She was but four at the time," he confides companionably.

Gwen looks up ahead. Aunt Nicola has reached a bend in the path. With no other direction in which to go, and no crossroad, the middle-aged Witch goes around the bend and vanishes from sight.

"How long is the road, Professor?" Gwen asks, a wave of cold terror rising from her toes, unable to take her eyes off the spot where Nicola had disappeared.

"We'll reach the hemisphere junction just around the bend, then from there it is about an hour's walk to the Monroe Gateway," The professor gestures with a hand down the road, with his scholarly voice on. When they finally get around the bend, the road continues for thirty feet before it comes to an eight-way intersection. Nicola leads them onward toward the junction.

"Hemisphere Junction? Do these paths lead to the four hemispheres of the earth?" Gwen looks to her escort as they step into the middle of the intersection. "Why are there four extra roads, then?"

"Because about every continent lies in two hemispheres. The four main roads here lead to the north, south, east, and west, hemispheres. While the ones between them lead northwest, southwest, southeast, and northeast." The professor gestures with his hand at each road. "If you want to go north you would simply turn back around and head back the way we came, only the road won't be the same."

"Interesting," Gwen says with an impressed look. "Once you choose a hemisphere, do you come to another intersection for the continents in that hemisphere, and from their regions and so on?"

"Ah, you got the idea. That is precisely how it works!" Vincent beams at her in approval, a cascade of dimples creasing his cheeks, and smile lines appearing around his eyes. "Since we're headed to Pennsylvania, which borders both the northern and western hemisphere, we'll be taking the northwest road."

Gwen glances at Leona just in time to see her irritated scowl before she looks away her mouth a tight line.

Apparently, our truce back at the Black Iris is already over, Gwen thinks to herself. *I can't look at her brother. I can't talk to her favorite teacher. I can't call Nicola "Aunt," and she gets a little crazy whenever I talk to Thayer. Sheesh! We're possessive, aren't we, Leona?*

Ignoring the other girl, Gwen watches as their traveling party moves around them, the shuffling of feet the only sound in this noiseless thoroughfare. Everyone follows behind Thoyen Nicola with utter confidence, several chatting convivially. Gwen smiles when she hears a small voice begin to sing what sounds like a Wiccan lullaby. She looks over her shoulder and spies the owner of the voice. It is a small girl about six years old with red hair and violet eyes walking hand in hand with her mother and her older brother. The child smiles shyly back at Gwen.

Gwen sighs and turns her eyes ahead as they all turn to the left and take the road between the northern and the western hemisphere path. Several of the other travelers have fallen out of the organized line and have moved ahead of them in the column, making Nicola and the others seem far ahead of them. Gwen's heartbeat quickens when she recognizes the slant of Jonah's shoulders ten feet ahead. She gets lost in thought observing the way he walks, neither a strut nor a lazy gate. Jonah's posture is straight, proud, and confident, yet without any hint of arrogance.

Jonah turns about, walking backward as he scans the procession, his eyebrows knit together in consternation until he finds her face in the crowd. Their eyes meet and for a long moment they are caught in each other's gazes, neither able to look away. One of his fellow servants taps Jonah on the shoulder, breaking their eye contact. Jonah turns his back to her as he engages in a conversation with the other young man.

Beside her, the teacher and pupil chat about their travels. "Professor, you're not originally from the Monroe Coven, are you?" Gwen asks at the first lull in the conversation between Vincent and Leona.

"Did my accent give me away?" The tall, dark-haired professor jokes. "Of course, I'm not. I'm from Ireland. The Galway Coven, to be precise." He smiles to himself as if a fond memory of home has just come to mind.

"Then why aren't you returning there? Why do you teach in Monroe?" Gwen asks, desperate to keep her mind and her eyes off Jonah.

"He's betrothed to Thoyen Zellah Bloodsworn," Leona supplies before the professor has a chance to open his mouth. Annoyance passes behind his light-green eyes, yet he maintains a calm, polite expression. "He came over from Ireland about ten years ago," Jonah's sister continues, self-importance showing in her smug smile.

"That's right," Vincent confirms. "We're to be wed after the winter solstice," he adds, a strange note in his Irish voice.

"Well, congratulations, Professor Leven!" Gwen smiles brightly, noticing that they have reached yet another intersection on the Lucifinian road. "Which way now? There are no signs. How do you know which road is which?"

"There are signs if you know where to look for them." Vincent unlinks his arm from Gwen to point at a set of symbols drawn on the ground before the path straight ahead of them. Looking around, Gwen notes that every road has a different set of symbols before it. "That road leads to the region that the Monroe Coven is in."

Ahead of them, Aunt Nicola turns to the road right of the main road without hesitation.

Gwen does not take the professor's arm again as they continue. As they pass over the white symbols on the road, Gwen bends down to examine them. Up close she sees that the symbols aren't drawn with chalk as she had originally thought but made of salt granules. One symbol is a circle around the shape of a flower with a ten-point star in the center.

"That's a Kalmia Latifolia, also known as the Mountain Laurel." Gwen looks up to find Professor Leven and Leona standing above her. The Professor bends down beside her and continues, "It's the state flower of Pennsylvania. It can be used as a poison or a remedy." He stands, extending a hand to Gwen. "That's the symbol for our Coven."

"I see." She takes his proffered hand, and the professor pulls her up to her feet. "Are all the Coven Symbols flowers of the region where they reside?"

"No. Some of them are local trees or animals. Each Coven has its own symbol. You'll learn all the symbols and names of every Coven at the institute amongst other things. In fact, I'm the Professor of Wiccan History and Culture."

"I look forward to learning more from you, Professor." Vincent Leven seems pleased by this remark.

Gwen spies Jonah looking for her again. *This time I won't let his mesmerizing eyes draw me in. If it's not going to work out between us, I can't lead him on. I must move passed him. Like you've already moved passed, Michael.* Her conscious whispers back to her. Gwen gulps down the guilt that the realization brings. *I promise this time I won't rush into another romance just to get over the last one.* She tells her conscience. *No more rebounds, for me!*

"I must say, Lady Gwenevere, that is a very lovely locket you're wearing." The professor nods towards Gwen's locket, which had fallen out of the neckline of her dress when she bent over. "May I ask where you got it?" he asks.

"Oh, thank you." Startled out of her thoughts, Gwen looks down at the locket. "My mother gave it to me," Gwen replies, a bit dazed, wishing she could hide from Jonah by slipping behind the tall professor's back.

"That doesn't seem very likely," Leona interjects.

"Excuse me? What's that supposed to mean? I think I would know if my mother gave me this locket or not better than you would," Gwen replies to Leona tersely.

"I think what she means is, as a pure-blood Wiccan, your mother would have given you a ring and your father a necklace, both with their own family crest engraved or filigreed on them."

"Exactly," Leona continues, nodding at the professor. "Wiccan parents only give their young children those two pieces of jewelry. Wiccan children don't receive any other jewelry until their coming-of-age ceremony at age twelve. Your father, not your mother, would have had to have given you that necklace and it wouldn't be plain, it would have his family name and crest on it."

"What are you, blind? My locket isn't plain! It has a symbol and my first name engraved on the face of it!" Irritated, Gwen grasps the locket and holds it up before Leona's and the professor's faces.

"I see nothing there," Vincent Leven answers, puzzled. His brow furrows in trepidation.

"Neither do I," Leona adds smugly.

Gwen looks at them, stunned as a wave of ice fills her veins. Confused, she looks down at the locket still in her hand, the weight of it hot against her cold numb hand. There she sees as she has

always seen, the word *Gwenevere* engraved over a burning rose inside an oval ring.

Am I mad? Have I always been the only one who could see the engraving? Gwen ponders, suddenly finding the nuns of St. Paul's refusal to call her Gwen not so unreasonable. *And all this time I thought they just didn't think Gwenevere was an appropriate Christian name!* Gwen traces the engraving on her locket with her index finger, the bumps, and divots of the design clearly real to her touch. *But why am I the only one who can see it? What purpose does an invisible name and symbol have on a necklace? It could be an enchantment,* Gwen reasons. Goosebumps form on her arms at the thought. *Who put the enchantment on my locket, and more importantly, what does the enchantment do? I've always believed my mother gave me this locket. Is that even the truth?*

The last dream she had with the blond guardian of her dreams comes back to mind. She relives the whole thing in a manner of minutes, mentally trying to dissect it into some semblance of sagacity. Nothing in the dream had anything to do with the locket other than the braided lock of gold and black hair in her mother's side-table drawer. An identical braid of hair has been coiled inside her locket ever since she wandered in the woods all those years ago. She finds her mind returning to the scene with the black-haired man and her toddler self in her childhood bedroom.

Was that my father? I wish I knew for sure who he was, Gwen cogitates. *Or that I could recall the symbol on the ring he gave me, or better yet, that I still had the ring now. I might know the symbol if I saw it again,* Gwen considers. *Certainly, there must be a record of all the family crests in the Wiccan Kingdom.*

A swell of hope fills her chest at the thought. Gwen retreats further into her thoughts. The shuffle of the travelers' feet around her melting into the hum of her own memories as the procession of Wiccans continue down the hidden paths.

Chapter Thirty-Two

Covenstead

An hour later, Gwen and her company come to the last junction on the Wiccan Luficinian road. The road ahead of them is blocked by a giant, green-tinted iron gate. A colonial-looking village is visible through its decorative scroll work. Aunt Nicola stops the procession. Everyone watches the older Witch as she stands on a raised black stone set into the road just before the Coven's gate.

"Speak and be heard, mother, sister, daughter, friend," commands a disembodied young man's voice above them. Gwen, as well as the younger children, look about for the speaker. The adults and seasoned travelers of these roads wait patiently, unimpressed.

"We, the children of the great mother and her consort, request entrance into the folds of Monroe," Nicola states with authority, addressing the gate itself.

"Only those of the blood may enter here," warns the voice in a formal yet foreboding tone. "Step forward and be received. If you are true in the blood, then pass through unharmed; otherwise, thou shalt meet a grim fate. The blood never lies."

"The blood never lies!" The crowd around her repeats the phrase in unison. At this, the gate splits down the middle, opening inward. A whoosh of warm air hits the travelers head on as the sounds and smells of the real world greet them. Compared to the grim silence of the Luficinian road and its unnatural glow, the village before them is boisterous and bright with the early afternoon sun beating down.

"What happens if you pass through the gate and you're not 'of the blood'?" Gwen raises her eyebrows for dramatic flair. The professor chuckles. Leona rolls her eyes.

"You know, I'm not quite sure, really." The professor leads the two young ladies on as the travelers pass through the gate as a column. "It's been a very long time since any outsider has even attempted to enter a Coven. I don't think it's something you would want to witness, though, Lady Gwenevere," he adds.

"I don't know, Professor. You'd be surprised by the things I can stomach." Gwen apprises the older gentlemen with a sideways smirk.

As the three of them pass under the gate, a deafening bell tolls just once, resonant, and deep, causing everyone near to cover their ears.

"What was that?" Gwen asks the professor, dropping her hands as the sound fades.

"That's the summoning bell." He sighs. "I'm not sure what Juniper wants this very moment that can't wait," the professor grumbles to himself. "I must leave you now, ladies."

"See you at Institute tomorrow, Leona." He turns and bows to Leona.

"Until tomorrow, Professor." Making a "W" with her fingers before her forehead, she curtsies.

"Lady Gwenevere." Vincent Leven takes Gwen's hand and places a soft kiss on her knuckles before relinquishing her hand. "Until we meet again." With that, he turns and stalks toward the main street of the town.

Gwen smiles after him. She turns to find Leona glaring at her with her hands on her hips.

"What?" Gwen asks throwing her hands in the air.

"You remember that he's engaged, right?" She quirks a superior blonde brow at Gwen. "And he's a teacher. You're his student. And he's an adult, and you're…"

"Cupcake let's get something straight. I am most likely a Glimmer, as you guessed back at the hotel. I'm not sure, however, if you realize that that means I have no control over the fact that

every man I meet will inevitably find me attractive or charming and likeable." Leona opens her mouth to speak but Gwen cuts her off. "I realized a long time ago that I could either hide my head under a paper bag and live like a hermit for the rest of my life or find a way to make the best of it and embrace what I am." Gwen gestures in the direction the professor went. "Accepting compliments and little flirtations isn't a crime, nor is it the same thing as flirting back or committing adultery. Also, I'm pretty sure that the professor wasn't hitting on me just now and might be a decent guy. You're reading way too much into him kissing my hand. Plenty of gentlemen used to do that. So, what do you say you worry your little blonde head about your own affairs." Gwen pats Leona on the top of the head in patronizing manner. "And I'll worry about mine." Gwen touches her hands to her chest. "Okay? Agreed? Fine. Good. Wonderful!" Leona glowers at her but Gwen doesn't wait around to give the younger Witch a chance to answer, turning and stalking off toward town herself.

"Whoa!" Gwen stops abruptly, looking up to find Jonah standing right in front of her; it takes all her coordination to keep from stumbling into the boy's arms. "I'm walking here. Do you mind?" Gwen moves to sidestep him without even looking up into his face. *I'm not ready to look into those big, gorgeous eyes just yet. In fact, I was not planning to look at, let alone talking to him in the near future.*

"Gwen." The tone of his voice grabs hold of her as surely as if he had grabbed her by the arm. She can't help pausing to look up at him. "Please. Just give me a chance to explain. Right now, isn't the right moment, I see that. I've got duties to attend to and you'll be interviewed by the Thoyens of the Coven right away." Jonah takes a breath. His eyes look like dancing water scanning over her face in earnest. "May I come by later after you've settled into Aunt Nicola's dwelling to talk?"

"I suppose," Gwen concedes, tearing her eyes away from his mesmerizing gaze. She runs a hand through her long, silky, black hair. "Although, I don't see what good it'll do." She makes a show of examining the few split ends of her hair before tossing her luxurious mane over her shoulder in an indifferent manner.

"There's just so much about Wicca and my family that you don't understand, and I think if you heard my side of things, you might not judge me so harshly." He looks down at her with contrition written in every line of his face. Against her will, Gwen feels her wall of icy disdain start to melt into a watery puddle before the power of his sincerity. "Or at least I hope so. I promise Gwen I never meant to deceive you in anyway."

"All right, fine. We'll talk later then." Gwen pushes on past him, fighting the urge to look back. With a deep sigh, she chooses instead to drink in this new world around her.

Somehow without her noticing the dirt path has transitioned into a stone street, looking oddly out of place amongst the old-fashioned village. The Coven's gate sits on the very edge of town, the main road leading from it to the opposite end of the township through a network of houses and buildings with the same grown-not-built appearance as Alcromech.

Men, women, and children step out of the buildings and onto the road to meet the new arrivals. Friends greet each other with open arms, parents hug children, and lovers embrace as they are welcomed back into the fold. Gwen spies Professor Leven followed by a chubby lad in servants' attire. Vincent makes a grand bow before a severe-looking woman dressed all in white with chestnut-brown hair cropped in a pageboy cut, straight bangs and all. When the professor straightens, Gwen notes that the lady is nearly as tall as him. With a haughty air, the woman listens to the professor, unimpressed before she allows him to take her by the arm and lead her farther into town.

That must be Vincent Leven's betrothed.

Scanning the crowd, Gwen finds Thayer and Leona being greeted with hugs and smiles by a middle-aged couple. The man, stocky and bald with a very generous brown mustache, slaps Thayer on the back. Meanwhile, his wife, a statuesque goddess with hair like fire curling and twisting around her rosy face and down to her hips, hugs Leona to her chest and kisses her forehead. When the lady lets the young Witch go, Gwen watches as a miniature clone of the woman steps up to embrace Leona, too, with a beaming smile.

Is that Isla? Gwen can't help but wonder, not wanting to know the answer. A short girl about ten years old stands next to Nicola. The girl receives a big hug from Leona, whom she gives a warm smile. She looks like Leona, but younger with short blonde hair styled in a bob. *This must be the littlest Crayborn, Cleo.*

"Welcome to Monroe!" The same disembodied voice from the gate speaks from Gwen's right shoulder. Gwen nearly jumps in surprise as she turns to find a striking young man of nineteen with long, flowing, golden hair. "You're a new face. Where do you hail from, sister Witch? I've never seen you in the capital." His golden Wiccan circle burns in contrast to his dark blue eyes as his gaze sweeps over her openly. "Are you from a Coven in the Mediterranean or Asia, perhaps?" The sunlight sends shimmers of gold through his hair. Gwen finds herself momentarily speechless.

He stands with a posture that a King might envy, tall, straight, and proud. The white cloak he wears looks both masculine and refined over his broad shoulders. His well-tailored white shirt and trousers look perfectly pressed and expensively made. Gwen notes the symbol over his left breast — a river running between two mountains encircled with a ring of white flowers. Lean yet muscularly built, the blond adonis before her has a face right off the cover of a romance novel. He seems better fit to join the cast of the popular Vegas all-male strip show, "Thunder from Down Under."

He could even pass for an Aussie, she thinks, bemused, a smirk pulling at the corner of her mouth. When their eyes meet, it is clear he is as impressed by her good looks as she is with his. *So, we both like what we see. What are we going to do about it?* Gwen has half a mind to say this aloud. *Wow, and just like that I'm ready to break my own promise to myself. You've got issues, Gwen. Serious ones!*

"No. I come from Rumford, Maine," Gwen supplies, coming back to herself. Gwen smiles at the young man politely, but not as seductively as she'd like to. "Or at least that's the first place I have any memory of."

"Ah, so you're a coon cat!" The blond youth proclaims as a display of dimples crease his cheeks and chin around a sparkling white grin.

"Excuse me? I have no idea to what you are referring." Gwen laughs lightly, unable to tear her gaze from his face. She steps forward to offer him her hand for a handshake.

"He's referring to the Coon Cat, the symbol of the Saco Coven." Jonah's voice speaks as he shows up beside them, startling them both. "That's the Coven in Oxford County, Maine. The one you should've been raised in," he says to Gwen while staring at the striking blond stranger, obviously an acquaintance.

Although the object of her infatuation of the last month doesn't look at her, Gwen can feel his displeasure as if steam is rising off his head. His aura dances around in a most aggressive fashion.

"Master Hardenbrook." Jonah's mouth tightens around the word "master" as if it pains him to utter. He gives the handsome young man a stiff formal bow.

"Oh, there you are, Crayborn." The blond has already regained his composure from Jonah's sudden appearance.

"What are you doing manning the gate?" Jonah asks. "Looks like you've been getting into trouble again"

"I don't answer to *you,* Crayborn. What do you want?" His tone agitated, his face creases between his brows with distain. He gestures to Gwen with a wave of his arm. "I'm busy, if you couldn't tell, making a new acquaintance."

"Let me formally introduce you, then," Jonah replies coldly. "This is Lady Gwenevere, ward of Thoyen Nicola Blackwool." Jonah stays in place between them, still refusing to look her in the eye.

What is wrong with him? A moment ago, he was begging me to meet with him later. Mr. Contrite and Polite has gone now, it seems!

"Ah-ha! So, *you* are the wild Witch everyone's talking about!" the other boy exclaims, a new level of curiosity entering his eyes as he studies Gwen.

"You have no idea how wild I can be," Gwen says, licking her upper lip. She only thinks the better of it the second after, and immediately wishes she could take it back.

Both the young men give her startled looks. Hardenbrook recovers first with a broad smile.

"Merry meet, Gwenevere. I am Drake Hardenbrook." He steps forward extending a hand. Gwen takes it and gives it a friendly shake.

"It is very nice to meet you, Drake." Gwen gives him a smile.

Jonah groans, stepping between them again.

"Fine. All right, you've met now. I must escort her to The Covenstead. Excuse us." Nodding in Drake's direction, Jonah takes Gwen by the arm and leads her toward town, not hesitating to ask for permission.

"We'll meet again soon, my lady!" Drake calls after them with an arrogant smirk across his beautiful face.

Gwen waves back to him with her free arm.

Drake whistles and a great big Tibetan Mastiff comes bounding up to him from the side of the coven gate. Drake leans down and scratches the dog behind its fluffy ears whispering something to the animal.

Gwen smiles to herself before turning on Jonah.

"What was that all about?" Gwen asks, shaking her arm free of his grasp. "You're acting like a jealous boyfriend. Stop it."

"You are acting like a wanton hussy from a pleasure house!" Jonah ripostes. "You stop it."

Gwen snorts. "That's rich coming from someone who flirts with other women when he's already engaged!" Gwen crosses her

arms beneath her breasts as she picks up her stride. It's no use, Jonah's legs are longer, matching her stride easily.

"You should stay away from Drake," Jonah advises, his tone calmer now. "He's a no-good, drinking, gambling, womanizing, pureblood snob. He'll chew you up and spit you out. Trust me. I've seen him do it before."

"Trust me, I'm more trouble than he is. I'm a no-good, deceiving, violent, no-circle, man-eating, wild Witch!" Gwen laughs darkly. "It sounds like we're a match made in hell."

"I am sorry." Jonah steps in front of her cutting off her path. Before she can duck around him, he puts his hands on her shoulders. "You're right. It's not my place to tell you to whom you can talk. I am NOT your boyfriend." All the fight seems to have gone out of him. Embarrassment shines through his aqua-blue eyes. "But believe me when I say he is NOT a guy you want to get involved with. I'm simply saying this as a friend trying to look out for you."

The pressure of his hands on her shoulders sends heat through her arms, across her chest, and down her spine. Speechless, they stare into each other's eyes. The tension is palpable between them. Her throat has gone dry, and Gwen swallows hard and moistens her lips. This draws Jonah's eyes to her mouth, and he begins to lean toward her. Gwen's breath catches.

"Jonah!" Thayer shows up beside them, startling the two of them apart. "What's going on over here?" Jonah's best friend asks

with a bright smile. His lime-green eyes barely conceal his frustration.

"Nothing, just..." Jonah scrambles for the right words. "Giving a bit of friendly advice," he replies with reddened cheeks.

"Then do it from a few more feet away. My sister is watching," Thayer whispers to Jonah, taking him by the arm and looking him earnestly in the eyes — a brother's warning.

Jonah nods, guilt written on his face. He and Gwen both glance over to see the Blackwool household standing just forty feet up the road. They all stare at them. Leona looks as though she has swallowed turpentine while Aunt Nicola glares at the two of them with open disapproval.

"Let me introduce you to my family." Thayer turns to Gwen with a kind smile. He gestures for Gwen to lead the way as he and Jonah fall in step behind her. A hushed exchange happens between the two friends behind her back, but she can't hear what their saying.

As she approaches the Blackwools, Gwen takes great pain to avoid looking into the eyes of the girl by Leona's side. The air seems heavy, her hands clammy. Thankfully, Thayer steps up to do the talking.

"Mother, Father, this is Gwenevere." At this, Gwen smiles awkwardly and bows her head, wondering if she should have curtsied.

"Gwen, these are my parents, Francis and Glendene Blackwool," he informs her with pride.

"Merry meet, Gwenevere." His gorgeous mother steps forward, taking Gwen into her arms and hugging her to her breasts. Taken back by this physical display of affection toward a stranger, Gwen is relieved when the lady releases her. She finds herself immediately embraced by his father a second later. Nervously, she pats the man on the back until he finally pulls back.

"We've heard so much about you from my sister," he declares, holding her at arm's length by her elbows. "You are welcome under our roof or around our hearth anytime!" Then, without warning, he spins Gwen to the right. "And this is our daughter, Isla Blackwool."

Forced to face the girl, Gwen is amazed by how small and childlike Thayer's sister looks. Isla peers up at her from somewhere around the level of Gwen's armpit. Gwen fights the urge to comb her fingers through the fifteen-year-old girl's wild mass of vibrant red curls, to force it into order.

"Merry meet, sister Witch." The girl child welcomes her with the single most radiant and genuine smile Gwen has ever seen. Isla's impossibly large eyes, identical to her brother's in color, drink Gwen up with pure joy. "You are so lucky my brother found you." Gwen stiffens as Isla embraces her and squeezes her tight, like being hugged by a baby doll with an iron grip. Gwen remains silent and still as the girl prattles on. "I can't imagine how terrifying and lonely your life has been without another Witch to guide you.

My, how lost you must've felt." Gwen breathes a deep gulp of air when finally, Isla releases her. "But all is well now that you're one of us!" She beams up at her suddenly, taking Gwen's hands in hers and squeezes. "We're going to be the best of friends, I know it! Oh! We should have her stay over tonight in the Dragon Hut with us! Don't you agree, Leona?" She practically bounces with glee, looking to her best friend for acquiescence.

"Why ... of course we should." Leona forces a smile while her eyes betray her horror.

No, no, no, no! For once, Isla, stop being the nicest person in the universe! She's the enemy! Gwen doesn't have to peek into Leona's thoughts to hear this.

Apparently Crayborns are very loud thinkers, Gwen muses. *I wonder if their parents were the same way.*

"As intriguing as a Dragon Hut sounds, I must decline your kind offer." Somehow Gwen manages to wiggle her hands free of the chipper Isla's grasp. "It's been a long day and I'd like to settle into Thoyen Nicola's dwelling. You know, to get used to the place. As soon as possible." Gwen forces a polite smile. "It's very nice to make your acquaintance."

Jonah steps up to the little girl who hangs by Nicola's elbow and ushers her over. "Gwen, I'd like you to meet our baby sister Cleo Crayborn."

The timid girl nods at Gwen as a greeting. Her clothes are all the brown third circle servant outfit. Her slim frame doesn't begin to fill out her clothes and her plain brown eyes dart about Gwen as if she is memorizing every detail of her. Gwen investigates the girl's aura and sees a blue glow with no flashing lights and just a one-toned hum. Even if her mind weren't wide open for Gwen to peer into, she would still know the truth about this girl. Cleo is human. She has no wiccan sunburst in her eyes, and witches never have brown eyes. Never. Her aura is even like the average human aura. Somehow the Wiccan spark just didn't cross over into Cleo's genetics. She must take entirely after her human mother.

How terribly out of place she must feel to be a human in a witch's world. "It's very nice to make your acquaintance." Gwen reaches out a hand to the girl. After a comforting pat on the shoulder from her brother, Cleo takes Gwen's proffered hand and shakes it weakly.

Something about her reminds Gwen of Kara, the little girl she lived with at the foster home back in Scranton, Pennsylvania. Maybe it's the look in her eyes or the timid way she holds herself. Yes, this girl has been pushed around and ignored in this world. She lacks self-confidence, Gwen senses from her aura. "Cleo is a very lovely name," Gwen comments, giving the girl a friendly smile.

Cleo looks up at her and a smile slowly forms on her lips. "Thank you. I'm named after Cleopatra, you know."

"Is that so?" Gwen asks with exaggerated interest.

"She was a Witch," Cleo informs Gwen. The girl's intellect seems to shine out of her eyes, her uneasiness melting a little as she speaks.

"I did not know that." Gwen responds with an impressed look. *She seems like a sweet kid.*

"I hate to interrupt the introductions, but Gwen still must meet with all the Thoyens at The Covenstead," Aunt Nicola interjects. "Come away with me, girl. We've got official Thoyen business to be about." All too eager for the excuse to get away from the overly friendly Blackwools and the others, Gwen quickly falls in step behind the Irish Witch as she heads up the main road.

"When you're done, you bring her to supper, Nicky!" calls out Glendene as she adjusts a woolen shawl about her shoulders.

"Aye, sister, we're making Hogseye Serpent stew!" Francis adds.

"In that case we'll be there directly!" Nicola calls back jovially.

"It was very nice to meet you all!" Gwen shouts, watching as they all turn and head down a side street. Isla takes Jonah by the arm, talking away as he smiles down, listening attentively to her.

Gwen tears her eyes away to stare at the symbol on the back of Nicola's shawl. It sways and dances as the woman makes her way through town. Gwen's chest clenches and her stomach flips. She shuts her eyes tight to hold the tears that threaten to escape.

I can endure this, Gwen soothes herself. *I must. I only have to stay for a little while. The Vampire conflict can't last forever, can it? The police will stop looking for me eventually, won't they?*

Gwen knows it's foolish to believe either of her predicaments will resolve soon. Instead, she chooses to turn her thoughts toward more pleasant things. *Like a blond-haired bad boy, perhaps?* Gwen hears a familiar little voice in her head. A relieved smile spreads across her face.

Well, I do like a challenge, Gwen sends back to Morna through their mental connection. *Listen to me talk! A couple of weeks ago my boyfriend was murdered, then I nearly fall for Jonah just to find out he's spoken for, and here I am already flirting up a new temptation! What's wrong with me?*

Nothing! It's just your unusual way of coping, Morna replies.

What? Are you saying I need a man in my life to be happy? I hope I'm not that pathetic! Gwen counters.

No, not at all. Rather that you need someone to take care of. It doesn't have to be romantic. You just like to be someone's hero. Taking care of other people makes you happy. Morna's words send a warmth through Gwen's troubled heart.

It's so good to hear your voice. You have no idea how worried we've been. I guess the cabin is closer to the coven than I thought if we can hear each other think like this. That's awfully convenient. Although, I wish you could've gone through the Lucifinian roads with me. It was trippy, and it would've seemed less strange with you there.

I'm sorry, Gwen. I have traversed those roads before between fairy nests. I don't blame you for not enjoying the experience. It takes some getting used to just like traveling by water.

Ugh, don't remind me of that! Gwen and Morna share a mental chuckle over the thought. *Nicola mentioned something about water scrying as an effective way for communicating between the tribes. As soon as I get a chance to come to the hermit's cabin, we can connect with Raven that way.* Morna seems comforted by the thought. *Did you have any trouble getting to the cabin? Do you have everything you need?*

I had no trouble at all. The Wiccans seem to keep their hermit's cabin stocked with the basic provisions just in case.

All the basics accept a bathroom, Gwen adds, sending Morna the memory of Gwen waking in the hermit's cabin three years earlier. She had just escaped Bec LaNuff by traveling by light and had to rush to the woods to empty her bladder thanks to the cabin's lack of modern amenities.

Although I do appreciate human's modern plumbing, I for one don't have qualms about relieving myself in the woods. Morna sends Gwen back a mental laugh.

"Here we are, child," Aunt Nicola announces, pulling Gwen into the present.

Gwen stops abruptly to find herself standing before a tall, black, twisted mass of trees and plants spiraling into the sky out of the cobblestone street. Nicola stands upon the wooden steps of this strange building holding open its triangular door, waiting for Gwen to step inside.

I must go now, Morna. I'll see you soon as I can. Gwen sends back through their connection.

I'm looking forward to it. The two end the mental connection between them. Gwen turns her thoughts to Thoyen Nicola.

"Where is here, exactly?" Gwen asks, looking over the foreboding structure with a growing sense of uneasiness.

"This is The Covenstead, child." Aunt Nicola responds with forced patience. "Here we will meet with the other Thoyens of the Coven and discuss what shall be done with thee."

"Thoyens are the council of Elders, right?" Gwen asks, stalling for time.

"That be right, dearie. Thoyen is another word for One of the Thirteen. Every Coven is run by thirteen Elders from the first circle," Nicola explains, reaching her free hand toward Gwen.

"Oh. That makes sense." Reluctantly, Gwen takes the lady's offered hand and pulls herself onto the first wooden step. Gwen waits for Nicola to enter first, but the lady stays by the door waiting expectantly.

"You two don't much like the unknown now, do ye? And you're none too keen on your own kind, are ye, lass?" Nicola wonders aloud with an inquisitive look in her light-green eyes.

"You two? I assume you mean Raven and me?"

"That I do." Nicola nods "He was just as fearful of entering the Werewolf Inn the first time as you are now to go into a building full of Witches," the Irish Witch observes. "You've been out on your own much too long, I'd say. Let's fix that now, shall we?" Nicola suggests with a reassuring smile as she wraps an arm around Gwen's shoulder and brings the teenager inside with her.

Under normal circumstances, Gwen would balk at such an intrusion into her personal space by a virtual stranger, but just now her throat is too dry to notice Nicola's touch. *And Nicola has done a few things for your benefit recently. Such as save you from the cursed flower, deal with an evil mermaid and help Morna get out of the trading post undetected,* Gwen reminds herself. *She's not the one you should be worried about.* Gwen swallows the wad of straw stuck in her throat made of her own cowardice. She nods numbly to her companion.

"Yes, let's get this over with," Gwen concedes. Entering the brightly lit entryway, she can't help but puzzle. What exactly does Nicola mean by *discuss what shall be done with thee?* Those words echo in her mind as she is led deeper and deeper into the Monroe Covenstead.

Chapter Thirty-Three

Pack of Strangers

*H*er heart sprints after her rational thoughts. They both attempt an escape in which Gwen cannot physically succeed. Inside the twisted root building, although large and spacious, she can't help but feel as if she's walking the stone tunnels of Bec LaNuff. Somewhere within the building she hears scratching, animals whinnying, and smells blood. She shivers.

"Are ye cold, lass?" asks Thoyen Nicola at her side. Jonah's adopted aunt still pulls Gwen along as though they are taking a friendly stroll and not walking into the gnashing teeth of a monster.

"I guess so. I seem to have forgotten my jacket," Gwen comments absently. Before her she sees a pair of nine-foot-tall wooden green doors at the end of the hall. Somehow, she doesn't need Nicola to tell her that this is the room where she will be judge

and punished. They approach the doors all too soon. The murmur of voices can be heard from the other side.

Gwen scrabbles to think of any reason not to go inside. Although she has had two weeks to mentally prepare for this, she had not thought her tribunal would be this soon. Part of her had hoped she would never have to face this moment.

"Here we go." Nicola takes a steadying breath and reaches toward the door. Instantly the doors before them open inward of their own volition like an automatic door in a store. Gwen knows that this is of course being done with magic, not mechanisms and motion sensors.

Her eyes lock with the cold gaze of a violet-eyed, dark-skinned Witch dressed in all green. Silence falls over the room within. Gwen goes numb all over as recollection and tortured memories surface. The lady in question stands rigid, wearing her rank in every muscle of her being. This is the Coven's High Priestess, the leader of the Thirteen Elders and the woman who refused to save Gwen's beloved Angelo two years ago at Bec LaNuff. Nicola enters the room, but Gwen is frozen in the doorway, unable to breathe.

Thirteen chairs reside in a circle on the opposite end of the room, before an ornate painted mural of a man and a dark-haired woman embracing. Rows and rows of benches line the walls all around the room facing the circle of chairs where a black stone altar sits in the center. Gwen absently notes a rack on the wall to her right with various kinds of brooms hanging from it. The chamber smells of incense, berries, and smoke.

The Witch in question stands before her chair just under the painted mural. She meets Gwen's stare, ignoring the other Witches and Warlocks that sit in several of the other chairs. Everyone else wears white with the same colorful shawl that Nicola wears but with their own house symbol embroidered on it. A few of the thirteen are absent, their chairs empty. Those present look between their leader and Gwen with curiosity and unease.

"Lass, you must come in." Nicola returns to Gwen's side with a forced sense of calm on her middle-aged face.

"I'd rather not, thank you very much." Gwen forces out the words through tight lips, tearing her gaze off her enemy. Gwen's eyes plead with Nicola to let her go.

"I'm afraid there's no getting around it, child. This interview must occur; you must be tried for your crimes," Nicola whispers softly, placing a hand on Gwen's which clutches tightly onto one of the green doors. Gwen releases the doorknob she wasn't even aware she had taken ahold of and steps hesitantly into the room. Nicola nods and smiles slightly in encouragement. She turns and leads her the way toward the circle of chairs and the black altar. With every step Gwen takes toward the High Priestess, she feels her skin grow hotter. Hatred gives fuel to the fire burning within. By the time Gwen steps into the circle with Nicola, she practically shakes with rage. The sunlight shining through the windows vanishes as the sky darkens without, clouds quickly forming over the sun.

"Enough! We can do without these theatrics." The High Priestess speaks in quick, clipped tones. She faces Gwen, her violet eyes unflinching, her dark black hair done in many braids and twisted into a bun on top of her head.

"Release the power you hold, child." Nicola turns to Gwen, visibly distressed but forcing her voice to stay calm. She slowly puts a hand on Gwen's shoulder as if frightened Gwen might bite it off.

"I thought you bonded her in a restriction spell." The high priestess inquires through tight lips. "Why is this child still able to summon a storm?" The violet-eyed witch points out the window at the gathering tempest in the sky.

"I did bind her. She is under the spell as we speak," Nicola explains.

"This shouldn't be possible, Nicola," one of the other witches in the room comments aloud shifting in the chair uneasily.

"She is very easily affected by emotions and her power very great. I believe she is still contained and unable to summon spells of her own will. Her heightened emotional state seems to manifest power of its own out of her control. However, I don't believe she can do anyone harm."

I don't know about that. After all, I have done it before. The image of Denis Keller's crushed body comes to mind. Gwen shivers inwardly. I had done that without my control, too.

"Ha, subconscious power, Nicola?" The priestess's tone holds skepticism. "Not only is this unheard of, but it is also highly unrealistic. No one can do such a thing. I suggest rather that your skill in casting spells has weakened with age."

Nicola swallows hard and her jaw clenches. "Everything I have learned of the girl and her history suggests that she is capable of such subconscious abilities," Nicola insists in a clear tone to the priestess before turning her back on the woman to look Gwen in the eyes. "This is a neutral place, lass. Everyone who enters this circle comes bare, without magic, without weapons or judgment."

"Somehow I doubt that" Gwen whispers back to Nicola. Still, she sighs and inwardly relinquishes the tempest of dark magic she hadn't realize she was gathering. I cannot be here in this room with that woman. I thought I could, Nicola, or maybe I just hoped she was no longer in this Coven, and I wouldn't have to face her again. But now... Gwen realizes belatedly that she had just spoken to the woman in her mind. The surprised look on the Irish Witch's face would be comical if it weren't for the tension in the room. Sorry, I...

It's quite all right, child. I don't usually leave any part of my mind open, otherwise I wouldn't have heard you just now. I should have tested you before for this ability, but...

It's not very common, is it? Gwen sees from the brief flashes of thought Nicola allows her to see that this is true. The woman just nods. Gwen also realizes that Nicola has great control over her thoughts and has a kind of mental shield that allows only what she wants out while protecting everything else from those who might pry into her mind.

"Is everything all right, Thoyen Nicola?" another Witch sitting in the circle asks, a woman with shoulder length light brown hair and teal-colored eyes. If it weren't for the Wiccan circle in her eyes, Gwen would say the woman looked like a soccer mom who belonged behind the wheel of a minivan, not a Priestess amongst Witches.

"Everything is fine, Agnes." Nicola smiles to the woman as she takes Gwen gently by the elbow and leads her toward the altar.

Nicola, no. I can't guarantee I can keep my head with that woman in the room.

It'll be all right, lass. Trust me. You've told me the sad tale of what occurred at Bec LaNuff. I understand your misgivings. I should've thought to ask the names of the witches that came to assist in your liberation. This is my fault. But don't fear. I've taken you under my name. I won't lead you astray or let others harm thee. Nicola's words are accompanied by a sense of warmth and understanding. Gwen feels her anxiety slowly melt out of her tense muscles.

The storm clouds outside seem to have vanished as quickly as they formed, Gwen notes, glancing out the windows. I was the one doing that, she realizes, cold spreading from her chest to every extremity. Perhaps I am dangerous after all?

"Gwenevere is ready to be seen by the council circle." Nicola turns to face the dark Witch at the head of the circle. "She's just tense, Juniper. It's been hectic the last few weeks with all this Vampire nonsense going on."

"I made my objections to this girl's admittance into our Coven known," Juniper replies coldly, still standing before her chair with the air of the Ice Queen. "As I find myself overruled by my King, I must allow you to take on this child's case and judge her of her crimes and give punishment as needs be. If she is found innocent, then you may have a trial period to tutor this wildling." The High Priestess looks at Gwen pointedly before adding, "I suggest you tread lightly."

"Don't I always?" Nicola replies with a lighthearted air. "Why me father always called me Feather as a child, I was such an easy babe, he claimed." Nicola winks at Agnes before taking the seat opposite Juniper on the other side of the black altar. Agnes smiles back before sighing and relaxing back into her chair. Juniper merely rolls her eyes at Nicola's remark but remains standing.

Gwen stands by the altar at a complete loss. Her hotheaded-self blisters at Juniper's words of warning. Meanwhile her rational side tells her she can trust Nicola and that lashing out at the High

Priestess will only do harm to her cause. After all, where will I go if they kick me out of the Coven? Back to Las Vegas where they're waiting to arrest me as a suspected serial killer? How long could I hide in the woods before I cross paths with another Forsaken, or worse a Vampire? With my luck that's exactly the scenario I would find myself in. Gwen hates to admit it, but, yet again, the fates have landed her between a rock and a hard place. Gwen sighs inwardly. You made Raven a promise, remember? Gwen squares her shoulders and faces the High Priestess with confidence and forced civility.

"All right, then, what is the procedure here?" Gwen asks the dark Witch. She slowly looks around to the other Witches and Warlocks in the circle. "I'm confused. Is this my tribunal or is this an interview of some kind? Ask me whatever you like. I have nothing to hide." Gwen is more than aware of all their eyes upon her body, examining her clothes and making appraisals of her from her appearance. No judgment, she says.

"We have yet to determine if a formal tribunal even needs to take place," Nicola interjects. "Think of this as an arraignment, just like the human's justice system in this nation. This is when you make your plea."

"Okay then." Gwen takes comfort form this thought. "Let's get started then." She raises her chin, throwing back her shoulders. "I plead not guilty, your …What do I call you exactly?" Gwen asks the black witch with a faint hint of snideness.

"You may address me as High priestess or Thoyen Jefferson. However, we wait first for the remainder of the Thoyens to arrive before we proceed with the council circle," Juniper replies, indicating the empty chairs with a gesture of her pointed chin. "Then a cleansing will be performed and then, and only then, will we hear what you have to say."

Before Gwen can open her mouth to reply, the green doors spread wide to admit Vincent Leven and a few others into the room. Gwen recognizes one of those that follow him to be his fiancée. Vincent gives Gwen a little smile as he steps forward to greet the other Thoyens present.

"Many apologies, everyone, I had rather hoped we'd put off any of the rituals and ceremonies until everyone had at least had supper." This gets him a chuckle and a nod or two from the other men in the room which there are only four, Vincent included. He exchanges a few bowed salutes with the other members of the circle before taking his seat.

"That's a man for you, always thinking with his stomach," Nicola announces, gaining several smiles and laughs from most of the nine Thoyen women.

"That's easy to say for someone whose brother does all her cooking," jibes another fellow, a half-bald Warlock with a long, gray beard, mustache, and the wildest eyebrows Gwen has ever seen. He reclines lazily in the chair three seats down from Nicola.

"I cook well enough when I must, Molasaba. Francis just has a better knack for it, and I a better knack for the craft," Nicola explains.

"Well, that explains why you're a Thoyen and he's not," interjects Molasaba. The wild eyebrow man busts into laughter at his own joke as the other Thoyens join him. Nicola makes a shooing gesture at the man as if dismissing a dog. The atmosphere in the room has changed drastically. The companionable relationship of the others seems to combat the cold hostility of their leader. For the first time since entering the building, Gwen's chest feels lighter, the air easier to breathe. Perhaps this whole thing isn't as dire as Nicola has led me to believe.

Juniper just stands erect in the same spot as she has been since they entered. Gwen notices that the priestess waits until the new arrivals have all taken their seats and the conversation has died down before she at last gathers her green silken skirts and sits in her seat of honor. The rustling and movement quiets as the other twelve of the council turn to look to Juniper.

"Let this session of the council circle begin," Juniper announces formally to the room. "As you have all been made aware from our communications over the last weeks, Thoyen Nicola has discovered a wild Witch amongst the human world." Juniper speaks with authority, her voice precise and schooled as her posture is stiff. She looks at the other thirteen and then turns her violet-eyed gaze on Gwen. "Child, yesterday we, the Thirteen, held council and had a vote on the matter of Nicola taking you on as her ward and the request that we hold your tribunal here in the Monroe Coven. The motion did not pass. However, in light of all that's happened in Alcromech the last few days and because of the Kings direct order, we now have no choice but to give credence to Nicola's requests." As she says this, she gives the Irish witch a not so pleasant smile. "Despite this, there are unsettling facts surrounding your background that give us pause to accept you into our fold, should you be found innocent of your crimes. As your guardian, Thoyen Nicola will assist you in the cleansing ritual and then we will use the circle to perform an Aegis spell to determine if you can be trusted."

"A cleansing of what?" Gwen asks with a curious brow quirked.

"Of you and your energies, lass." Nicola steps up to Gwen's left shoulder to stand beside her at the altar. "It helps to separate you from the negativity that you carry with you. It helps the Aegis spell take greater effect and is also a kind of protection." Nicola looks to the corner of the room and snaps her fingers. Gwen follows Nicola's gaze. Several brown-clad Wiccan servants step away from the wall as if they were part of the woodwork. They had stood so still she hadn't noticed them next to the wall of brooms.

"Protection from what? For whom?" Gwen asks Nicola as she watches the five servants hurry to a cabinet near the mural and retrieve several items from its shelves. They turn to the circle in unison and weave their way through the chairs to enter the center of the circle. They each place their collected items on the black altar. The servants retreat with bowed heads back to their corner, never once looking anyone in the eyes.

"Protection for everyone, from each other and the negative forces without," Nicola whispers to Gwen. She rearranges the items on the altar, a different-colored candle set at all four edges of the tabletop. Yellow on the east edge, red placed in the southern position. Blue is to the west, and brown to the north with a silver candle in the center. Nicola places a white, unlit candle right before Gwen on the altar. Recognition dawns on her as years of reading every book on Wicca, pagan religions, and the occult resurfaces. The set up on the altar looks like the setting for a space-cleansing ritual with a few extra items that she knows to be commonly used in a self-cleansing ritual.

Yes, that green powder in that bowl smells distinctly of sage and that's a Thurible with a charcoal block in it. She has never heard of the Aegis spell before but from the sounds of it, it must be a special kind of truth or protection spell.

"Before we begin, do you have any jewelry on your person?" Nicola asks. Her eyes flicker to the gold chain around Gwen's neck. Gwen feels the weight of the pendant between her breasts. The cold metal familiar against her skin hiding underneath her black lace bodice of her dress. "All jewelry must be removed before the ritual." Nicola must see the hesitance in Gwen's eyes for she adds, "Some metals and gems effect the Aegis spell poorly."

"Yes, I wear my locket." Gwen hesitates, putting a protective hand over her chest. "But I always do, and it's never interfered with any magic spell before." The idea of handing this precious piece of her past over to Nicola makes her heart race.

"The Aegis spell is different from regular spells. You must be bare of all negative energy and all things that might interfere. That's why we cleanse you first," Nicola explains, holding a hand out for Gwen to deposit her locket. "I promise you will receive it back at the end of the Council Circle before you leave."

With a deep sigh Gwen pulls the chain up over her head, the locket slipping out of her dress along with it. Quickly Gwen hands it to Nicola, forcing her hands down to her side before she is tempted to snatch her necklace back again.

"Good. Thank you." Nicola stows the locket away in one of her dress pockets. Gwen watches it disappear with a strange sensation of abandonment. She realizes suddenly that she can't remember the last time she went without her locket. She's even slept with it on for as long as she can remember. "Now do you know what to do with the white candle, child?" Nicola asks when Gwen finally takes the candle from her.

"Yes, I think so." Gwen feels her old child-like curiosity and thirst for knowledge overcome her. "If what you practice is like what human Witches do, then I'm supposed to use the white candle

to light the charcoal block inside the Thurible. I sprinkle some sage incense powder over the lit charcoal, then I walk the Thurible around the alter to release the sage smoke. Then I use the white candle to light the silver candle in the center of the altar, after which, I focus on the light of the candle and breathe in the incense, clearing my mind and relaxing my energy." Gwen looks to her elder Witch with a look of satisfaction on her face.

"Ah, but first you most draw the circle around the altar, dearie," Nicola corrects. Gwen's smug look disintegrates into annoyance.

"Why, of course. I meant after drawing the circle." Gwen tries to recover her mistake. Gwen spies a small bowl of salt on the altar. This must be for drawing the circle. She picks it up. While walking slowly backward around the altar, Gwen sprinkles the salt on the ground in a trail. When she's done the line of salt makes a complete circle around the altar. Gwen places the bowl of salt aside and takes the white candle in her hands. She takes a deep breath and lights the white candle "Flar Mes Roara," Gwen utters, intending to light the wick of the white candle in her hand when suddenly the entire candle bursts into flames. Gwen yelps instinctively, dropping the wax fireball to the floor where it immediately sets fire to her long black lacey skirt.

"Downstae, revolk!" Nicola shouts quickly, extinguishing the fire from both the candle and Gwen's dress, smoke billowing around them. Several of the elders have coughing fits before the smoke makes its way towards the open window.

In shock, Gwen hadn't time to react to her clothes being aflame before Nicola acted. Shaking slightly, Gwen stares down at the white puddle of wax at her feet, the smell of her singed newly made gown thick in the air. All at once a searing pain spreads across the flesh of her right palm. Slowly she raises her shaking glove-covered hand before her face, completely oblivious to everything outside of her pain, the shock, and the humiliation. She stares at the burnt holes in the fabric of her black glove, sees the reddened and blistering flesh of her hand beneath. Some part of her is vaguely aware of Nicola's hands on her shoulder, shaking her. Several voices yell around her. They seem to be either speaking at her, calling her name, or yelling about her amongst each other. Gwen cannot decipher any of it. She suddenly is transported to another time and place.

* * * * *

Heat is all she knows; fire consumes everything around her. She hides beneath her mother's bed, curled up in a ball in the farthest corner against the wall. Her mother's lifeless hand dangles off the side of the bed. Blood dripping down her delicate fingers into a pool of red. Oddly, it complements the green paint caught beneath the edges of her fingernails. Beyond the hand, she sees the

fire dance across the floorboards toward her. Remembering something her mother said before hiding her beneath the bed, she begins to chant over and over to herself. Somehow, she knows that if she keeps repeating her mother's words the fire cannot touch her. Shutting her eyes tight, she lets the words consume her own fear, taking away the pain of her mother's loss, leaving her numb.

Closing her eyes again, Gwen sings the old, familiar song of healing and comfort.

"*Dade winda cura longa, babeta lavota,*" she intones sweetly, imagining the pain in her hand away, letting the words consume her nerves and relieving her of the suffering. "*Babeta lavota, lavota, babeta. Dade winda cura longa, babeta bae, babeta bae la ru mamina lavota uon!*" The images in her mind are still there as she feels herself resurface to the present. The little girl she once was opens her eyes, no longer afraid, only to see violet eyes staring back at her. "You can't hide from me, little nymph." And a pale hand thrust forth to grab her.

"Gwen! Gwen!" Nicola shouts at her, shaking her by the shoulders while a room of strangers sit in a circle of chairs staring at her, all white-faced and unnerved.

"What? What!" Gwen shrugs Nicola's hands off her, retreating away from the altar until she finds herself outside the circle before the door she entered by. "Stop it. I'm fine! It's all right, okay!"

"Nothing is all right," Juniper responds coldly, standing once more before her chair, gripping the arms of her seat with white knuckles. "You lit a candle with a ball of fire!"

"Flara is the word used to light a simple flame. Don't you know anything, girl?" Molasba adds on top of the High Priestess.

"This is why we don't allow untrained children to go about practicing Witchcraft on their own," Zellah Bloodsworn chimes in, her straight brown bangs falling at congruent angles as she inclines her head. "How she was ever left so long out there in the world without being discovered is beyond me!"

"I beg the council to reconsider allowing this wildling into our midst," Agnes pleads, her once-ordinary face transformed by the gleam of distrust and fear in her eyes. "Even if she isn't guilty of the crimes laid before her, she will be a danger to the children and expose us all to great peril."

"I tried to warn you all." Juniper raises her voice above the others. "Now we have seen what she really is capable of."

"Clearly, she is dangerous. I agree." Vincent Leven stands, hands raised as if in surrender. "But am I the only one that noticed that she performed the Lavota charm with perfect execution?" Vincent stalks across the room toward Gwen. "Here, let me see your hand, Lady Gwenevere." He beckons her to reenter the circle of twisted root chairs. Gwen hesitantly steps toward him, taking his proffered hand. She allows the professor to lead her back into the middle of the circle to the altar. Once standing before Juniper, he

takes her right hand and gently removes the singed glove, letting it drop to the floor. He turns Gwen's hand over in his own, examining it. "See, not a mark, no reddened skin, no swelling or blistering of any kind." He holds up Gwen's immaculate hand for the High Priestess to see. "Clearly this is not the work of an inept child."

"She has the healer's touch — that is certain," Nicola agrees, coming to stand on the other side of Gwen. Discreetly, she takes Gwen's left hand and squeezes it in reassurance. "The fireball was clearly a nervous mistake, nothing more." Nicola goes on turning, pleading eyes on all her fellow council members. "She has been through a lot in her short life, not mention in the last few days! She has a lot to learn, no one's denying that, and it won't be easy at her age to relearn the proper methods and rituals of the craft. But should we reject her, she'll be on her own amongst the Eden spawn when the Vampires let loose their fury on mankind."

"It's intolerable cruelty to leave one of our own helpless amongst so many enemies." Vincent picks up Nicola's reasoning. "She'll also be perceived by the Vampire to be a violation of their terms, as opposition to their claimed rights made clear in their declaration." Many of the others in the circle nod at this. "She was the one the vampires enlisted a daughter of the Mer-people to abduct and bring to them. Clearly, she is in danger out there and she needs our protection."

"What are you proposing then, Thoyen Leven?" Juniper asks with a quirked brow as she folds her arms across her chest.

"Do as we have already discussed. Let Thoyen Nicola take full responsibility for the child, only bind her in an oath of obedience to our esteemed council member, giving her power to moderate the girl's power and uses of it."

"Now hold on a minute!" Mollified by her mistake and shocked by her flashback of that dark night she became an orphan, Gwen has been left speechless until now. She steps back from Nicola and Vincent looking at them both in turn with suspicion. "We will do no such thing! You know some of my past. Have you forgotten already how I was forced to live under … Legion's control in Bec LaNuff?" Gwen forces her former husband and tormentor's name to pass her lips as though the word is a tangled ball of needles and thorns. "You would dare ask me to bind myself willingly to another?"

"This is not the same thing, lass; I promise it won't be…"

"Nicola, you speak of something you have never known," Gwen insists, shaking. "But I do. I've been too trusting once before, too stupid to see evil before my own eyes…" She tears at the glove on her left hand, flinging the elbow-length kid glove to the floor and thrust her hand up into the air for them all to see. "And I paid dearly for it!" She wiggles her four fingers to demonstrate her missing ring finger, the nubby stump twitching. "Send me away if you're not up to the task of training me. Be just like everyone else and judge me only on your own fears. I'm used to that sort of thing by now. But understand this: if I stay and learn from you, I

do it as an independent soul. I cannot, and will not, be caged again."
Gwen lets her hand fall by her side. Looking all her elders in the
face by turn, she leaves Juniper for the last. "Everyone makes
errors. You can't expect to leash me like a dog because I made one
mistake. Did none of you ever say a wrong word when you meant
another? Make a wrong decision that took you down terrible roads?
Is anyone here perfect?"

A pregnant silence hangs about the room as the council
members look at one another uneasily. Some just stare off into
space, or down at their hands as if lost in thought. Only Juniper
looks Gwen square in the face without seeming affected by her
speech.

"Thoyen Nicola." After what seems like an eternity the High
Priestess finally speaks. "Are you sure you are willing to take full
responsibility for this child's teaching as well as pay the
consequences of her mistakes?" Her eyes linger on Gwen until the
last word, turning her head only slightly to address the Irish Witch.

"Yes, High Priestess, I am." The note of finality and assurance
in her voice gives Gwen a modicum of comfort.

"Well, then, please continue the cleansing ritual. We have a lot
of work ahead of us," Juniper concedes, resuming her chair once
again. From this perch, the High Priestess watches Gwen as Nicola
instructs her step by step through the ritual. Gwen feels the heat of
the woman's eyes upon her like the noonday sun in the desert. Still,

she remains calm, and does exactly as she is told, her arrogance swallowed up for the time being.

Once the cleansing is finished, Gwen feels as though she has been spiritually cleansed, just the way she felt after Morna cleansed her aura the night she rescued her from Lynette's cage. The thought of her friend makes her ache to get this whole thing over with and get to the hermit's cabin at once. However, there are still more rituals to preform, a truth spell to submit to, and answers to provide before that can happen.

After the Aegis spell is finished, Gwen stands before the Thoyens feeling as though she is pure in heart and mind, suddenly all her worries gone from her.

"Let us proceed," Juniper instructs stiffly from her chair. "Gwenevere, you have been caught in the act of preforming sacred rituals and spells along with exposing the secret existence of the Werewolf tribe and the Fairy tribe all before humans for personal gain. What have you to say for yourself?"

"Remember you are under the Aegis spell." Professor Leven speaks up from his chair in the circle. "Do not try to lie to us, for it will cause you great pain. The more you try to resist telling us the truth, the more severe the pain will become." He says this formally but Gwen senses he means it as a friendly warning.

"I did perform real magic disguised as illusions in a show in Las Vegas. I did ask my friends Raven, a werewolf, and Morna, a fairy, to be part of my show." Gwen answers truthfully, with the

bluntness of a child. "None of us had any idea that this was against any laws. We figured we weren't hurting anyone. No, I did not do it for personal gain as I don't need the money. You see, my old boyfriend, Angelo … you remember him, he's the vampire you let burn to a crisp?" Gwen pauses for a moment, looking to Juniper for some acknowledgement. When the witch just stares blankly back, Gwen shrugs and continues prattling on under the influence of the Aegis spell. "He left me a lot of money when he died so I'm set for life financially. I did it for fun, because I like to perform, and I love using magic. I also figured it was a good cover for a witch in the human world." At this Gwen finally stops talking and looks about the room expectantly.

Nicola gives her an encouraging nod. Gwen smiles back, as carefree as kindergartener.

"You see." Vincent Leven stands addressing juniper first before turning to speak to the others. "Can there be guilt when you are unaware a law is being broken? Gwenevere may be nearly the adult age, but in experience she is like a child."

Somewhere in the back of Gwen's mind, she balks at this.

"I believe not." Nicola agrees. "And since the girl is obligated to tell us the truth under the Aegis spell, clearly she isn't speaking in falsehoods, or she would be wailing in pain right now."

This causes a stir among the elders. Several nod and mumble agreement.

"I vote that the child Gwenevere be declared innocent of all wrongdoing and the tribunal dismissed." Leven declares to the room. In unison, every head turns to Juniper.

"As do I," Nicola announces, standing from her chair.

"A vote has been proposed. Those amongst you who vote in favor of absolving Gwenevere from guilt of the crime of performing witchcraft before humans, please stand," Juniper instructs.

Chairs scrape against the floor and fabric rustles as slowly members of the council begin to stand. First one, then two, until five women and two men stand. Gwen notes that one of the women is Agnes. Zellah Bloodsworn remains seated with the remaining four Thoyens including Jupiter.

If Gwen thought the High Priestess could look any more severe, she was mistaken. Her expression somehow becomes even more sour. Gwen is suddenly reminded of the Mother Superior from St. Paul's Orphanage. The two are so alike in mannerism and attitude that it leaves Gwen with a sick feeling in the pit of her stomach.

"Nine have voted in favor. Thus, the Wild Witch Gwenevere is found innocent of all wrongdoing by this council circle. So, let it be known," Juniper announces with a face of stone.

Gwen turns to Nicola with a triumphant smile. Nicola gives her a wink back. Those who voted in her favor step forward to

shake Gwen's hand and congratulate her. Some even welcome her to the Coven.

"In our next Council Circle, we will discuss the terms of your trial tutorship in our Coven, Child. In the interim, you are to be accompanied by either Thoyen Nicola or a member of the Blackwool household. Furthermore, you are not permitted to wield any magic outside of the classroom and your personal tutelage under Thoyen Nicola. Is that understood?"

"Yes, High Priestess." Gwen nods.

"Nicola, you may release the girl of the restriction spell put upon her and return her power to her," Juniper instructs.

"Yes, High Priestess." Nicola turns to Gwen with a formal look about her. "Magquec inablee, rea strique revoke, pro vaer inablee!" Nicola chants and, with a twist of her hand, the spell is lifted.

The wall of blackness that has separated her from her power for two week is now gone. Energy surges through Gwen's body, filling her to the brim. Gwen takes a deep and contented sigh.

"Is that all? May I go now?" Gwen asks Nicola first. She turns her gaze on High Priestess Juniper Jefferson.

"Not quite yet," Juniper declares before Nicola can speak. "There is still the matter of your mysterious lineage to address."

"Yes, I for one want some clarification on this subject." Zellah Bloodsworn speaks up from her chair. "I have never once heard of the heritage basin being unable to determine the lineage of a

Forsaken's blood before." Her tone seems to suggest that Gwen falsified the results.

"Yes, Nicola, are you sure that there wasn't some mistake?" Molasba adds to his fellow Thoyen's statement. "The whole thing is highly irregular."

"I swear there is no mistake. The populace agent even administered the test twice. However, since Gwenevere is missing her binding finger, it wasn't as conclusive as they would've hoped."

This explanation seems to satisfy some but not all the Thoyens.

"And Gwenevere has no memory of her childhood?" Professor Leven asks.

"From what I can tell, no she does not. She seems to have a mental block on her mind surrounding her early childhood memories," Nicola explains to the other Thoyens.

"Like a suppressed memory from trauma or an actual magical block?" Agnes interjects, a thoughtful look on her plain face.

"I believed it was just the trauma of watching my mother's murder and the pain of dealing with it that caused me to forget the first five years of my life, but now…"

"But now it seems as though something else might be responsible." Professor Leven finishes for Gwen.

"Impossible. Spelling someone to forget that much time for this long would require the caster of the spell to feed the spell

power continually. It simply couldn't be done," another member of the thirteen points out.

"Unless the spell was anchored into an object rather than a person," Nicola supplies after a long thoughtful pause.

Several of the Thoyens perk up at this and look around at one another.

Gwen feels the effects of the Aegis spell wearing off. The realization of what Nicola is suggesting hits home. Her emotions and logic returning to normal, and she feels panic creep up her spine.

"Why would an object be able to maintain such a spell when a person couldn't? Wouldn't the Witch that cast the spell have to maintain the spell's source of power either way?" Gwen asks quietly.

"If the spell was simply on a person, then they would need to do this because a person changes." Professor Leven answers, his voice slipping into his scholarly tone. "The mind evolves and grows. The ability to retain vast amounts of information and to comprehend complicated notions grows in time. This mental growth would literally outgrow the spell unless the power feeding it was maintained."

"But an object doesn't change it doesn't grow in the same way the mind does," Gwen finishes for the Professor. He nods in reply. Gwen gulps a lump in her throat the size of Texas. Both curious and afraid, she asks the question she is dreading to have answered. "Could my locket be such an object?"

Nicola's head snaps up at this as though it was the most obvious thing in the world, and she just figured it out. "Yes, child, it could, especially if it had something that belonged to you and the caster of the spell in it."

"And she would have to wear it all the time both morning and night. Any prolonged time away from it would lessen the spell's power. Overtime it would fade entirely," Juniper interjects.

"How often do you wear this locket, lass?" Nicola asks.

"All the time. I have for as long as I can remember."

"And is there anything inside the locket?" Professor Leven asks Gwen. She nods slowly.

"Where is this locket? Have it brought to me immediately?" Juniper interrupts. She had stayed all but still as a statue through the whole conversation till now.

"I have it, High Priestess," Nicola answers. She fumbles in her pocket for the object in question. When she pulls it out from its hideaway, something in Gwen yearns for it. It takes everything in her to keep from dashing across the room and swiping it from the Irish witch. Gwen's eyes follow it almost hypnotically as Nicola carries the glinting gold pendant on its ornate gold chain to lay it into Juniper's hand.

"Humph." She raises it to her eyes and examines it closely. She mutters a few words under her breath and then waves her other hand over the locket. Nothing seems to change about the locket, but Juniper's face does. "There is an enchantment on the jewelry. In fact, there might be two different spells at work here," she announces. She rubs her fingers over the locket and reacts in surprise. "Also, an engraving is hidden to the eye." With a click she opens the clasp and pops open the front. With her free hand, she pulls the braided lock of hair out to hold before the room to see. The two contrasting shades of hair interweave into the braid. Golden blond and midnight black. "Where did you get this locket, child?"

When the dark-skinned witch looks up at her, Gwen is frozen in place. Her own fear paralyzes her. Gwen shakes off the feeling and mumbles, "My mother gave it to me when I was a baby, I think."

"And whose hair is in this braid? To whom does it belong?" Juniper demands.

"The black hair is mine. The gold hair is hers. My mother's hair."

For a moment, the room seems to go still as the other Thoyens wait for Juniper or Nicola to say the first word.

"Then your mother most likely is the one who cast this spell that has blocked your memories all this time." Nicola vocalizes what everyone is afraid to say.

"But why would she do that?" Gwen asks incredulously.

"To protect you," Nicola supplies.

"But from what or who? How is forgetting who I am and who my parents are supposed to protect me?" Even as Gwen asks the question, her mind recalls her last dream with her blond, blue-eyed guardian angel. He had given a reason, she realizes. His mother was the one who killed her mother. She was the one Gwen's mother was trying to protect Gwen from. *What if she made me forget as a way of hiding me from the woman who killed her and from myself?*

"That's what we intend to find out, Lady Gwenevere," Vincent Leven informs her.

"For now, it's probably best that you do not wear the locket," Nicola adds.

"Yes, this would be wise and as well she should be given a Rainbow Fluorite crystal to help open up her suppressed memories and improve her overall health," Juniper orders in clipped words as she coils the lock of braided hair back inside the locket and closes it. She hands it back to Nicola, who waits before her. "Take this and put it somewhere safe so that we might examine it more and unravel the enchantment on it."

The Irish witch bows and backs away from the High Priestess with the locket firmly clasped in her hand. Gwen panics a little inside as she watches Nicola stuff her locket back into her dress pocket.

Gwen is about to go stir crazy if she stays in this room one more minute. She needs the locket back in her possession. It is the

only thing she has left of her mother. But if it's the thing holding me back from remembering my past … The thing keeping me from getting the answers I've always yearned for… Gwen lets the reality sink in and reconciles herself to letting the locket stay in Nicola's care, for now.

"That will be all for now, Gwenevere. Nicola, you may take the girl home with you," Juniper instructs.

Every cell in Gwen's body screams to get out the Covenstead and away from all these people. Juniper turns her face away and begins speaking to the other Thoyens, as though Gwen had already left her thoughts.

Nicola takes Gwen by the arm and turns her towards the doors quickly. The rest of the Thoyens take their seats again, their attention back on their High Priestess. Gwen takes a deep breath of air as they hurry down the hall toward the Covenstead's front entry. She had dodged a bullet, she realizes. However, she suspects that she has not seen the last of Juniper Jefferson's disapproving glare. And now I must live day in and day out under her command. Gwen finds herself leery of the terms the council will decide on for her duration in the coven, feeling the prisoner once more.

I'll see you soon, Morna. Gwen sends the mental message to her fairy friend, along with the memory of the entire meeting. Although grateful to have Morna as some blue sky in the gathering storm that her life is becoming, she still can't help missing her other best friend.

Oh, Raven. I sure hope you're doing better than I am, she thinks, wishing her friend were back beside her once more. At least where you're at, you have family to welcome you. Meanwhile, I'm stuck here playing "Simon Says" with a pack of strangers.

Chapter Thirty-Four

Lost Kin

At the sight of the gateway at the end of the road ahead, Raven heaves a huge sigh of relief. Not that he's claustrophobic or anything, but four hours of walking down a never-changing, quiet, and unnatural road made him homesick for the real world. They left Alcromech with ten additional Werewolves. All their traveling mates except one are gone now. The new wolf left with them is a forty-something fellow named Gideon, an old friend of the Caddo family. The others disappeared along the way as they all split off into smaller groups at different forks in the road.

Raven hesitantly approaches the golden filigree vine-covered gate, his companions ahead of him. Gideon steps forward and kneels upon a black circular stone in the road. His bald head reflects the unnatural light within the tunnel-like passage. His flannel shirt taunt across his hunched shoulders as he prostrates himself. In a manner quite reverent, he puts his hands palm down to the dirt and presses his forehead between them. As he rises, he scoops up some dirt between his hands and rubs it on either side of his tanned face. Specks of dirt cling to his salt and pepper beard and mustache.

"From earth we came, to air we ascend. Let thy children enter, Great Spirit, sheltered by thy shadow. Protect us from the eyes of Eden and its spawn," Gideon chants. The twins, standing on either side of Raven, whisper the words along with him.

The golden gate opens of its own, creaking from lack of use. The vines covering it crackle and snap with the movement, leaves falling to the ground. As they open wider, natural sunlight and a gust of wind break through the opening. The scents of the forest beyond bathe the four travelers. The woodlands smell of sugar maple, American beech, red oak, dogwood, and ferns. Raven also picks up the scent of seawater, sand, and various wildlife.

Gideon takes an exaggerated deep breath of air and sighs contently as he exhales. He looks over his shoulder to the three younger men.

"You smell that, Ulfs? You know what those smells are, Raven?" The gray-bearded man turns to address him. After an awkward moment of silence Raven realizes that Gideon wants an answer. Confused, Raven looks to the twins for help on either side of him. Each wears a suppressed smirk with something like amusement and excitement in their golden eyes.

"Forest?" Raven shrugs.

"No, son, that's the smell of home! You're coming home at last, oh heir of Mahiingan!" Gideon smiles broadly. Grabbing Raven by the arm, he pulls him out of the tunnel and into the woods. "Another master of beasts returns to the den!" Gideon announces in a booming voice up to the sky as the twins follow behind them. "Welcome to Wolf Island!"

Raven can't help but smile — Gideon's enthusiasm contagious. Raven looks back to the twins and notices that the gateway and the Luficinian road have vanished. No traces remain. All that lies behind Thunder and Lightning is more woods.

"Where did the gate…"

"It's enchanted," Thunder responds smugly. "You can't see it from this side of the Luficinian road."

"Not unless you're a member of the tribe and are looking to leave again," Lightning adds, adjusting his pack on his back. "Then it'll reappear; otherwise, it might as well not exist."

Raven nods, returning his attention to the woods around them as they cross through the tall summer grass. They continue walking for about fifteen minutes without any change in the surroundings. Raven stops abruptly.

"So where is this den of yours? I sort of expected we'd step out of the Luficinian tunnel and right into a Mohawk Indian village," Raven admits to his companions.

Gideon guffaws and the Twins chuckle.

"It's just on the other side of the forest," Gideon confirms, slapping Raven on the back.

"You may not know this, brother, but not all Indians are wolves and not all Werewolves are Indian," Thunder informs him in a placating tone.

"Actually, I was aware of that fact, Thunder," Raven says in a dry tone that might even rival Gwen's gift for sarcasm. "This isn't the first pack I've ever been a part of, you know?"

Lightning laughs at this. Thunder just shrugs. "Hey, you're the new pup around here, buddy." He takes his pirate's baseball hat off his head and runs his fingers through his brown tuft of hair before placing the hat back on his partially clean-shaven head. "You better get used to everyone telling you stories and sharing little factoids about our culture."

"That's right. And don't forget that yesterday you didn't even know who your parents were, what pack you belonged to, let alone that you're a Mahiingan," Gideon supplies. "There's a lot you don't know about your father's clan, Ulf."

"Gideon, did you know my father or know of anyone who met him?"

"Jacy Mahiingan was one of my closest friends," the middle-aged man at his side admits. "I used to follow him and his crazy brothers everywhere they went. I even dated your Aunt Jaralyn for six months when we were sixteen."

"And how did my father and his brothers feel about that?" Gideon gives Raven a sideways smile, a dimple appearing in the middle of his right cheek just visible above the line of his beard.

"They were supportive of our relationship, only not very friendly once we broke up. Except Jacy, of course." This time Gideon smiles to himself as if remembering a time long ago and far away.

"What was he like? My father, I mean," Raven asks as they pick their way through the ever pines and elm trees, sap, dew, and moist earth mingling with the trees' heavily scented needles. Raven can feel the rhythm of the wildlife about him, scurrying in the trees, burrowed deep in the earth, and soaring through the branches above.

"He was a good man, the 'strong, but silent type,' people called him," Gideon replies. "You take after him, you know?"

"I hope that's a good thing." Raven smiles nervously.

"Oh, it is. It is," Gideon answers with a quiet smile.

The woods around them take on a mystic air as the sun begins its descent over wolf island. Raven hangs back, letting the twins and Gideon take the lead. His thoughts turn to the two women who have occupied his life for the last several years. Two women couldn't possibly be any more different than Gwen and Morna. Yet somehow, they make the best of friends, both tugging at his heart in their own way.

In the weeks that Morna was missing, Raven had worried endlessly. The only thing that could distract him from this was Gwen's uncertain safety in Alcromech and her precarious situation with the witches. When the news of the incident with the cursed flower reached his ears, he was sent on high alert. Since that moment he's barely slept and hardly ate. Instead of staying at the Captured Moonlight with the werewolves, he had snuck out every night to sleep outside the Black Iris. He made his camp behind the building within the woods with Gwen's bedroom window in clear sight. He hadn't told Gwen this, of course. He knew it would only worry her and make her feel guilty. He didn't mind sleeping outdoors. It was more comforting being near her than on the other side of the trading post with the Caddo twins snoring loudly in the next room.

Mentally preparing himself for the next attack against Gwen, Raven ran through hundreds of scenarios. He used the strategic training he had learned during his time with his old pack to produce solutions to overcoming every possible enemy. Despite this, nothing he had planned prepared him for what happened.

He had never been more frightened in all his life than when he heard Gwen scream and turned to see his best friend being dragged into the water by some sort of monster. Springing to her rescue, he strained every muscle to pull Gwen from the beast's grasp. Only his superhuman strength was bested by this creature. He felt the wolf urge him to turn but realized immediately that his animal self

would be useless against an aquatic assailant. Being a werewolf gave him amazing abilities. None of them made him an exceptional swimmer or gave him the ability to breath underwater. He never felt so helpless. It was in that moment of doubt that Gwen was ripped from his grasp, disappearing under the surface of the river before his eyes.

Panicked, he had not a moment to react before a blinding light suddenly burst from midair. The force of it knocked him on his back into the bank of the river. When the light faded, he saw Morna standing in the midst of it. Wings extended; she was glowed as if made of something incandescent. Any joy he might have felt in at last finding his missing fairy was quickly forced aside. She turned to him and barked, "Go get Nicola Blackwool!" Before he could stammer a response. The five-foot fairy dove into the water, taking with her the luminescent glow. Scrabbling to his feet, he took off running for the boarding house. Nicola had answered on the first knock, somehow already awake and aware that something was wrong. She followed him with no question. The witch conjured up a spell to locate Gwen which produced a floating ball of light that took off into the night. Raven and Nicola followed it down the river.

The relief he felt when Gwen and Morna appeared on the bank in the strange bubble of water was immeasurable. It popped on the bank dumping Morna, and the mermaid wrapped around Gwen, like a boa constrictor. It took everything in him not to attack the creature with all the ferociousness the wolf had to offer. It proved unnecessary as the mermaid lost her strength on dryland. She released her hold on Gwen as she turned human and weak.

In that moment Raven wasn't sure who to rush to first, Gwen or Morna. He suddenly knew that what he told the Caddo twins about the two women in his life wasn't entirely a lie. He realized right there on the riverbank in the most inopportune moment that he not only felt something for Gwen but Morna, too. Gwen had been teasing him and dropping hints about him and Morna hooking up for ages now. Somehow, she had seen it. *Strange how intuitive Gwen can be about others while being entirely oblivious about herself or my feelings for her.*

A twig snaps behind him and suddenly Raven is all too aware that someone is following them bringing himself back to the present. Alert and ready, he spins around to face the stalker. What he sees is… nothing. *Blasted sunset*, he grumbles inwardly. The magic hour had passed and now the fading light of the sun leaves the landscape in a state of visual limbo to all wolves. It was the worst moment to confront a possible foe. Until the sun went down entirely, he was halfway between his human sight and the super night vision of the wolf. Someone in the shadows could be right before his eyes and Raven wouldn't even know it. Reaching out with his superior hearing, he searches the forest. Nothing. No heartbeat, nor the rhythmic breathing he expected to find.

I'm losing my mind; I could've sworn that I felt someone. He stands there a few moments more, uncertain until the sound of his companion's movements fading farther in the distance forces him to choose. Turning around, he jogs down the forest path, the twins' backs only visible now and then between the trees.

Abruptly a force collides against him. Blindsided he is sent flying off the path into the underbrush. The world flips upside down and bones crack as he hits the ground. The impact of such a force depletes his lungs of oxygen like a balloon being squeezed in a tight fist. After the initial shock wears off, Raven is bombarded by a sheering pain all up his left side and a throbbing headache. He gasps for air and struggles to get to his feet. He stands slowly, scanning the forest for his attacker. The shadows lengthen as the last rays of sun vanish behind the treetops. Nothing stirs in the woods.

"Who's there?" Raven asks aloud. No one answers. The birds chirp in the treetops nearby; bugs and animals slither and scurry all around him. But no personage is present. *How can this be?* Then realization sinks in and the hairs all over his body stand on end. *Vampire.* But how many he can't know, not until the sky goes dark. He might not be able to hear them since they do not have a heartbeat and need not breath. He may not be able to smell them as they have no scent. However, there will be nowhere to hide from the wolf's sight.

I can take one maybe with my injuries, but more? Vampires are swift, as he just experienced, and this makes him doubt his chances with more than one foe in his current state. *A year ago, I wouldn't have thought twice about taking on a couple of vampires myself. But then I had a death wish at the time. Thinking Gwen was dead had really messed me up. Things are different now. I'm this close to meeting my family. I can't afford to be careless now. If I try to call for help, I'm done for. If I try to run, I'm dead.* The only way to alert his friends of the danger and give himself the best chance of survival is to become the wolf. He is stronger and deadlier as the animal than he is as the man. Letting his animal-self take rein, Raven wills himself to change. He draws upon his anger, giving into every dark emotion within him.

He crouches down on his hands and knees. With great restraint he forces himself to remain silent as the transformation twists his every bone and muscle. The experience is painful. Every. Single. Time. Even after ten years and thousands of transformations. Retreating into a far corner of his mind, he focuses on changing over without screaming out and alerting his stalker of what he is doing. Raven lets go of himself and slips away into the mind of the wolf.

＊＊＊＊＊

The world is aglow with a silver light. The sky now dark, the world around him turns silver as the life force from every plant and creature shines from within. This inner glow of all things is visible only to werewolves. Curling back his teeth, the animal begins to hunt his hunter.

The wolf takes hold of the situation without fear. He creeps forward slowly through the tall grass. He stays low to the ground, his belly scraping rocks and twigs.

Just to the right of the path Raven walked a moment before, the wolf detects movement. The silhouette of a man glows behind some trees.

Eager to tear into flesh, the beast lunges forward. The man darts away, his glow streaking across the forest with incredible speed. The wolf gives chase. His paws beat across grass, rock, and twig as he soars through the woods. Throwing back his head, the wolf howls into the sky. The other wolves will join him soon. Up ahead he sees a large boulder in the man's path. Veering off to the left, the wolf bonds towards it. He covers the distance swiftly. Climbing up the boulder, he reaches the top just as the man passes. With a growl the wolf, leaps off the rock and onto the back of the vampire. The wolf hits the ground with his prey pinned beneath him.

Immediately the creature begins to fight, bucking and squirming his way out from under the wolf's paws. The wolf

scratches and bites at the thing to get it to stop, to scare it into submission. The man's shirt is tattered. Blood spills out of the deep gauges in his back. With a grunt and a hard push off the ground the vampire throws the wolf off his back. The moment he is free the creature leaps toward the wolf.

The wolf swipes at him with his claws. The vampire darts about trying to get around him. The wolf knows better than to ever let a vampire get behind him.

Before the wolf knows what's happening, something grabs hold of him from behind. *There's another one!* The wolf bucks, snarls, and thrashes trying to break free. The effort and the pressure of the arms around him aggravates his injured ribs. Frantic, the wolf tries to nip at his assailant as he is lifted off his feet into the air. The vampire in front of him gives him and evil grin of satisfaction as he watches. His captor flings him through the air. Soaring over the tree tops high in the sky, it takes him the wolf awhile to come back down.

As he starts his descent, the wolf realizes that the impact will kill him. Calling upon the man inside him, he retreats into the corner of his mind. The transformation takes place mid-air. Howling in pain, the wolf's body rearranges back into a man. As the transition completes, Raven comes abruptly to the surface of consciousness plummeting to the earth. The forest below rushes up to greet him. Raven shouts in terror as he collides with the trees. Scraping bare skin on bark and branch, Raven frantically tries to

grab hold of something. With a jolt, Raven stops falling, his hand clinging to a branch. He finds himself hanging naked eight feet above the ground. Heaving a huge sigh of relief, Raven lets himself fall. He lands on his feet with a jolt and collapses in an exhausted heap in the foliage. Swallowing hard, he stares up into the story night sky, the moon nowhere in sight.

Three wolves howl in the distance. Raven jerks up to a sitting position. *Gideon, and the twins.* Raven scrabbles to his feet. Every bone and muscle in his body screams for him to rest but he pushes past the pain. He hurries towards the sounds of the wolves, knowing his friends will face a terrible foe.

Who knows how many vampires are roaming these woods? They'll need all the help they can get.

Raven runs on, lungs burning and ribs aching. When he bursts out of the woods on to the path. Spinning around he looks for any sign of his friends. Nothing. He hears a commotion up the path and takes off toward it. His bare feet thud on the dirt path. Veering off the path, he breaks through the trees into a clearing.

A golden-brown wolf rolls on the ground with a vampire, the two embraced as they bite and claw at one another. Nearby two black wolves, identical in every way, circle around the other vampire. Raven recognizes him as the one he had chased down. Suddenly the twin wolves attack simultaneously. Caught between two wolves, the vampire can't escape. Raven watches the Caddo twins rip the vampire to shreds. Blood, flesh, and entrails spill out into the dirt. The vampire only managed one scream before they snuff his life out.

A yelp draws Raven's attention back to the other combatants. The wolf lies whimpering on the ground as the second vampire stands before him.

"Hey!" Raven yells as he charges toward the vampire. The creature looks up sees Raven coming, sees his friend is dead, and bolts. By the time Raven gets to the brown wolf's side, the Vampire has vanished into the trees. He considers going after him. He glances down at the wolf and sees a deep gash running a crossed his belly, blood matting his fur.

"It's okay, brother, I'm going to get you some help. But first you need to let go of the wolf." The wolf looks Raven in the eyes and understanding passes between them. With a howl that melts into a shout, the wolf shifts from animal to man before Raven's eyes.

* * * * *

"I'm just saying there's no reason to feel inferior. It was just you and two vampires. No one will think you any less of a wolf for failing miserably," Thunder mocks as he leads them down the path. His puffed-up sense of pride shows even in his strut.

"That's very generous of you to say," Raven replies dryly, rolling his eyes.

With an arm over Raven and Lightning's shoulders, the two carry their injured elder Gideon between them. With a makeshift bandage wrapped around his stomach, Gideon wears his shirt unbuttoned as he limps along with the younger men. He sweats and grits his teeth as they move. Despite this, he laughs at every idiotic taunt the twins have thrown at Raven since turning back into men.

While the twins were transforming, Raven found Gideon's pack and helped bandage him and get him dressed. As soon as he was taken care of Raven, headed down the path to recover his own bag. Grateful for the comfort of clothing, he headed back to his friends. When he arrived, Thunder and Lightning immediately started tearing into him, boasting, and posturing about their triumphant kill and saving his and Gideon's asses. *And they haven't shut up since.*

"How much longer till we get to this den of yours?" Raven asks impatiently. "Gideon needs a doctor."

"We're already there," Lightning tells him from the other side of Gideon. He nods, indicating that the place they seek is up ahead.

"This way, boys," Thunder announces boisterously. He heads toward a massive chunk of volcanic rock the size of a boulder. Besides being an unusual rock for this area — there being no volcanoes in the region — the boulder also seems out of place by the way it protrudes out of the forest.

"Follow you where?" Raven asks, confused as Thunder strides right up to the strange chunk of black glass-like rock.

"Here is where the Fenris Lykaios, the Werewolves' council, meets," Lightning announces.

"How do we enter?" Raven asks, tearing his golden eyes from the rock's solid surface before him. He looks between his companions.

"Just step toward it. The den will open itself to us, sensing our blood, knowing Lords of Wolves from other men," Gideon the eldest Wolf instructs Raven. "I think I can take it from here, boys. The path into the den is narrow and I'm feeling up to walking on my own now."

Gulping down his nerves, Raven nods, then follows slowly after the other three Werewolves. The hairs on his skin prickle with tension as Lightning takes the last step before colliding with the volcanic mound. The ground shakes and rumbles startling Raven. Yelping, he jumps back as the rocks shift, dirt crumbles beneath the rock, and a crack forms a vertical opening before them in the once-perfect, smooth, black rock. Thunder shakes his head at Raven with a smirk on his face before he turns to follow his brother and Gideon, who have already entered the opening. Raven hesitates just a moment, looking back the way they came, before he hurries after the others. As they enter, the crack deepens into a doorway, then into a tunnel leading deeper into the den, the way before them uncertain.

"Raven, are you coming, Ulf?" He hears Thunder shout, his voice echoing off the cavern's walls and back to him.

"I'm right behind you!" Raven calls out.

Once he is several feet in, the dirt shifts and a rumble alerting him to change just before the opening behind him closes off, throwing him into complete darkness. Instantly his supernatural senses adjust his sight. Raven moves on. The floor slowly inclines downward, sloping deeper into the earth as it curves and winds, the tunnel's end ever out of sight. The air is musky about him, moist, yet not oppressive. The density of it changes as he turns a final bend, seeing a dim light ahead.

Before long he steps into a yellow light and out into a large chamber. Filled with men, women, and children of every age and ethnicity, the den bustles. All are dressed in every fashion imaginable. From traditional Native American dress to modern blue jeans and t-shirts. The people all mingle with one another around a large ring of stones in the center of the room. The yellow glow of light comes from a massive stone set into the ceiling just above the circle of standing rocks. Doors and windows line the stone walls. Occasionally a face peeks out or a person exits into the main chamber. It reminds him of something out of the history books of some ancient civilization. He can smell dozens of meals cooking from beyond the walls, mingling with the distinct animal/man smells that only Werewolves have. Raven looks about as he walks toward the center, like a wide-eyed tourist seeing Times Square for the very first time. Thus, distracted by his surroundings, Raven collides with a solid mass.

"Oh, excuse me." Red-faced Raven looks down to see a young man with an aqua fauxhawk hairdo tumble into the dirt at his feet.

"Watch it, will ya!" cries out a female voice in annoyance as the person before Raven dusts off their flannel shirt and loose-fitting jeans, her face downturned.

"Oh, crap! Sorry, I didn't see you there. Let me help you up." Raven reaches down and takes the unsuspecting woman by the hips and hefts her to her feet. She gives out a startled yelp and shoves his hands off her as she steadies herself.

"I can take care of myself, thank you very much. You've done enough, you big bru…" She trails off as she looks up at Raven. Golden eyes alight on him, and her face changes. In an instant he sees the family resemblance to the twins. She has the same strong nose, full brown brows, and creamy skin. She's about as tall as her brothers, too. Perhaps five feet eleven inches — tall for a woman. She has long skinny limbs, and no curves to speak of.

"I'm sure you can. I didn't mean to suggest otherwise," Raven replies, apologetically. "I'm sorry I picked you up, an old habit, I guess."

"So, you're used to manhandling women, are you?" she quips after an awkward moment of staring at him as if she didn't understand him at all. She puts her hands on her hips and gives him a sideways smile.

"Not exactly." Rave laughs, scratching the stubble on his cheek. "I just know a Fairy that tends to always find herself in my

way and didn't mind being picked up or carried about whenever I happened to knock her over," he admits with a blush and a fond smile.

"Oh. Your girlfriend, huh?" The woman's face changes again and her shoulders slump.

"Well..."

"That's right, sis!" Thunder confirms as he steps up between the two of them.

"He's also dating a Witch!" Lightning adds, slapping Raven on the back as he appears on the other side of him. Raven's blush deepens despite himself.

"Oh, you're very popular, it seems." The woman gives Raven a forced smile before turning to Lightning with arms wide open. "Welcome home, brothers!"

"Good to see you, baby girl!" Lightning gives her a big hug, picking her up off her feet before she insists, he put her down. The moment she's out of one brother's embrace the other twin scoops her up and repeats the same greeting. Her face grimaces when Thunder calls her "Baby Girl" as well.

Clearly, she doesn't like being reminded that she's the little sister, Raven surmises.

"Hey, where's Gideon?" Raven asks as he scans the chamber for their injured companion. "He needs to see a surgeon right away."

"He went straight to the healers already," Lightning reassures.

"Wait, what happened to Gideon?" The woman asks, face incredulous as Thunder puts her back on the ground to stand on her own two feet once more.

"We had a run-in with some vampires just now in the woods," Thunder supplies

"Vampires here? On wolf island? Even they aren't that stupid," their sister says, disbelieving.

"It's true, sis. They went after Raven here and we saved him," Lightning says with a smug a smile anyone could boast.

"Really?" Again, the twin's sister looks at them, unconvinced.

"We even killed one," Thunder adds.

"That's right — we tore him to shreds!" Lightning continues.

"With claws and teeth…" one twin begins.

"…Blood and guts everywhere!" The other twin finishes.

"Okay, okay, I get the picture." The aqua Mohawk woman raises her hands up in the air, stopping the twins from describing the slaughter further. "I'll believe it when I see the corpse. But for now, don't you think one of you ought to introduce me to your friend?" the Caddo girl inquires.

"Meet Raven Mahiingan, lost son of Jacy Mahiingan," Lightning announces with a flourish.

Raven puts out a hand in greeting. The woman looks at her two brothers as if awestruck, ignoring Raven completely.

"Raven, meet the runt of the Caddo family, our little sister, River," Thunder adds, nudging his sister with his elbow and indicating Raven's outstretched hand with a nod of his head.

"Whoa, the rightful heir to the Lykaios throne is this guy?"

The twins nod in unison. This seems to free her from her shock. Stepping up to Raven, she takes his hand in both of hers and gives it a vigorous shake. A big smile spreads across her face. "I've got to say, Raven, you certainly look the part! Wow, welcome home!"

"Gee, thanks." Raven smiles awkwardly. "Umm, I have no idea what you are talking about," he explains to River, looking at the twins with a confused expression. From his peripheral, Raven notices several people pointing at him and whispering among themselves.

"Wait, these lugs didn't tell you?" River exclaims, dumfounded. She goes as if to smack the baseball cap off Thunder's head. Anticipating her, he quickly takes her hand in his grasp and bats her away.

"It wasn't our place," Thunder rationalizes in their defense.

"We thought he might have already heard of the Mahiingan bloodline. We thought he knew they were the Werewolf equivalent of royalty," Lightning adds.

"And you also assumed he would know he was the next in line for the throne and the rightful Chieftain of the Werewolf Tribe?"

She gives her brothers a look that only a sister could give. "Why would anyone assume that?"

"Wait, hold on." Raven throws his hands up to get the Caddo siblings' attention. "There's been some kind of mistake. I'm not heir to anything. I'm just some orphan, looking for a pack."

"You just came from Alcromech, didn't you?" River asks Raven.

"Well, yeah," he admits, scratching the back of his neck as he tries to get his brain around the situation.

"And they administered the Heritage Blood Test at the Tribal Populace Center, right?" she continues.

"You mean that thing with the needle and the Gargoyle bowl that comes to life and everything?" Raven clarifies.

"Yeah, that's the Heritage Basin, that's the Heritage test," River confirms as her brothers nod in affirmation on either side of her. "And the test confirmed that you are Jacy Mahiigan's son?"

"That's what they told me." Raven shrugs. A crowd is slowly gathering around them.

"The blood never lies," River informs him with a shake of her head, amazed.

"Your father was Chieftain after your grandfather passed on the honor to him," Thunder injects. "Once Jacy passed away, your uncle, Deganawidah, took on the role."

"But now that you're here, and obviously alive, and the only son of the eldest son of clan Mahiingan..." Lightning takes up where his brother left off.

"That means ... you're it," River finishes with a shrug.

The idea seems preposterous; I can't be...

"Where is my boy?" a woman shouts. Everyone turns to see a Native American woman in her sixties standing in the doorway to the adjacent chamber. Her long black hair hangs to one side in an extravagant braid all the way down to her hips. Behind her Raven sees Gideon, who whispers something to the woman. Suddenly, her eyes lock on Raven. She beams as though the sun just raised just for her. Wrinkles deepen around her eyes and her bright smile. She wears a white button-up blouse and a flowery yellow skirt that swishes as she makes her way across the room. Several long necklaces and bracelets bounce around her neck and clatter on both of her arms as she walks. The crowd parts before her, every head bowing in respect to the Lady.

Raven finds himself riveted to the spot, unable to take his eyes from the stranger as her gaze holds his. All too soon the woman steps up to him, scanning his face for something. He doesn't know what. He stands there, confused, stunned, and brimming with emotions he doesn't understand.

The older woman holds her two hands in fists in front of her, tense. Slowly she opens her hands and raises them up to take his face gently between them. Her hands urge him to bend down, bringing his face inches from hers.

"It's as if the Great Spirit has given me back my son," she whispers, her eyes moist. "Welcome home, my dear boy."

"Hello." Instant love burns in Raven's chest, and he fights the sudden urge to weep. "Who are you?"

"Forgive me." The lady laughs softly. Suddenly embarrassed, she releases his face and grasps his hands in hers instead. "I am your father's mother."

"You mean, you're my grandmother?" He struggles to control his voice.

"Yes, Ulf, I am. My name is Tala Orinda Adams Mahiingan."

"My mother, she named me Adam." Raven finds a trembling inside of him, yet somehow on the outside he is still. "I wonder was that for you. I mean, for your maiden name?"

"Yes. It was your father's wish for his first born." Sadness crosses behind her gentle eyes. "If she hadn't run off after your father died, if we had known she was pregnant ... we never would've..." Tala's voice cracks and she closes her eyes as if in pain.

"It's okay. No one's to blame here." Raven swallows hard. "I'm here now, and please call me Raven. That's who I am now."

She opens her eyes and smiles up at him. Raven gathers her into his arms, hugging his grandmother to his chest. Something

inside him clicks and an overwhelming sense of joy floods through him. After a few moments she steps back and smiles up at him.

"I'll call you whatever you want, just as long as I can call you, my grandson." She turns back the way she came with his hand clasped in hers. Raven lets her pull him along after her toward the room she had entered from. The crowd around them bow their heads to him as they pass by. He just smiles and nods nervously back at them, not sure how the heir of a Chieftain heir should behave. They cross through the standing stones and under the glowing yellow rock above.

"Grandmother where are you taking me?" he asks hesitantly as they approach the doorway. He can hear people talking in the next room.

Tala laughs sweetly and squeezes his hand. "We're going to introduce you to all of your lost kin."

Chapter Thirty-Five

Venom

Stumbling down the cobblestone path on exhausted feet, Gwen finally catches sight of Nicola's home. It stands on the very edge of the coven and the forest, where the protective barrier begins. A true Wiccan treehouse, it is a two-story brown and red structure that looks like something out of a fairy tale. Instead of siding or brick, it is made of bark. The red windows look naturally grown into the trunk of the building, with tinted glass. The second story is comprised of tree branches angling into the different wings of the house. The roof is made up of hundreds of red leaves. It sits encircled by a green patch of grass, and a circular wall enclosing it with a gate in front.

Nicola opens the gate and walks down the steppingstones leading to the red front door. Gwen sighs deeply, suddenly wanting nothing more than a bed to collapse on. Following her new guardian into the wooden structure, it doesn't surprise Gwen when the house lights up instantly with glowing orbs of light in every room.

Just like the house in my dreams, Gwen reminds herself. *My mother's house. My house.* The thought brings to the surface the flashback she had at the Covenstead. Not ready to examine that suppressed memory, she shoves it back into the recesses of her mind.

The front door opens right into a great room comprising of the living room, dining room, and kitchen. The floors are wooden, and wavy in pattern. The walls are rounded without corners or edges and lined in a grayish bark. All the furniture is made of twisted roots, vines, branches, or stones. It smells of plants and berries. With the fading light of day streaming through the tinted glass windows, the house has a very homey and pleasant feel about it.

"Your room is up the stairs to the right." Nicola scurries off into the kitchen. Rummaging in a cupboard, Nicola calls out, "Hurry and get change, lass, we've got dinner at my brother's place waiting for us!"

Gwen's appetite disappeared hours ago back at the Covenstead. Something about facing the Thoyens, defending her own actions, and seeing the flashback of her mother's death just left her feeling nauseous. She feels oddly out of place without her mother's locket hanging around her neck. As though it was the one thing keeping her down on earth and she might just blow away with the first gust of wind. Gwen shakes these thoughts away.

"I don't feel like being around people tonight," Gwen calls back as she climbs the winding stairs up to the second floor. "Can't you just go on without me?"

"No, I can't leave you unattended, dearie. It's part of the arrangement with you being my ward."

Gwen groans as she comes to the landing at the top of the stairs. Three doors lead off it. One straight ahead of her, and one on either side. Gwen pushes open the one on the right. In a flash of fur, a Persian cat darts out of the room and thunders down the stairs. Gwen watches it go before going into the bedroom.

The quarters are small, the room barely big enough for the wardrobe and twin-size bed. On top of the red and orange bed spread sits Gwen's red duffle bag and Angelo's violin case. Gwen sighs with relief and shuts the door. The room has a round window looking out over the coven. She draws the curtains closed and quickly peels off her charred black lace dress. The fire ball she accidentally made of the candle earlier burns up a good chunk of the dress's lower skirt. *Maybe they can alter it into a knee length dress.* Gwen tosses the ruined garment aside. Walking over to the wardrobe, Gwen opens the doors. Within, she finds the all-black Wiccan collection of clothes she purchased at Allianne's dress

shop back in Alcromech. Quickly she locates a pair of black leggings pants and a long sleeve black lace top. *I don't care what anyone says, I am wearing pants tonight.* Once dressed, she dons a pair of black socks and witch boots and adds a waist length velvet cloak to her assemble. Satisfied with her choices, she hurries back downstairs.

She finds Nicola waiting in the kitchen sitting at a stool before the bar-height table. The Persian cat Gwen saw earlier eats food from a wooden bowl on the table. Its tail sways happily as its owner scratches its back.

"Who's your friend there?" Gwen asks as she sprawls herself onto the living room couch. She stretches her arms and legs and settles into the couch to rest.

"His name be Killian." Nicola gives her a look that Gwen reads all too well. With a groan, she swings her legs off the couch and sits up right.

"I'm not hungry, Nicola. The only place I'm going tonight is to see Morna at the cabin."

"The fairy can wait. We've got dinner plans and it'll be suspicious if we don't attend."

"If I'm not going to see Morna, then I'm not going anywhere at all," Gwen declares, folding her arms across her chest as if to signal that her decision is final.

"Nonsense, child, we're going to dinner. I'm in charge of you now, and that means I must make sure that you eat, and I don't cook." Nicola hops off the stool and crosses over to Gwen. Taking Gwen's hand, she helps the teen up to her feet. "Come on, let's go." Nicola grabs her own cloak off a hook and opens the door.

"Then what do you do for food? Conjure it up with magic?" Gwen asks incredulously as the woman shoves her out the front door.

"No. Although you can, it's just too time consuming and not really worth the effort. No, I just eat all my meals over at Francis and Glendene's place."

Jonah's house, you mean. Okay, it's not really his house but he lives there. Gwen groans inwardly. *How exactly am I supposed to get over a guy I see not just everyday but also have to sit across the table from for every single meal? Oh, and let's not forget that his fiancée will be there, too. Every. Single. Meal.*

Gwen shoves her hands into her cloaks pockets and follows Nicola begrudgingly through the coven. The way to the Blackwool house takes them past the institute and an inn. The residents of Monroe scurry about as the sun begins to set. In no time, Nicola leads Gwen to her brother's home.

The Blackwool house is a larger home, made up of multiple trees lined next to each other all melded into one another like one solid mass. The structure seems to be two stories as well. It has tinted blue bark and green ivy windows with green leaves for the roof. The chimney smokes, and lights glow from within the tinted glass windows.

The walk wasn't nearly long enough. Gwen finds herself ill prepared to face Jonah again. A ball of nerves bounces around in her stomach.

All the stress she's feeling over the awkward encounter is forgotten the moment Nicola opens the door. Her brother's family and the Crayborn siblings occupy the dining room and kitchen. However, the first thing to catch Gwen's eye isn't Jonah. There lying on the couch in the living room is a real-life bear, asleep. As they enter the room, Gwen realizes that other strange animals are in the Blackwool home.

A beautiful red fox trots along after Francis Blackwool wherever he goes. Perched on Leona's shoulder is a toucan bird. At Isla's feet by her chair is a giant tortoise. A crab sits on the mantle of the fireplace, while an otter is curled up on an end table napping.

"What's with the zoo?" Gwen stands in the middle of their living room and asks no one in particular. "Is that an actual bear?" She lowers her voice; suddenly not so sure she wants to wake up the beast.

"Yes, it's a real bear," Nicola replies. "Have you never heard of the practice of keeping a familiar?"

"I've heard of it. I've just never seen it before," Gwen admits.

"Let me introduce you to everyone's familiars then. You've already met mine, that was Killian. The otter belongs to Thayer; his name is Kevin." Gwen gives Thayer a look at this, but he just shrugs. "Icarus is a toucan and obviously belongs to Leona. Darya the giant tortoise is Isla's Familiar."

"And the crab on the mantle…?" Gwen asks.

"He's mine." Glendene raises one hand while stirring a giant pot over the old stove in the kitchen. "That's Cadmar. He's very friendly if you want to pick him up." Thayer's mom calls from over her shoulder, never taking her attention off dinner preparations. At her side, her husband chops ingredients for dessert. His fox waits patiently at his feet. Occasionally, Francis offers the fox little bits of food. A couple raw pieces of meat and then a bit of celery. The fox happily eats these offerings.

"I'm not sure I want to risk it." Gwen laughs nervously. "I've never heard of a friendly crab before, and I'd like to keep all the rest of my fingers."

This gains her a quizzical look from several of the company, but no one says anything. Gwen can feel Jonah's eyes on her but elects to turn her attention back to her guardian.

"And who does the bear belong to then?"

"That's Angus, he's mine." Jonah speaks from behind her. Gwen tenses. Nicola gives her a look that seems to say, *now be nice.*

Gwen smiles weakly back at her. Nicola gives Gwen's arm a comforting squeeze as she passes her to go into the kitchen.

No, Nicola, don't leave me alone with him. Slowly she turns around to look up at Jonah. He stands inches away from her, much

too close for the situation and the people present. Gwen peeks over his shoulder to glance at his fiancée, Isla. The little red-headed teen sits chatting with Leona as they play a card game. She's completely oblivious to the two of them. Gwen sighs. *Poor simple girl. If I weren't so darn decent, I'd have a mind to steal him right out from under your nose. But...*

"Huh, so why a bear and why Angus?" Gwen schools her tone to be as conversational as can be while ignoring the searing heat Jonah's closeness produces on her skin.

"The witch doesn't choose the familiar, it's the other way around," Jonah informs her. "Angus, I chose it because it means "one strength" It seemed appropriate."

"So, you choose the name? How does Angus feel about that?" Gwen asks dryly.

"The witch or warlock gets to choose their familiar's name, but the animal has to approve it," Jonah clarifies.

"So, you can speak to him?"

"It's more of a feeling in my mind, or images we send to one another. If you'd grown up in a coven, you would've gotten yours when you were eight years old."

Gwen thinks back to the raven who helped her after she tunneled herself out of the rubble of Bec LaNuff. He had communicated with her in the same manner as Jonah and his familiar. *Hmm. I guess that means the bird was a familiar. But is he my familiar or someone else's?*

"Will I still get a familiar?" Gwen asks curiously.

"Of course. Once you've finished your third-level studies, you'll go through the ceremony," Jonah answers with forced nonchalance in his voice. His tense posture and the look in his eyes speaks volumes about how he really feels. Gwen pretends not to see this and takes a step back from him to cross the room and take a seat in an armchair.

"That's very interesting."

He follows, grabbing a stool from a desk nearby and setting it before her chair. *Great. We're going to have that conversation now, aren't we?*

Jonah gives her a surprised look, still not used to the idea of hearing someone else in his head. It takes him a moment to collect his thoughts enough to reply. *Yes, I feel like I owe you an explanation. I'm expected to marry Isla — it's what my parents wanted. It's a part of our traditions, it's…*

It's fine, Jonah. Really. I just wish you said something before. That I didn't have to hear it from Nicola instead of you.

I know and I'm sorry about that. I just … didn't want things to change between us. I wasn't expecting to feel the way I do about…

Jonah, stop. Gwen interrupts him. *Don't say something that you'll regret. Don't say something that's only going to make things more awkward between us.*

But if you've been hearing all my thoughts all this time, then you already know how I feel. How can saying it to you do any more

harm? The earnestness in his aqua eyes burns her soul, with a deep and painful remorse for what she must do.

It will. Thinking something to yourself and saying it to me are two different things. This seems to silence Jonah. A look passes between them, expressing all the unspoken longing they each feel. *I just want to put the last month behind me and move forward from here. I just want to be your friend. Nothing more.*

Then I won't say anything more about it, Jonah concedes, sadness radiating out of him. Breaking eye contact, he firms his jaw gets up, walking away.

"Gwenevere!" Cleo comes bounding down the steps in the living room from the second floor. Her blonde bob bounces around her heart-shaped face. Her brown eyes alight with the sweetness Gwen felt from her before. Gwen notes that Cleo like her siblings is not wearing the servants' brown attire. Instead, she wears a pink knee-length dress with white and purple butterflies printed on it. *That's a human garment,* Gwen realizes. Cleo wears a pink butterfly plastic beret in her hair as well. Neither Jonah nor Leona wear human clothes but casual wiccan attire with actual colors in them instead of the boring white, black, and brown Wiccans usually wear. *I guess when it's their free time and they're indoors with the Blackwools, the Crayborns don't dress or act like servants. Jonah did say that they were treated like family.* Gwen's glad to see that this is true.

"Hello again, Cleo." She greets the ten-year-old as she practically hops across the room to Gwen. "Please call me Gwen."

"Okay." Cleo shrugs. "How are you liking Monroe so far, Gwen?"

"Well…" Gwen tries to think of something nice to say. "It's the most unique town I've ever lived in. Everyone has such interesting pets here, too." Gwen gestures to the animals in the room with a swoop of her arm.

"They're called familiars, not pets." Cleo laughs good naturedly.

"I know that. Nicola was just telling me about it all. Where's your animal?" The moment the words leave her lips, Gwen wishes she could take them back. The uncomfortable look on the girl's face hits Gwen to the core.

"I don't have a familiar. I'm not a…"

"A witch? Yeah, I know." Gwen bats a hand as though the whole thing were no big deal. "You know, humans keep animals all the time and they can't do a lick of magic."

"Huh." This seems to lessen the girl's embarrassment. "I guess you're right. I never really thought about having one because it wouldn't be the same as it is with Jonah and Angus or Leona and Icarus."

"You can't communicate with them mentally, so?" Gwen puts it matter-of-factly. "It doesn't mean you can't still share a bond

with an animal." The thought seems to intrigue the girl. "Say if you could have a pet, what animal would it be?"

After some thoughtful consideration, Cleo answers "I really like monkeys and iguanas, but I think I'd have to say an elephant."

"Really? Why is that?" Gwen inquires, all her discomfort in being here under Jonah's roof dissipating in the simple pleasure of a regular conversation with an uncomplicated and delightful person.

"Because at least I can get a ride on it if ever I'm stranded." Gwen laughs at this.

"That makes sense. I can't argue with that logic," Gwen concedes.

If it were not for Cleo sitting beside Gwen and prattling on the whole meal, the dinner would've been a painfully drawn-out affair. Despite Cleo's charming company, all Gwen really wants to do is to slip away. The hermit's cabin seems both all too near and a world apart. Instead, she must sit across the table from Jonah and Isla, while the girl basks in his glow for what seems like an eternity.

I'm ready to see my friend Morna. She'll be restless to see me. Gwen mentally lets Nicola know as they finish eating the main course.

Not tonight, dearie, Nicola replies coolly. *Tomorrow is soon enough. It'll be dark soon and we really shouldn't venture out of the coven at the wee hours of night.*

Gwen groans internally.

When at last dinner is through, Gwen excuses herself to the other room to get some space from the congenial bunch. Thayer's family are nice enough people. Throughout the evening they have included Gwen in their conversations, but Gwen isn't particularly interested in pleasantries right now.

Gwen leans against the far wall watching the Crayborns and Blackwools gather around the thirteen-foot wooden table. Laughter fills the room. The smell of Hogseye stew wafts through the kitchen and dining room. Leona and Glendene Blackwool scurry about cleaning up after dinner. Isla and her father Francis pass out plates with dessert on it. It looks like some kind of tart. Thayer and Jonah take a dessert and sit back down at the table. They listen attentively as Aunt Nicola spins a tale of her childhood in Ireland and the coven, she grew up in. Cleo sits beside Nicola, her head resting on the woman's shoulder.

Gwen sighs irritably. Closing her eyes, she opens her mind to commune with her fae friend without the coven.

She expects to find a cheerful and happy Morna waiting for her on the mental wavelength. However, the sensation she gets radiating from her friend is fear and pain. A prickly sensation travels over her skin, and the side of her neck burns as if bitten by something poisonous. Gasping, Gwen grabs her neck in reflex, only to find nothing wrong. She feels Morna's pain. She senses her friend's fear. That's when Morna's voice penetrates Gwen's mind.

Nicola, we must go, now! Gwen shoves off the wall and launches into the next room. Grabbing the older woman by the shoulder, forcing her to look Gwen in the eyes. Mentally Gwen sends the message that Morna sent her.

"I'm not feeling well, Thoyen Nicola. Would you please escort me back to your house? I fear I won't remember the way back in the dark." Gwen asks in as convincing a voice as she can manage.

"Of course." Nicola nods to Gwen, understanding showing in her lime green eyes. *Don't worry, lass. We can handle this opposition easily enough. It's nothing I haven't done before.*

"Sorry to leave early, Brother." Getting up from her chair, Nicola makes eye contact with the others. "But we're off."

"Of course, I hope you feel better soon, Gwenevere." Francis declares. The others make similar statements. Gwen barely manages a smile and a nod as a farewell before she bolts for the door. Nicola follows behind, out into the dark and windy night. As soon as they are out of sight of the Blackwool home, Gwen spins to face the older witch.

"What's the quickest way to get to the hermit's cabin without anyone knowing we've left?"

"We'll travel by water," Nicola answers. Before Gwen can speak, Nicola pulls out a vial of water from one of her dress pockets.

"What's that?" Gwen asks as Nicola uncorks the vile and tilts the fluid out onto the ground between them. The water does not soak into the dirt — it stays in a puddle at their feet.

"It's enchanted water. It's useful for when you need to a quick exit but don't have a body of water nearby to enchant for the traveling spell," Nicola explains before she utters a spell. The water takes on an oval form and grows at their feet until the magical puddle is big enough to encircle them both. Then they sink into it. As they enter the watery passageway, Gwen catches a glimpse of Jonah turning a bend in the road and witnessing them vanish.

* * * * *

The chirping of crickets sounds without the cabin walls as a breeze blows through the open window. Morna sits before the fireplace on the rug. Her head rests on her knees. The wings folded into her back are still without a flutter. The glow of the fire casts her golden hair and eyes in an even brighter hue. She stares into the flames. Her mind travels on the wind, her spirit out of her body barely tethered to earth.

Dusk falls over the forest. The golden rays of the sun fade behind the mountains as the sky turns red and indigo. Beneath it, the landscape blends with the shadows of the night encroaching. Fearing discovery by the Coven, Morna can only fly in this fashion

keeping an eye out for Gwen's arrival. With the light of day fading, Morna must retreat to her earthy self.

With a gasp, Morna jerks into her body. Her every muscle aches, and her skin tingles. After several steadying breaths, she stops shaking. It takes a moment for her eyesight to readjust. Closing her eyes, she stretches out on the rug on her stomach. Her wings arch above her before settling onto her back. She releases a sigh but stays in this position for several minutes.

Gwen is not going to visit tonight, it appears. She probably could not get away so soon after arriving. After all, no one can know that I am here, Morna reminds herself. She reconciles herself to the notion that she might be alone in the hermit's cabin for several days. This is little comfort, but the reality of her current arrangement. *At least we are close enough to each other that Gwen and I can talk through telepathy.*

It had been a relief to Morna when she felt Gwen emerging from the Lucifinian road. She had her mind open in preparation for it, hoping she might be able to feel her friend even beyond the coven's protective barrier. Morna wanted to speak to her friend right away. As it happened Gwen was preoccupied with not one but two boys upon entering the coven. After that, she was being introduced to half the coven, it seemed. Gwen had unwittingly left her mind open, too. She must've been too distracted with everything happening around her to realize she was leaving her consciousness vulnerable. After that, she closed her mind and

Morna hasn't been able to make contact since. Morna is anxious to hear Gwen's report of her meeting with the Thoyens. Most of all she wanted to know when Gwen would go before the tribunal.

A sound in the woods has Morna on her feet in an instant. With a sigh of relief, she hurries across the room and throws open the door. The landscape before her is dark, the wind blowing in the trees. Straining her eyes, she scans the woods. The shape of a woman walks on the dirt path through the clearing toward her. *Gwen!*

Wings fluttering behind her, she sprints forward and takes flight. Soaring across the field, Morna touches down just a few yards in front of her. Morna rubs the stone pendant of her necklace whispering an incantation. The stone illuminates a bright light that casts a glow over the path. The woman standing before her is not Gwen. Instead, she finds herself face to face with a tall woman dressed in a burgundy pantsuit with long blonde straight hair. The stranger's unimpressed smirk and her silver eyes tell Morna that she is not surprised to stumble upon a fairy and that the woman is in fact a vampire. The woman gives her a toothy smile, flashing fangs.

Morna spins around and jumps into the sky. With a jolt, she is yanked out of the air and thrown to the ground. The force sends her rolling down the path a few times before she lands in a crouch.

Gasping for breath and aching from a dozen cuts and bruises, she faces her enemy with fire pulsing through her veins. Gathering

the anger inside into a ball of energy in her chest. Morna puts forth her hands and casts a spell.

A gust of wind bursts from the fairy's hands, shooting out to the vampire. The woman's smug look vanishes as she finds herself struggling against the wind. Shielding herself with one arm, the female vampire tries to push forward, her high heel shoes digging into the dirt path. Finally, the force proves too much for her. With shouted curses, she goes tumbling feet over head up the path and out of sight.

Satisfied, Morna releases the spell. *I must warn Gwen that a vampire is here.* She spins on her heels toward the Coven. Something blocks her path. A man towers over her. She looks up into his face, surrounded by shoulder-length brown hair. His silver eyes flash as he gives her a fanged sneer.

"Well, hello, little fairy. That wasn't very nice what you just did to my beloved. I'm afraid recompense must be made." He speaks with a Spanish accent. Before she can even move, the man has her neck clutched in one hand, and his other arm wrapped around her waist. With his hand crushing her windpipe, Morna can only croak and gasp. He lifts her off her feet, bringing her neck to his mouth. He bites, the venom in his fangs burning the skin. A numbing feeling spreads from the wound down her neck through her body, temporally paralyzing Morna.

Gwen! The Vampires are here! They somehow found me at the cabin. There are only two of them. Please come, bring help. Morna shouts mentally, sending the message towards Gwen's consciousness, praying that her friend has her mind open at that moment. Just before the venom hits her brain, cutting off all ability to think clearly. Morna hears a reply.

I'm coming. I'll be there soon.

After that Morna's vision blurs and simple thoughts become difficult to form. Suddenly the Spanish vampire holding her removes his mouth from her neck and drops her like a sack of potatoes. She slumps to the ground in a heap, her eyes glazed over, her expression vacant.

Above her, the blond vampire's face comes into view as she stands over her.

"This must be the witch's little fairy friend that Brielle told us about. She's pretty and blonde. You know ... just the way you like your women." The woman sneers at the Spanish man. He wipes the blood from his mouth on a white handkerchief, folds it into a triangle, and stuffs it back into his suit's front breast pocket.

"Don't be petty, Peyton. I'm not looking for your replacement, although I have heard amazing things about fairy mating practices." He raises his eyebrows at her when he says this.

"It such a shame they had to go and kill poor Brielle." The woman called Peyton makes an exaggerated sigh. "I guess that's one less ex-girlfriend of yours that I don't have to kill myself." She smiles darkly.

"Are you two done with this lovers' quarrel? Some of us have better things to do than listen to you two bicker." The voice of a young girl asks from beyond Morna's line of sight.

Just then more faces appear above her, surrounding her on all sides, their faces illuminated in the glow of her enchanted stone pendant. Each one of them has silver eyes and fangs. Mostly men, a few women, and a little girl. Something about the child is familiar.

Lynette. Morna hisses in the back of her mind. Unable to move or react, unable to send telepathic messages, she can only lie there and seethe inside. *We thought you died in Bec LaNuff with Legion and the vampires. You should have died. You will soon enough.*

Lynette looks down at Morna and tilts her head to look in her face. "It's nice to see you again, although you might've forgotten all about me by now." Lynette laughs, her brown curly hair bouncing around her face. "Looks like I've caught you again, only this time you won't escape."

"What's this talk of you catching her? That was us," Peyton mocks, gesturing between her and her boyfriend. "You've got no claim to this fairy anymore."

"You cannot speak to my mother that way." A twenty-something handsome man steps up to Peyton, a challenge in his tone and countenance. "Mother says the fairy was once hers and if Mother wants it, she shall have it."

Two young women and another man join the first man, stepping between Peyton and Lynette. Their hostile expressions are identical to the first.

"Call down your dogs, Lynette," the Spanish man orders.

"Don't worry, Dante, I can take on these puppies," Peyton tells her lover, never taking her eyes from the line of young people defending the child vampire. "You new vampires have no respect for the hierarchy of our society. The child might be your maker, but she's sworn fealty to our King. You will learn to respect his soldiers and officers like Dante and me. If not, you'll meet your final death before long." With this, Peyton walks around Morna to stand next to Dante, threading her arm through the crook of his.

"Fine, whatever. Can we just kill the fairy and feast on her blood already? I'm starving," Lynette concedes with a pestilent grumble.

"Maybe the king would like to keep her?" Peyton suggests to Dante. He shrugs.

"He doesn't have to know about her." Dante smiles.

"How long till the witch shows up, do you think?" One of the other men in the group asks. His face is scarred with burned tissue, his head bald. Morna can't quite place his accent.

"If not tonight, then tomorrow maybe. We'll wait in the cabin till then," Dante replies. "Jameson, Sarah, we'll need a way to transport the witch once we have her, some way that will seem inconspicuous to witches. Maybe recruit a human servant to help."

A man and woman nod and take off in a blur. "Markus, Neil, fan out in the woods to the west. Brian, Luke, you take the east." Instantly those vampires named take off to do their leader's bidding. "Lynette, send two of your children to the north and the other two to the south. Have them watch the path."

"You don't boss my people around," Lynette hisses. This earns her angry glares from half the group.

Dante and Peyton's soldiers, Morna surmises.

"As right hand to the Vampire King, I outrank you, little one. Don't cross me, or I will have to tell the King that you did not serve him well during this little mission," Dante warns Lynette in a cold tone. "You wanted to make your own little army of vampires, fine. But don't think for a moment that they can save you from the wrath of Lazar Taudero, The Black Russian."

Lynette presses her lips into a tight line before stomping her foot in a very immature fashion and screeching. "Fine. Do what he says." Lynette turns to her four vampire children and commands in a huff, waving them off in either direction of the clearing. Morna notices the way the four youths look at Lynette with awe and utter respect and cringes mentally.

An army of loyal servants bowing to that sadistic child monster....

Dante smiles, satisfied, and then barks out to the two remaining men standing by. "Boris, Malcom, bring her." He turns toward the cabin with his girlfriend attached to him.

Morna faintly feels someone pull her to her feet and heft her over their shoulder. She dangles head down, jostling up and down as the man carrying her walks. His feet her only view. She hears the shuffle of footsteps behind her.

"What about the wolf?" Morna hears Peyton asks "Lynette, what was his name again?"

"They call him Raven," Lynette replies, her voice coming from behind the man escorting Morna.

Morna's heart skips a beat and starts racing. *What about Raven?*

"Raven, right, that's it." Peyton's voice sounds muffled until the man caring her steps over the threshold of the cabin. Morna hears the shuffles of the others' feet as they follow. Morna feels a man's hands around her waist as she slithers off his shoulder and plops down on the straw bed on her back. In this state, she can only stare up at the ceiling of the old cabin.

"How long until Julian and Andrew get back from Wolf Island?" Peyton asks. "I'd like to get a look at this Werewolf. Brielle made him sound scrumptious. I've never had a werewolf before." The woman laughs.

Morna goes cold inside. *Gwen! They are going after Raven, too! Gwen get word to Raven! He is in danger!* Morna hears nothing back. The venom still affects her, rendering her telepathic abilities useless.

She fights to break free of the venom's mental and physical prison she finds herself in. Nothing she does changes her state. The fear inside her builds. The uncertainty is unbearable.

"Barring any difficulties, they should be back with Gwenevere's Werewolf boyfriend tomorrow by noon," Dante replies casually.

No, no, NO! Gwen will be here soon, prepared to fight two vampires only to find sixteen. Somewhere far away Raven could be either fighting for his life or already captured. Oh, Gwen, I hope you bring someone with you, or this could be the end of us. Morna writhes inside, captured in her own body, a prisoner of the mind. She can do nothing but wait for the eventual decline of the effects of the venom.

Chapter Thirty-Six

Last Act on Earth

*T*he water bubbles and ripples in the pond hidden in a thicket of trees. The moon shines silvery light along the water's surface. Two heads break through the surface. Nicola and Gwen emerge up out of the water, momentarily cold from their watery passage. Treading to the bank, the magical spell that brought them quickly dries their clothing. They move quietly through the dark, weaving through the trees. The only light to see by is the moon. A strong wind whistles through the forest, bringing with it a chill to the air.

A storm brews within Gwenevere, a tempest made of a multitude of emotions. Anger, fear, regret, anxiety, and frustration build one onto the other until she brims with dark energy she can barely contain.

Nicola leads the way. The older witch trudges forward out of the forest into a clearing. A small cabin is nestled in the center

of it with a path leading through the woods. Firelight glows from the windows. Shadows move within. Cutting across the clearing, they make their way to the cabin.

What's the plan, Nicola? Gwen sends to the other witch. Nicola does not respond at first, her mind hidden by her mental shield.

Let me do the talking. Follow my lead. Don't even think about uttering a spell until I say so. Don't worry, lass, this isn't my first rodeo.

This is not what Gwen had in mind. Her pride bristles at Nicola's condescending tone. This only adds fuel to the fury within. Gwen grits her teeth, her jaw clenched, her hands balling into fist so tight her fingernails burrow into the flesh of her palms.

I'm not about to just sit back while you have a chat with a couple of vampires when my best friend's life is on the line.

They round the side of the cabin to approach the front door. The hermit's cabin dates to colonial times. The windows are without glass, with full shutters to shut off the openings in case of a storm. The shutters are open, and they get a glimpse inside as they pass. Morna lies motionless on the straw mattress of the bed. She stares up at the ceiling as if comatose, her blonde hair splayed haphazardly around her head. Her blue skin looks pale and sickly. A woman with long blonde hair wearing burgundy lounges at the head of the bed stroking Morna's head. She plays with strands of her hair as if Morna were a doll, a plaything. A man with tanned skin in a grey suit with shoulder length brown hair stands beside the bed. He watches the window as if he knows they are coming. For a moment Gwen locks eyes with him. He smiles. Gwen sucks in air and holds it in, willing herself to keep herself under control.

Nicola knocks on the cabin door. A moment later the door opens inward, and the grey-suited man stands at the door.

"Well, hello." The Spaniard greets with the air of a host at a dinner party. He gestures with a sweep of his hand for them to come within.

"You can only imagine our surprise. Here we be finding a couple of Vampires occupying our Coven's *secret* isolation cabin." Nicola declares pointedly. "This is supposed to be a safe place for Witches and Warlock. Those who need their space from the others for a spell." Gwen would laugh at the pun if it were said at any other time. She does love a god bad joke, after all. However, just now she feels no mirth. Trapped between terrified thoughts and murderess inklings.

Nicola waits for the Spanish vampire or his lady to respond, but they stay silent. Nicola forges on, "It is not meant to be used by anyone without the permission of the Monroe Coven. The Fairy was invited to stay in the hermit's cabin. You, however, are trespassing in Wiccan territory."

"You must be Gwenevere. My king wishes to have a word with you." The man looks over Nicola's shoulder at Gwen, ignoring the older witch all together. "Please, won't you join us inside? You can warm yourselves by the fire."

Whatever you do, don't step inside the cabin. Nicola warns. *Make them come out to us in the open.* The thought makes Gwen's skin prickle. *Stay behind me and don't say or do anything, lass!*

"Is that why you're holding my friend? How did you even find her?" Gwen asks. This gains her a sigh from Nicola. "You're the ones who sent that mermaid after me at Alcromech, aren't you?"

"Well honestly, finding the fairy was just a bit of luck." The Man stuffs a hand in his pant pocket and leans against the door frame causally. "One of my people knows the fairy and recognized her scent the moment she left the trading post. Then we followed, staying far enough back to not catch her notice. Luckily, the scent of fairy lingers a long time." He smiles smugly. "The mermaid was, as you guessed it, another one of my associates."

"Well, I hope you're proud of yourself, because you got your associate killed." Gwen smiles sweetly at him and adds, "You'll be joining her shortly."

"I am the girl's guardian. If you have a message from Lazar Taudero, then you can deliver it to me." The man gives Nicola a sardonic smile. Nicola adjusts her Thoyen shawl and adds, "Or better yet, have your King contact ours, as that's how things are supposed to be done, *lad*."

"He tried that. Your King refused to turn the girl over to us. She must do penance for her crimes against the Vampire tribe. So, he felt he needed to take things into his own hands. That's why we are here."

"Well, now you've got our attention. You can let the fairy go. Your quarrel isn't with her." Nicola points out.

"The fairy is all yours, provided that Gwenevere goes along with us peacefully to go see the King." The man answers congenially.

Nicola glances over her shoulder to Gwen. "And should she refuse?"

His female companion joins him by the door in a flash of burgundy. "Then we'll kill the fairy and the werewolf, too," Peyton replies with a sideways smirk.

Gwen lurches toward the lady vampire. Nicola tries to hold her back, but it is already too late.

The vampire woman before her gasps as she is lifted off the ground. She looks to the man in surprise. Gwen reaches out a hand and closes it into a fist. Simultaneously, the woman begins to choke. She grabs at her throat, trying to fight off invisible hands.

In a flash the man is at the bed with Morna in his arms. "Release my love or I will tear your friend's head off!" he threatens.

"*Impeda resistee!*" Nicola shouts with a flourish of her hands. The Spanish vampire freezes in place. His eyes go wide as

he finds himself unable to move. "There'll be none of that tonight," Nicola declares.

Gwen looks at the vampire woman, and suddenly she flies and hits the wall of the cabin. She falls to the ground in a dazed heap. Gwen rushes to Morna. Halfway across the cabin floor, Gwen feels a piercing pain in her side. Crying out, she stumbles forward and falls to her knees. The room goes blurring and hazy. She clutches a hand to the source of the pain. Something protrudes from under her ribs. She pulls her hand away looking down to see a dart sticking out of her black tunic.

Nicola screams her name as if from the other side of a long tunnel. Gwen glances back toward the other witch and loses her balance. She lands on her back, knocking the air from her lungs. Rasping for breath, she fumbles at the dart in her side.

Get it out, Gwen. Get it out! she demands. Her body seems slow to answer her command. She grasps the alien object with fingers made of rubber, hands without strength. A child screams nearby. A woman yells in pain. Something falls to the ground with a thud.

Suddenly a memory flashes before Gwen's mind from two years earlier. She sees the scene before her as if she is living it all over again. There she was, fifteen years old fighting, an Elf, a Giant, and a Dwarf in the back alley of an old warehouse behind a park in New York. First, she knocked the dwarf off his feet and out of view with a gust of wind. Then she had entered the Giant's mind and taken control of him while trying to fight off the magical missiles thrown at her by Vinita the Elfin woman. In all the hubbub, she had forgotten about the Dwarf until it was too late. She found herself struck by a dart in the neck, the assailant who had shot it at her, the Dwarf she had underestimated. She had been foolish then and she feels foolish now.

As the feeling leaves her body her hands fall to her side, the dart still inside her body. Helpless she stares up at the ceiling.

Will you never learn to think before you act, Gwen? At first, she thinks it is her asking the question. Then she realizes she hears Nicola in her head. She had seen the memory in her head as Gwen did, her mind left vulnerable because of the drug in the dart. *I told you not to enter the cabin.*

Nicola, help me. I can't move. Gwen pleads.

Neither can I, lass. Images flow from Nicola's mind into Gwen's. She sees herself from the other witch's view, witnessing the dart hit her and herself crumble to the ground. Nicola moves forward looking to the corner of the cabin to see a small girl hiding in the corner with a dart gun in her hand. *Lynette! That's impossible!*

Gwen would recognize that doll face surrounded in brown curls anywhere. That evil glint in the eyes of someone who looked so innocent always seemed unnatural. Before the child can turn the gun on Nicola, she sends a ball of fire at the girl. In an instant she is engulfed in flames. Her screams fill the cabin with deafening force. Just as Nicola turns to hurry to Gwen's aid, something grabs her from behind. A pain shoots from her neck through her whole body as sharp teeth tear into her flesh. Nicola yells before she hits the ground, completely paralyzed by the vampire venom, her mind the last thing to go numb. Gwen feels Nicola's consciousness fading from the physic connection until she is alone again in her own mind.

＊＊＊＊＊

Something is wrong. He could not shake the feeling as Jonah watched Gwen and Nicola excuse themselves from dinner and hurry out of the Blackwool's house. It nags at him until he finds himself rushing for his coat. He turns at the door and explains that he had something of Nicola's that he had forgotten to give to her. Before anyone could question him, he is out the door and into the night.

He dashes in the direction of Nicola's home. Not far from the Blackwool's house he catches sight of the witches he seeks. He watches Nicola and Gwen slip behind a building on the edge of town near the woods. *That's not the way to Nicola's place.* Following them, he came around the corner of the building only to see the two-woman standing in a puddle of water that didn't belong there. Before he can call out, he witnesses the two sink into the water and vanish. Gwen's eyes lock on his at the very last moment. The look on her face sends a chill into Jonah's bones.

Something is wrong. Why are they traveling by water? Where are they going? His instincts told him he needed to go after them, but not alone. Turning on his heel, he made his way back to his family. *Leona will know how to track the spell. Together we can find them. I just hope we're not too late!*

* * * * *

Feeling grows slowly through her body. The stiffness of the paralysis fading from her limbs, Morna ventures a twitch of her fingers first. It works. Taking a small breath, she pushes out with her mind, her thoughts becoming clearer. Gwen and Nicola are here. As she feared, they came alone and had quickly been ambushed by Lynette and the vampires with her.

If anything happens to Gwen because of me, I'll never forgive myself. She must do something. She must move fast. Only the element of surprise will be in her favor. Vampires might not have much in the way of magical abilities, but they make up for it with superior speed to any of the other tribes of Cain. No one can match them.

Morna listens to the movement in the room. More vampires have entered the cabin.

"What happened to our mother!" a young woman demands. Her shrill voice comes from the far corner of the room.

Does that mean Lynette is dead? Morna can only hope. Vampires are not so easily killed.

"She was hit by a fire ball," Peyton answers, the slightest hint of sympathy in her voice. "The old witch was faster than we expected. Or Lynette wasn't fast enough."

"Can you help her? What can we do?" a young man asks, desperation clear in his tone.

"Ask Affray. He's lived through a similar experience," Dante interjects from somewhere near the door.

"I recommend you bury her. If she's not dead by tomorrow evening, then she might pull through. But it'll take years to recover." Morna recognizes the man's voice as the one with the burns on his face. The voice tugs at familiarity but Morna cannot figure out how she might know this vampire.

"Yes, of course. We'll do anything you say," another young man replies. Morna hears the shuffle of feet and a pained groan, Morna assumes from Lynette. She listens as those carrying the child vampire exit the cabin. Their foot treads fade as they depart.

Gwen, can you hear me? Morna ventures a physic thread toward her friend. She finds nothing. *Did they take her away already? She cannot be gone. If the vampire king gets her, I will never see Gwen again.* She knows that something has happened to Gwen, but she can't be sure what. They shot something at her.

Morna heard the gun shot, heard Gwen's cry of pain. She heard Nicola scream, too, and then she had heard nothing for far too long. *I must see what is going on.*

Morna slowly twists her neck, careful not to be too obvious in her movements. Luckily, no one is watching her. She still lays on the straw mattress on one side of the one room cabin. There are several vampires in the room. Lynette is gone along with her four spawns. Presumably, they have taken her somewhere to bury her for the night. Dante and Peyton stand by the door speaking quietly with one another. At their feet, a middle-aged woman lies on her side, her eyes stare widely at Morna. *Nicola.* Morna can detect no mental activity from the woman. If she is coherent inside, she hasn't the ability to show it from without.

If only I had Gwen's gift of telepathy, I could communicate with Nicola. Not that she could me help me at this moment.

Morna notices that the vampire with the scars on his face, Affray, she believes he is called, stands only few feet away from Nicola but his attention is distracted elsewhere, a strange look of anger and longing in his silver-white eyes. Morna follows his gaze. Against the right wall, two men bend over the body of a woman dressed all in black, her midnight black hair and pale face barely visible as the men bind her arms and legs. Morna glimpses her face for just a moment. A gag is wedge in her mouth. Her green eyes are open but stare blankly at the ceiling. She doesn't protest as the men lift her up.

Gwen! Desperation fills Morna's chest and panic threatens to overtake her. *No, I must remain calm. I need a plan. The time to act is now.*

She thinks of something she hasn't done in a very long time … a spell that is a great fairy secret. It will take a great amount of her energy to accomplish. She does a semblance of this spell every time she has to assume the appearance of a human. That trick is hard enough, but what she must attempt is harder still. If she is successful, it will give her the advantage she needs to outsmart and outmaneuver the vampires. *After all, they cannot bite what they cannot see.*

Closing her eyes Morna chants the words in her head. Immediately she feels the spell draw from her physical strength.

I will not be able to hold the spell long. Hopefully it will be just long enough to save my friend.

When the last word of the spell passes her lips, Morna feels the shift. Although she cannot see it herself, she is aware that the spell has taken hold of her.

Morna holds her breath as she gets up from the bed. On tip toes, she creeps across the floor. No one notices that she has vanished from view. If she is lucky, no one will look at the bed until she is long gone. She follows the two men escorting the comatose Gwen out of the cabin. They walk out the door. Quietly, Morna follows passing by Nicola, Dante, and Peyton. She glances regrettably back at the Irish witch lying on the floor.

We will come back for you, Nicola. I promise. With that Morna slips out the door into the night.

The sky is full of a multitude of stars. This far from human civilization, they shine brilliantly. Out in the grass she doesn't have to walk slowly to avoid detection. No one will hear her footsteps now. The clearing around the cabin would seem serene if not for the deadly creatures stalking about. Besides the two male vampires, she follows, four more patrol the edges of the forest. Nearby, Morna hears someone digging in the woods.

Lynette getting her well-deserved final rest.

Morna is surprised to realize that a black car awaits on the dirt path. *Something they call a two-door sedan,* she thinks. When they brought a car, she cannot fathom. She never heard it pull up. The men detaining Gwen lead her toward this vehicle. A woman in her thirties wearing regular human clothes jumps out of the passenger side door. She hurries to the back of the car and opens the trunk. The vacant space within glows with a fluorescent yellow light. The car waits to swallow Gwenevere whole and carry her far away to a certain and terrible end.

It is now or never.

Sprinting forward, Morna angles towards the man holding Gwen's feet. Resisting the urge to give out a battle cry, she rams into the man's side silently. He is a skinny man, and average in height. If he had been a bigger fellow, she might have bounced right off him. With a surprised yelp, he drops Gwen's feet and tumbles into the grass. Morna nearly falls over the man but catches herself. The man holding Gwen's arms is a bulky, broad-shoulder fellow who wears a beard despite being bald. He seems older than the other man physically by ten years. He spins around as Gwen's body suddenly sinks to the ground, dragging behind him. Incredulously he looks to his comrade.

"Neil, you stupid fool. What? Did you forget to tie your shoelaces?"

"I didn't trip on my laces Marcus. Something pushed me!" the man called Neil protests as he gets to his feet and dusts off his jeans.

"Pick the witch up! We've got to get her the hell out of here before someone realizes she and the other witch are gone. Hurry…" The vampire named Markus abruptly stops talking, giving out a startled cry of pain. His nose spontaneously cracks and begins to bleed. He drops Gwen's arms, letting her hit the dirt as he clutches his face in agony. "Something just hit me."

"See, something is here!" the first man declares. "Sarah, Jameson! Hurry come help me get the witch into the car. We're under attack over here." Neil shouts to the occupants of the vehicle.

The woman waiting by the open trunk of the car turns her head and whistles. A second later, the driver side door of the black sedan opens. In a flash a third man hurries to the woman's side. Tall and lean in muscle, he has dark tan skin and a military style haircut. Jameson looks capable and deadly.

"What is it? What attacked you? I don't see a thing." the man asks incredulously. He flashes across the grass, appearing by Gwen's motionless body. He looks around the clearing, his eyes scanning with cold determination. His body stiffens, and he takes a deep breath. "You smell that?"

The other vampires all sniff the air or inhale. Their eyes each widen, and they turn to one another. The woman speaks first.

"Fairy," she murmurs and the others all nod. They dart glances all about the clearing.

"But fairies can't go invisible, can they?" Markus asks as he wipes the blood from his face, his broken nose already healed.

"Maybe it just shrunk and then attacked?" Neil suggests.

"Either way, we better warn the others that the fairy is loose," Jameson advises. In a flash the vampire appears across the field next to one of the sentries. He exchanges words with the man before the man hurries off to speak to the other vampires patrolling the field. Then Jameson turns and flashes across the clearing and into the cabin.

"Sarah, you keep a look out while we grab the witch," Marcus orders. The woman nods, glancing about constantly as the two men shuffle toward Gwen.

Out of nowhere a gust of wind knocks the female vampire off her feet and flat on her back. A moment later another blast of wind hurls the vampires Neil and Marcus through the air. Each roll across the grass several times before they finally stop.

Morna hurries to stand over Gwen. She lies there, still in an immobile daze. That's when she sees the dart in her friend's side. Bending down, Morna gently removes it. Gwen gasps in pain around the gag. Her eyes flutter. Morna tosses the dart away and kneels next to Gwen.

"Gwen, you must get up. I could really use your help here," she whispers taking her by the shoulders. Morna shakes Gwen gently. Her friend only moans and rocks to her side closing her eyes tight as if to shut out the world. *Gwen! Can you hear me? Can you get up? Can you fight?*

Morna can connect to Gwen mentally again, but the inside of the witch's head is a mass of foggy thoughts and memories. *The effect of the drug may take some time to fully dissipate,* Morna realizes woefully. *That's all right. We'll just fly out of here instead.*

Morna glances around. The female and two male vampires she just struck down are still recovering from the blasts. They will be on their feet soon. The different sentries stay in their position but stare into the clearing now instead of at the woods. Across the field, Morna sees the man called Affray run out of the cabin and into the woods. *He's going to warn Lynette's people, no doubt.*

Just then Jameson exits the cabin along with Dante. These two head toward Gwen. *It's time, Morna,* she tells herself, taking a deep breath. Positioning her arms under Gwen to heft her up into a cradling position, Morna flaps her wings. She lifts Gwen off the ground with her as she hovers into the air.

Something flashes in the corner of her eye, and then Morna feels a hand clasps around her calf. Morna looks down to find Jameson has a hold of her leg. Dante is closing in.

"I think I've got it," Jameson calls out to his companion.

With all the strength she can muster, Morna beats her wings faster and faster. The gust of air created by her wings pushes against Jameson. He stays on his feet, but his grip begins to slip. Grunting in frustration, he flings out his other hand blindly. He manages to brush her other leg with his knuckles. In an instant he has the fairy's other leg in his grasp and tugs downward. Gwen's body is suddenly snatch from her arms by Dante.

The moment Gwen is out of her grasp, Jameson spins Morna around by her legs and vaults her over the car. When she lands on the dirt path with a thunderous boom, Morna feels all her strength leave her. She loses hold of the invisibility spell and crumples in a heap. Gasping and coughing, pain racks her slender frame.

Now visible the vampires converge on her. Their faces appear around her as they had before. Only half of the vampires are currently present. Dante bends down on his haunches to look at her, a mocking glint in his eyes.

"Tsk, you were so close to saving your friend and now you've failed her again." He shakes his head, his dark hair bobbing around his shoulders. "You're a brave little sprite, I'll give you that. But you're also stupid. If you could vanish from sight, why not just

save yourself? Why risk your life for this one witch? She is no one of importance. She has no name, no family. Surely saving her will gain you no great reward. So why do it?" Dante asks with genuine curiosity.

"If she's of so little importance, why do you want her so desperately?" Morna croaks as she attempts to shift herself into a crouching position. Her body might feel like pulp, but her wings are perfectly operational. If she attempts to leap into the sky now, the half dozen vampires encircling her will likely tear her to shreds before they let her escape again. Morna realizes this with bitterness. A cough wrenches from her and she doubles over in pain. When she wipes her hand across her mouth, it comes away with blood on her fingertips.

"She's important to my King and, as you well know, she killed many of my kind a few years ago when she destroyed Bec LaNuff. One of these vampires happened to be my Queen and Lazar Taudero's beloved Evaling. Killing the Queen is a serious crime. One that demands a serious consequence be paid," Dante informs her in a clipped tone.

"Well, Gwen is important to me. You could say she is more than a queen in my eyes, and I cannot let you take her without a fight. I'll die if I must, but you are not going anywhere with Gwenevere," Morna declares in a dark voice.

"That's very noble and loyal of you, little fairy." Dante shakes his head as he stands. Hovering over her, he looks down on her in pity. "It's too bad that all your suffering will be for nothing." As he turns to leave Jameson stops him.

"What do you want us to do with it?" Jameson asks with a nod in Morna's direction.

"What we should've done in the first place. Kill it," Dante replies, buttoning his jacket as he turns to walk back to the black sedan.

"So how should we do this? Any preferences?" Jameson asks the other vampires in the circle. Morna doesn't hear the response. Her attention is stuck on Dante. She watches as the vampire Markus appears behind the car with Gwen slung over his shoulder. He unceremoniously dumps her body into the open trunk of the car. Gwen grunts when she lands. One of her arms shoots out weakly as if to stop the door, but it is too late. Dante slams the trunk closed and it locks with a click that echoes in Morna's skull.

When Morna looks back at the vampires surrounding her they have produced a plan of execution. As they all moved toward her, Morna fills her lungs with air and screeches. The banshee cry she emits belies the daintiness of her fame. It strikes out around her in a shock wave. Piercing the ear drum of every vampire nearby. It sends them to their knees or writhing in pain on the ground. Wasting no time, Morna shoots into the air. Out of the ring of predators she arches towards the black sedan. Dante and Markus have buckled to their knees, clutching their bleeding ears behind the car. Morna descends towards the trunk.

A gust of wind is all the warning she has before something hard and large strikes her. The jolt not only knocks her out of the sky but the wind from her lungs. Her head spinning, she tries to halt her falling, tries to pump her wings. Pain spikes from her wings into her back. Crippling, blinding pain. In agony like nothing she has ever felt before, Morna crashes to the ground, bouncing and rolling as if a pebble skipping the surface of a lake. When at last the shock of the impact wears off Morna lifts her head to see a bolder resting only a few feet from her head. It hadn't been in the clearing before. This is the missile that shot her out of the sky. Groaning, she tries to sit up but the pain in her wings still throbs. Glancing over her shoulder she finds what she fears would be there — a tear in right wing. No spell in her arsenal is strong enough to heal a wound this dire.

She hears yelling, cursing, and voices. Morna looks up and across the field. The rock sent her across the clearing to the edge of the woods by the cabin. The black sedan seems small now in the distance. The vampires recovering from her banshee screams, get to their feet and head for her.

If Gwen were awake, we could link our power together and I could send her far away traveling by light. But Gwen is not awake, not really. Morna can feel Gwen's befuddlement even now. *One giant blast of light ought to do it. It'll blind the vampires and give me a chance to get to Gwen. It might kill me, but it is better than nothing. The light from the blast alone will surely draw the attention of the entire coven. Someone will come to help.*

Morna gathers all the energy left in her tattered frame and surges it into a ball of light in her chest, ready to unleashes it once the vampires converge on her. She can sense even as she prepares to utter the words that this will be the last spell, she ever casts. Her weakened body is too frail to withstand being consumed by it. This will be the last time she ever wields magic. Her last act on earth.

Chapter Thirty-Seven

Twisted Darkness

*J*ameson bursts into the cabin, his military stoicism lending him an air of importance.

That he doesn't deserve. Affray thinks.

"The fairy has escaped," he announces to the room. Concurrently Dante, Peyton, and Affray all look to the straw bed. It is vacant. Their captive indeed gave them the slip.

"Clever little fairy," Affray murmurs almost to himself.

"How the hell did she do that?" Peyton asks no one in particular.

"It's invisible," Jameson supplies, "and it's already attacked us while trying to free the little witch. She got the best of Marcus and Neil pretty quick. She's not likely to give up anytime soon."

"Then we better find her. We can't have her ruining everything. I've worked too hard to catch this girl only to fail my

636

King now," Dante declares, a grim set to his brow as he turns to follow Jameson out of the cabin.

Peyton moves as if to follow, but Dante stops her.

"No, my love, someone must keep an eye on the old witch. She'll recover from the venom soon." Peyton sighs but nods agreement.

Dante grabs her chin and brings her toward him for a quick kiss. Affray rolls his eyes at this. Dante and Jameson swiftly exit, leaving him alone with Peyton.

Instantly Affray heads to the door.

"Where are you off to?" Peyton asks incredulously.

"Someone has to warn Lynette and her children," Affray answers. Peyton shrugs and waves him away with one manicured hand.

Affray ducks out into the night. He makes a beeline for the forest where he watched the four new vampires carry the wounded Lynette. He finds them not far into the woods, a child-size hole already dug, and their mother cradled in one of the young woman's arm's. One of Lynette's son's leans on a shovel next to a mound of fresh earth. *Where did they find a shovel?* Affray shrugs it off as immaterial. Lynette still writhes in pain, gasping for breath. Her skin smells of charcoal. They all pay him no mind as the children say comforting words to their invalid mother.

"The fairy got loose. Dante says to go and help Jameson and the others find her. She's invisible so she could be anywhere,"

Affray informs Sean, Clark, Elizabeth, and Ashley. The four newfangled vampires look to him shocked and alarmed.

"They can do that?" Ashley, the youngest of them all, asks. Her eyes round and her glance darts from tree to tree.

"Apparently," Affray confirms.

"Wouldn't it just leave? If I were her, I would," Clark questions moving away from his shovel to take a defensive stance next to Elizabeth. She cradles Lynette's small frame to her chest as though she were her babe rather than her maker. In her diminished state, Lynette seems more childlike than ever before. *And I was there when she became vampire.* Even as a whimpering human child she was more formidable.

"She's loyal to the witch Gwenevere. Trust me, she'd rather die than leave her with us. She already attacked Markus and Neil trying to free her."

"What about Mother?" Sean asks, perplexed and torn.

"Leave her with me. I'll finish burying her. You all go on ahead. I'll be there as soon as I'm done."

Elizabeth gently places Lynette inside the grave before she and Lynette's other children race through the trees toward the cabin.

Once the fools are gone, Affray turns his attention back to the grave and the emaciated Lynette. Her glazed eyes search for him, only half seeing her surroundings. Affray knows because this is what happened to him. At first, he couldn't see, couldn't move.

His body wasted to almost nothing, was useless after he was charred.

"I'm sorry, Lynette, that this has happened to you. But I couldn't have planned it better myself. It's almost as if fate has given me the answer to all my problems."

"Affray?" The child vampire grunts and shrifts her head to look at him. Her vacant, burnt eyes look right through him. "What do you mean? Where is everyone? Clark? Elizabeth? Sean, are you there?" Lynette tries to call out, but her frail voice doesn't carry far. Affray smiles sardonically at this.

"Oh, they've all gone off to fight some battle they can't possibly win. Most of our vampire comrades are going to die tonight, your beloved children included." He paces back and forth at the foot of the grave. He folds his arms behind his back, his posture straight and refined.

"What's going on here? If anything happens to my children, I swear I'll…"

"Kill me? There's not much chance of that now that you're hanging onto your life by a thread. You'll meet your final death soon enough." Affray cuts her off.

"What do you want? How will my death solve any of your problems? I thought we were friends. Why would you do this to me?" Lynette prattles on, half delirious.

"I needed a way to get into the King's favor without him knowing who I really was," Affray explains in a conversational tone. "If he knew my identity, he wouldn't be very forgiving for the part I played in the circumstances that caused the untimely death of his beloved Queen. He'd hold me responsible on some level and surely would kill me." Affray shakes his head with a *tsk*. "It was better he believed I was dead and that I assume a new identity. However, I still needed a way into his court, and as an unknown vampire with no background or reputation to go on, that would be impossible. Then I realized the solution to my problem. You. So, I looked for some hint of your whereabouts. When I found you, I sent an anonymous tip Lazar's way that there was a baby vampire stalking the Vegas strip."

"That was you? You bastard! How did you even know I was still alive?" Lynette asks bitterly. "You went down with the mountain and, as far as you knew, so did I."

"Except that I saw you leave. I saw you run away like a scared little child as you left your maker and your sisters to die."

Lynette stiffens at this. She doesn't attempt to deny the crime but doesn't seem to have any word to say in her defense.

She's already tearing herself up over it, Affray deduces, launching into a monologue.

"Back to what I was saying before I was so rudely interrupted…" Affray clears his throat for dramatic effect. "I just had to wait for the King's minions to catch you. Once they did, I needed an opportunity to make myself known to you and gain your trust. Through you, I would get my admittance into Lazar's Court.

That is if he didn't kill you on the spot." Affray shrugs as if to say it mattered little to him. "Imagine my surprise when finding you should also lead me to my Gwenevere. I believed until then that she too had perished in the destruction of Bec LaNuff. I was overjoyed at the prospect of seeing my long-lost love once more … only it appeared that she had completely forgotten me and moved on. And on, and on. She'd been a busy girl. I didn't much like that. Not that I'm a jealous man, but…"

"You killed Gwenevere's little hipster human boyfriend, didn't you?" Lynette interjects in a wheezing voice as the realization occurs to her.

"Well, yes, and all the others too, but let's not get sidetracked here," Affray admits before going on. "After having my fun with Gwen's boy toy and watching her misery over him, I was content to watch your hatred for her help unravel the girl's whole world. I knew you would tell Lazar about Gwenevere to save your own skin. I knew he would use you to help obtain her and kill her for his Queen's death and the destruction of one of the greatest fortresses in his kingdom. Getting to tag along for the hunt was just frosting on the cake." He stops pacing to look down at Lynette. "The only problem was that you knew who I really was. And I realized over the last couple of weeks that I'm not quite ready to give up on my beloved little witch after all. So, for my safety and to guarantee that neither the King nor Gwen ever knows my secret,

I'm afraid I need you out of the picture, cherub. I hope you understand."

"Ha, you'll never get away with this. My children will come back for me. If they see that I'm dead, then they'll turn you over to the King or hunt you down themselves."

"Ahh, but what you and your little children don't know is this: In order for you to survive you need to drink lots of blood immediately. A dozen children or four grown men in your case." His face askew in distaste. "Then you sleep underground for an exceedingly long time. The longer you go without blood the less likely you are to survive," Affray clarifies. "All I have to do now is fill your grave and walk away. By the time your precious children dig you back up, you'll be as good as dead. Without new blood, you cannot regenerate or heal. The hunger and your injuries will eat at you until you are finally dead and are reduced to ash." He smiles at this. "Problem solved."

Lynette twists in rage. Yelling and stumbling, she attempts to get to her feet. Her charred legs buckle beneath her, and she collapses to the ground. When she attempts to try to climb out of the grave again, she is pelted in the face by a spray of dirt. Lynette looks up to see Affray pushing the mound of dirt next to the grave. With ease, he fills the hole with its original soil. Lynette shouts, curses, and screams, but her weakened voice has no power in it. Her cries fall on death ears.

Quickly, dirt covers Lynette. First her feet, then her legs, torso, and last her little curly head. Affray glimpses the absolute horror in her eyes before he dumps the last of the dirt on top of her. His work done, he smiles to himself and walks away. Affray leaves behind his past and his secrets where they can't ever resurface. He stuffs his hands in his pockets and hums an old familiar French tune. His attention drawn to the pin picks of light above the forest canopy, he meanders back toward the cabin.

* * * * *

Blackness surrounds her. The smell of leather, fabric, and oil is in the stuffy air of her enclosure. Gwen is vaguely aware of the fact that she is inside something, remembers falling into this capsule and the pain that came with the impact. Recalls the world going dark and being alone. However, she can't remember much else.

A thread of thought surfaces in her haze. Not her thought, but someone else's. Emotions come with it. Desperation, pain, sadness, regret, loyalty, and love. A deep and endless love for Gwen. This catches her attention and tugs at her consciousness. Someone's mind is connected to hers. Someone whose mind is as familiar to her as her very own. *Morna!*

She plans to do something desperate, something dangerous to save Gwen.

 643

Save me? What do I need saving from? What's going on? Where am I? These thoughts push at the fog in her mind. Some clarity begins to register. The last thing Gwen can remember is standing in the doorway of the cabin. Morna laid on the bed and someone was threatening her life. *Vampires.*

This shakes some more of the fog away and Gwen pushes further. *Wait, where is Morna now? How did I get in here? Where's Nicola?* Gwen tries to reach out to Morna's mind, to speak to her in her head but she can't push her mind that far. The drug in her system won't allow it. *Don't do anything stupid, Morna. I'm coming. Wait for me. I'm getting out of here.*

Gwen suddenly becomes aware that there is a cloth stuffed into her mouth. She tastes the rough, dirty fabric. When she tries to reach up and take it out, she realizes that her hands and feet are bound. The ropes itch at her skin. Shaking her head, she pushes with her tongue against the unwanted item. Eventually she manages to eject the gag. It lands next to her half damp from her saliva. Gwen spits out the taste and coughs.

"Morna!" She shouts despite her dry throat. Her voice echoes off her metal surroundings but doesn't carry. Gwen listens waiting for her friend to reply. Nothing. Then something shakes her capsule. Thunder rumbles from outside. People scream and shout.

What's going on out there? Gwen tries to connect with Morna again but only feels the fairy's side of the connection. She can't seem to push her thoughts toward her friend. Morna's pain is unbearable, her despair crippling. Gwen tries to reach for the source of all magic and feels only a trickle of the energy in her grasp. *Wait, Morna. Wait for me!*

You must break out, Gwen. You must overcome this drug in your blood, Gwen demands of herself. *Get angry, Gwen. Be the instrument of fury and destruction that everyone thinks you are. The time for control is gone.*

The words pull at her inner self. The demon inside the angel. She delves into the darkness, looking for the power that destroyed a fortress. The power that crushed a man while she was barely alive or aware of what she was doing. The self-preservation that has kept her alive all this time. Gwen pulls from all her darkest memories her most terrible moments and lets this fuel the tempest building inside her. When she surfaces to the present, her mind hums with power. Her skin almost vibrates.

Now what to do with this reserved power? Only useless English goes fleeting through her thoughts. I

"*Paraoxem!*" Gwen yells. A blast bursts forth from her, tearing the roof of the trunk from its hinges with a deafening creak. With a boom it hurtles off and out of sight. The cloudy night sky is revealed above her, unobscured. A storm surges overhead, lighting flashes, and thunder rumbles. Fresh air surges in and Gwen inhales deeply. With the open air comes clearer and stronger sounds of the tumult happening outside.

Gwen quickly turns her attention to the ropes constraining her. "*Flara*," she commands. Smoke rises from the ropes as a blackness spreads a crossed them. Then flames erupt into life. The moment the ropes are weak enough, Gwen wrenches against them and flings the enflamed ropes off. Pushing off the bottom of the trunk, Gwen leaps out of the car. She lands on the dirt path in one fluid motion.

What she sees before her is outright bedlam. Between her and the cabin across the clearing, several skirmishes are in progress. More than a dozen vampires dart and flash about the clearing to attack or avert multiple magical spells and projectiles. The source of this onslaught is half a dozen men and women. It takes Gwen a moment to recognize them in the faint glow of the moonlight. A flash of lightning lights up the field and Gwen gasps.

The Blackwools and Crayborns sprinkle the field amongst the vampires. Each flourishes their hands in different gestures as their mouths move with uttered spells and chants. Gusts of wind shoot forth from Thayer's outstretched palms. It knocks down two male vampires who charge towards him. They claw at the dirt to keep from being blown away.

Nicola summons lightning from her conjured storm above. It strikes a female vampire about to leap on Thayer's back. The woman crumples to the ground with a startled cry and a puff of smoke. The scent of burnt flesh hangs in the wind. Gwen is relieved to see that the Irish witch is alive.

"*Gainien raisa,*" Leona shouts. Gwen witnesses as the levitation spell hurtles the blonde woman in the burgundy suit. The lady vampire shoots into the sky so high she disappears into the storm clouds. Her startled shouts and curses fade with her as she ascends out of view.

Francis and his daughter Isla stay together back-to-back as they each face their own foe. "*Haultia emmitula!*" he yells as a twenty-something; scrawny man leaps towards him with claws poised to strike. The spell hits him and suddenly he goes stiff. Stuck in his pose, the man plummets abruptly to the ground unable, to move a muscle.

A man with a beard and shaved head suddenly darts toward Isla. In a flash of fabric and skin, he blurs and melds into the dark landscape. The man is only visible when the lightning flashes across the sky.

"*Gainien raisa! Gainien raisa!*" Isla yells repeatedly in a shaky voice as she attempts to capture the man in her spell's grasp. His lack of visibility and his incredible speed make this very trying. With each failed attempt to capture him, the vampire advances toward her. Suddenly the man is upon her. He lifts the timid and small Isla off her feet.

"*Evata Madota!*" Gwen hears a familiar young man's voice call out. Just before the vampire can sink his teeth into the teenage girl's neck, an orb of light shoots toward him. It strikes him with a sizzle and absorbs into the bearded man. Stiffening, he releases Isla and arches his back in agony. Writhing and screaming, the vampire falls to his knees and curls into a ball on the ground, twitching.

Gwen spins to find Jonah behind her farther up the field. He clearly sent the orb that saved Isla. But his attention is swiftly averted from the girl. He twists around, hurtling orbs of light left and right at several vampires who dodge and weave around him.

Wait, where's Morna? Gwen scans the field and sees no sign of the fairy. Pushing her mind out, she listens for Morna's mental hum. The effect of the drug has either worn off or the amount of power surging through Gwen forced it out. She's not sure which, but she can connect with Morna's mind again. It takes her a moment but finally Gwen finds her. The hum is faint. Her friend is very weak, injured, and unconscious from sheer exhaustion. She needs healing and fast. But Morna is on the other side of the clearing and there is a war separating her from Gwen.

Just then Gwen hears a woman yell and looks up in time to see the vampire in the burgundy suit fall out of the sky. She crashes through the roof of the hermit's cabin. The structure is so old and simply made that the impact causes the entire roof to collapse. The sound catches the attention of one vampire, a man with shoulder length brown hair — the Spanish vampire who answered the door when Gwen and Nicola first showed up at the cabin. He ceases his assault on Jonah. Abandoning his fellow vampires, he flashes across the field. Nicola attempts to strike him with lightning as he passes her, but to no avail. The man makes it to the cabin without interference and rushes inside.

I hope he finds his girlfriend's bones shattered to dust Gwen thinks before she turns her eyes back on the pandemonium before her. *This has gone on long enough. Morna needs me and I don't have time for this nonsense.*

"*Lau Nch Raisa!*" The spell sends Gwen into the air in a huge bound. The arch of her descent should drop her near Morna on the other side of the field. As Gwen soars above the melee, the battle seems both epic and minor all at once. The Vampires are losing, the cursed ones either frozen in place or writhing in pain about the field. Their comrades struggle on with a determination that defies reason.

They're relentless! Clearly, they are out matched even with having more than twice the numbers. Why haven't they run away? Why are the vampires still here? Gwen can't help wondering as she witnesses the brawl going on below her. Then it hits her. *They must fear failure more than they fear death. More than they fear us. Their King sent them on this mission. If they fail to bring me back with them, there will surely be consequences. They won't stop until either they're all dead or my friends are. I'm the only witch they'll let leave this place alive.*

Gwen looks up just in time to see a male vampire leap into the sky, heading straight for her. "*Dainien gounda.*" As he nears her, she evokes, the spell sending him back down to the earth. But

 649

it's too late. Abruptly he collides with Gwen. Wrapping around her, he takes Gwen with him. Both yelling and unable to stop their descent, they plummet, landing in the middle of the clearing. Luckily, the man hits first, breaking Gwen's fall and taking the brunt of the impact. With a grunt, Gwen tries to push off him and out of his grasp. The vampire immediately tightens his hold on her. With a cry of pain, his fangs extend out of his gums. He comes at Gwen with the intent to bite. Gwen grabs a hold of him by the throat with both hands. Attempting to choke him with all the strength she has, she manages to keep his fangs away from her neck.

Flashes of memories from another time and another place appear in her mind's eye. Gwen grabs hold of the vampire beneath her with magic and begins to crush him in on himself. He cries out in surprise. His eyes bulge as the force of her magical grip shatters bones, punctures lungs, flattens arteries, and pulverizes every inch of him. When he goes completely limp, he resembles a raisin more than a man. She gets to her feet, leaving the wasted remains of the vampire behind her.

She left her foster father in a similar state after he tried to violate her in a drunken fury. Those memories used to haunt her. Surge her with doubt, fear, and guilt. Right now, she feels none of that. The darkness inside feeds on those memories now. It fortifies her, gives her confidence in what she can accomplish. *She is unstoppable. She is all powerful. She is everything.* Gwen stops in her tracks. *Am I referring to myself in the third person now? What's wrong with me?* She shakes the strange feeling away as if waking herself from a bad dream. *I'll worry about what just happened to me later. Right now, I must get to Morna.* Gwen breaks into a run, her speed picking up as she moves.

Several vampires break off from their assault on the other witches to chase after Gwen. Realizing this, she picks up her pace. Heart racing, blood pumping in her ears, she glances behind her and sees three vampires on her heels.

Before she can utter a spell, they tackle her to the ground. Colliding with the grass face first, Gwen finds herself with a large male vampire on her back, pinned and stunned by the impact. Breathing is all but impossible. She gasps, twisting and struggling to get the man off and out from under him. The man reaches a hand around her mouth and holds tight. Gwen bucks and writhes. His hand does not come loose. He's not giving her the chance to utter one word of a spell.

"Hurry. I need an injection now! I dropped my needle," the vampire practically yells in her ear as he speaks to his companions. "We must keep her sedated. Affray said it was the only way to catch her and not get killed in the process. He's seen her in action. She's too dangerous."

"Here, Jameson, I've got a needle," another man announces, standing just behind them. Gwen hears the man fumble in his coat for something.

Who's this Affray person? When has he seen me in action? Was he a vampire from Bec La Nuf I didn't know about? The name doesn't seem familiar to Gwen, but she has bigger concerns. Whoever he is, he's obviously the vampire behind the dart gun idea and has supplied them all with needles of the same drug she was injected with earlier. She realizes now that it's the exact same thing she was shot with when she was captured in New York by Vinita and her friends two years ago. *Yes, this Affray fellow was at Bec La Nuf and has aided in my capture once before. Now he's helping another vampire leader try to do the same thing he did for Legion.* The realization gives Gwen new resolve. *I will not be a prisoner again. Never again!*

Gwen shakes her head until she manages to move the man's hand just enough. She bites down hard with all her might. The vampire lets out a howl. In pain and injured, he moves his hand out of her bite by reflex.

"*Flemay banna!*" Gwen croaks. The spell turns her flesh to fire that burns anyone who touches her. The vampire on top of her leaps back, screaming. Suddenly free, Gwen flips onto her back. Jameson is now completely in flames and running across the field like a chicken with his head cut off. Gwen is left with the other two vampires. One lunges at her with a syringe in his hand, ready to stab it into her. Gwen takes a deep breath and with it a surge of power.

"Fro no altae!" As the words leave her lips, Gwen flourishes her hands toward each man. A spray of gelatin-like liquid hurtles out of thin air onto the two vampires. The liquid hits them and they both freeze in mid step. The liquid instantly hardens, leaving them encapsulated within its cold embrace.

Her mind hums again with power, her skin practically radiating with it. A kind of wild giddiness comes with it that has Gwen on the verge of madness. Hatred pumps in her blood, frustration, anger, and jealousy all piling on top of it to fuel the growing darkness in her soul. The magic is intoxicating. Gwen feels tempted to take it all in and swim in it. Drown in the ecstasy of absolute power. To become one with absolute darkness.

Back on her feet again Gwen turns back toward the sensation of Morna in the back of her mind. Her friend's presence and memories soothe and quell the storm of emotions inside her. She holds it back from the brink. *Morna needs me. I'm trying to save her, not get revenge.* Pulling all the energy into her that she can muster, Gwen runs across the field. She senses a fire burning inside her, a heat greater than the sun. More memories flutter into her skull. She sees another battle fought years ago with other vampires. She remembers how she dealt with those vermin.

Gwen had given into the power then and lost a little bit of her mind in the process. But during that momentary insanity, she had conjured a spell so terrible that it annihilated an entire room full of enemies. But she had no control over it. It had been a wild kind of power she knew not how to recall again. Or did she? Words come to mind. A new spell constructs itself in her imagination. She doesn't know if it'll work but it's worth a try. Adapting three spells together, she could possibly recreate that spell again.

Her speed picks up as she moves. Four young vampires in their twenties, two men and two women, emerge from the edge of the forest ahead of her. *Reinforcements coming to join the fight?* The leader of the group, a handsome guy with a quarterback build, blazes toward the battle. He stops when he recognizes Gwen and veers toward her. His friends behind him follow his lead and turn into blurs advancing at her at breakneck speed.

They run head-on at her as if they are playing a game of chicken with her. Their speed is three times her own.

"*Calabrae Suna, Flemay Madota, incen urate!*" Gwen chants. The spell bursts forth from her as a beam of pure sunlight shoots like a laser from her outstretched hand. The four vampires before her haven't time to react before they are encompassed in the beam. Instantly, they incinerate in mid-stride. Their whole bodies go red as if made of molten lava, they simply burn out of existence into nothingness. Not even ash remains.

The beam bathes the field in light. It is as if the mid-day sun shone on them for just a moment and then went back to sleep in an instant. The light startles everyone on the field. Everyone's eyes turned to the source in time to watch Lynette's four vampire spawn be consumed in Gwen's beam of light. The vampires look at one another. Unspoken words communicate in their looks.

Panting, Gwen stumbles forward, exhausted, and physically spent by the power she just expended. She turns to look behind her, curious why the sounds of the skirmish have ceased. In the clearing, everyone stares in her direction. The witches look exhausted, but none are injured. There are only five vampires left standing. These five suddenly run for their fallen comrades. Hefting them on their back or carrying them in their arms, the vampire head toward the woods. In a flash, they each leave the clearing with their wounded as if running from the devil himself.

Gwen turns her back on them and hurries onward toward where Morna should be, the faint hum of her consciousness almost a whisper of sound. Gwen sees a hint of blue ahead and races toward it. There on the edge of the woods, Morna lies on her stomach, out cold. Her body is bruised and cut, and one wing is torn. The terrible state of her friend sends a chill through Gwen's veins.

Kneeling, Gwen places a hand under Morna's blonde head, and the other on top of it. Closing her eyes, Gwen calms the raging torrent of emotions inside to bring the power of healing to her touch.

"*Dade winda cura longa babeta lavota.*" Gwen sings the words to the old tune, the one memory left clear to her from her childhood. To give the spell more power, Gwen reaches into her happiest memories. Moments of joy, kindness, friendship, and love. All these memories have either Morna or Raven in them. Gwen sends the healing power through the fairy's entire body. When at last her work is done, Gwen releases Morna and slumps back on her heels, feeling emotionally and physically spent.

"Gwen?" Morna stirs, mumbling her name as if speaking in her sleep. Slowly the fairy pushes off the ground to sit up. Disorientated, she sits there a moment as if shaking off a sleepy haze. Then she finally opens her eyes and looks at Gwen.

"Thank god." Gwen exhales with relief, lunging forward to wrap her arms around Morna.

"No, wait, my wing…" Morna flinches away but stops to look at her right wing. It is whole once more, no sign of the tear left. She looks to Gwen with gratitude written clearly in her golden eyes. She squeezes Gwen tight to her, burying her face in her black hair.

"What happened to the vampires?" Morna asks, looking over the clearing. Gwen follows her gaze and realizes that there isn't a vampire in sight. The rest of the witches seem to be searching for Gwen. They call out her name, each looking exhausted in their own way.

"Our friends came just in the nick of time and sent them running for the hills," Gwen replies with a tired smile. Morna nods at this.

Gwen helps Morna to her feet and pauses for a moment in shock. Gwen catches sight of a face in the woods. Her heart skips

and her breath catches. *You're seeing things, Gwen. It's not possible. He's dead. You were there. You watched him die. My mind is playing tricks on me because I'm here at the hermit's cabin. The last time I was here it was with Angelo just after escaping from Bec La Nuf. Being here again must've shaken me up more than I realized,* Gwen rationalizes. *Why else would I be seeing the face of a dead man?*

Gwen doesn't tell Morna what she sees. She doesn't want to say it and seem any crazier than she already feels. She turns her eyes away from the forest. Throwing a comforting arm around her little fairy friend, Gwen leads Morna toward the other witches.

"What will we do now, Gwen?" Morna asks breathlessly.

"We'll sneak you into the Coven with us somehow. You can't stay out here. The cabin is destroyed and it's just not safe enough."

"Now you tell me," Morna quips. Gwen snorts at this.

"We won't be taken off guard again," Gwen promises. "One way or another, Morna, I swear I will keep you safe."

"Yes, but who is going to keep you safe, Gwen?" Morna asks, suddenly serious as they stumble forward across the grass clearing under the starry sky. Nicola's storm is gone now, nothing obstructs their view of the pinpoints of light in the black blanket above them. "With the Vampire King sending all his minions after you, it's only going to get more and more dangerous for you from now on."

"I guess I'll just have to kill all the vampires then, won't I?" Morna smiles wanly as though this is a joke and turns her gaze on the wrecked remains of the hermit's cabin. However, Gwen isn't joking at all. Now that she's started to perfect her secret weapon, there's no telling what she just might be capable of doing.

Gwen smiles wickedly to herself. A male voice deep in the darkness of her soul laughs a disturbing and triumphant laugh. Gwen doesn't really notice, too distracted with thoughts of vengeance. Her mind is too consumed in the ecstasy of power that comes from her own twisted darkness.

Chapter Thirty-Eight

The Decree

He knocks on the old farmhouse front door. The rapping of his knuckles on wood sounds like cannons firing in the quiet stillness of the night. There is no animal chorus from the barn. No horses braying or hoofs clopping. The cattle do not stir. Not even a dog barks on the farm.

Affray takes a deep breath and sniffs the air. The scent of blood hangs thick around the place. Lights flicker on shining through the windows and frosted glass on either side of the front door. Affray watches as a blurry shape approaches the front entry. He hears no footsteps.

The door creaks open just slightly, and half a face is visible in the crack. A silver eye examines him a moment before stepping back. A hand removes the chain from the lock above. The door swings inward to reveal Sarah, one of the female vampires in

Dante's drove. A woman in her early twenties, the vampire is rail thin with barely any curves to speak of. Her dark red hair hangs in a straight bob around her plain pale face. With no freckles despite being a ginger she does sport a birth mark just above her lip on the left side. This gives her a slight Marilyn Monroe flair, but the mark is the only part of her appearance that could be mistaken for beauty. Her generic t-shirt and jeans hang on her emaciated form, as she puts a hand on her hip and regards Affray with a suspicious air. Thick reddish-brown brows furrowing.

She stands aside as Affray strides into the house without invitation. *At least one of the humans who lives here is still alive and under vampire control,* Affray notes to himself. *Otherwise, none of us could pass over the threshold.* A witch had made this possible thousands of years ago, with a very clever little spell. Even to this day the threshold of any completed house would stand as a barrier that no vampire could pass. That's why they never lived in the typical home unless they had control over the human who lived there.

"Where the hell you been?" Sarah asks, closing the front door and locking the deadbolt along with the chain latch. "When everyone was getting hammered by the witches, you just disappeared." She points out in her usual ill-bred, unsophisticated voice. Affray has always found her manners wanting and wouldn't mind if she had been one of tonight's casualties.

You can't have everything. Some things will come in good time. But it had been a good night for him on the whole. Gwen still lives and is free, but he at least knows where she is. The vampires sent by Lazar had been mostly destroyed or badly wounded. He survived and could use this to gain further trust and power with Lazar. And, best of all, Lynette was dead or would be soon enough. His secret would die along with her.

"I was helping Lynette's children bury her somewhere she could heal in peace. I sent them to help once the fairy escaped. Unfortunately, by the time I finished filling her grave, the witches had already won the fight and the rest of you had high-tailed it out of there. I wasn't about to face half a coven of witches all by my lonesome, now, was I?" he points out in his usual arrogant droll.

"I guess not," Sarah responds flippantly. She walks past him down the hall. Affray notices that the back of her hair is singed clean down to her scalp. Here the flesh is red and blistering.

"What happened to you? Your hair…"

"I was struck by lightning. It wasn't fun," she informs him with a bitter scowl. "The others are around the place. If Lynette recovers, only nine of us survived. The witch Gwenevere got away and those hurt have fed and went underground for the night to heal."

"Except you, it seems," Affray points out.

"Yes, I'm still awake to assist Dante. He lost Peyton tonight. After I help him put her to rest, I'll go to ground myself," she

informs him with a touch of sadness in her voice.

Oh, that's right, I forgot. Peyton was your maker. That's explains a lot.

"He's going to need a new second in command. And he chose you," Affray comments aloud.

Sarah nods solemnly.

"How did that old witch get away from Peyton? When I saw her last, she was unconscious on the cabin floor with Peyton keeping watch. Next thing I know, I see her making storms and shooting lightning bolts."

"Ugh, don't remind me," Sarah interrupts him. She shakes her head as if shaking off the memory. Then winces in pain. "All I know is that we were just about to tear the fairy limb from limb when she screeched at us, and my head felt like it was gonna explode. Apparently, it did the same thing to all of us."

"I think I heard that screech. I just assumed it was a dying owl," Affray comments.

Sarah goes on as if Affray hadn't spoken. "Then she tries to fly away. Jameson, badass as always, managed to recover fast enough from the pain to throw a boulder at her." Sarah snorts at this. "It knocked the dumb fairy to the ground. That's when the other witches suddenly showed up. They just appeared out of nowhere and started demanding to know what we were doing there and if we had the old witch and

Gwenevere."

"What did you do?"

"We all just started attacking." She shrugs. "No one really gave the order, it just happened. I guess everyone figured it was better to strike them first before they had a chance to use their magic on us. Turns out they're quick with their hands and muttering their spells." Sarah makes a face at this, waving her hands in mockery.

"Yes, but how did the old witch escape? You still haven't touched on that part." Affray points out.

"Right after everyone started fighting the witches, Peyton comes flying out of the cabin window and lands in the middle of the field on her back. A moment later, that witch pops out and a storm starts above us. I think the witch pretended she was still paralyzed and only attacked Peyton when she was distracted by the fairy's scream." Sarah's mood seems to change, and her voice turns somber. "That's the only way I can imagine the witch getting the best of Peyton. She's never been careless before. She was fastest vampire I've ever seen and one of the most cunning." She concludes with a look that says volumes about how she feels about the woman who made her a vampire.

"Who else did we lose tonight?" Affray asks after a long pause. It seems the proper thing to do in such a case as this. He must at least seem to care about his fellow vampires.

"Jameson, Boris, and all four of Lynette's sorority vampire spawns," she answers dryly. "The only great loss was Jameson.

Boris was a sexist pig and Lynette's kiddos were all morons. They weren't going to last long as vampires anyway. I'm surprised Lynette's lasted as long as she has." Sarah stops in the hallway. Her eyes keep flickering to the shut door at the end of the hall.

She's stalling. She's never bothered to talk this long with me before. She's avoiding something or someone.

"I should probably go see Dante before I turn in for the day." Affray speaks up, breaking Sarah from her distracted mumbling.

"Yes, of course." She straightens. "That's what he would want. I'll take you to him."

Affray follows the twenty-something woman down the hall to the door she was just anxiously watching. She raps on it once and waits.

"Come in." They hear Dante's voice speak from within the room. Sarah turns the knob and opens the door. They step inside the dark room. Dante stands looking out a large bay window with the curtain drawn back. Outside, the moon shines high in the sky. It casts the Spanish vampire in silver tones and harsh, contrasting shadows. As they come farther in the room, Affray realizes that there is a body lying on the window seat before Dante. He looks down on his beloved Peyton. Her tall, slender form fills the window from one end to the other. Her long blonde hair cascades down the side of the wall beneath the window. Her eyes stare wide into nothingness. Her body is covered in blood and riddled with shards of wood. Some jut out of her at various angles. A few pierce all the way through her body. One such beam protrudes straight out of the center of her chest.

Affray stays still, waiting for the other man to acknowledge him. *A stake through the heart. A vampire doesn't survive something like that. It's one of the things the legends about vampires got right.* From what he understands Dante and Peyton had been together over a hundred years. *A man doesn't get over a love like that easily. It's perfect. A bitter and vengeful Dante suits my purpose just fine.* After a long silence, Dante stirs turning slowly to look at Sarah and Affray.

"You're not dead. Good," Dante comments with a thoughtful nod. "I will need your help."

"Anything you need I will do gladly," Affray professes in as convincing a tone as he can manage. Humility was never his strong suit. "What can I do for you?"

"You can tell me everything there is to know about this witch Gwenevere. Did Lynette share all her dealing with the witch?"

"Of course. Lynette spoke with such detail about Gwenevere I feel like I know her better than anyone. Better than she knows herself," he boasts.

"Good, because after tonight I will do everything in my power to see that she meets a bloody and painful death."

"What about capturing her and taking her to Lazar? Won't the King be angry if you kill her instead?" Sarah interjects, her fear of her king written clearly on her alabaster face.

"Her death is better than an outright failure to capture her at all," Dante replies. "And accidents happen all the time." He smiles darkly.

Yes, this night couldn't have gone better. I might just get everything I want after all.

* * * * *

By the time they reach Nicola's house at the very edge of town, Gwen is dead on her feet. Weakened by the amount of power she wielded in the battle tonight; she feels all but hollow inside. Now hidden within the folds of Gwen's long black hair, Morna's little voice calls out, "Is this Nicola's house? The big brown place on the edge there, the one standing apart from the rest?"

"Yes, it is," Gwen answers in a whisper. "Why is it separated from the other houses like that, I wonder."

"All Thoyens live in the houses that make the outer ring of the Coven," Morna informs Gwen in her ear. "Their homes help maintain the protective barrier of the wards that hide the Coven from the outside world."

"There's a ward? How does it work? How do you know

all this any ways?"

"My mother made me study the histories of all the other tribes. Even fairy princesses are expected to be knowledgeable in all things," Morna explains before continuing, "The ward is like an invisible shell that makes the Coven look like the rest of the forest from the outside. A human wandering in the woods will see nothing out of the ordinary. However, they will feel a strange sensation when they get near the wards that compels them to go around it or go back the way they came."

"So, it gives them the creeps, the chills, or something like that?" Gwen asks, her curiosity piqued as she looks about the edge of the forest willing herself to see the invisible barrier. She sees nothing. However, as she gets closer to Nicola's twisted root tree house, she senses the energy of an enormous spell, its magic seeming to hum around them. "I can feel it, I think."

"Me, too," Morna admits. "Although, you must feel much more keenly than I."

Gwen nods at this. Ahead of them, the Irish witch leads the way. Her shoulders sag and the woman shuffles her feet with the same exhaustion that plagues Gwen. *Conjuring magic takes a lot out of a witch.*

I forgot to ask; how do you feel about animals? In particular, cats? Gwen asks Morna mentally.

Most animals I don't mind. Cats are terrible creatures I avoid at all costs.

What exactly is so terrible about cats? Gwen communicates through their mental bond, her amusement evident even in her thoughts.

Trust me, if you were a fairy, you wouldn't find it funny at all, Morna insists. *Cats are among the few predators that Fairies cannot disguise themselves from. They can smell a Fae from miles away. Our scent drives them wild and induces a carnivorous drive in them.*

I see. So, you smell like catnip, I take it. Gwen laughs inwardly.

Ha, yes something to that effect. Why do you ask?

Well, sorry to be the bearer of bad news, but Nicola has a cat. He's called Killian, but don't worry, Morna. I'll protect you from the scary kitty cat! Gwen mocks.

Morna gives Gwen the mental equivalent of sticking out her tongue.

A bubble of laughter bursts out of Gwen despite herself.

Nicola opens the gate leading into her little walled-in lawn. Gwen and Morna follow as she starts to ascend the steps to front door.

Nicola opens the door. Smiling, the middle-aged witch steps a side to let Gwen step in before her.

"There's no need to be shy, dearie. You live here now. Please treat my home as if it were yer own," Nicola requests, her curly auburn hair bouncing about her shoulders as she

adjusts her Thoyen shawl.

"Of course," Gwen concedes. "Thank you, Nicola, for your generosity. You've done more for us than we have any right to expect." Gwen steps into the living room and Nicola closes the door behind her.

Once inside, Morna shoots out of Gwen's hair and zips about the room. She heads into the rafters and lands on a beam. Peeking over the edge to look down at them, Morna's little blonde head and blue face poke out. Thus distracted, it takes Gwen a moment to realize that Nicola is still waiting by the front door.

Nicola seems to be at a loss for words and in deep thought. Gwen sees sympathy and gentleness in the woman's face.

"You've lived an exceedingly difficult life, child. I don't blame you for being skeptical of me or unable to believe in the kindness of strangers. But I want you to know that I am someone you can trust. Someone on whom you can rely. You and Morna both, of course."

"Thank you, Nicola, we appreciate that. And thank you for convincing the others to keep Morna's presence here a secret. We realize what you're all risking in doing this." Gwen smiles weakly.

"It's nothing, really. We'd do it for any of our friends," Nicola reassures.

Gwen yawns. "It's late and I don't know about you, but I'm exhausted."

"Yes, of course, let's get off to bed." Nicola ushers Gwen up

the stairs. Morna swoops down from the beam to land on the top of Gwen's head.

I don't see this cat you spoke of. But the house reeks of him, Morna informs her. Gwen suppresses a smile.

Nicola waits for Gwen to enter her room before she passes by to open her door across the landing. "If there's anything you need, don't hesitate to ask." Gwen smiles appreciatively. Morna nods. "Goodnight, Gwenevere. Goodnight, Morna." Nicola bows her head slightly in farewell before slipping inside closing her door.

Gwen shuts her bedroom door and turns to the dark room within. The lights don't magically appear in the rafters as before. Gwen doesn't want light and the house senses this. Instead, Gwen moves by the light of the moon shining through her circular window. It casts a soft glow over her narrow bed.

Morna hovers off her head and lands on the coverlet. She walks about, sniffing and wiggling her little nose.

"Let me guess, the bed reeks of cat, too?" Gwen asks with a sardonic smile.

Morna nods and flutters up into the air. She swishes over to land on the windowsill. She looks out into the night at the coven. Wonder and curiosity hum in her mind.

With a deep sigh, Gwen changes out of her black Wiccan clothes into a pair of sweatpants and a baggy tee shirt from her red duffle bag.

Before slipping under the covers, Gwen retrieves a black book from her bag. She flips through it. Drawings in ink and pencil fill its pages with scribbled notes and thoughts interspersed amongst them. It looks just like the notebook Douglas gave her back when she was still at St. Paul's orphanage as a child — the sketchbook she filled ages ago. This is just the latest version in a long line of successors to her original artist journal. A pen holds her place in the book. The new blank page awaits her to express herself upon it.

With the pen in hand, Gwen unloads the turmoil of the last few days onto the page in words or in sketches of the things that have taken place. As she does, each stroke alleviates her soul of the stress that has been building within her. Her life isn't going to get less complicated any time soon. She realizes this. Rather than dwell on it, she focuses her mind on better times. Those from the past and those yet to come. She misses Las Vegas. Performing in the magic show, the freedom of being separate from the world as she Morna and Raven had been then.

When done, Gwen stows her notebook away and pulls out the little drawstring bag that holds Morna's belongings. She pulls out the old jewelry box from her time in Bec LaNuff. It's an old present from Legion, but she's kept it despite this. This is where Gwen first hid Morna after rescuing her from the cage in Lynette's room two and a half years ago. She places it on the nightstand by the bed and opens the lid. Inside, a mass of black hair is coiled into a kind of nest. It's not all Gwen's hair. Raven's hair helps make up Morna's bed as well. The smell of witch and werewolf will help disguise Morna's scent from those who prey on fairies.

She whistles at Morna. The fairy turns from the window and flutters across the room to land on the nightstand. She looks at the jewel box and then at Gwen with a big smile. Then she hops into the black nest within. She stomps around on the black hairs in a circle before plopping down in it. Curling up into a ball, she calls out, "Goodnight, Gwenevere."

"Goodnight, Morna." Gwen yawns and, pulling the covers up, she turns onto her side to try and fall asleep.

She doesn't want sleep, though. She wants to dreamwalk. She suddenly needs to see *him*, the one she calls her guardian angel. The strange, blue-eyed, blond-haired boy from both her dream world and her past life. She has so much to tell him. Although it's only been a few days since she saw him last, so much has changed.

Remember, Gwen, the world can be turned upside down in just one day. And for you it's happened more times than you can count, she tells herself as she drifts to sleep. She sends her consciousness into the dreamworld with the one she seeks on her mind. This is the only way she knows how to find him. Hopefully, she won't find his mother lurking in the dreamworld instead.

Gwen can't help wishing that things were simple again. Just like they had been before Jonah, Thayer, and Leona showed up at her show. Before Michael died and Gwen found herself a wanted woman once again. Before all the vampire nonsense started when they made the decree.

Writers depend on their readers.

Thank you for taking the time to read my book! The Decree is book three in the Thirteen Tribes of Cain series. To keep up to date on the releases of future volumes follow me at any of the following:

www.rjcraddock.com

http://rjcraddockauthor.blogspot.com/

https://www.goodreads.com/RJCraddock

www.facebook.com/RJCraddockAuthor

https://twitter.com/RJCraddockwrite

https://www.instagram.com/r.j_craddock_author/

Your feedback is appreciated.

A story not read is a story not realized. You, the reader, give my words life; your imagination brings them one step closer to reality. If you enjoyed getting to know Gwenevere and reading about her world, please leave a review on the following sites:

https://www.goodreads.com/RJCraddock

http://www.amazon.com/dp/B00DQA9OZI

http://www.barnesandnoble.com/w/the-forsaken-r-j-craddock/1115287679

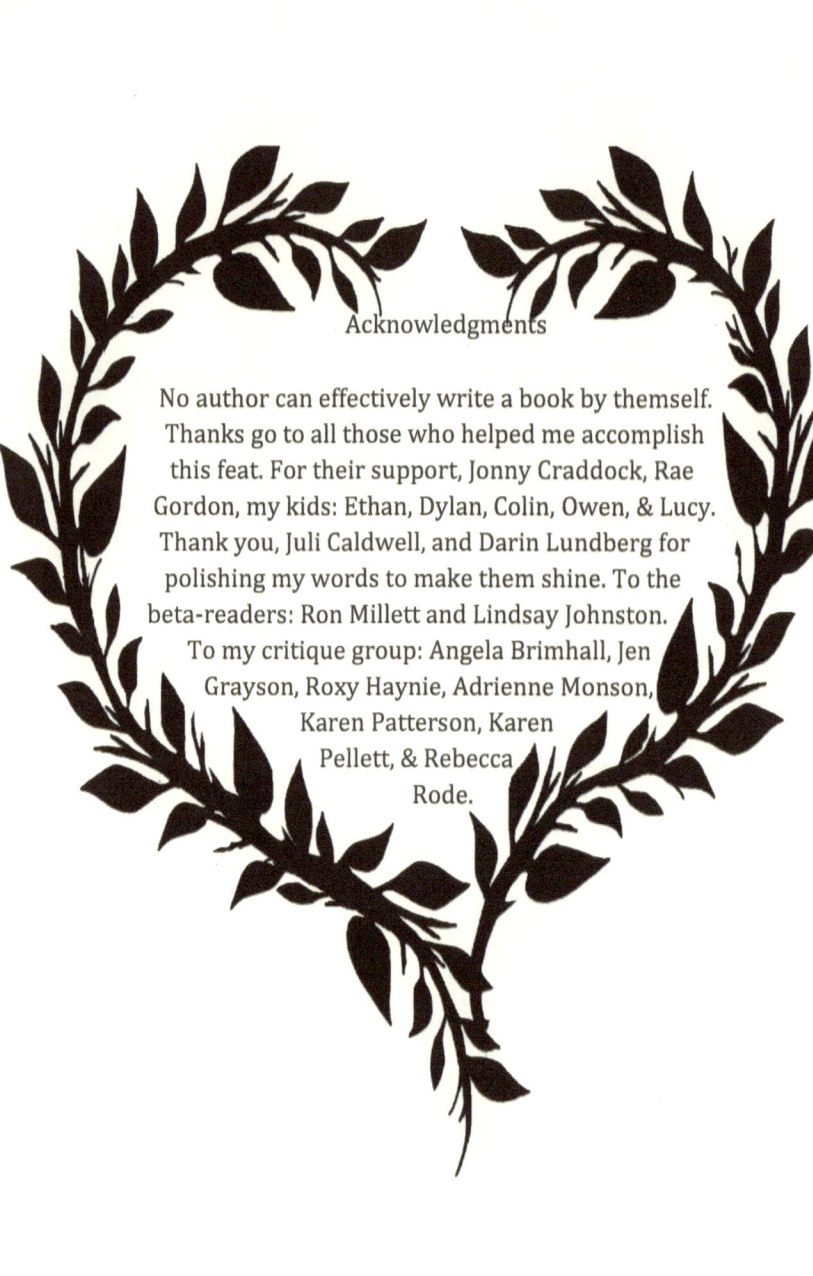

Acknowledgments

No author can effectively write a book by themself. Thanks go to all those who helped me accomplish this feat. For their support, Jonny Craddock, Rae Gordon, my kids: Ethan, Dylan, Colin, Owen, & Lucy. Thank you, Juli Caldwell, and Darin Lundberg for polishing my words to make them shine. To the beta-readers: Ron Millett and Lindsay Johnston. To my critique group: Angela Brimhall, Jen Grayson, Roxy Haynie, Adrienne Monson, Karen Patterson, Karen Pellett, & Rebecca Rode.

R. J. CRADDOCK

Born Ruth Jerraisetti Harris in Oka Tamuning, Guam, Ruth is the youngest of eight children. As a young child she began telling stories, developing unique characters, and conjuring fantastical worlds in her mind. As she grew older, a thirst for reading overcame her and she devoured all kinds of books, finding kindred spirits in classic novelists such as Dickens, Bronte, and Fitzgerald. She started writing her first novel at age eleven. After high school she attended the Art Institute of Phoenix to pursue her other great passion: Art. Ruth now lives with her husband, four sons, and daughter in Texas. Her published works include the first three volumes of The Thirteen Tribes of Cain series as well as The ColorKids picture books.